JULIA FITZGERAL[illegible] Wales, and rais[illegible] Yorkshire. She is the author of thirty historical novels, including *Royal Slave*, *Slave Lady*, *Venus Rising*, *The Princess and the Pagan*, *Firebird*, *The Jewelled Serpent*, and several written under the pen names Julia Watson and Julia Hamilton. Her writing has recently won her an international award from the magazine *Romantic Times*.

Julia Fitzgerald lives in Chester with her husband, who also writes. She has a son who is at college, and her daughter, Juliet Hamilton, is a fashion designer.

JULIA FITZGERALD

Taboo

FONTANA/Collins

First published in Great Britain by Century Publishing Co. Ltd 1985
First issued in Fontana Paperbacks 1986

Made and printed in Great Britain by
William Collins Sons & Co. Ltd, Glasgow

We make our fortunes and we call them fate.

Benjamin Disraeli

Contents

Taboo

PART ONE

The Peacock Dancer

Many waters cannot quench love, neither can floods drown it. A man might well barter his house and all his possessions for love, yet consider the cost trifling.

Song of Songs

Heart's blood and bitter pain belong to love,
And tales of problems no one can remove;
Love thrives on inextinguishable pain,
Which tears the soul, then knits the threads again.
Islam and blasphemy have both been passed
By those who set out on love's path at last;
Love will direct you to Dame Poverty,
And she will show the way to Blasphemy.
When neither Blasphemy nor Faith remain,
The body and the Self have both been slain.
Begin the journey without fear; be calm;
Forget what is and what is not Islam;
Put childish dread aside – like heroes meet
The hundred problems which you must defeat.

Farid ud-din Attar, 12th Century

Chapter One

The peacock shimmered, swirled, the silken susurration of its plumage rustling like crisply lacquered leaves in autumn. Sapphire, cerulean, emerald, jade, indigo, twisting, flashing, iridescent, mesmerising the senses. Chink, clink, went the tiny gilded bells as the peacock whirled round, faster and faster, the scent of attar of roses billowing out towards the gaping audience. Loosed, a shimmering feather ascended, fluttered, gyrated its way down towards one of the men who reached out to crush it in his sticky palm, his face growing hot.

Down sank the iridescent creature, so gracefully swirling that no one could believe that the dance had ended. There was stark silence for long seconds and then the loud cries of delight began, the clapping hands, the clink of coins being thrown at the dancer's bare brown feet.

Mishaal raised her head cautiously. She was in another world when she danced, far from the confines of the house of pleasure, somewhere radiant, mystical – and safe. Seeing the shiny faces of the men, their damp lips, their ogling, greedy eyes was always a sharp and unpleasant shock to her system as if someone had slapped her and said, 'See, there is beauty only in dancing: the real world is a threatening place, and yet it is your true home. Face it, Mishaal, face it, and say goodbye to your dreams.'

Rising, eyes averted, she withdrew behind the silk hangings, sweat clamping the peacock robes to her body. Matiya was there with the cup, as she always was. Taking it, Mishaal drank deeply, not tasting the ambergris-flavoured sherbet. Having reached her room, she stripped off the dancing outfit, plunging her hands into the bronze bowl of cold water sprinkled with rose petals which stood nearby.

'You live like a great queen, you have every comfort available,' ZouZou was fond of telling her. 'Everything is here for you, all riches and luxury, silk robes and soft beds, parchment to write your verses on . . . what queen could want for more?'

Matiya held out the linen when she had bathed, her expression rapt. She worshipped her young mistress: who would not? Mishaal was special, the sacred one, different from the other harlots who lived here and who thought only of their bellies and their purses. Mishaal was far removed from such low life; she was pure, her spirit shone. She had brought enormous good fortune to the house of pleasure where Matiya had been a drudge of all work until Mishaal had elevated her to the rank of personal maid. But for the beautiful dancer who performed like one possessed by the old gods of Arabia, Matiya would still be scrubbing floors and linen and rising at dawn to bake bread.

Mishaal's eyes were reflective as she dried herself. Seventeen years of age, she dreamed of romance and finding her own happiness, and of the day when she would dance as an artiste, far, far away from the brothel. It would not be easy, she knew that; but she would strive to make her dream come true. There were so many dancers who performed only to gain money, and who sold their bodies simultaneously; they were throwing the art into great disrepute, and she did not wish to become like them, the *'ālmahs*, whose name was now synonymous with immorality. Yet what hope did she have of evading that stigma if she remained at Rhikia's house?

When Mishaal was born, her mother had left her in the care of Rhikia, her old, dear friend, and to Rhikia she owed her life and all its comforts. There was no greater shame than a decent, honest woman bearing a child out of marriage after taking a *nasrani* as a lover, and this had happened to Mishaal's mother. She too had been a romantic and had fallen in love with a handsome American who was in Arabia to study the Arab customs and way of life. He was American, he was handsome, and he was a writer; that was all Mishaal knew about her father.

She could remember nothing about her mother. Rhikia had told her so much, yet it was all at third hand; not the warm and tender reminiscences that a daughter should have of the woman who had given her life. Rhikia said that her mother was dead; that she could not live with the shame of having been abandoned, unmarried, and with a child who could have *nasrani*, Christian, blood. She could not return to her family for her father and brothers had cast her out. That was the custom. She had been lucky to avoid a public beating for her fornication.

'Stay here with me,' Rhikia had begged. 'Stay and live with us. You need do nothing that would be unacceptable to you,' but Mishaal's mother had refused, out of shame and pride.

The house of pleasure was in its infancy then, but it had grown swiftly. Rhikia chose her girls carefully; they were always beauties, renowned for their grace, their elegance and sophistication. Rhikia's standards were high, even though her living was earned immorally. From the age of five Mishaal had joined the girls when they were dancing in their leisure hours. Rhikia's treasured adopted daughter displayed her talents early. Not for her the stumbling, awkward legs of the five-year-old, nor the stubby, clumsy body of the child. Every tiny muscle worked in sinuous cooperation, the hands were as lithe as the wings of birds, the neck could sway and undulate like the head of a cobra, the feet glance along the floor weightlessly.

ZouZou saw her dance that first time and insisted that her sister have the child trained.

'Think what fame we shall have . . . She dances like one from the temples of the East. She is light as a grain of sand, her flesh is like honey. Rhikia, you cannot keep her hidden! She must be allowed to dance for our customers. You are having her taught to read and write, though I see no reason for that, yet you refuse to have her coached in a skill that will make our fortunes!'

ZouZou had been persistent, and eventually Rhikia had capitulated. The little one was taught to dance. The lessons were begun early before muscles tightened and posture sank into its own individual stance. Backs must be straight, necks, too; nothing must sink or sag, grow crooked or stunted. And the same must be said of her mind, for Rhikia was determined that Mishaal would acquire all the learning that she would have had in her blood mother's home.

Of the tutoring, Rhikia was proud, but of the dancing lessons she had grave doubts. The house of pleasure had thirty girls and they must be considered, too, as must she and ZouZou. All were dependent on Rhikia for their living. They could have hired a dancer, or brought one to live with them, but why do that when there was one sent to them as if by the hand of Allah Himself?

Mishaal sat on the stool before her mirror, a silk wrap round her soft honey-coloured shoulders. The face which greeted her in the mirror never failed to take her by surprise. Was that what she truly looked like? Inside, she was not like that at all. Inside, she was reflective and spiritual, dreamy and distant: living in another time and place which were unnamed and unnameable. Tourmaline eyes were unexpected against the molten-honey skin, the result of the mating between white American and brown Arabian. Her hair was thick and dark as the eyes of night, or so Matiya liked to say as she brushed it; her forehead straight, the hair neatly limned as if it had been painted carefully on the amber brow. Her lashes were thick and straight, dropping like fans across the glowing eyes.

Who was it who looked out at her from those eyes? She did not know. Perhaps she never would. It was not Mishaal, of that she was sure, not the Mishaal who was familiar to her. Peering closely into the glass, she tried to see into the clear green eyes, really see, deep, piercingly beyond, through the colour, the orb, the veins behind. Who was in there? Who was it whose eyes stared at her in the glass?

'Mistress!' Matiya's voice sounded disturbed. She did not like Mishaal to stare into her mirror like that. It made the hair on the nape of her neck tingle.

Mishaal's thoughts sped back from the unnamed place. The heat, the sounds, the scents, were sharp and heady, almost palpable to her after her withdrawal. Slipping into the robe which Matiya held out, she lay down on her bed of cushions.

What had her mother really been like? She knew that her skin had been brown, her eyes very dark, her hair the colour of aloes, for Rhikia had told her all that, but what of the inner woman? Why had Maryam left her family and followed the American, allowing him to take advantage of her outside the bonds of marriage, and then abandoning her child?

'Did she love me, Rhikia?' Mishaal had once asked.

'Of course. Too much. That was why she left you here with me. She could not give you good food and a roof to keep you dry. She had nothing of her own.'

'Why did her family not care for her?'

'She went against their wishes. She was to have been married to the man whom they had chosen. She refused; she ran away. They said that she had disgraced them.'

'And was it thus?'

'For love, all is possible. Who would condemn a young girl in love? If we do not act on impulse then, when shall we? One day you will know that what I say is true, Mishaal. One day you too will fall in love and wish to spend the rest of your life with the man of your choice.'

Rhikia was a romantic at heart, despite being the successful proprietor of a brothel, or perhaps because of it. She had grown up with Maryam, exposed to the same beliefs and creeds. It was only later that their paths diverged. Rhikia had watched the man she was to marry die of a wasting disease, and, from that moment, she had vowed that she would live alone, remaining faithful to her lost husband. She had stayed true to her vow, and so when she had inherited a sum of money from a relative, she had founded the house of pleasure in the Street of the *Jijims*, desiring to give others what she had denied herself.

Mishaal's eyes were questioning when Rhikia assured her that she would find a husband. How would she do that when she saw no man save for the customers who came to buy the girls for pleasure? She did not even speak with them, for Rhikia would not allow it. She danced, on a raised dais, then vanished behind the curtains like a *houri* returning to paradise.

'You think that I am a silly old woman, Mishaal, that I imagine such things, but where is your faith? One day, he will come, and you will see that I am right.'

Rhikia had concealed her tears. She did not know if she spoke the truth. She had a certain conviction, but was that enough? For all she knew, she was projecting her own dream on to the girl whom she loved and cherished as a daughter, yet it was not in her nature to look on the negative side.

'No, never silly, Rhikia, good and kind and very dear to me,' Mishaal had replied, tears in her own eyes.

Was it proper that she should have her own dreams? Mishaal had never been too sure about that. Never having known her own mother and father, or their parents, she had to guess at so much, and create the rest of it. What would they have been like, her family, had she known them, and how different would she herself be if she had been raised in their affectionate bosom? The stigma of her wayward mother hung heavily upon her at times, like a bad dream from which she would wake only to find that it was reality.

Shrouding her face in her arms she tried to clarify her thoughts, to untangle the fears and the doubts from the truth. Soon, she would be ready to write some of her verses, but not yet. Like *kahwe*, they must brew before they were ready.

The noises of the house faded, the stillness of late evening descending soothingly. Some evenings, she would dance a second or third time, but not tonight. A few days ago she had turned her ankle on the stairs and it was still a little painful.

She curled up on the cushions, smiling at Matiya as her servant pulled the covers higher around her shoulders before tiptoeing away to go about her chores.

Outside, she heard the creak of a footfall on the boards. It woke her from that slumbrous state of near-sleep and the vivid dream that had been growing in her mind. Surprised, she heard ZouZou's voice through the door.

'Mishaal, please open the door. I have something of great interest to show you.'

Mishaal's reaction was automatic. Pulling on a loose robe, she obeyed ZouZou's request. Rhikia was away for the night, and ZouZou was probably lonely. For all her acid tongue, ZouZou needed people, although she would never admit it.

Before the door was half open, ZouZou was in the room. Her face was rich with colour, her eyes sparkling, but she seemed nervous. The clink of coins filled the air as she moved about the room, almost gabbling her words.

'Mishaal, this is a great moment for you, the moment when you will realise that ZouZou has been right all along. Rhikia means well, but she cannot see what is best for you. It is vital that you secure your future. Do you want to end your life poor and without the means to support yourself? A dancer's life is soon over; she cannot continue to delight her customers when her bones have stiffened and her face is wrinkled. Just a few more years are left to you, Mishaal, and then you will have no choice but to sell your body. Yet who will want an old woman with drooping breasts and belly? You will have to work hard to support yourself, doing menial chores, and you will long for the days of your youth when you could have secured a fortune.

'Do you know how desperate Rhikia is for money, yet you could make her rich overnight? How can you say that you love her and yet refuse to help her?'

'I have not refused! I help her all I can . . . I dance and bring in the customers, you know that well enough, ZouZou.'

'Yes, and they throw a handful of the smallest coins at you when you perform,' ZouZou sneered.

'It is better than nothing!'

'It is an insult! Rhikia has not told you the truth. She has been so sick with worry over our poverty that it has affected her health. She did not go away to hire another girl but to see a physician. She fears that she is dying, but she did not wish you to know. There will not be enough money to pay her physician's bills, Mishaal. She will have to suffer alone.'

'No! That cannot be true!' Mishaal clenched her fists, unable to believe what she was hearing and yet remembering the strained expression on Rhikia's face of late; the dullness in her eyes. 'If I thought that was true then I would . . .'

'Do anything to get the money for her? Yes, I hoped that you would say that, child. Allah, but I have despaired of you showing Rhikia the love that she deserves!'

'You know I love her deeply, ZouZou.' Tears glittered on Mishaal's lashes. Her foster mother dying, and she had been dreaming her hours away in childish whimsy . . .

'Then you must prove it. There is someone outside who has watched you dance many times. He will pay generously for your attentions. He wishes to be the first, Mishaal. You will not disappoint him?'

Mishaal's heart lurched into a twisting, searing movement that threatened to take her consciousness, but she fought the wave of panic and struggled for calm.

'He? Who is he?'

'A very wealthy man, a merchant who has dreamed of having you in his arms. He is handsome and he will be gentle. He says that you have nothing to fear; that he believes he loves you already.' ZouZou couched her words with the romantic phrases that young girls needed. Speak of love and she would come like a lamb to be deflowered. In ZouZou's pocket gold coins chinked again.

'How old is he?' Mishaal whispered, her legs weak as paper, her whole world changing.

'Thirty.' ZouZou's mouth clamped shut.

Mishaal swallowed. That was not too old; he would not be hideous and pot-bellied with decaying teeth, yet still she held back. One hour ago she had been so safe, so sure of herself; now she was shaking with dread.

'Come, child, we cannot keep the man waiting all night. His patience will be at an end by now. Think of Rhikia.'

Meekly, Mishaal nodded her head. 'Let him in.'

ZouZou grinned an enormous curving grin, and rushed out of the room leaving Mishaal standing facing the door, her knees so frail that she thought she would fall. Any moment now the door would open and the man would come in. He would want to kiss and embrace her, take off her robe and his own clothes and lie with her on the cushions. Then he would . . . Goose pimples rose on her arms and prickled along the flesh. By morning, she would no longer be a virgin.

The door opening slowly, she saw the face of the man who would deflower her. He was tall and very dark-skinned with a spotless white robe sashed with green, and a small, neat white turban which slipped to one side of his head as he came through the low door. His eyes were very wide, looking as if he had been startled; his nose flattish and devoid of a hook, his mouth thick and gaping to reveal big white teeth. Mishaal thought that he must have Moorish blood. As he came closer she smelt attar of roses, and, beneath that, another smell, far from acceptable. She could not help but wrinkle her nose, yet he seemed unaware of her distaste.

Outside she heard the clinking of coins and knew that ZouZou was listening to hear that all was going well. That woman had got what she wanted at last.

As the long, muscular arms curved round her, Mishaal wanted to scream, to fight and scratch and kick, but she thought of Rhikia and the physician's bills, thought of them so hard that her body became rigid.

'I shall not hurt you, dancer. Do not fear me. I have watched you dancing night after night and three times I have asked to come to your room, but always I was told no, until now. Last night I swore I would never return, but here I am, and my prayers have been answered. Allah smiles on those who trust Him.

'Are you not going to speak to me, little one? I vow that I shall not cause you any pain. It is a beautiful thing to take a maidenhead. With gentleness, it need never hurt. You will enjoy it, I promise you. Would it help if you knew my name? I am Ali Ben Mahommed, and I am a merchant. I sell silks and spices, leatherwear and silver. If we meet regularly, I will bring you valuable gifts.'

He did not add that he was interested only in virgins and that she would never see him again after tonight. He had contracted a virulent disease from whoring, and his physician had told him that there was one sure cure: he must deflower as many virgins as possible. It might take ten or twelve to effect the cure; he would know when his symptoms had vanished.

Mishaal would be the sixth.

Gently Ali Ben Mahommed led her to the piled cushions where he sat down beside her, and began to fondle her breasts. She sat as if frozen, feeling nothing but revulsion and the beginnings of nausea. That smell, what was that hideous smell? The fingers that were squeezing and nipping her breasts were spotlessly clean and heavy with rings, and the mouth that stopped hers was clean, too, and scented with violet cachous, yet beneath it all she could smell something rotting.

'Speak to me, little one, tell me that you do not find me unpleasant. Feel what I have to give you . . . Is that not beautiful?' His hand came out, gripped Mishaal's and thrust it down between his legs. She felt something terrifyingly rigid and larger than she could ever have anticipated. It would hurt; surely it would hurt? Oh Rhikia, Rhikia!

'Do not draw back. My gift is pleasing; it will make you a woman.' His voice was raw with desire now, and his lips shining with moisture.

Mishaal shuddered. She could not help herself. This was worse than she had imagined; the man was being patient but it did not give her courage. She wanted to run and not stop until she was lost in the desert where no one would ever find her. She did not want to be sold like a piece of cloth or a basket of dates; she wanted to give herself in love, not loathing.

The man was pressing her back on the cushions and kissing her hungrily, her cheeks and mouth and neck, then lower to her breasts, tearing aside her flimsy robe and gripping her shoulders. When she whimpered, he did not seem to hear. So much now for the gentleness he had promised. Pain shot through her left breast. He had bitten her! She could not believe it. Suddenly she was struggling wildly, and crying out to ZouZou, but the man's huge, dark hand crushed over her mouth and muffled her screams. Stars flashed vividly across her vision; he had slapped her face to quieten her. Oh, this was horror of the worst kind: this was no man but a demon, and how could she defend herself against one who came from Satan?

The thick hard bar was stabbing at her thighs and between them, bruisingly sharp, and there was only a section of torn silk preventing him from breaking into her. It had tangled round him and now he was cursing as he tried to free himself. White-cheeked, she stared down at the huge dark weapon jutting from its nest of curls. It was not dark all over but covered in pale patches, brindled in the strangest way, and yet for all she knew, all men might be brindled like this. She had never seen a man naked. Rhikia had protected her from all that.

Again the suffocating, fleshy mouth clamped down on hers, and the man began to thrust, then he was urging her to pull up her knees so that he could enter more easily. She was clammy with sweat, her heart thundering so hard that she felt she might die, but it was terror, not passion.

'Ah, that is better.' Breathing heavily, he jabbed into her, but she had brought her knee inwards and he struck against her thigh. It hurt her a great deal so it must have been agony for him. Groaning, he panted a little and then raised his hand to punch it into her face.

The vase made a deafening sound as it smashed on to the man's head. But for his turban he might have been killed, for Rhikia had attacked him viciously. Pieces of coloured pottery clattered on to Mishaal as she lay there not believing what she was seeing.

'Get up, my darling, get up and away from him!' Rhikia's face was suffused with blood, her eyes distended. 'ZouZou, Matiya, get him out of here . . . Throw him into the street before he recovers! ZouZou, throw his gold after him: I want no repercussions of this night. Mishaal, my beloved child, are you hurt? Was I in time? Did that filthy man harm you?'

Slowly Mishaal got to her feet, and slipped on the robe

that her foster mother was holding out for her with trembling hands. The nightmare was over; she had been saved; Rhikia had come back early and she was free!

ZouZou's face was crimson with fury as she helped Matiya to half-pull, half-drag the man's body out of the room and down the stairs. Her little plan had failed because her half-sister was so cursedly suspicious that she had returned unexpectedly; now she would lose all the gold that she had pocketed for herself so gleefully. How could that stupid old woman be so sentimental about a mere girl? In the name of Allah, what was a tiny flap of skin? Men were stupid; they could be fooled into buying Mishaal as a virgin for some years; ZouZou knew all the tricks for replacing maidenheads so that the customer was always satisfied. Now Rhikia had spoilt it all, the old hag. But ZouZou would have her revenge, oh yes, and soon.

Rhikia cradled Mishaal in her arms as she sobbed out her relief, and when she spoke of having agreed to lie with the man so that the physician's bills could be paid, Rhikia held her at arm's length.

'What physician? What bills?'

'For your illness! ZouZou said that you, that you were going to die, she said –'

'Die? *Me?* I have no intention of dying, nor am I sick! Tired, yes, but not sick!'

'But ZouZou said . . .'

'That witch lied to you! She hates not having her own way; she has been pestering me for months to sell you. As if I would! We have other plans, daughter of my heart.'

'How could she lie about something so important? How could she *do* that?'

'It is her way. She is ruthless when her plans are blocked. You don't know the half of it, my treasure, but I am back now and the ordeal is over. That vile man . . . I would not have let him have any of the girls, let alone you. You know I was going to take on another girl?' Mishaal nodded. 'Well, she is very young, younger than you, and she was a virgin. I thought that her presence might take some of the heat out of ZouZou's demands. That man who came here tonight . . .

he took her virginity, the poor creature, and now she is sick with a most loathsome disease. Her mother gave me his name so I would be forewarned and . . .'

'You are a fool, Rhikia!' ZouZou stood before them, hands on hips, her mouth slanting downwards grimly. 'You treat that child as if she is gold yet she costs us a small fortune in food and drinks and dancing clothes, and what return do we see for it? I am nearing the end of my patience. How much longer do you think I will stay here in this hovel agonising over our poverty? So you thought another girl would improve the situation, did you, but would she not be another mouth to feed? These young girls eat like horses and bring in little money. They all want fine clothes and you, Rhikia, cannot bear to say no to any of their requests. Your soft heart will be the finish of you and of me too, if I let it!'

'ZouZou, I shall never forgive you for what you have done tonight!' Rhikia rose to her feet, her face stony. 'That man was vile – diseased – and you did not trouble to check, did you? All you cared for was lining your own pockets. You did not worry about Mishaal's health at all.'

'So if his disease is all that makes him unsuitable, I'll find one who's healthy!' ZouZou growled, thrusting out her jaw.

'You speak as if you knew . . . Did you know he was sick? *Did* you?' Rhikia's face flamed.

'Of course not! Allah, do you think I asked him such a personal question?'

'There are ways of finding out discreetly. How do you think my girls stay so healthy? It is *not* because I allow any men into them, and they too can see if anything is wrong.'

'So could she!' ZouZou pointed at Mishaal who was listening white-faced. 'She is not so helpless as you think. She can take care of herself.' Jealousy narrowed ZouZou's eyes.

'Yes, normally perhaps, but not when you have put her in the impossible situation of telling her that I am dying and she must pay my physician's bills! That was vile, ZouZou, vile and abominable. I shall never forgive you for this, ever, nor shall I forget!'

'I never told her you were dying! What nonsense!' ZouZou lied boldly. 'She is stupid; she misunderstood.'

‘So now she is stupid, eh?’ Rhikia glared. ‘You told her that I was dying, and she believed you. I would never have thought you could sink so low, tricking a young girl in this brutal way.’

‘She always comes between us, Rhikia. Now you believe her rather than me, yet children always lie their way out of a corner. That is what she is doing, lying to you and you prefer to trust her rather than me! No, Rhikia, it is I who shall never forgive you, or forget!’ ZouZou flung back her shoulders dramatically, head in the air, then swirled on her heel and vanished through the door.

Rhikia collapsed against Mishaal, sobbing brokenly. She hated discord; it always upset her. That was why ZouZou had always had her own way until now.

‘What are we to do, Mishaal? Oh, what are we to do? I cannot manage without her housekeeping and yet she is so cruel that I fear something terrible will happen soon if she does not get what she wants.’

‘There is nothing to fear, mother of my heart.’ Mishaal stroked Rhikia’s hair gently. ‘I shall never listen to her again and you must not give in to blackmail. It will all blow over, you’ll see.’

But that was not what she was thinking. ZouZou never gave up when she had her claws into some plan. She became shrewish and demanding until Rhikia surrendered for the sake of peace. Once, there had been a cosy harmony in the house, so that it was warm and welcoming as a home should be, and now it was filled with arguments and bitterness. And she was the cause of it. Staring, unseeing, over Rhikia’s head, she came to the only possible conclusion.

If she was not there, then the hostilities would end and Rhikia could enjoy her home once again.

Chapter Two

'It cannot go on much longer!' ZouZou stood with feet apart and hands on hips, accentuating her short and stocky build, the broad face, jaw thrusting, the cheeks flushed with more than rouge. 'You saw how the men looked at her tonight . . . Ah, when I think of the money they will be willing to pay!' She clicked her fingers together, jerking her hand up into the air. 'How many virgins have they bought here? One, two? I doubt even that. When women come to us, or we select them, they have forgotten what virginity is!'

Rhikia was pale, her mouth stretched tautly against her teeth. This talk always made her heart jump and twist as if it were gulping for air.

'Do not say any more, ZouZou, I shall not listen. You know my thoughts and you have known them for many years now not to mention the other night. They will not change. She is not for the house! She is my adopted daughter, and she will have all that I can give her. Not for her to give me anything, certainly not *that* sacrifice out of marriage. If you think that you will beat me down, sister, then think again. You are wrong. I am right. She is not like the others.'

'Ayiee, you breed dreams like a fevered madman! You imagine that she is your flesh and then you treat her like a queen . . . You have ruined her, made her spoilt and selfish! She is already destroyed, and no one, certainly not you, sister, can recreate what has been taken from her. Night after night, all those eyes on her and the admiration, the applause. It has gone to her head, she is proud and arrogant now. No man would want her for a wife.'

'ZouZou, you are dreaming. If Mishaal is arrogant, then you are a camel!' Rhikia splayed her fingers in exasperation.

'Camel, am I? Then what are *you*? Blind as a lizard at night! Men who are greedy for conjunction with a beautiful girl will tolerate her arrogance, but a husband will not. Will she rise willingly from her silken bed to make his pilaf, and grind the flour for his bread? What if his *nabidh* turns sour and she cannot tell because of her ignorance? You have taught her nothing of domestic affairs, save for an occasional visit to the *souk*, nor have you prepared her for the outside world. Is it that you expect her husband to visit her here in the house, to sip her charms like a customer before creeping back to his own home?'

Stung, Rhikia gritted her teeth. ZouZou was the daughter of her father's second marriage; in many ways they were incompatible. Her sister had inherited much of the rawness of her blood-mother's family who were notorious for their squabbling and feuds. ZouZou had quarrelled with their father and his brother, offending them so deeply that they had told her to find her own roof. She had left with such suddenness to join Rhikia that the latter suspected the whole matter had been staged; that ZouZou, having heard of the profits her half-sister was making, wished to share in them. Nonetheless, despite her venal and mercenary leanings, Rhikia had loved her for they had been as one on many of the matters imperative to the successful running of the house; it was only over Mishaal that they bickered, taunted and goaded one another. Now, Rhikia could not say that she loved her half-sister; not after the horror of her appalling deception; instead, she felt a sick loathing when she looked on her face. Their relationship would never be the same again.

'What I have done with Mishaal is entirely my own business. She is in my care, not yours. Have you forgotten how much you owe me, ZouZou? Where would you be with your vindictive tongue but for me? I have suffered you under my roof for many years now, and yet still you interfere.'

ZouZou flounced her head, looked about to leave, but changed her mind.

'I heard that our father is sick. That he wishes to see me before he dies.' ZouZou inserted her words neatly and stunningly into the conversation. 'Soon, I shall not need your charity, *sister*. I shall stay in Father's house most happily and I shall suffer no regrets for leaving you.'

'*Mashallah*, sister, *Mashallah*.' Rhikia turned away, her chin quivering. She did not turn back as she heard ZouZou leaving the room. Was it true that their father was ill and that he had not asked to see her, Rhikia? She was the eldest; she should be summoned first. Why should she be excluded? Had not ZouZou lived here with her in the pleasure house for many years? If their father remained incensed at the taint of sin, did he not consider ZouZou despoiled, too?

Mishaal was so young, so innocent and tender-hearted; she must not discover that the world was harsh and painful. Outside these walls there were many who would think as Rhikia's father; that any association with a house of pleasure was shameful and to be condemned. Arab women of good families did not soil their hands with trade; there was no need. Their men brought in the money and gave them comfortable homes where they need do nothing beyond bearing children, preparing meals and waiting upon their husbands and sons. Mishaal would be asked where she had spent her childhood, where was her father, her mother, her relatives . . . She would have to lie, out there in the brutal world of reality.

Rhikia curled up on a cushion. Her bones were aching, throbbing away like a bad tooth. So far her health had been excellent. What ailed their father? He too had enjoyed a radiant vitality. She tried to picture him as he had been when she had last seen him. He had averted his eyes from her as if she were leprous; he had said that her name would never issue from his mouth again; that she was dead as far as he was concerned. Yet he had asked for ZouZou . . .

'Father, I was a good daughter! I loved you, truly I did!' The child in Rhikia wept, while the aging bones twinged.

Rhikia closed her eyes, seeing in her imagination the swirling iridescent peacock dance which was Mishaal's most popular performance. She could not have loved the child more if she had given birth to her; there was something thought-provoking about her . . . She made one look twice, think, reflect.

Maryam had begged that her daughter be named Mishaal, which meant Torch, for one day, so she had said, Mishaal would light the way for the people of the Land of Mirages.

Those words came back to Rhikia now; perhaps because her pride was hurt and she was vulnerable – as Maryam had been that day.

The Land of Mirages bordered their city. At one moment there was the chaos and clutter of the streets, the tradespeople, the houses and the souks, and next moment the clamouring silence of the desert, stretching endlessly, farther than the eye could see or the mind could think. It was called the Land of Mirages because of its aridity. The nomads lived a pauper's existence, searching for water, dreading that yet another well had dried up. When times were worst for them they came to the city to beg. Rhikia always gave generously, as the Prophet had ordained. They were proud and undaunted people, those who endured in the Land of Mirages. They could have found places for themselves in this city or another, yet they stayed out there in the iron wilderness, subsisting, eking out a bare living.

Why should Mishaal be their torch? Rhikia had never understood what Maryam meant, putting her words down to the woman's derangement, yet on occasion she had recalled the assurance in Maryam's voice, the glow in her dark eyes.

'One day, Mishaal shall light the way for the peoples of the Land of Mirages.'

She had not told ZouZou; how could she explain without being greeted with derision?

She pulled her tiny medicine cabinet towards her. Inlaid with mother-of-pearl it was securely locked and the key was round her neck. Open, the cabinet rested on her knee as if to say: Take my contents, down them all, and suffer no more! She brushed a hand across her brow. The anguish of not being summoned to her father's sickbed was a pain in her head, her breast. She was the eldest; it was her right to be present at the most important family events whether they were happy or tragic. All she had in the world was her father, Zou-

Zou (who favoured those who possessed wealth), and Mishaal. . . .

Suddenly she had a vision of ZouZou telling Mishaal that Rhikia lay dying but that Mishaal could not see her because she was not related by blood. Unhappy, distressed to have been excluded, Mishaal would be vulnerable. She would succumb to ZouZou's insistence that she sell her body, that she owed this to the others in the house. There was only one way to satisfy ZouZou. If Mishaal could earn as much by dancing as she could by selling her body, then ZouZou would be silenced. But it was not possible. Men came to leer, it was true; but mainly they came to fumble, kiss, and pillage soft, scented bodies: it was for this that they paid the highest prices.

If Mishaal were dancing in the city of the Sultans, or at the Grand Turk's court, then she would be rich in no time; here, for all its pretensions to sophistication and worldliness, there was no excess of wealth. They were, after all, only the length of a foot away from the Land of Mirages. Starve, thirst, languish unto death, but enjoy the most rapturous mirages in Arabia, that was what they said about it.

If only there were some desert Amir or chieftain who visited the brothel to enjoy Mishaal's dancing, to fling gold coins and gems at her feet.

Rhikia knew that if she encouraged Mishaal to go out into the world and sell her talents as a dancer, then she would lose her virginity swiftly. How could she fend off the ruthless and the debauched? ZouZou saw everything so clearly in monetary terms, with no emotional shades in between. The brothel was suffering from lack of money; business was poor of late. Mishaal could change all that. For a night with the peacock dancer, men would, in theory, pay enormous sums.

Child of my own flesh, Mishaal has been like the child of my own flesh, Rhikia thought, and the spears of pain lancing her bones increased. Was this how her father's illness had begun, with pains like these? Now he was bedridden, waiting for his heavenly reward. Would she, Rhikia, be next to die? Then what of her adopted daughter's fate?

She opened her eyes, conscious of another presence in the room. Mishaal had put her head round the door, anxious to speak with her.

'*Salâm*, mother of my heart,' Mishaal said, her voice low. 'Are you sick? Your face is pale.'

Kneeling beside Rhikia, she took her hands and kissed each one, gently, reverently.

'Only sick with the knowledge and burdens of age, my treasure, nothing more serious.'

'ZouZou has been talking to me again, mother of my heart. Is it true that the house is in financial trouble, that we shall have to close down soon?'

'She told you that? Allah, she is vicious! It is her greed which speaks, but not the truth, my treasure. The truth is that we must tighten our belts, but do not the Beduin do this regularly? We must be like them and budget. We spend too freely, we indulge ourselves too much.'

'You would not mislead me, mother?' Mishaal's jewel-green eyes tried to gauge Rhikia's thoughts. 'I would hate it – loathe it! – but if my joining the other girls would ease our money problems then I shall do it. That much I owe you, mother of my heart.' Again she kissed the stocky little hands with their henna-painted nails.

'No! I shall die before I see you despoiled. One day a husband shall be found for you. If I must rise from my deathbed then I shall find you one! *Inshallah*, God willing, you shall have all that any other girl expects.'

'But I am not any other girl, Mother. You do not need to shield me. How can you? I am adult now. All my life I have felt different because I have been treated differently. I look different! My skin is too dark for the West and too light for the East . . . I have green eyes! Whoever heard of an Arab with bright green eyes? Do you think I cannot see that people treat me as an outsider? On the dais while I dance there is nothing that they can say, no insult that can be levelled against me. Those who wish to call me *nasrani*, Christian, or half-breed, have their tongues stilled while I perform. It is as if all the evil in the world were suspended while I dance. Only when I stop, and step down from the dais do I see the real world waiting there for me, the derision and the barbs, the suspicions of one who is not the same as others.'

Mishaal leaned her head against Rhikia's shoulder, her cheeks flushed, her upper lip dewed with the sweat of remembrance.

'My treasure, you are gentle as the breeze from Mecca. How could you protect yourself against such unpleasantness if you joined the other girls? There would be no dais to raise you then. You would need a heart of bronze, a mind to match. I shall not have my sweetest child thrown to the carrion!'

'Mother, how can you prevent it if I wish it?' Mishaal's jaw jutted a little, her fists clenched.

'I would close down this house if you tried to defy me!' Rhikia gripped her adopted daughter by the shoulders and stared into her face, shaking her gently. 'Do you hear me, little rebel? I would close down this house before seeing you despoiled!'

'What – what if I said that you were keeping me from my destiny, Mother? Preventing me from finding the pleasures that the other girls enjoy, and a place here as one who is sought out by men . . .?'

'Sought out by men? Aiee! The only thing that a man shows when he seeks out a girl for his bed is that he is driven by the lusts of the flesh, and enjoys rutting, my sweet, rebellious child! It does not show that he cares for you, that you are important to him, or that he will never forget you. Far from it. You will become one of many, a tiny seed pearl snatched from an oyster's shell for a man's brief enjoyment and then flung to the bottom of a jewel box to gather dust and lie in darkness.' Rhikia plunged her head into her palms.

Mishaal held a hand to her mouth, watching her foster mother weeping, not knowing why this subject made her so distraught. A tiny, insistent pulse was beating in Rhikia's temple, like a finger tapping impatiently.

Uneasy silence shrouded the room, dulling the scents of jasmine and attar of roses and the mimosa unguents which Rhikia loved, stripping life from the tapestries on the walls so that the birds and beasts and mythical creatures looked stiff and unyielding, clutched by the passionless fingers of time. A pair of brocade slippers at the foot of the cushioned bed lay as if engraven on the floor, as if they had no form, no shape, no space for feet to slip inside.

Impasse spread over them, mute, irretractable, the one who would yield all too willingly and the other who would rather die before she saw her daughter sullied outside of marriage.

Outside the door ZouZou stood, knuckles bunched into her cheeks so that scarlet patches would remain for long minutes. Emotions were rearing through her mercilessly. Jealousy was like pins stabbing. Those two were so close, so loving. She was excluded, always excluded, when what she most wanted was to experience and feel and enjoy affection like theirs. They held her at arm's length and despised her wishes . . . Rhikia did, anyway, if not the girl. How could anyone become so unbalanced over the subject of a maidenhead? Rhikia was like one demented, possessed by *jinns*, whenever the matter was raised. There they sat in that room, so close, so intimate and sharing, even if they disagreed strongly, while ZouZou was treated like some abomination because she was sensible enough to see the only possible solution to everyone's problems. The child would go to her fate and never turn back. Why should she? The money would gather into piles and the house would be saved. Think what the men would say of the chance to bed a girl with such pale skin, a girl of *nasrani* blood. Mishaal was a jewel, *their* jewel, to use as they wished.

Saliva formed into a droplet at the corner of ZouZou's mouth. She wanted to rush into that silent room and scream and kick and order those two imbeciles to obey her. For one short, searing second, she almost followed her instinct. Forcing breath into her wooden lungs, she moved unsteadily away, down the narrow, dim corridor, her feet stabbing as if they were being freed of pins and needles. Her eyes were watering. No, it was surely tears. This was the day when she would visit her dying father and he would place his hand on her head and say that she was forgiven. She could not bear that! She did not want his mercy. She had been out in her hinterland too long to return to the soft, childish delights of daughterhood, of obeisance to a man whom she could respect. Of late, that type of man had been non-existent. Who could respect men who had the flush of lust upon their cheeks, damp, slippery hands and pounding hearts, their minds obsessed with but one thought?

Sell Mishaal! Her head was seething with those words. Far from being dismayed by the foiling of her plan, she was spurred on all the more. She was determined that Mishaal would make her fortune, so that she, ZouZou, could be free of this place and Rhikia's nauseating charity; free of their father too and his rigid demands. The girl would command a high price; she had proof of that. So next time, she would ensure that the man involved was in perfect health, but man there would be, and soon. Why should the girl not be auctioned? Let them barter . . . In their public greed, they would pay a far higher sum than in private. Yes, that was it. The idea was brilliant; it sparkled in her mind. She would make Rhikia agree if it took her weeks of argument and pressure. But submit she would in the end, come what may.

Chapter Three

A caravan had arrived, travellers hungry and parched from the Land of Mirages. ZouZou was hopping from foot to foot, her eyes glittering, her face flushed. The travellers had brought Turkey carpets, leather, bolts of silk and brocade, caskets of valuable unguents and oils, and spices, to sell in the rambling souk a few streets away from the house. Then, pockets clinking, they had headed for the most renowned establishment in the land.

There were not many caravans trekking through the Land

of Mirages these days. The shortage of water had seen to that. Some said there was a curse upon that stretch of desert, that all the water would vanish in a very short time. Wells had dried up, so had oases. No one knew why, and those in the city had cared little until their trade began to diminish. In this bleak and arid place what else could aid their survival if not trading? For 400 years, the city of Abeesha had flourished. Whether entering or leaving the desert, travellers paused there and refreshed themselves, and it was to this city that they brought their wares for sale. Once, the house of pleasure in the Street of the *Jijims* had echoed to the sound of happy visitors, men wishing to make love to girls before vanishing into the tortuous wastes of the iron wilderness, or men who had not set eyes upon a female for long weeks.

In ZouZou's mind there was only one solution: fewer customers must mean that prices should rise, so that the few who came paid more so that their income did not diminish. Many times, Rhikia had explained that the customers' incomes did not rise simply because there were fewer of them, but ZouZou could not accept this. Whatever the raw realities of the outside world, she did not want them to intrude here. She had deserted her father, shamed herself and displayed a most unholy avarice, and to retract now was impossible. If she did not have this roof to shelter her, where would she go? Who would marry an aging woman of forty-five years with a past like hers, unless she could provide herself with a handsome bride price?

Money was security, power, energy: she could not live without it. Her savings must grow higher by the month; nothing less would placate her. One day she would retire, buy a little house far from Abeesha and disclaim any connection with its house of pleasure. She may even select a new name for herself, and ever after, she would say, 'Rhikia? Abeesha? No, I never knew that woman and I never lived in that city.'

The travellers were settled on their brightly-coloured cushions, feet tucked beneath their knees. Soon the spangled curtain would be drawn to one side by Matiya, and Mishaal would appear in all her peacock glory. That was what the men had paid for, and that was what they would see. After they would choose the girl who most pleased them and take her to one of the small, luxurious rooms on the upper floor, then silence would reign, the silence which ZouZou associated with the accruing of her wealth.

The lute began to pipe, sweet, bright, delicate notes, then the drum joined in, patted and coaxed by old Imja, the most ancient member of the house. For long, taut moments the music played, while the men shouted and slapped their palms together, banged their heels on the floor and shouted Mishaal's name repeatedly. Coins were thrown on to the dais, and the colour in ZouZou's cheeks deepened. It was she who always collected these offerings when the dance ended.

Finger cymbals clashed, a board creaked. Mishaal was coming. The audience roared their greeting, and then the swirling, iridescent peacock filled the dais, glittering, spangled feathers whirling, floating, as if she were flying. Once, twice, she lifted her arms so that the blue-green veiling was transformed into wings, peacock wings with bright and piercing eyes. A feather was loosened by the movement and floated out towards the audience. Two men cracked their heads together trying to catch it. While they groaned, a third trapped it in his palm, grinning broadly, his eyes luminous with longing. The impact of their lust struck at Mishaal so sharply that a tiny, fierce pain stabbed between her brows.

Tonight, for some reason, she was not as detached as usual, the audience swelled before her like a herd of restive, over-heated oxen, bulky, ungainly, too strong for her safety. How long would she survive beneath their hooves, crushed, trampled, tossed from curving horn to curving horn? Sweat was fresh on her skin; she wanted to run.

Rhikia was watching from the corner, her lower lip drooping, one stocky, henna-painted hand clutching her veil beneath her chin. If she had not held that same infant in her arms when she was tiny, and watched her grow, serene, innocent, and radiating affection, then she would have bitten on her lips and called to Allah to protect her now. There was all the supernatural magic of the *jinn*, of the spirits of power and greatness in Mishaal's dancing tonight. On the dais, she was weightless, seeming wild, yet firmly disciplined, vibrant, shimmering, lithe . . . Rhikia closed her eyes. She could watch for just so long before she was dazzled. So much beauty, so great a talent. She knew that whatever Mishaal did, whether she stayed here dancing virginally, or was married to the wealthiest, most loving man, she would be wasted. She had been born for more than that, much more. She thought of Maryam's strange prophecy, that Mishaal would one day light the way for the people of the Land of Mirages. Was it through her dancing that she would achieve this?

The drum and tabor were droning to a halt, the peacock crouched on the dais, beautiful, untouchable, yet eminently desirable. A man leapt to his feet and headed for the dais, trying to snatch at the outspread fan tail. Old Imja, for all his advanced years, got there first and the man retraced his steps sheepishly, to hurrahs from his friends. How they were applauding now!

Later, when the refreshments were being served, ZouZou watched the men attacking the food and sherbet, her expression benign. Behind that mask she could be thinking anything, one never knew. Last night she had visited her father and returned with her eyes sunken from weeping, unwilling to speak about it, even to Rhikia. Now she was composed as ever, that thin, glowing smile on her face, as it always was when she was collecting money.

Studying her half-sister, Rhikia tried to penetrate her mind, but it was a wasted exercise. If their father had told ZouZou that he would disinherit her, then that would account for her tears, but Rhikia would have to wait for ZouZou to tell her. Questions would achieve nothing. A dark grey mist wavered around ZouZou tonight; sometimes it was stronger than at others, but always it repelled Rhikia.

Rhikia did not know it but she could see auras. Around Mishaal she could see a pure white, pearly sheen, quite the opposite to ZouZou's. She believed that everyone could see the coloured outlines round people, unaware that only a chosen few had this ability. Gleaming white for the pure, who could never be tainted by evil, and a rather unpleasant grey for her half-sister who was venal in heart and soul. To embrace auras like that surrounding Mishaal was heavenly (not that she had ever seen another so pure) while others were repugnant, coarse, evil and dirty. People who displayed those were to be kept at leg's length.

The curtain had fallen behind the vanishing Mishaal. Matiya would be handing the girl her refreshment now and she would drink like one in a trance, as if the sherbet were ambrosia handed to her by the one true God. Rhikia came forward, ready to assist as the men began to select their partners for the night. Over and over, as always, she had to repeat that the peacock dancer was not for sale.

'Alas, you know how it is, unfortunately she is an artiste; she concentrates on her dancing. But we have other lovely girls . . . Let me introduce you to Lalla, and Fira, or would you prefer Madela? She has Circassian blood; look at her creamy skin and light brown eyes . . .' On and on she would chatter, soothing, coaxing, cajoling, turning men's thoughts away from Mishaal. Once there was a man who would not be dissuaded, but he had turned out to be a genuine admirer of Mishaal's dancing talents and in the end she had performed for him in a private room, with Rhikia on hand as guardian. The man had paid well, but others were not interested in her dancing accomplishments, they wanted a warm, scented body to clutch in their grasping embrace, and rouged mouths to kiss. The city possessed very few terpsichorean connoisseurs. If only it did!

One customer could not make up his mind between a girl with black hair which had been soaked in henna and had an auburn sheen to it, or one who had black hair streaked with silver-white, and Rhikia had to mediate. She was so successful that the man took both girls to bed, and ZouZou had to clamp her lips on a burst of exuberant laughter. If only more men were so lusty then they could double their fortunes overnight . . .

In her room, out of sound of the clamour, Mishaal sat cross-legged recovering from her performance.

Matiya was bringing in the beaten copper jug of water and the linen, but on seeing the expression on her beloved mistress's face, she withdrew, making her way to the cupboard where the oils, unguents and herbs were stored for their health and aphrodisiac properties. Incense for happiness. Where was it? The jar was empty, more would have to be prepared. Matiya emptied a little from each phial into a bright brass bowl: rose, ambergris, sandalwood (the red variety), jasmine oil from Persia, gum Benjamin, the resin of trees from the East Indies, all fragrant and comforting.

Matiya whispered a prayer over the mixture, then shook the bowl from side to side before returning to Mishaal's room where she emptied the contents into the censer which stood near her mistress's bed. Reaching for the tiny brass tinder box, she struck a light and then stood back as the pungent odour of burning incense wafted into the room. This would bring her mistress happiness, she knew it.

An admirer had given the censer to Mishaal. Heavy, ornamental brass, laced with heart-shaped holes and star and moon shapes, it was suspended on delicate gilt chains. The small brass tinder box which accompanied it had come from a place called London, so he said.

The scent of the incense drifted, languorously, round the room, so that Mishaal half-closed her eyes dreamily. Already her mood was brightening and she was filled with a sensation of anticipation, as if something extraordinary were about to happen. When Matiya brought in the mint tea and a bowl of fresh figs, she bit into the fruit absently, her thoughts far away.

Night had drawn in, and the streets of the city were quiet. Everyone was safe beneath his own roof now, whether it was plaster, stone, wood or the rough shelters of the poor. From her highest window, Mishaal could see a star which always seemed friendly. There was an extraordinary fulsomeness about its glow, as if it were trying to transmit a message to her. Peace began to eddy into her mind. She could forget what was happening in the other parts of the house. How far removed all that seemed, nothing to do with her; had it ever been? Somehow, she had escaped the reality of the house in which she had grown up. A pleasant euphemism, 'the house', which Rhikia called their home where others were more direct. Bawdy house, or brothel were truer titles, and no doubt outsiders referred to Mishaal's home by those names. Only here, in her small, snug and colourful room was there any essence of the word 'home'.

The walls were draped with brightly hued rugs, in peacock greens and blues, her favourite shades. A carved bench stood to one side, its seat scattered with blue and green woven cushions; nearby was a small table of gleaming brass, on which stood a shapely vase with a narrow neck, a bulging middle, and grasses and ferns bowing from its top. The bed was pile upon pile of cushions over which lay a blue rug and a furred coverlet. On the floor were scattered rugs of woven wool fringed with blue and green which could be easily pushed to one side when Mishaal was dancing.

The burning incense was sending out little gusts of pirouetting smoke which danced and twisted until they vanished dizzily into the atmosphere. The hot mint tea had flushed Mishaal's cheeks. Watching her mistress sipping the tea and staring out at the stars, Matiya believed that she could see those stars reflected in Mishaal's eyes. She knew that her mistress was different from others, special, even unique. Her mistress had the biggest, warmest heart that Matiya had ever known. She was proud to serve her.

The star was trying to tell her something. Its twinkling scintillation was brighter, more urgent. Mishaal half-closed her eyes, trying to translate the message. What were the words she must know? They were vital, yet she could not comprehend them.

'Do you think that there are people who live on the stars, Matiya? They say that there is a man living on the moon, but I do not know whether to believe that. The moon looks so cold.'

'Perhaps we too are a star, *sitt*, and others are now staring at us in the same way and pondering whether this world is inhabited.'

'Matiya, how interesting that is! I had not considered that. We too might be a star just as bright as that one. How I long to know the truth – what the star is trying to tell me!'

'Has that old bitch ZouZou been at you again, *sitt*? Believe me, you do not need to listen to her. She is a poison, a sick camel! Because she is tainted, she wishes everyone else to be the same, but you, *sitt*, you will never be, never!'

'Matiya! Do not speak of ZouZou like that. We owe her a great deal. She has worked here for years, and improved all our fortunes.'

'Only to improve her own! *Sitt*, she envies you. She is poisoned with her envy of your youth and innocence and beauty, and she is jealous of your love for the one who took you and reared you as her own. You think the best of people, you see only the good, but I, Matiya, I see the dross behind the smiling face.'

Mishaal had gone pale. Closing her eyes she tried to wish herself back in time so that she need not have heard the truth, because she knew that Matiya was right. For all her plain and humble appearance, Matiya was acutely perceptive about character, so perceptive that some considered her a seer.

Matiya chewed her lip. It was uncomfortable to be a prophetess. It made her feel uneasy with herself at times, so that she longed to be free of her skin. People listened to her, lapping up her words, so that she felt responsible if matters did not turn out well. Yet she could not clamp her lips on the prophecies which came, nor on the character judgements which rose to her tongue. What if she stayed silent and a tragedy occurred? Yet what if there was disaster because she spoke? Ah, who would be an oracle, even on such a small scale?

Rising to her feet, Mishaal swished the hangings across the high window so that the star was excluded. ZouZou was bitterly jealous, yet had she not known that all along? She did not want to face it. There was no harmony when unpleasantness must be countermanded. It upset the balance which was so dear to her heart. Besides, what could she do? She did not trust ZouZou; regularly she thanked the one true God for having given her into Rhikia's care, because she knew that ZouZou would not have had the patience, tenderness or understanding to raise her so happily. She had been fortunate in her foster mother, and in the gift which God had given her, the grace to dance, the talent to write verses, yet those blessings were as bitter as aloes when placed against her bastardy, the fact that she was a half-breed.

'Let me be the cause of happiness, not misery,' she whispered, as if she were alone. 'If my existence is causing such disagreement, then take me away from this house, dear God! Take me where there is only harmony and joy.'

Matiya shrugged. Her mistress was a dreamer, she longed for all the best in life. Some would say that her desire for harmony was weak, displaying a character unable to cope with unpleasantness. Matiya could not agree. It was a virtue to desire harmony, so how could it be a sign of weakness? There was no escape for Mishaal. Wherever she went, she could not escape that she was born of mixed blood, half-white, half-Arab, without parentage or honour. That was how Allah had willed it in His immense wisdom.

There was a tap at the door.

'Mishaal, dear one, we have a customer who wishes to see you dance and hear you reciting your verses. He is a stranger, a *nasrani*, so you may refuse him if you wish, but he is rich and tall, and oh, so good looking! He has heard of your talent and he wishes to see you for himself. Will you say yes, my daughter?' Rhikia's face shone. The man had obviously made a great impression on her.

Mishaal's heart twisted in her breast so that she swallowed painfully. A *nasrani* like her American father, a man who would be taller than Arab men and whiter skinned, with light-coloured eyes and hair. She had never danced for a *nasrani*; they disdained to travel in this foreign area.

Matiya was scurrying around collecting anklet bells and veils, the peacock robe and headdress. She had no doubts that Mishaal would say yes. Who could he be, the *nasrani*? How far had he come and why? Just to see her mistress dance? Thanks be to Allah, her fame was spreading wide.

'Shall you, my daughter?' Rhikia licked her lips. There had been such tranquillity in the little room that she felt like an interloper, rudely disturbing such peace: Mishaal could emit the most powerful calmness. But Rhikia had liked the look of the man or she would not have come now to ask this favour. He was very tall, strong in the face, with a powerful gaze and authoritative demeanour. A man who was important in the land where he lived, she could tell; someone who was accustomed to being obeyed. When he had asked for Mishaal, she could tell that he had not even considered that the answer might be no despite the lateness of the hour.

It was a sharp curiosity which made Mishaal agree, and begin to dress in the peacock robe while Matiya brushed her hair until it shone, and curiosity winged her feet as she made her way to the chamber where the *nasrani* awaited her.

The *nasrani* sat cross-legged on a scarlet cushion tasselled with gold. He had been given a white silk robe so that he could relax. His jacket and cloak and hat were on a bench nearby. Mishaal did not notice them.

All she saw was the *nasrani* sitting there like a prince, waiting for her to perform for him. Her heart jumped again. It felt loose, as if it might fall. She lost her breath; she could barely inhale. Excitement tore through her blood, making it sing.

He was so beautiful, like a god, his face so magnificently cut, sharp, lean, strong planes which spoke of strength and courage, integrity and honesty. His hair was bright as the moon, pale gold, thick and wavy, cut shorter than an Arab's, his eyes a determined and heart-stopping russet brown, not the deep, dark brown of the Arabian. She could see his hands linked on his knees. They were clean and well cared for, the nails cut neatly across, the backs broad, again suggesting strength, as did the shoulders. He was tanned, yet she could see how fair he was compared to the other men she knew. That burning-sun hair could not be acquired with chamomile rinses. He must be a prince in his own country. Suddenly she was convinced that he was an important, famous man, respected and admired, even if he worshipped the Christ whom Muslims considered only as one of the prophets. Yes, even despite the fact that he was a *kaffir*, an infidel and non-believer, Mishaal liked him on sight. Maybe because she had some *nasrani* blood; maybe the blood of Christians was so alike that they recognised one another on sight and felt no suspicions or doubts regarding one another?

The drum and tabor players were late and Mishaal stood

there for long moments feeling awkward and embarrassed, her cheeks flushing. Standing as if she were on show, unable to move, was deeply humiliating. She wanted to look closely at the stranger, explore him with her eyes, yet she had to look away when his gaze met hers. Those bright brown eyes were overpowering.

At last the musicians arrived, their *kuffayiahs* crooked and their faces red. They must have been with girls in the upper rooms. How they would have cursed to be disturbed.

As the first reedy notes of the music began, Mishaal swayed into her peacock dance, every muscle lithe and sinuous, the breath returning to her lungs as if summoned by *jinns*, her feet light, strong and capable. She danced more beautifully than ever before, eager to impress, to prove to the man that whatever he had heard about her talent was true. She could not bear that he should come all this way to find her a disappointment. As the dance progressed, he began to smile, and she wanted to smile, too, she felt so elated. She had never been so overjoyed; she felt as if she were flying, twisting, streaming through the air like silken ribbons.

The stranger was smiling more widely and leaning forward as if he could not see enough of her. A girl brought a tray of sweetmeats and *kahwe* in an ornate brass pot, but he waved it away so that he would not be distracted from the dancer.

Mishaal wished that the musicians were more competent. Their music was sufficient for the ordinary customer but not for this great man who must surely be a connoisseur of artistry and style. Now and again, a discordant note was emitted and Mishaal wanted to cringe, and cry out an apology.

The soles of her feet were burning by the time she sank to the floor in her finale. She had twirled round so fast that her skin was raw with the friction. She did not care; she had never been happier or more exultant. The *nasrani* applauded her loudly, for a long, long time. Sinking down, she bowed her head in gratitude and to hide her blushes. Now she must recite her verses, and speak as carefully as Rhikia had always insisted. She had been taught to read and write by an old man who, having been disgraced in his former position, was eager to teach in return for his food and a bed. He had died the year before, but not before Mishaal knew everything that he knew and more. Rhikia had seen to her elocution, wishing her to speak like a lady. Would the man comprehend her Arabic? What if he could not understand her? Again she felt breathless, helpless, wanting to stay and yet wanting to run, not knowing which was best for her.

> *'For each man there shall be a bride*
> *Who, in love's matters, he shall guide*
> *And for each bride there shall be a man*
> *Who shall protect her for life's span . . .'*

She halted, unsure as to whether he could understand. He was staring at her piercingly, leaning forward, fists clenched as if preoccupied. She wished that he would speak, complain, accuse, anything rather than that unnerving silence.

> *'It is the will of God that man and woman share*
> *The kisses, comforting and care,*
> *For if a man shall hate his wife*
> *Then he shall be a* kaffir *all his life . . .'*

At that, the stranger threw back his gold head and roared with laughter, clapping his hands together. Was he angry, did he think her verses stupid? Mishaal trembled, her legs almost giving way. She wanted to run, get out before he made insulting remarks about her poor talent. She could not bear the delicious spell to be shattered, so that he became foul-tongued as any ill-humoured Arab and she the recipient of his disdain.

Suddenly the man was on his feet and coming towards her. Gasping, she drew back. So did the musicians, fearing that the *kaffir* was going to try and take her by force. They knew that they would be thrown out if they did not protect her, yet the man was hugely tall and powerful and they small and skinny by comparison.

'Mishaal is your name, honey?' Mishaal nodded jerkily. 'You are a treasure, little dancer, a treasure. If only I could take you back home, and show you to my folks! Do you know where I come from?'

'No, *yâ sîdi*,' Mishaal croaked, hanging back, away from this great towering figure who could speak almost perfect Arabic.

'Have you heard of the New World, the land of opportunity and fortune? America, have you heard of America? That is where I hail from. Have you not met an American before?'

It was then that he saw the colour of her eyes and his mouth fell open.

'Goddammit, you've got white man's eyes! How the hell did you get those, honey?' Then he laughed at his own words, throwing his head back again and shouting with delight. Before she could prevent it, his hands were gripping her shoulders and he steadied her before him so that he could confirm his first impression. Yes, her eyes were brightly green, as jade or peridots, freshly sparkling as new young fern tips. She saw puzzlement in his gaze, and what could only be recognition – what was he seeing in her?

His grip on her shoulders was making the room spin. The scent of jasmine was so thick in the air that she could not draw breath. This man, this foreign infidel, who was he, why was he here? She refused to believe that he had come all this way just to see her dance.

'I have not met Amr'eecan before . . .' she said slowly, while memories raced back into her mind of all that she had heard about her own father, the faceless, nameless man who had disgraced her mother.

'I am the first you have ever known, that's it, is it not, little green eyes? Am I so ferocious that you flinch from me? I mean you no harm, I assure you.' Realising that he was the cause of the colour flooding her face, he stepped back. There was a harsh sigh of relief from the musicians.

'You are the first,' she whispered, staring down at the floor while the muscles of her calves jerked in the most dismaying fashion and she wondered if she would lose her balance.

'Allah be praised!'

She gasped at his words, then saw that his eyes were

dazzling with humour. He was no believer: did she really expect him to be? He was teasing her, and perhaps he was being unkind and taking advantage of her innocence? No, be frank: her ignorance. 'I come from a place called New Jersey. Have you ever heard that name?' She shook her head. 'I live in a beautiful house called a château – I don't expect that you will know what château means? No, I thought not. It is French for house. You see, my home was built by a Frenchman, the Chevalier Jean de Bretanne. He was one of the early settlers in my homeland, but during the Revolution he remained loyal to England, where relatives of his had been given refuge during the French Troubles, and so his château came into our family. One day, one day, little green eyes, you will see it. I promise!'

Again his hands were gripping her shoulders so that she wanted to cry out, wanted to pull away, yet part of her yearned to be his, truly his, belonging in mind, body and spirit. Already she knew that he was the man of her tenderest romantic dreams: her beloved rescuer.

'Mishaal, where did you get such green eyes? Was it from your mother or your father?'

Blushing, she replied that her mother had been dark-eyed. 'My – my father gave me his eyes, I was told.'

'And who was he? Not Arabian surely?'

'I know little about him. He – he was from your land, the Amr'eeca, a great rich lord, but I never knew his name.'

'And you're about seventeen, eighteen years of age, honey?'

Mishaal nodded, wondering what all these enquiries were about.

'Allah be praised!' The American grinned again. 'I knew it!'

And then he was crushing her to him and laughing, and suddenly his mouth was on hers and she knew what it was to be loved.

Chapter Four

'Allah has spoken, Rhikia, you cannot deny! It would be insane to do so!' ZouZou stood with bunchy hands on hips, feet planted firmly apart, her neck flushed to the shade of geranium petals. She clamped her palms on her hips because she wanted to put them round her half-sister's throat and throttle her. Rhikia was beyond reach now, her mind had turned. She had screamed at ZouZou until the veins stood out like worms on her neck and now she had shut herself in her room and ZouZou was having to shout through the door.

'Go away, ZouZou, go away or I shall break every vase in this room!' Rhikia screamed, the blood throbbing behind her eyes. 'Leave me, leave me!'

'Not until I have your answer!' ZouZou screeched, battering at the door with her bunched fists. Ah, how that made them ache, how the pain screamed down her arms making her wish that she had not done it. Rhikia would never damage the ornaments in her room: she had collected them over a lifetime and she treasured every one. It was yet another empty threat.

No one was more dismayed as the sound of smashing pottery echoed round the room. Then something crashed against the fragile planks of the door, and Rhikia's screams followed. Had she cut herself? Was she bleeding to death? ZouZou cried out, 'Open the door, sister, open the door!' But her reply was the gusty sound of despairing sobs.

A firm hand fell on ZouZou's shoulder and pulled her aside. Mishaal had arrived back early from the souk and her face was white with rage.

'Rhikia, Mother, open the door for your daughter!' she cried, her hands clenched round the handle, positive that it would open on the instant. It did not. There was silence from inside the room. 'If she has harmed herself because of you then may the angels of darkness haunt you for ever more!' Mishaal said through gritted teeth.

ZouZou fell back, jaw gaping. She had never seen such passion in the face of the young dancer. The eyes were sharp, green and merciless. Her heart forgot to beat, then jerked twice as if it were made of soft pulpy material without muscle to support it. Her breath staggered in her lungs and she could not speak. But rage was rapid on the heels of her shock and, gathering her strength, she placed her hands solidly on Mishaal's chest and shoved with all her anger.

Mishaal's cry of alarm, the sound of her spine smacking against the polished wooden floor boards, made Rhikia open the door, as ZouZou had known it would. Sister faced sister with hatred and loathing, and then Rhikia was on her knees cradling the dazed Mishaal in her arms.

'Hush, little one, my darling little *jijim*, my precious pet, that is the last we shall hear from her. Now she will leave us alone, will you not, woman who has disgraced our family name?'

'*I* have disgraced our family name?' ZouZou tossed her grey-curled head. 'Bitch, you did that years ago when you opened this godforsaken harlotry! You, you are the one who has bought shame down upon our heads!'

'If that is so, then why are you here, ZouZou? What brought you to this place and this company? Was it love for us or ruthlessness, mercenary desires which have separated you from us? Where is your charity, your compassion? Gone, all gone with your common sense! You want to sacrifice this child to fill your own pockets with *drâhim*. How can you do that when she is like our own child? Where is your heart, one-time-sister-of-mine, where is it?'

'Sacrifice? What witless, emotional nonsense! A flap of skin that is all it is, a flap of skin, not her life, in the Name of Allah, not her life!'

'Go, leave us alone,' Rhikia spat. 'Do not stand over us

crowing like some she-*jinn*. You are no longer of our name, ZouZou. *Go!*'

'Why, you old hag, you bitch, you will be sorry for this!' ZouZou was white beneath the eyes and round the lips. Her heart was no longer beating steadily; it was jerking painfully backwards and forwards. She leaned against the wall, sweat icing her face.

Rhikia had turned her back, and was stroking Mishaal's forehead. She was only dazed, thank the one true and merciful God. Soon she would get up and step into Rhikia's room and they could lock the door behind them. She heard ZouZou walking away, slowly, haltingly. She did not glance back.

When Mishaal was recovered, she lay down on Rhikia's cushion bed and slept a little, then woke and drank a herb tincture made with loving care by Matiya: chamomile, dried in the sun, to soothe and calm, comfrey to heal the bones should they have been split, and lemongrass to refresh. Then, while Mishaal sipped the tincture, Matiya ground together reviving spices and incense to burn in the censer in Rhikia's room: camphor, galbanum, for Mishaal's natal sign, Libra, and also for Jupiter which was rising at her birth, and saffron, also for her natal sign; thus would restorative strength be radiated to her and her alone.

The scent issued gently round the room, nurturing the air as Mishaal breathed. Soon, her colour was returning, but her eyes were bleak.

'This has been brought to pass because of me, Mother of mine. Were I not here then you and your sister would be allies. It lies heavily on me that I am the cause of your dissension. I wish to bring peace and harmony to you, dearest mother, and joy.'

'And you have, my *jijim*, you have. Who dare say otherwise? When you were placed in my arms by your poor mother, Allah protect and guard her memory, I began to live for the first time, truly to live, to know contentment and happiness. Who can bestow a greater gift?'

'Mother, never say that! ZouZou is no longer young; where could she go? How would she find a home? I shall go. This has made up my mind.'

'No!' Rhikia flung herself across Mishaal, tears bursting from her eyes. 'No, do not leave me! I knew that you would say this one day but I beg it unsaid! Allah, have I not loved you enough that you would desert me now?'

'I shall visit you, Mother. I shall never forget you. The time has come when I must go out into the world.'

'*This* is your world, Mishaal. Outside there is danger and unhappiness, and diseases, dreadful diseases. You will be sick, you will long to return!'

'If that proves to be so, then return I shall, Mother.' Gently, Mishaal took the bulky little brown hands in hers and kissed them tenderly in the age-old gesture of a dutiful, loving daughter, and fresh tears followed the first, flowing down Rhikia's hot face.

'Stay just a little longer . . . I can change her mind, I know I can. Promise me that you will not leave yet. I – I must get a dancer to replace you. You would not leave me without someone to entertain the customers, would you?' Rhikia's thoughts were far from such selfish objectives but it would gain her time to coax Mishaal into staying. Young ones could be hotly foolish and do impetuous things which all would regret. What if she was despoiled by some lying stranger and conceived a child and the whole sad and miserable sequence began again?

'Mistress, let *ya m'allmi* sleep now,' Matiya whispered, showing courage beyond her station to protect Mishaal.

Sighing, Rhikia swept a cloth across her soaked and burning cheeks, tasted the salt of her tears and knew that it would not be the last time. How was it that her daughter could be ready to leave when her mother was nowhere near prepared? Allah, give her fortitude in the weeks ahead . . .

The American came back that night. It was explained to him that Mishaal was unwell, that she must rest, but it was promised that he could see her dance the next night. He went away and returned with his arms filled with flowers, fresh and bright and sweet-scented; where he had found them no one could guess. He brought expensive sweetmeats too, and almonds crisped with sugar, and these he said were for the dancer whose performance had so delighted him the night before.

ZouZou and Rhikia were not speaking, and it was the former who saw the *Amirika'ni* and took the gifts from his arms. Tall, far greater in height than any Arab she knew, he emanated vigour and courage, and instinctively she felt that no one would be able to prevent him from achieving what he had set his mind on. She knew a little of *Ama'rika*, the country which the Turkish called, *yen'ki du'nia*, the New World.

'Mishaal will be eager to see you tomorrow night, *yâ sîdi*.' ZouZou bent her head, keeping her expression solicitous. 'She has the great delight to dance for you again. It is never often enough that she has such an audience to appreciate her art.'

'Please give her my good wishes for a speedy recovery. It is nothing serious that ails her?'

'Nothing, *yâ sîdi*.'

'I am pleased to hear that.' The *Amirika'ni* smiled broadly, his eyes glowing. ZouZou saw that their colour resembled polished sandalwood.

'You will stay and be entertained this evening?' ZouZou had scented wealth. The infidel's clothes were sumptuous, finely tailored, hugging his masculine form in that fashion so favoured by the unbelievers of the West. In Araby, men wore the bernouse and the flowing robe tied with a sash to keep the material out of their way when they rode and worked. In the West, they wore jackets which to ZouZou's eyes looked ready to split at the seams, and strange, hugging *shalwar*, so that every muscle and sinew could be clearly seen. She found this indecent. There had been those who had visited the house in such attire, sweat glowing on their faces and their cheeks russet-red, while this man wore the Western clothes with dignity and coolness, and, flung over them with insouciant gallantry, a bernouse of soft greyish-gold cloth edged with gold braid. She was almost shivering with greed, the saliva filling her mouth. This man could make their fortunes, she knew it.

'There is no need,' he smiled carelessly, turning away to leave.

'We have other girls, beautiful, shapely and willing, *yâ sîdi*,' ZouZou tugged at his cuff, her throat tightening in dismay that he would go and never return.

'I am sure that you do, but they do not interest me. I shall return tomorrow night.'

The door closed behind him and ZouZou's mouth dropped open. For long moments she stood there, feeling as if she had been given a pouch of gold *drâhim* only to have it snatched away. Now the thief was running into the night with her treasure and her feet were leaden and would not leave the ground.

The room smelt of roses and violets, reminding him of his youth in England: Kent, where the fields were more emerald, the skies a brighter blue, the air tingling with the fresh sweetness of fruit and flowers. Briefly, he felt emotion form into sharp pins and probe behind his eyes, searching for escape. Gritting his teeth, he put the memories of Kent aside.

They were keeping him waiting tonight. Policy, no doubt. He was being treated to various drinks, fermented figs in water: the drink approved by the Prophet because it was non-alcoholic. Perhaps that was why he found it so unappetising. If it came to it, he preferred mint tea although they tended to make it of sugar and a smidgin of mint. He did not have a sweet tooth.

A girl brought him refreshments, placing the polished brass tray at his feet and then throwing herself to the floor before him as if he were a pasha. Her hands had been so deeply dyed with henna that they were bright ginger, making him think of the spice cake he had eaten as a boy.

'*Yâ sîdi* has all that he wishes?' The girl's voice was husky as if she had a sore throat.

'All except the lady who is late in arriving,' he grinned.

'Soon, she comes. All must be right, the mood, the time, all.' The girl pressed palms and fingertips together, touching them to her forehead, then to her breast before walking backwards out of the door.

Huntington wanted to laugh. Not even as a lord in England had he been treated with such esteem and obeisance. It was vastly amusing, and all that his employer had promised it would be.

The curtains moved, and his heart leapt. She was coming out now, the vision which had haunted him for three days: Mishaal, the Peacock Dancer, that was what she was called by the people who spoke of her with awe and admiration. She was no lascivious *bintilkha'ta*, fallen woman. All those who knew of her knew that she was untouched, and wished to remain thus, because of her art. Her origins were mysterious; she was illegitimate, nothing in that, so were thousands of others, but it would seem that her father was a wealthy infidel (and concerning that, he had his own ideas). There had been talk of something concerning the water supplies hereabouts; he had not understood it, and the old man who was trying to tell him could not explain himself properly. Those listening to old Abdul had laughed him into silence, so Huntington had only half a story. Wells running dry, water being short and disappearing for ever unless a precious store were discovered by the hand of an unbeliever.

He had received the impression that the tale of the water shortage was linked with Mishaal, but how he could not recall. He would have liked to find out more, but city Arabs were not the full-hearted, talkative ones of the desert, and Abdul had been jeered into closing his mouth, while threatening eyes were turned on Huntington and those signs made which were believed to ward off the evil eye. He had left, desperate to know more.

Mishaal's appearance was like that of an angel swaying towards him on bared feet, glittering wings outspread. His breath was trapped in his throat, clutched in a tight, unwieldy knot. Without hesitation, he knew that she was the one for whom he had been searching, the woman who would illumine his days and warm his nights. She was lissom, with a delicate, fluid grace which gave her weightlessness and a mesmeric agility, a *rara avis* indeed, he smiled to himself. He had seen ballerinas in St Petersburg, twirling on satin toes, and Spanish dancers whirling in Aragon and Castile; the cream of English aristocracy dancing in the royal palaces of London and the castles of Scotland; gypsy girls spinning and gyrating in Andalusia, seductive belly dancers in Morocco and Tunisia and the infamous *ghauzeeyehs* of Cairo, who sang and danced wearing nothing but *shinteyaun*, loose trousers of transparent gauze. He had been accosted in Alexandria, where no women were allowed in the *kahwe* houses save for gypsies and *shermoodeh*, eager to sell their bodies, willing to cavort naked so that lustful young men could press gold coins to their sweating bodies when they came close, then swiftly snatch them off before they danced away. All this he had relished in his formative years, and more. And now . . . all of it was swept into the distant past, forgotten, nullified by the exquisite grace and radiance of Mishaal the Peacock Dancer, with her jade-green American eyes, eyes that exactly matched those of his employer, Lord Tavenish.

Was it that air of unapproachability she possessed? Her expression was serene, unstained by sin or worldliness; he was sure that she had never known a man, possibly never even been kissed. His lips quirked into a smile. All men were Muslim at heart when it came to desiring that their chosen women be virgins. Could it be that she was, even here in this house of ill repute?

Mishaal's heart was twisting and shaking in her breast, missing a beat now and then so that she was momentarily breathless. She had never moved so gracefully, never been so inspired, despite the stiffness in her spine from the fall. He was there, the *kaffir*, with his sunburnt white skin, that aureole of glowing moon-gilt hair and his bright russet eyes filled with laughter and delight. Tonight, over his dazzling hair he wore a *kuffayia* with an *aighal*, the white kerchief of the Arab, held in place with a twisted cord. Her heart stopped its acrobatics, in fact it stopped completely, causing her not a little panic until it thumped into life again. How was it that this *kaffir* had such an extraordinary effect on her? Was he not human but a *jinn*, a spirit come from the other world to watch her dance?

Once she had told Rhikia that she feared Allah might envy her the love she had for her dancing and verse writing. It was often said that one must not tempt the envy and jealousy of the evil spirits for fear that they took some terrible revenge. Rhikia had laughed.

'Allah sent your gift: He, Himself, the one true God, breathed your gift into your very body. Why would He be envious of His own handiwork?'

What if He were, though? What if she had not been grateful for her gift and He was angry at her ingratitude? Allah, forgive me if I have not shown You my thanks! she said silently as she lifted her hands to either side of her face, forefingers and thumbs almost touching, her other fingers stiffly raised like fans, and swayed her head towards her left shoulder, then to her right, in that impossible looking movement born of practice from childhood. As if it possessed no bone to anchor it, her head undulated to left then right, then back again repeatedly while her feet sped over the shining ivory and jade tiles of the floor, lifting and elevating her vibrantly. Now the music was in her veins, singing along her nerves like tingling flames, until she was the music, each note her breath, her heartbeat, her pulse.

When that moment came, when she became the music, those who had thought she danced like an angel would be stunned into silence by the increase in her agility, grace and interpretation. Many had been enraptured and thrilled, or aroused by her gift, but few had been capable of appreciating it like Lord Huntington. Infidel he might be, but not where the arts were concerned. This bird of paradise was straight from God, he was sure of it.

In God's name where had she learned to dance like that, so that it deprived him of breath and reason? Those beautiful bare legs peeping out now and again from the bright blue-green feathered costume, were enough to drive a bishop to commit a sin, yet she was not deliberately tempting him, he could tell that. She was unaware of herself when she danced, of the effect she must have on all full-blooded males. Suddenly he was stricken by the thought that many men must have seen her dance like this, here in this house of pleasure, and many must have wanted to bed her. How many had? Was innocence painted on her face to hide years of debauchery? He clenched his fists at the thought, a hollow feeling rising from his stomach. He had seen the child prostitutes of Arabia, behaving like women of thirty, draped in the gold coins that they had been given by their customers; from the time they took their first step they were taught coquetry and the arts of tempting. Was Mishaal one of these, the innocence of the young lamb flaunted to captivate those who would rather not think of all the men who had been there before them?

The music was typical, reedy, undulating, passionless. The musicians were less inspired than their dancer. She was performing to a rhythm which none but she could hear, or so it seemed. The repetitive banging of the drum was only a little faster than his heartbeat as the shapely brown legs curved into view then vanished again behind the glittering feathers.

Mishaal wanted to dance for ever; she did not want to stop, to face what must surely happen next. He would offer money to buy her body; that was all he wanted. Coins to purchase his entry, then, when he was satiated he would leave, not looking back. The sexual desire was the briefest of desires, causing so much agony when it arose, demanding satisfaction and then fading until the next time. Who remembered the woman he bought in a house such as this? Which customer fell in love with a whore? The sexual act was purchased here, like a roll of silk, a purse of spices or a dish of *kahwe*, then the *kahwe* was consumed, the silk made into a robe, the spices tossed into a bubbling pot and who ever remembered the first delights in the possession?

If she were not of cross-blood she knew that she would feel differently. Had she been wholly Arabian, then she would have settled to her destiny with the same belief in fate that the true Arab exhibited. There were so many Arabic phrases all concerning Allah's divine will: *Inshallah*, Please God, let us hope! *Allah yhannik*, May God prosper you. *Daheelek*, For the mercy of God. *Istafarallah*, God forbid! The true Arabian could accept whatever came his way and never rail against it; Allah be praised, he would say when disaster befell him. It is the Will of the one true God, Allah is His name!

She knew that it was her mixed blood which prevented her from enjoying this calm acceptance. *Kaffirs* were impatient and hasty, and there was an old Arab saying that haste came from the Devil. The unbelievers were wild and desperate, refusing to accept their fates and striking out blindly into all manner of trouble and problems. She was like that, so she knew that it was because of her infidel blood. She had been raised a Muslim, but Rhikia had never forced the religion upon her, believing that she could make her own choice when she was mature. All the same, not wishing to feel different over that, too, Mishaal had worshipped like the others in the house in the Street of the *Jijims* yet always with the sensation of being there under deception. What did Allah think of the half-caste daughter of a *kaffir* saying her prayers to Him, even if He was the same God of the *kaffir* holy book? *Kaffirs* believed that Jesus Christ was their God; they worshipped him as vitally important to their creed; they worshipped his mother, Mary, too, while in the Muslim holy book, Jesus was simply one of the prophets of Allah.

There were dangers, terrible dangers, in consorting with *kaffirs*. The lack of faith spread like disease and tempted the heart away from Islam, that word which meant submission to the Will of Allah. Some Muslims could overlook this and offer hospitality, giving all they had to spare to a guest even if he were a white-faced infidel; particularly in the desert amongst the nomad tribes this was practised, yet there were others who would not so much as talk to a non-believer, let alone invite him into their tents, for fear that his lack of faith would spread to them in the night.

The arrival of the *kaffir* with moon-gilt hair and eyes the colour of the bronze censer in her room had awakened all Mishaal's deepest doubts and insecurities. Was it a sin in the eyes of Allah to dance for an unbeliever? Would she be punished? Or did Allah not consider her a Muslim so she was not committing any sin? She did not know which was preferable, to be sinless and free to dance for this enchanting man, if it meant that she was a *kaffir* like him, or to be punished for dancing for him, which would mean that Allah considered her as one of His own.

'*Ya Allah,* let me not offend thee . . . Keep me close to thee so that I follow in the path willed by Thee . . .' she intoned beneath her breath as the final coruscating notes of the music sounded and she began to whirl round and round, faster, faster so that the cerulean, indigo, emerald and sapphire hues of her costume glittered like a thousand eyes, lids closing, slowly closing as she sank to the ground, wings cloaking her head and body.

The silence that followed was agony. Slowly Mishaal rose, uncoiling sinuously, not daring to raise her head and meet those penetrating eyes. Was he displeased? He was not applauding her! She must look up, she must!

He was unmoving, as if paralysed, the smile vanished from his beautiful face, that face which surely had been cast by angels?

She could not help herself. Her hand came out as if beseeching him to speak, to clap his hands, her silent entreaty apparently moving his heart for he did indeed begin to applaud, crying out her name and then the praises fell from his lips, so that she blushed hotly and her throat went dry. Matiya appeared as if from a cloud, bearing a dish of sherbet, yet it was not seemly to allow the *kaffir* to see her gulping the drink which refreshed her. Bowing her head, she slipped behind the beaded curtains and drank deeply. She could feel Matiya trembling beside her, but she did not wish to meet her eyes. Magic was taking place, the great magic of love; he, the *kaffir*, had enchanted her. She was beneath his spell and wishing with all her heart to stay there until the end of time. *Yah Allah*, she was an unbeliever! It had been decided for her.

Heart thudding, she stepped back into the room and slowly, cautiously, went to join the *kaffir* who was sitting cross-legged on a woven mat, drinking from a dish of mint tea. They exchanged a clinging look as she took her place beside him. The decisions was made; she was his.

PART TWO

The American Lord

In this vain fleeting universe, a man
Of wisdom has two courses: first, he can
Direct his time to pray, to save his soul,
And wallow in religion's nectar bowl;
But, if he cannot, it is surely best
To touch and hold a lovely woman's breast,
And to caress her warm rounded hips and thighs,
And to possess that which between them lies.

Bhartrhari

What lights the world is in the world, but how to seek it no one knows –
The fishes in the sea are unaware the while it ebbs and flows.

Hayalî (d. 1557)

Chapter Five

Who would she pray to for courage now? she wondered as she clung to her lover's back. His Arab mare was taking them far away from the city where she had grown up, and towards the Land of Mirages, the open desert where they would have no companions but the stars and the lonely moon. Mishaal was alight with happiness. This was the solution, the cure. She loved this beautiful man who had led her by the fingertips into the garden of paradise; she wished no one to suffer anger and the loss of a loved one because of her. Now ZouZou and Rhikia, who had not spoken for three weeks, would be reunited and there would be no more harsh quarrelling and tantrums. She was sure that somewhere in the *Qu'ran*, the Muslim holy book, there must be the words warning that it was a sin to turn believers against one another. She had never done it deliberately; it had always upset her when the two women argued: Rhikia, the mother of her heart, whom she could not have loved more had she been her true mother, and ZouZou who had never shown her affection but who had hitherto behaved in a dutiful and exemplary manner. Not everyone could show tenderness and make the move to embrace another; some could only show their love by good deeds and hard work: who would despise them? Certainly not she.

Now the house in the Street of the *Jijims* would be peaceful once more, free to return to the happy days when she was a child. She could be pardoned for thinking that sexuality was at the root of all troubles, but not love, never love, and this was what she felt for the tall, dashing American who was spiriting her away into the desert.

The night air was like warm honey against her face. Tonight the moon was new, *hilal*, the time for fresh beginnings, for casting off the old and outworn: her childhood, her doubts, her Arabian blood. She was no longer of the Mohammedan peoples; she was free, striking out into a new and exciting life with her handsome lover.

Oh, what days of bliss they would enjoy together beneath the desert stars, and that sliver of a platinum moon, enduring as love, faithful as her *kaffir* lover. But now she must not think of him as a *kaffir*, for she too was of his race, and must prepare herself for taking her place in his life with his *nasrani* friends. He was a Christian, as were his family and kin; she too would don that faith to be his beloved, and she would never regret it.

How brilliant were the stars when viewed from the unfolding desert, like polished diamonds swollen with their blinding brilliance. She could see them pulsing, the glitter seeming to dim slightly and then burst into light once more, with renewed power. She could not see her guiding star though she twisted her head round to look for it, that star which she had admired from her highest window, feeling such deep empathy, as if it spoke to her, telling, confiding; warning, too, sometimes. Where was it now? Did stars hide? Could they come and go as they wished or were they always in the same place?

The scent of the desert was heady. The sand was dark, the colour of *kahwe* in this light, and the sound of the desert the most stunning silence that had ever clamoured against her ears, the silence of the great golden wastes, the emptiness, the strangeness; yet she felt no fear whatsoever, not with him beside her, her American viscount, Drew Huntington. His father was English, his mother American, and it was her country where he had made his home.

'Who would want to live anywhere but the New World?' he had said, his eyes glowing with memories. 'You will love it as much as I, Mishaal. After my work here is completed, we shall return to New Jersey and there you will be my bride, my lovely Lady Huntington.'

She did not understand all that he said. An English lord

was something like the Arabian Amir, he explained, but it was the tender kiss on her forehead which she remembered from that night and not the fact that she would become Lady Huntington when they were married. Titles, money, meant nothing to her: what dialogue had she had with money while in Rhikia's house? Few coins had ever passed through her hands. Everything she needed was provided generously; she had never dreamed of becoming rich, as ZouZou did. Identity, and the love of the man of her dreams, were all that she had desired and now she had both.

She was not an Arab; she had never been an Arab. She was a *nasrani*, a Christian of the white Western blood like her beloved Drew. She had never felt so serene, so sure, in her whole existence.

They rode until the horse was weary, and then they made camp. Drew put together their makeshift tent in moments, then stood back to see that it was steady. Eyes shining, Mishaal unpacked the cooking pot and hung it on its tripod over the fire of sticks and branches which she had gathered. Drew took out a tinder box which had belonged to his father, engraved with the initials G.H., and soon the little fire was flickering energetically, the water in the pot bubbling. They had goatskins of water, sacks of meal and fruit, dates and figs, fresh and dried, and some *laban*, the buttermilk that Mishaal loved. Matiya had said it was good for the complexion, and must be drunk daily.

Poor Matiya. She would miss her, but her servant had been the only confidante in the secret plan to escape. She had wept, but with joy, for she was assured that the American, infidel though he was, was the right man for her beloved mistress. Had not her premonitions told her that this man would lead her mistress to the greatest happiness on earth?

'Happiness, all happiness go with you and may the blessings of Allah fall upon your heads and those of your children,' Matiya had whispered as Mishaal was about to slip out into the dark night.

'No, not Allah, Matiya. I leave Him behind here with you. I go to my new life now. Think of me and I shall think of you. Be happy, Matiya!'

Then she had pressed into her servant's hand the note that she had written for Rhikia, and the note for ZouZou, and within a few moments she had left the house in the Street of the *Jijims*, never to return.

The water bubbled, and Drew produced a small gilded casket. Inside was black, dusty powder.

'It is called tea. The English are famous for drinking it, my darling.'

Mishaal giggled. She was watching his beautiful brown hands. There was a world of strength and power in those fingers and the broad, sunburned backs where golden hairs lay like fleece. Those hands had held hers, stroked her cheek, rested lightly on her shoulders, and smoothed back her hair but as yet they had not touched the more intimate parts of her body. Silently, she willed the beautiful hands to leave the tea-making and come to rest on her body, caressing, stroking and holding.

In Arabia, women and servants made the coffee and mint tea, not the master of the house, and *never* the Lord of the house. To see her American going about this humble ritual made her embarrassed and impatient. She must learn to make his English tea exactly as he liked it, and present it to him whenever he wished to be refreshed, even if it was the custom in England and America for men to make the tea!

Out of the saddlebags came two little porcelain dishes and into this was poured the black fluid, steaming hot. Mishaal sipped and felt the tip of her tongue go numb.

'Wait a little for it to cool, then drink.' Drew's russet-bronze eyes were mysteriously dark in the midnight hour. She could not tell what he was thinking. Did he not wish to embrace her, pull her close and shower her with kisses? *Ya Allah*, how she wanted him to do that! *Allah?* No, she had vowed to remove His name from her thoughts! What was the name of the God of the Christians?

'What is the name of your God?' she asked solemnly, and wondered why Drew threw back his golden head and roared with laughter.

'My sweetheart, why so solemn? Who wishes to ponder upon God at such an hour?'

Hotly she blushed. 'I have displeased you?' she whispered, her chin trembling.

'No, my little lamb, never that. We shall talk of God in the morning. Tonight is for us alone.'

Then his mouth was on hers and all the stars were dipping down towards her, closer and closer, dazzling, blinding, robbing her of breath and all control, the moon swimming across the indigo skies like the gleaming coronal of some ancient goddess of the night, and her heart was bursting with joy.

'Sweet little lamb,' he was whispering in her ear as he cradled her head in his palms, her hair rippling like liquid ebony. 'Even in this dark night your eyes glow like jewels. Are you truly mortal or some female *jinn* come to tempt me beyond reason?'

'I am no *jinn*!' she cried, alarmed that he should think such a thing and then she recalled how she had thought the same of him but a week or so ago. A foreign devil, she had called him in her mind, mentally testing her true picture of him.

Bronze eyes stared deeply into jade, a frisson springing between them. Fingers touched, invisible sparks dancing along Mishaal's arms and straight up to her heart. This was her adored one, her *mahbûb*, the one she had waited for all her life, the stuff of her dreams and yearnings made into strong brown flesh, the lips she had ached for, the eyes filled with passion, the arms made to hold her, the heart beating wildly because of its longing for her . . .

Then he was caging her so that she could not move, nor did she wish to, and the mouth she loved with all its sensual curves and soft, tender flesh was covering hers, so that the movement of the Heavens and of time itself came to a juddering halt, and in her mind's eye she saw her very own guiding star pulsing and twinkling, telling her that this was right, oh so right, that this was what she had been born for: the love of this dear infidel. The last few vestiges of doubt flowed away as that first lingering kiss changed her life, changed her, and destiny.

'God of the Christians, thank you,' she said silently and

then the kiss was chasing all thought from her head save for aching longing and that searing yearning which had been gathering since she had first set eyes on her *mahbûb*.

Kiss followed kiss, dreams turned into the flesh of reality and she thought that she would faint from the ecstasy of the touch and taste of her lover's lips. As he placed her gently on the sandy earth, the scent of crushed herbs filled the air, and the mournful cry of a desert vixen floated towards them. The vixen had lost her mate, but she, Mishaal, had found hers. Her arms went round Drew's neck, clasping tightly behind his head and tugging him down to her so that his lean, sun-bronzed body curved into hers like flame devouring her senses. Such excitement soared in her that she moaned, sighing his name like a prayer, willing him to make love to her now.

He was gentle, taking his time. 'Patience is the key to gladness,' he whispered in her ear, eyes twinkling. That was an old Arab proverb which she would surely know. *Iṣṣabr' miftâh ilfa'rah*. 'Haste tempts the devils of the desert to overpower us,' he went on, knowing that she would listen and heed. She was very young, a virgin, as ZouZou had assured him when trying to bargain with him over the price of that virginity. That he should buy this beautiful girl! God forbid!

'They must shut their eyes for shame at watching us,' she whispered, holding him so tightly that her arms throbbed. 'Kiss me again, *ya mahbûb*, kiss me!'

Laughing, he obeyed, running his hands over her curvaceous body, the full, high breasts, the tiny waist and dancer's hips, round and strong. Again she gave a little moan, knowing what would come next. How could she have been raised where she was without knowing the outcome of such white-hot kisses? The girls talked freely of their customers, their needs and desires, and she knew so much – and yet so little.

Drew's hands were gently exploring, pulling away the soft material of her robe, the silk cord which was knotted round her waist, so that he could see the creamy swell of her breasts. They were fair as an English girl's, white opal moons, soft as satin yet warm as only flesh can be. He kissed them urgently, his tongue slipping over the soft silkiness so that she shuddered in his arms, her head rolling against his shoulder. Soon, she would be his, this *rara avis*, the most intriguing and unique girl he had ever known in all his years of travel and adventuring.

His entry was cautious, easy, taking account of her virginity. He did not wish to cause her undue pain. He was not a pillager of innocents. Oh, the feel of her warm, pulsing flesh against his, the desperate desire to be deep inside her, cushioned in that unequalled haven. She did not appear to be frightened; she was a brave creature, and for that he admired her greatly. Bold as the desert, she was a world away from the simpering, prudish females of English society, or the blowsy, debauched females of New Orleans where he had lost his own virginity as a boy. She was quite different from anyone he had ever known and he could but do his utmost to treat her properly.

Mishaal was flushed, her heart leaping. She could feel the burning pressure of him between her thighs and it was paradise. Heat was flooding her body, sweeping through her at hectic speed. The pressure was increasing, burning, like fire flickering inside her, but what delicious scorching heat it was, and she wanted more, all of it, every iota. She clasped her arms round his back more firmly, her knees clamped at his sides and thrust herself up towards him as he thrust down. Sweat shone on their faces, the rocky ground forgotten as was the lonely cry of the vixen who had lost her mate to the *fáhd*, the brown and red-brindled wild cat.

Then the barrier was vanquished and for the first time Mishaal experienced the feel of the man she loved deep within her. It was such bliss that she doubted she would survive; virgin ground tilled for the first time, as a Muslim would say, yet which gave no hint of the ardour and the ecstasy involved.

There was such intensity in his kisses and the movements of his hips that she did not see how he could hold back, yet he did, and it was divine waiting. He was not out of breath yet she was panting like a young gazelle desperate for water, her tiny breaths fanning his cheek. His strong hips were crushing hers, his chest pinioning her, yet she would never complain. This was what she wanted, what she had dreamed of. No longer was she a virgin: now she was a woman, mature, full grown, and this act was no longer the mystery it had been.

Still he did not stop, his face buried in her neck. She heard him moan her name, say something in English which she could not understand, then revert to Arabic and call her his beloved, his darling, his little lamb, and her heart soared. This man was her first and only love; one day he would be her husband; she held paradise in her hands and she would be grateful.

Soon after, he shuddered, clamping her tightly and then coming to a halt. Their bodies were scorched with sweat as they lay together while he gathered his strength.

'That was beautiful, little lamb.' He kissed her neck. 'It will get better for you, I promise. The first time is rarely the most heartening of experiences.'

'It was paradise, my heart,' she sighed against his face. 'If it improves then I shall die of it.'

He drew in his breath, then laughed aloud. 'What shall I do if that happens, my lamb? You had better not enjoy it again!'

Then they were kissing, and rolling in the sand, laughing and teasing one another, while Mishaal kept thinking over and over, 'I am a woman now, I am a woman!' And this was her man, her beautiful man, her young god from the far country.

The night was growing cooler, the stars and moon turning to ice. They went into the little tent, protected as it was on one side by a high undulation of the sandy plain, and, wrapped in one another's arms, they fell asleep.

Mishaal had never woken in the open air. The sounds of birds roused her, twitterings and squawkings of the winged creatures as they carolled their territorial rights. Something slithered past the tent, causing the hem of it to shake a little. Mishaal clung to Drew. What if it were a giant snake come to eat them? But the slithering had ended and it was safe again, and Drew's lips were on her neck and cheek, the tip of her nose.

'We are safe, little lamb, quite safe. I have these, look.' He lifted the corner of the pillow to show her two sharp, curving daggers and a pair of pistols, gleaming metal which smelled of raw cold grease and death. Instinctively she shuddered, more uneasy at the sight of these killing weapons than at the thought of a snake nearby. It was natural for a snake to kill, he must do so to survive. What made man kill when he could more easily make allies? Had this beautiful infidel murdered another human being with these guns? She could not ask. Her lips would not move to form that question. No, she decided, he must have used them for the procuration of food when there was no other method of obtaining it. He would never kill one of his own kind, not her darling.

'See, we are safe.' He had not understood her alarm at the sight of the weapons. He was hugging her close, and soon kisses were eliminating alarm. Now it did not matter if storms whipped at the tent, or wild animals scurried close by, for she had her love. This time, she was not quite so tongue-tied, and she dared to whisper his name, trying to say it in English as he had taught her but she did not know how to say 'beloved' in his language, so she said, '*Ya mahbûb, ya mahbûb*,' then blushed hotly for fear that she had been too forward. Whatever else she had learned at Rhikia's house, she had also been taught how genteel females spoke and behaved. Only where payment was involved were women forward and lustful, Rhikia had said. Then a question rose in her mind: was this passionate, uncontrolled response the same as lust? Was she behaving shamelessly?

'Little brown lamb, what is troubling you?' The russet eyes were soft with tenderness.

'I fear . . . I fear that you will think me a, a . . .' She could not say that word: *bintilkha'ta*, fallen woman, harlot. 'I am pure!' she cried, twisting her head away.

'Of course. After last night how could I suspect you of being anything else? Besides, I knew that you were untouched. That was all I heard from those two women who guarded you like the Crown Jewels!'

'They might have been lying. How many times did I hear that virgins bring in more *drâhim*?' She could not look him in the eye.

'In my country too, though our women are not veiled and shut away in back rooms like the women here.'

'Not veiled? All decent women must wear a veil for fear that men will be overcome with desire and attack them!'

'In my country there has never been such an arrangement, Mishaal. Faces are unveiled, and, believe it or not, men can control their ardour reasonably well!' His eyes twinkled. 'When I take you back to New Jersey, you will not be required to hide behind a *yasmak*, my love, nor live in *purdah*. You will be beside me at all times as my wife.'

Silently she digested these words, trying to imagine herself walking as freely as a man and without hindrance.

'There will be no harem quarters for me? What of your other wives? Will they too be happy with this situation?'

She did not know why he was laughing so uproariously, but their love-making was temporarily halted as he considered what she had said. She had never seen anyone so highly amused. He must think her a fool . . . Would she ever learn all that there was to know about his way of life? She feared not.

'Mishaal, my sweet angel, in my country we have only one bride, and that is for life. That has always been the custom and always will be. You shall be my one and only wife, for ever and always. Do you hear?' He gripped her by the arms and looked into her eyes, but there were crinkles of laughter round his and his mouth was twitching. 'Nor shall you be locked in any harem quarters as you call them. You will have the freedom of my home, and you will share my bed. I shall not ignore you while dallying with my concubines, as they do here, then expect you to welcome me into your arms with a honeyed smile. How I detest such morals!'

She laid her head against his shoulder, puzzled yet feeling so secure, so content. She would be his one and only wife; she would share his home, walk where she wished, leave her face unveiled to the sun, wear the clothes of his country, be honoured as his bride. Suddenly, everything that she had accepted as normal all her life became alien. How could women tolerate being one of many wives and concubines? As they aged, a man was likely to bring home a younger, prettier bride and there would be nothing that the older ones could do. Now that she saw such customs as cruel and barbaric, she was prepared to put them aside as if they had never been. She was American now like her man: American.

Soon, they were celebrating the dawn in one another's embrace, as the sky flared from dark to pale then bright, the sun rising upwards like a cobra's head, aureoled with blinding orange flames, bringing with it heat, life, and, here in the Land of Mirages, such a stark aridity that the stones seemed scorched, the sand bleached. They were near water now, for there were wells here, but the farther they ventured from the city's perimeters the drier the land would become and the fewer the wells.

It was heavenly to feel her beloved's hands on her body like gentle fires, caressing, smoothing. It made her tingle unbearably from her mouth to her toes; she could not keep still yet if she continued to squirm and wriggle so violently, Drew would not be able to go on with what he was doing. Ah, this was bliss too beautiful for mere mortals to endure . . . Lines of verse floated into her mind, drifting, dancing.

'Ah, stars of the desert your brilliance pierces my heart
While the man whom I love cages me tight in his arms
Sun crowned with flame warm me, nurture me,
Give me my heart's dearest desire: a lifetime of love . . .'

To be one, it was everything that she had hoped; there was no disappointment, no anti-climax, nothing but ecstasy as the cobra-headed sun splashed the sky with rose-gilt hues and the terracotta earth began to heat.

This might be the last birdsong that they would hear for days, yet even this was feeble compared to places far from the desert's moistureless reach. The desert owl had wailed but they had not heard it for they had slept too deeply after love-making. Spring was close, the brief, dewy paradise grasped feverishly by the desert nomads before it swept into scorching, sand-choking summer. Now there would be buttermilk in plenty and the herbs and grasses would shoot high; there would be fresh, sweet milk when the camel-cows had calved, yielding their infants silently into the silence of the desert.

Drew and Mishaal could not have been setting out into the Land of Mirages at a better time, and yet the wells and the oases were running dry, one by one, although they did not know it . . .

Chapter Six

Two days later they paused at an oasis where a little caravan-serai stood amidst stocky, sun-resistant palms. Close by, there was a small, swampy pool at which the horses gulped eagerly. Watching them was a man with narrowed eyes, the hood of his bernouse pulled low over his gaunt features. Instinctively, Mishaal drew her veil across her face.

The man continued to stare ruthlessly. She saw that one of his eyes was closed, gummed together. Perhaps he was unable to see properly. He had a sorry little donkey with him; it looked as if the weight of the world hung on its moulting, scraggy haunches. Mishaal's heart went out to the animal and she yearned to pat it and murmur words of comfort into the scruffy ears.

The water in the pool was drinkable and yet she did not feel like filling her goatskin flask from it. How many creatures had dropped their snouts into these very waters? What of disease?

Drew was apparently unaware of such thoughts for he rapidly filled the larger flasks and his own hip flask, and then, grinning, led Mishaal into the modest caravanserai. Its walls were ashen white, crudely painted mud and twigs, with straw mattresses to lie on, and no barriers for modesty between each palliasse. Nor was there a section for women, and she being the only one, Mishaal wondered where she would rest that night. Four of the mattresses were occupied with snoring males. One woke as they entered, hitching himself on to his elbow to gawp. She blushed beneath her veil, trembling slightly as she gripped the material. Drew's hand tightened round hers, and he gave her a reassuring glance.

There was sand everywhere, crunching beneath their feet, knotted into the straw of the mattresses, in the jugs and bowls of water, the dishes of exhausted dates and dried figs handed round by a fat old woman. She tittered when she saw Mishaal with the *kaffir*, and Mishaal glared back at her, pushing away the proffered bowl of hard and gritty figs. Shrugging, the woman limped on to the next customer. What was it to her if these travellers starved?

Mishaal had never been stared at under such circumstances. In the souk when shopping for ZouZou, she was just another heavily veiled woman. On the stage, dancing, she expected to be scrutinised yet she knew that she was safe. Here, she was not too sure herself what she was . . . and this increased her fears and uneasiness. A veiled woman with a *kaffir* . . . would people think her a whore? Her heart lurched and sweat broke out on her face behind the stuffy veil.

With the insouciance of his race Drew had noticed nothing. He was accustomed to the ways of the New World, not this old, old, land.

A man hurried in, waving his arms furiously, pointing at Mishaal.

'No, not to be here! Outside, woman outside!' He barked in gruff tones, his English lumbering yet competent.

Drew uncurled his lean body, standing over the man who did not even reach so high as his sternum.

'The lady is with me. She is my bride.'

'Outside, all woman outside!' the man repeated, his eyes shiny, dew forming in them so that he looked as if he were about to burst into a fit of weeping.

'I said the lady is my bride,' Drew repeated grimly, while Mishaal was swept with the burning heat of embarrassment and shame.

'Woman outside, in woman's quarters. *Ḥarâm, ḥarâm!*' The man jutted his jaw, fists clenched beneath his chin. 'Forbidden to be here, forbidden!'

'Who is going to remove the lady?' Drew said, jaw equally jutting.

'She will escort herself!'

'The lady will not escort herself. Are you planning to carry her out bodily? What of the laws of the *ḥarâm*? No man may touch another's wife or sister. The punishment for so doing is severe, I believe?'

The man was gaping. Now there were tears trickling out of his eyes. Was it anguish or sand irritating them? Mishaal watched, fascinated.

'Bring a screen. You must have a screen of some kind? Place the screen wherever you wish, and my bride and I shall remain concealed behind it. But neither of us shall leave the shelter of this place.'

The man looked beaten. The screen was brought. It was sturdy and needed four men to carry it. Drew, acting the benevolent overlord, tipped them handsomely, and then he and Mishaal retired behind their portable haven and prepared to sleep. Once, Drew caressed her shoulder, kissing her lightly on the cheek, but she could not bear the embarrassment of his making love to her when only a screen separated them from a room of men no doubt all of whom were keeping their ears peeled for such sounds. Thankfully, Drew understood how she felt and soon they slept, locked in one another's arms, sweetly comfortable.

Before leaving the oasis, they stocked up with water, filling the leathern sacks that were hitched to the horses' saddles, and cramming saddle bags with dates and figs, nuts and raisins, for which Drew paid an extortionate sum.

There were hostile stares as they left. Mishaal knew that her countrymen could be tolerant and hospitable, or abusive and insulting to *kaffirs*, depending on their interpretation of the Qu'ran, and how they had been raised. She had once seen a white man stoned in the streets of Abeesha for which she had known a terrible sensation of shame and helplessness. All men were kin beneath the skin, of that she was sure, and yet there were those who said that infidel ways were contagious like disease and even sleeping nearby a *nasrani* was enough to make one lose one's own Muslim faith.

But her case was different. She was already part *kaffir*, so what did it matter? How could she lose what she had never had? As for faith: surely that was never lost if it was firm? The fact that she had put aside Islam so eagerly had revealed to her that it was not the correct religion for her. Yet she knew very little about Christianity. Drew would tell her all that she needed to know.

The glare of the desert was a harsh and unremitting apricot glow, splitting the eyeballs, and if one raised one's lids the sun blasted its shrivelling heat. They rode for three hours then paused when the sun was directly overhead. Drew put up the little tent and they crawled inside to rest. It was airless and muggy, and their clothes clung to them as if they were drenched, yet anything was better than the flaying heat.

'Wither thou goest I will go.' Drew was musing aloud as he looked down at Mishaal's face in the gloom.

'What are those words?' Mishaal cuddled close. Here was her heaven, her earthly paradise, in this man's arms.

'They are in the Christian Bible, the Good Book as it is called in the New World. A woman spoke them to tell of her love and devotion for another. She said, "Wither thou goest, I will go . . ."'

'It is a woman's place to be beside her husband.'

'You may agree, but there are many who do not. In the country where I was raised, and in the one where I now live, women frequently decide that they wish to go their own sweet way and heaven help their men!' He gave a rueful smile.

'Drew, have you loved a woman who went her own sweet way?' Mishaal stared into his russet eyes, trying to gauge what he was feeling, but his eyes were dark and shadowy in the tent.

'You could say that!' He gave a burst of laughter. 'Yes, I guess you could say that.'

'Did it hurt? I mean, when she went her way without you?'

'A little, yes, I guess it did, but why should I look back to that? I have you now, my little brown lamb. Other women have ceased to exist for me. You followed me out here into the desert without one word of complaint or criticism. Even now, you do not ask questions about our destination. That's what I call loyalty, honey.' He kissed the tip of her nose.

'It is for your book, that is what you said. You research for your book. There are things that you must know about the Land of Mirages. So there we go . . . or rather here we are now!'

'A book about the desert . . . Does that not sound strange to you? Would you not like to question me, ask me what will be the chapter headings? "The Blazing Sun", "The Choking Sand", "The Waiting Vulture"?' He gave another rueful smile. 'You of all people must know what they say about this desert. Its reputation for aridity and bleakness; the fact that earlier explorers have not returned from its iron heart. Yet you followed me eagerly, and that I admire. You have no idea how much. There would have been scenes and storms if you had been raised in New Jersey, even if you were willing to risk your delicate drawing-room complexion!'

The air was hotter and closer by the minute and soon they had no alternative but to sleep, as nomads and desert dwellers everywhere were sleeping until the sun began to descend, away from its scorching peak. Mishaal woke with a parched, gritty throat and, reaching out for her water flask, she pulled out the stopper and drank. Warm, as if it had been boiled, the water was not at all refreshing. Thrusting her arms round Drew, Mishaal kissed his neck, his chin and cheeks until he woke. How dark and mysterious were his eyes in the tented gloom. He seemed a stranger, forbidding, a little frightening, but it was only the effect of the gloom. How soft and sensitive was his mouth on hers, like flame-touched satin, velvet, yet dewy and gentle. She had never suspected that her mouth could be so responsive to a man's lips. Aching, stabbing sensations sprang from their kisses, darting through her breasts and between her thighs, urging her to lie with him. She was helpless in his hands, and oh so willing. Love was life and life was love. Nothing else existed.

They had fastened the tent securely, and yet there was gritty sand everywhere, in the folds of their clothes, on their skin, in their noses and mouths. Mishaal could feel it pressing into her stomach and thighs as Drew lay on top of her and pulled her close.

Eagerly she moved her knees apart, longing to shelter him inside. Her wide hips were made not only for childbearing but for supporting the weight of this man whom she adored. Impatient, she tugged him into her, and he thrust forward swiftly, smoothly, entering the silky haven of her body as if he were fashioned especially to fit. How could there be any sweeter bliss than this? Could carols of angels and shining spirits, and all the rewards of *janni*, the Muslim paradise, be more thrilling than this? She knew that they could not. If she had forfeited her heavenly rewards, Muslim or Christian, then so be it. She had chosen Drew and she had chosen rightly.

They were oblivious of the parched and suffocating heat as they moved against one another, Mishaal tugging at Drew's hair, he with his arms clamped round her waist. How lithe and forceful he was, how deep and penetrating were his movements, and how passionate hers, so that sweat pearled her face and dripped down her neck, and she lapped the sweat off his cheeks with her tongue.

An hour might have passed, or a few minutes; she did not know or care. What was time anyway? Man's measurement of the immeasurable. He was so deep inside her that she felt she was being recreated by his love making; its urgency and its rightness were sharp in her mind: yes, they had been fashioned for one another by God; their bodies fitted neatly, perfectly, his manhood shaped to fill her womanhood, so intimate that they might never again be free of one another's bodies.

'This man and this woman whom God has put together, let no man separate them.' Drew had said that words like that were spoken at the Christian wedding ceremony. Perhaps it was an allusion to this moment of intimacy?

Drew was whispering in her ear, telling her that her smile was the sweetest he had ever seen, and that her body was fair as opals, her hair suited to the Queen of the Night's own ebony tresses, her eyes like dewy jade, bright and green and clear. His praise made her blush; she was not one to need flattery, if flattery it was, yet he spoke with sincerity, and why should he lie? She must forget what the girls at Rhikia's warned, that men would say anything, promise anything, in the heat of passion, and recall nothing of it when they had got what they wanted.

Words of ZouZou's came into her mind, unwelcomed.

'When it is lust, then man will pay the bill; when it is love, the woman pays.'

Was there truth in that, harsh though it sounded? ZouZou could be very cynical, yet sometimes she struck right at the heart of the matter.

'My love, where are your thoughts? How can they be absent at a time like this?' Drew was gazing at her as if she had injured him.

Crying out, she took his face in her palms, returning his look with one of fondest adoration.

'This is love, real, true love, Drew, like in your New World? In New Jersey, they feel like this?'

'Yes, this is real, true love, but I doubt that many feel it as powerfully as this. Honey, some are made for love and some for lust. I would say that those who regularly experience one fail ever to know the other.'

His words were echoing her thoughts. He loved her, so it could not be lust. Ah, if only she knew more of the world, of man and woman! It was only now, in the bleakness of the desert wilderness, that she was coming to understand that she knew very little, especially about men.

They reached their finale together, Mishaal feeling so close to Drew that she could only wonder at the strength of their emotion. They lay coiled in one another's arms, dozing lightly while the sun took pity on them, beginning to drop slowly from its merciless height so that they might breathe again.

*

Mishaal tended the fire while Drew went in search of their food. Although he took one of the guns discreetly, thinking that she was not looking, she saw him pick it up, his fingers caressing the metal. She did not like the thought of the gun, not for killing people or animals, yet she had eaten meat often enough and never thought of its origins or how the animals had died. Now this was brought home to her. Birds, lambs, gazelles, they must all be killed before they could be cooked and eaten. How were they killed? Hacked to death with axes, stabbed with knives? Did their terror and melting fear, their anguish and helplessness, radiate through them so that it was borne into their flesh and thus into the person who ate it? The sight of Drew's gun, harsh cold metal, had made her contemplate this for the first time. There was a cold grey light round the weapon when she looked at it; she shivered and looked away quickly. Death was in that gun, yet she could not accept that anyone or anything had died from Drew firing it.

The fire was crackling merrily, snapping at twigs and parched branches from the low, storm-whipped bushes growing in a hollow nearby. The small black cooking pot was suspended over a tripod of metal and inside it a few inches of water were beginning to bubble around the herbs and green roots that she had picked herself from the part-soil, part-sand streak of earth running through the hollow. The sky was a vibrant orange-gold, and in the distance sand dunes rose like the billowing robes of a desert giant. She heard animals moving close by and flinched at the thought of their being killed so that she and Drew might eat. The Christian God spoke of love, forgiveness and tolerance to all mankind, but what of His little creatures?

This was the first time that she had been alone in the desert, yet she did not feel lonely or afraid. This was a place she was rapidly coming to love; she felt that she had been here before, lived here, even, and been happy. Because her mother was of nomad stock? She knew so little about her parents, and it was too late to find out now.

Stirring the pot, she sat cross-legged like a Beduin woman content in her family's camp. A bird flew overhead, slender and dark. It, too, was searching for food. She did not feel that its actions were against the way of nature; far from it. Animals and birds had been ordained by God to behave as they did; humans had a choice, and thus could commit evils.

Drew's voice came to her ears. He was standing on the sandy rise in front of her, waving and grinning broadly. Something was hanging from his hand. It looked like a rat. She shuddered.

'Do not look,' Drew said, sitting down beside her so that he could skin the creature. The creature was dead now; it would feel nothing. Nonetheless, she was feeling for it.

Into the bubbling water it went, cut into tiny pieces so that it would cook all the quicker. The smell which rose from the pot was delicious, and her stomach gurgled in the most unromantic way. She smiled ruefully. Drew laughed, patting her cheek, and told her that there would soon be the tastiest meal she had ever eaten.

He was right. She wanted to refuse the food, say that she could not eat one of God's creatures killed for her, but her hunger was more powerful, and she gobbled the meat. He would not identify it; he seemed to know that she was offended by her first experience with death.

When they had eaten, she felt painfully full. Despite her guilt, she could not survive on roots and berries. The Beduin tried to and became gaunt and thin-faced; when their hunger was severe they tightened their special belts to make their stomachs feel smaller and full.

Tea was refreshing; she was coming to like it in the plain way of the English, without mint or sugar. Black and acrid, it made her tongue feel furry, yet it revived her instantly.

'That was a sumptuous dinner,' she smiled. 'You know the ways of the desert so well. You have been here in this land many times?'

'I came here two years ago, and had one devil of an experience, if you want to know how I learned survival.' His eyes twinkled. 'I set out with a party of your countrymen, two guides and every possible piece of equipment to keep us comfortable. Afer a week, one of the guides decided he had seen enough of life and dropped dead. The other became deranged and spoke of curses and evil, and the *jinn* of the desert. He would not stay. By this time, we were somewhere to the north of here and it was too late to turn back. One morning I woke to find that half the equipment had been stolen in the night. The men trickled away one by one, until only myself and my English servant were left. It took us seven weeks to make it back to Najran. I had run out of bullets and so we were forced to live on roots with the taste and texture of badly cured leather, a few shrivelled berries when we were fortunate enough to find any, and the remains of the figs that we had brought with us. Figs, day after day after day!' He grimaced. 'You have no idea what a diet of figs can do to a man! At least it kept us on the move, back to civilisation.' His grin flashed. He was never unsmiling for long.

'Not all of my countrymen are thieves!' Mishaal had flushed when he told of his equipment being stolen. 'Some may be, and there is no excuse for it, but most are honest men.'

'Of course, my love, I had not meant to cast any slur upon your people.' Drew took her hand and kissed its soft palm. 'My God, we have enough thieves and vagabonds in America! England, too, for that matter. Human nature is the same the world over.'

'I know it. The *Qu'ran* is very firm in what it teaches Muslims. They must be considerate of those who are less fortunate, give alms to the poor and have charitable hearts. Allah . . .' Her voice faltered. Allah had dominated her life for as long as she could recall. Where was He now that she had forsaken Him? Did the forsaking mean that He ceased to exist? But no, how could He, when He was also the God of the Christians but by another name? Oh, how confusing it all was! 'Allah smiles upon those with generous hearts. Mohammed, the Prophet of Allah, says that the worst evil is meanness. He said, "Every Muslim who clothes the naked will be clothed by God in the green robes of Paradise," and that there is nothing greater or stronger than a good man giving alms, and that he must give with his right hand and conceal it from his left, and in that way he would overcome all things.' Mishaal's body was taut. She did not want her lover to believe that Muslims were bad, for then he would be biased against her people, and include her in that bias.

'And he also said, "Every good act is charity, smiling in your brother's face is charity" and an exhortation addressed to your fellow men to do virtuous deeds is equal to alms-giving. Putting a wanderer on the right path is charity, assisting the blind is charity; giving water to the thirsty, also. You see, I have read the words of the Prophet.'

'You know all this? You have read the *Ṣuwar*?' Mishaal gasped.

'I have, and not in their translation, I might add.'

'Why, why did you do this?'

'I am a writer, do not forget. They embrace the world, or rather a good writer does. I could not keep a closed mind to another religion, especially not when I am writing about your countrymen. I want the world to know about the Arabs, the noble savages that they are.'

'Noble savages? Do you think then that I am a savage?' Mishaal's face was scarlet. Throwing down the teapot, she leapt to her feet. 'Do savages learn that the greatest act of all is to give water to the thirsty and alms to the destitute?'

'Honey, I mean nothing against you personally! My countrymen have a fine and gallant image of your people as noble savages. They call them this because they rise above the harshness and indignities of their life in this desolate land and carry themselves with composure. So much of our learning originated in Arabia. A thousand years ago, Arabia was the centre of all wisdom and knowledge, did you know that? We have words in our English language which came from your tongue.'

'You do?' She paused, wanting to hear more.

'Yes. Your word *al-jabr* gave us algebra. Your *kafur* gave us camphor, the aromatic gum used in liniments. *Sifr* gave us cipher, *al-iksir* gave us elixir, and from your *nazir* we took nadir, the lowest point, and from *samt* came zenith, the highest. So you see, we owe your peoples much. Medicine too . . . Philosophy, mathematics, astronomy and astrology. Did you know, for example, that there was a school of medicine in Jundishapur in Persia, in the eighth century, when my own countrymen were savages indeed? In the centuries when learning became more widespread, the language of knowledge was Arabic, and the greatest scholars were Arabic.'

Mishaal's green eyes were wide. She had never guessed that the teachings of Arabia had borne fruit throughout the world.

'Did any women take part in this learning?'

'Indeed they did. Maysun, the Beduin wife of the first Umayyid Caliph, was a poetess. Listen:

'"*Breeze-flowing tents I prefer*
to ponderous halls
And desert dress
to diaphanous veils.
A crust I'd eat in the awning's shade,
not rolls,
And watched by a dog that barks
not a cat that smiles,
I'd sleep to the wind's tune,
not to the tambourine.
A youth's impetuous sword,
not a husband's wiles,
Uncouth slim tribesmen I love,
not corpulent men."'

'So, even the Beduin write verses. I had no notion that they were so sensitive. From what I had heard, they are hardy and stern of temperament. Tell me more, my Drew. What else did my ancestors do?'

'In the tenth century, Ali-ar-Bashman wrote his Book of the Stars, while my ancestors were running around in rough skins and living in mud huts! It was he who gave the constellations their animal identities, the zodiac. Nearly a thousand years ago, Al Birani wrote an encyclopaedia suggesting that the Earth might move round the Sun, not vice versa. We went on burning men at the stake for centuries because we insisted that the Sun moved round our Earth, and that we were the centre of the Universe.'

'So my Arab forefathers knew all about the stars and planets. Did they know about the brightest star which I used to see from my window? Would they have given it a name?'

'That is probably Venus, named after the Goddess of Love.'

Drew's eyes glittered as he pulled Mishaal to him. 'A fitting star for you to be ruled by, my child of love.'

She melted into his arms, tiny spangles of enjoyment dancing along her flesh. Her feet seemed to float above the ground as he held her. She had all the learning that she needed for life: she loved him and he loved her.

One more day and they would reach the oasis of Nargis where they could refill their water bags and sleep under a roof. They packed up their belongings and set off.

'Tell me more!' Mishaal called out as they urged their mounts into movement. 'Why did the Arabs write so much about the stars?'

'In ancient times, people believed that they were ruled by the stars. They navigated by the stars, so they were extremely important on sea voyages. The Arabs invented the astrolabe with which they could chart a voyage and check on all the planetary positions. And the compass was improved by the Arabs, although it originated in China. I know a poet whose work you would enjoy: Omar Khayyam. He was born in Nishahpur in the eleventh century. What of this, honey?

'"*Come, fill the cup, and in the*
Fire of Spring
The Winter Garment of Repentance fling:
The Bird of Time has but a little way
To fly – and Lo! The Bird is on the wing.

'"*Alas! that Spring should vanish*
with the Rose!
That Youth's sweet-scented Manus-
script should close!
The Nightingale that in the
Branches sang,
Ah, whence, and whither flown again,
who knows!"'

'That is very mournful. The death of youth . . . when I have barely begun it.' Mishaal wrinkled her nose.

'In my land, a poet would be likely to read a hundred books

before he embarked upon writing his own verse. Very few pour it from the heart like you, Mishaal.'

She averted her eyes, her cheeks turning pink. What was her scholarship compared to his? Not wishing to offend, she told him nothing.

That night they camped in a hollow close to what had once been a rushing *wadi*. Now it was dry, bleached and scorched like everything else in this desert. Small round stones filled the base of the hollow which they pushed aside to make a softer sleeping area. Caravans had come through here frequently; Mishaal could see a trail of polished rocks where they had travelled. The evening sky was rosy-mauve, delicate and pastel, giving no hint of the ferocity of midday. A breeze was mounting, whistling along the stones at the top of the hollow in the most eerie fashion, casting sand with energetic abandon.

The fire was fluttering and Drew had gone in search of meat for the pot. The horses had been watered and given their bags of oats and Mishaal found herself contemplating her ancestors. She had been desperate to discard her Arabic ancestry because she believed it to be unworthy of her future life. Now she was not so sure. All the great sciences and the arts, poetry and music, the stars which even now were glittering like new-minted dinars above her head: her old tutor had never told her that the knowledge of all these had been perfected and sent round the world by her forefathers. It was a stirring vision.

The horses were tugging at the tiny frizzled bushes and munching on them stolidly. Her skirt was filled with sand, she could taste grit on her mouth, and feel it itching in her eyes and nose. Life? What did it all mean? High above were those stars which circled the Earth like a Caliph's robe, and men had been steering their ships by them for centuries. Who had put the stars there so that men might find their way at sea?

Allah was the answer to that if she were the faithful Muslim she once had been. What would the *nasrani* say? His God, of course, the God whose Son had died on the Cross so that the world would be saved from Hell. That was what Drew had told her. Why did one man's death save the world? She could not comprehend such an act.

The stewing herbs smelt of fresh pasture after rain. She thought of the tiny patch of lawn in the court of Rhikia's house where she walked knowing that no one could accost her, and where, in clement weather she would practise her dancing.

Rhikia, dear Rhikia. How swiftly life sped by and took the ones you loved . . . The wind gusted again, and she shielded the pot with her hands. There was a chink of sound behind her, like a heel flickering on stone. She turned, but there was no one there. Her skin pricked sharply. Desert *jinns* . . . they were said to be particularly vicious and destructive. Closing her eyes, she tried to quiet her pounding heart.

Again that clinking noise, and the clatter of small stones. She rose to her feet, and stared in the direction of the sound. How dark the sky was now, with a dense shadow that seemed to be closing in on her. She put a hand to her throat, whispering, '*Istafarallah, istafarallah!* God forbid!' Although she could see nothing, she had the crawling sensation of someone or something approaching, reaching out to her, to grasp and imprison her.

'No! *No!*' she cried, thrusting out her arms and preparing to flee. 'Drew! Drew! Where are you? Help me, help me!'

Chapter Seven

A hand on her shoulder startled her so much that she screamed.

'Honey, it's only me. Who else did you think it was out here in the desert? Did you think some rapacious nomad was come to rape you? I would shoot him first.'

'Oh!' She fell into his arms, shivering and crying his name. She had been so sure that she would love the desert in its every mood, but this experience had unnerved her. Moaning winds, sand flying from nowhere and the sound of footfalls when there were no feet to be seen. Night spirits? If so, she never wanted to be alone in the dark again!

'See how the moon glows and the stars glitter. While they light the world, you will be safe,' he soothed.

'Everything went dark, like a great shadow falling over me. I could not see the stars or the moon! It came like a veil, a great veil . . .'

'Women's imagination . . . How fertile it can be. Food will alter your outlook. See what I have brought.'

Opening the pouch of his belt, he pulled out a long, thin coiling rope. Mishaal realised with horror that it was a dead snake. This was too much to bear! She flung out her hands, whimpering, 'No! No!' over and over while tears rushed down her face.

'God above, so you're petrified of snakes. I might have known it. Women are the same the world over. Look, it's dead, quite dead. Feel it, touch it, cold, dead, ready to be broiled in that pot. Snake meat tastes like chicken, very pleasant. I've eaten it in the American desert, too.'

'You have killed it!' Mishaal wept. 'It is dead!'

'Yes, that's what I said, so you're quite safe. Come on now, Mishaal, stop this blubbering. I'm ravenous.'

Choking, she turned from him, but the image of the dead snake remained imprinted on her mind. She had seen snakes before. Once in the souk a man had played on his *madruf*, a reed pipe, and the cobra had undulated out of the basket set before him, swaying and dipping like a woman's arm, slender and gleaming. How she had enjoyed watching that performance. She had gone back the next week, but the man had moved on. She had talked to Rhikia of introducing a new dance, of dropping the peacock idea and making a costume of silk imprinted with snake scales. Perhaps she could even use a live snake in the dance?

She would never forget her foster mother's expression.

'A *live* snake, *jijim*? Over my corpse is the only way that you will get a live snake into this house! And corpse it might well prove to be if you did bring one here!'

The cobra had been beautiful, a wild yet gloriously domesticated creature. The man threw it food, and it slept in its comfortable basket. She thought that such an arrangement would please it even though it would not have the chance to find a mate . . . But to see one dead, that richly graceful form and shape hanging limp like tattered rope, all life sped away, so that its meat could be cooked! She pressed a hand to her breast. She felt as if her heart had been pinched. Poor snake, one of the creatures of Allah and now it was dead because they had intruded on its territory.

Sighing impatiently, for he was hungry, Drew chopped the snake into rings and flung them in the steaming water. Soon there arose a succulent scent of cooking meat. Drew sat cross-legged to eat his dinner, but Mishaal would not join him.

'Come on, you're being stupid. You're as hungry as I am! Fresh meat will give you the strength for the journey. What are you afraid of? Snakemeat will not upset your stomach.'

'Maybe not,' she muttered, but she knew that it would, and not only her stomach. Her heart and emotions would be upset too. She did not know why; perhaps she was being unreasonable and idiotic as he said, but she could not help herself. The snake had been beautiful, wild and free, and now it was dead. Was that not enough? Must she eat its flesh, too?

The oasis of Nargis was tiny and shabby. An old woman, wizened and with one eye missing so that the flesh hung over the empty hollow like a brown pouch, welcomed them warmly.

There was a small group of men there, and to Mishaal's surprise they too rose and came to welcome them. Grinning, Drew began to talk, and Mishaal realised that this meeting had been arranged. The men did not appear to be unusual in any way except that they were somewhat unsavoury. How could they help Drew with his book? They were babbling together in Arabic now, so fast that she lost the thread of their speech. Yawning, she took a seat on the rush matting spread out by a low tray-like table. An old woman, happy to serve her, brought her goat's milk, *laban* and *harisa*, meat and flour mixed together like stew with hot butter poured in the centre. It was filling and rich and she enjoyed it.

Mishaal was sleepy. Folding her bernouse around her, she felt sleep creeping over her, her head nodding. Drew had not noticed; he was still rapt in conversation with the men. Now they had brought out sheets of crackly parchment; maps she thought; and were peering closely at them.

She jolted awake as Drew came to sit beside her.

'If my lady wishes to sleep sitting up then she can, but there is a bed prepared for us in the back. How did you dine with your *yasmak* in place, little one?'

She giggled sleepily. 'It helps to strain the food. I lift it up and eat beneath it, of course.'

The room was sparse and layered with sand, the walls were crude mud and twigs, daubed together to form a structure which would withstand the weather, and roughly smeared with white. On the floor was a rush mat, just big enough for two, and close by was a shiny brass tray on which stood a jug, battered mugs and a dish of figs. Mishaal did not care that the floor was baked mud, uneven and bone-bruising. Lying down, she swept into sleep in an instant, unaware of Drew's lying down beside her, his arm scooping her waist.

Dawn was pure nature. Here there were no roofs or minarets, no prayer towers or smoke, to interfere with the beauty created by the God of the Muslims and the Christians. Lush delicate peach came first, the wing of an angel spreading victoriously over the darkness of night, and then the sun, pulsing with fire and heat and the passion of eternity, making her think of the dead snake so that her eyes filled with tears.

She was standing at the door of the caravanserai with Drew's arm around her. They had breakfasted on pomegranates and goat's milk, unleavened bread and dates. The old woman had served them eagerly, her face split with smiles so that the hollow pit where her eye had been was deeply crinkled. Before and after serving them she salaamed, half bowing as if they were royal. Mishaal wanted to smile. What had they done to deserve such attention?

Outside, the morning air fragrant as herbs in his nostrils, Mishaal asked Drew why the woman was so humble.

'The men say she is a seer. Perhaps she knows that I am a lord in my homeland and that you will be my lady when we reach there?' He squeezed her hand.

'Perhaps, if she is a seer. She did not look as if she had the sight to me.'

He looked down at her in surprise. 'Can you tell?'

She bit her lip. Would he think she was boasting?

'Well, can you?'

'I . . . Yes, usually I can tell when anyone has such gifts. How, I do not know.'

'So you are possessed of unearthly perceptions?'

There was a strange look in his eye. She did not like it. It chilled her, changing their relationship in a way that she did not wish. He had thought she was bragging.

'Oh no, what opportunity have I had to exercise such a talent as that, my Drew? I tease you, that is all.'

But the look remained in his eyes. For all that he said, he was like the Muslim men who did not want a wife to excel them in any way. All the same, she had the gift. She had always had it. She would just have to conceal it from him, that was all. Matiya had taught her how to use it wisely, and how to nurture it.

'Can you perceive eternal truths, my Mishaal? Do you know what is fact and what is fantasy when men speak of matters such as history and philosophy?'

He was waiting for her reply; she could feel the tension in him.

'My Drew, I cannot even spell those words let alone know what truths they contain. How can you award your untutored Arabian girl such gifts? She does not possess them, I assure you. Such talk is wild. How can anyone see what is not there?'

Yet, the night before she had sensed, felt, almost seen, some looming evil, palpable as flesh before her, blotting out the moon and the stars. The dawn was ruined for her; cold spangles were furrowing along her spine. Nothing will be the same again, Mishaal, no man likes a woman who possesses qualities he cannot understand or share; he will change his mind about you now; he will not love you . . . Her throat was closing, her heart aching, and there were fresh tears in her eyes.

'Mishaal, honey, I did not mean to upset you! God, but women are sensitive! Come here, little one, see, I am not cross with you. Why should I be? You be a seer if you want it so much, but do not forget that you might end up old and ugly and with one eye missing!'

The chilling moment was over; laughing, she fell into his arms.

'Where are we heading now, my Drew?' They were setting out again, bags packed with dried dates, water, *laban* and pomegranates shrivelled to dark brown with age.

'The next oasis, where else?' He grinned at her disarmingly.

'Where is that? Is it far? Do we meet other men there?'

'So many questions, my little one, my seer of the desert . . . If you have the gift, then you tell me.'

He was laughing, telling her nothing. What was he hiding? Why should he conceal their destination? She thought of the night before, the men arguing over the maps. She was convinced that Drew had a private destination, a secret goal. The Muslim in her told her to close her mouth, to be obedient and silent, but the woman whom he was schooling for life in the New World wanted to speak out, demand to be told. For a time they rode in silence.

They had exchanged their horses for camels, and this new mode of travel was more than enough to occupy her thoughts; a world of swaying, lurching and the animal's loud belches. Now here was an ugly beast, she thought, yet he could exist for days in the desert without water, surviving on little more than a few shoots. Mishaal's camel was a dingy brown, shabby and sorry looking with bald patches, but its hump was solid with water. She was surprised to find that it was female.

'The female is tougher and bolder,' Drew told her. 'Surely you knew that? Males for carrying goods, females for long journeys. We can milk this one for she recently gave birth.'

'Where is her calf?'

'I believe it died.' Drew's eyes were on the horizon.

He was far away from her in thought, more distant now than ever before. He was discovering that she was not as perfect as he had thought; she could tell that she was displeasing him in little ways, almost daily. But at night all was forgotten as they lay in one another's arms: then she had his full and dazzling attention.

Their horses had been quiet at night, but camels belched and snorted. After a few nights, she became accustomed to this but still occasionally woke with a jolt. Drew insisted that no one would come near them; that they were quite safe here.

'Why are we safe here? What is special about this part of the desert?' she asked. 'It looks much the same as any other part.'

'Yes, it may be to you, but it is deserted. Had you not noticed? This area is taboo. You know that word?'

'I – I may do, I am not sure.' Better to sound ignorant and let him feel important explaining things to her.

'Taboo means forbidden, to be avoided at all costs. The nomads have a legend about this area, some old mumbo jumbo about its being a place of pagan worship in ancient times, sacred to a goddess.'

Tingles were scoring along Mishaal's skin. She felt suddenly cold, as if a winter wind were blowing.

'Why must we come here, my Drew?' she whispered.

'For my book, my love. I told you. Research for my book, "Treatise on the Morals and Mores of the Arab Nation". This is the important part!' He turned glittering eyes to her.

She did not know what he meant by mores, but morals – proper behaviour, fidelity, loyalty and honesty – how could any of these be found here?

'I know what I am doing, Mishaal,' he went on. 'In a few hours we should see a ruined building, a temple. My readers will be eager to hear all about it.'

'Of course, my Drew.' Hiding a sigh, she rode on beside him.

She felt it growing colder, yet it was morning and should surely be growing warmer. The pricking sensation on her skin had returned, and her senses spoke of danger, but she was being stupid and must not let her lover see her disquiet. It would irritate him and he would look at her in that cool, detached way which she could not bear.

Midday now and in the distance, shimmering in the blazing liquid-silver heat haze, lay what must be the ruined temple. Once it must have been a glorious place for pagan worshippers to come. In the days before Mohammed, there had been 400 pagan gods and not until the Prophet had forbidden their worship had Allah risen, the one true and exalted God. Was this a temple where those pagan gods had been honoured, or did they each have their own temple?

'Whose temple was it?' she asked, shielding her eyes against the glare.

'One of those dark and evil pagan goddesses who demanded blood sacrifices and promiscuous rites: connected in some way with the golden calf worship, I think. In our Bible, the Jews turned away from God and fell into sin, making sacrifices to an idol called the golden calf,' he explained. 'It was the symbol of a god whose name I do not know.'

'The *Qu'ran* says that Allah will not tolerate idolatry, and that the pagans prayed to females. What does your holy book say?'

'Females? I do not know of any references to female gods in the Bible – they weren't important enough to be in the Scriptures. The pagan goddess worship was unearthed by archaeologists, and it became obvious from the deciphering of the tablets found – the writings, that is – that her priestesses were prostitutes, women of great immorality who would lie with any man who wanted them. They were called "*qadesh*".'

'I have heard that word before! It means holy, not prostitute!' Mishaal could not help herself, the words were out before she could stop them.

'*Holy?* Women who would lie with any man, even beggars who came to the temple? How could they have been holy?'

'Yes, you are right, of course, my Drew. How could they have been?'

They were like the women at Rhikia's house, harlots, fallen angels, and as such deemed the lowest of the low. To Mishaal they were warm, pulsing, emotional human beings, many of whom had endured heartache and destitution before coming to her foster mother's house. Sneer at them, judge them as immoral? She would never do that.

'The pagan ways are most unsavoury, and merely excuses to indulge in the perverted pleasures of the flesh, to sacrifice young girls to heathen gods who were figments of lunatic imaginations.' Drew's russet eyes glittered. 'Thank God that we have left those times behind. We are enlightened now and that is entirely due to God's good grace.'

'Yes, my Drew.' And Mohammed's, she added silently.

'I think we should rest now, and drink.' He reached behind him for his water flask, opened it, drank deeply and then replaced the flask at his hip.

For a few brief seconds, Mishaal felt as if she had been forgotten. He had thought of his own thirst first, leaving her to fend for herself. In her country, that would be normal, but in his, so he had led her to believe, men prided themselves on putting ladies first at all times. There was an intricate system of what he called 'etiquette' which said that ladies should be given the first serving, the first seat, the first attentions at every opportunity.

Either Drew was no gentleman, or else – Allah forbid the thought! – he did not think her a lady.

She drank from her own flask. Warm and tepid, the water tasted of goat hide. Her camel seemed restive, throwing its head up and down, scraping at the ground, and snorting in an ear-splitting and embarrassing way. *They* had never heard of etiquette or restrained behaviour.

Patting the beast's neck, Mishaal spoke to her camel.

'Hush, brown one, you are soon to rest. Now, will you get down so that I may step off your back?' She waited until Drew was ready to help her down, then tugged at the camel's reins in the way that Drew had shown her, so that it began to sink to the sand, lurching and swaying so that she had to grip with her hands and knees or be catapulted off. Once it knelt, she took hold of Drew's hands and slid off the animal's hump. Her back felt as if it had been pummelled; her buttocks were inflamed with the pressure of so many hours' arduous riding. She had not suffered this way with the horses; how genteel they were compared to this great wild and unruly beast. How could the Beduin love their camels and nurture them like pets?

What enormously long lashes her camel possessed, protecting her eyes against the sun, and how round and limpid were the eyes. Before she knew what she was doing, she was hugging the neck of her mount. It looked surprised, alarmed even, but no more astonished than she was at her gesture.

'Women.' Drew was watching her antics with a half smile on his face. 'I suppose you will want to dress it up next? A ribbon for its hair and curling tongs for that moth-bitten fur, eh?'

'Are there any camels in New Jersey?' she asked innocently.

'Camels in New Jersey!' Drew guffawed. 'No, only high-nosed ladies who think they are too good to speak to poor folks, but they exist the wide world over, honey.'

'You said there was a desert in the New World? Is there no camel for that?'

'No. We manage fine with mules and horses.'

'Are horses different there? Can they carry water inside them like camels?'

'No, my little inquisitor. The deserts are not as arid and grim as out here, but bad enough all the same.'

'How is merchandise transported through them?'

'By wagon train or mule. Can you imagine a large square wooden box on wheels, covered by a white canvas roof, pulled by horses? That is a wagon. The pioneers of America are famous for their wagon trains. They pack all that they own and set off across the Rockies and the deserts to face Red Indian heathens, shortage of water, cholera, smallpox and all manner of other killing diseases, just so that they can find their own little homestead in a free country. Once they find a plot of land they drive a stake of ownership into the ground and it is theirs. After that, it's struggling against wildcats and hungry bears and the elements, to name but three little problems.' He grinned. 'I was fortunate. I had the money to buy a ready-made and very beautiful homestead.'

'Tell me about your home, my Drew.'

They were sitting cross-legged on goatskins, eating *laban* and sipping camel's milk while the camels themselves attacked the rusty roots nearby, great upper lips crunching savagely.

'It is just one hundred years old, of brick, with three storeys, that is, levels, and wings at either end with two storeys each. Not the wings of birds, but named because they are attached to a house rather like wings are attached to a bird at the sides, and outspreading. Each of these wings has its own entrance, and inside each has seven chambers. The main part of the house has a massive Dutch door, the planks of wood formed into Vs. It's set back quite a way from the main street, and there's a wide lawn to the front, and some beautiful old trees framing it. You will love it, without doubt.'

'I cannot wait to love it, my Drew! Tell me, shall we go on our travels often, or is this all that you need do for your book?'

'You are here now because I found you here, my little one. A wife's place is in the home. Besides, when you have children you will not be able to leave them.'

'So you will be leaving me often?'

'Often? Now I did not say that, did I?' He took her hand and kissed each fingertip. 'Perhaps once more, twice at the most. Believe me, you will be more than occupied with our family. I would like four sons and two daughters.'

She suppressed a giggle. Her man might claim to be a *nasrani* and a Westerner but she knew better. Men were all the same religion beneath the skin: that of Islam.

Her camel was behaving strangely again, tossing its head and rolling its eyes. Mishaal took water for it and risked her fingers as it drank gustily and roughly from a dish in her palms.

'What ails you, unruly one?' Mishaal whispered in its ear. 'Do you want to be back home? Comfortable in pastures of green grass? It will not be much longer before you are free of us.'

'It is only a camel, Mishaal, not a child,' Drew remonstrated. 'It cannot understand what you are saying. Even if it could, do you expect it to talk back to you?'

Smiling, she left the camel and returned to her place by Drew, at which he looked relieved. He was jealous, that was it! He wanted all of her attention, just like a child. Well, why not? If he needed her enough then he would not leave her behind when he went off on his expeditions, however many children they had.

It was late afternoon when they set off again, with Mishaal singing beneath her breath to keep her camel from snorting and tossing its head. The animal seemed to be calmer when she sang.

'Carry me over the gilded sands, beast of inner beauty,
Take me to my destiny, bear me with your high back;
Worship with me in the temple of the pagan goddess and when you have done your duty,
Our rewards shall be so rich that wealth, money and love we shall never lack . . .'

Drew looked at her sharply. 'Where did you learn that?'

'I just made it up now as I went along. It is nothing, just a silly verse, a nonsense, that is all, my Drew.'

He looked taken aback and there was that chill in his eyes. Was it her mention of the pagan goddess? Or her attention to the camel?

Two hours later, stiff-backed and desperate for *terra firma*, Mishaal begged that they make camp for the night. The sky was swarming with shadows, steely-grey and watery-ebony streaks.

Drew stopped when he saw a suitably sheltered but rocky dip in the ground. They made camp swiftly, for the sky was stark ebony now, ominous with the threat of a storm. They secured their tent with extra firmness, weighting its edge with the largest rocks they could find. Then they hobbled their camels, Drew tying their forelegs together just above the foot, the traditional method of ensuring that an animal did not stray. Snorting and puffing, the camels watched them vanish inside the tent and tightly secure the flap.

Inside it was cosy and intimate and, wrapped in their sleeping blankets, they waited for the storm.

The wind steamed along the desert surface, scouring, screeching, smashing against rocks and stones tempestuously. Mishaal felt that they might not survive its attentions. She heard the camels baying, then thudding to their knees for shelter.

'They are used to this, unlike us,' Drew said, reading her mind. 'Tell me, have you changed your mind about coming into the wilderness with me? Is it too frightening for you, honey?'

'No! Not with you beside me.' She rested her head on his broad shoulder. 'I would follow you anywhere even if there were storms every night! But I wish . . .' She paused.

'What do you wish, my love?'

'I wish that we had room for the camels in here with us!'

The wind screamed until midnight, sandblasting them so that when they tried to climb out of the tent at dawn they found it half buried in sand. Nonetheless, Drew said that it was only a minor windstorm compared to some he had seen. Mishaal herself had heard such a wind in the distance from Rhikia's house when gazing out of the window above the roof tops and minarets to see sky the colour of sand as great veils of grit and dust were scooped into the air. The *simûm*, they called it, the hot, dry, scouring wind that found its way into men's hearts. They said that if a Beduin were opened up after death, his body would be filled with sand. She could well believe it.

There was grit all over her face and in her eyelashes, up her nose and in her mouth, down her dress and in her nails. Slapping and shaking it away, she stopped suddenly.

Last night had been the first night that they had not made love since they had set out together.

Chapter Eight

'By the morning hours
And by the night when it is stillest
The Lord hath not forsaken thee.'
The Qu'ran 93:1–3

Ahead of them the temple shimmered, surreal and glowing. Mishaal glanced at Drew's face. His expression was that of a man who anticipates a meeting with Allah and his angels. He was urging on his camel fiercely, and she was biting back her anger. How could he hit the poor creature with his stick and stab his knees into its sides? Did he not know that animals had feelings too?

The more they travelled towards the shining ruins, the more distance there seemed to be between them.

'It is an illusion that we get no nearer . . . Something to do with the light here,' Drew explained, but his jaw was tightly clenched and he was restless in his saddle.

Nonetheless, after another three hours they were no nearer their destination. The sky was dimming, and the painful white light that turned the sand to ghostly beige was fading fast.

'Goddam weather!' Drew hissed, then, looking ashamed, he apologised for his words. 'This country is blasted in every sense of the word! What the hell's happened to the light?'

Was another storm on the way? No, it did not seem to be for the atmosphere was fresh and cool, the air serene. Mishaal sniffed. To her surprise it was scented. She could smell frankincense and myrrh, cinnamon and jasmine, rose, musk and ambergris, one after the other. She recognised them all from Matiya's mixtures. How light-hearted she felt now, joyous and exhilarated. All would be well; happiness would come, but not yet, not until difficulties and dangers had befallen her . . .

'Mishaal, stop dreaming! I said, do you want to stop now? We might as well.'

'Stop now?' She turned a dreamy face to her lover. Where had she been? What had happened to her just then? First she had smelt the spices and the incense and then words had floated into her head as if spoken by an invisible voice, a woman's voice, yet if she was asked to describe it, she could not. It was soft yet strong, authoritative yet gentle, loving yet distant. The desert *jinn* were affecting her wits!

'Yes, shall we make camp and eat?'

Drew was already tapping his camel on the neck with his stick so that she would halt. Next he was gripping on for dear life as she flung herself to her knees without warning, almost bucketing him over her head.

'Cussed beast!' he scowled, turning his frown to a grin when he saw Mishaal trying not to laugh. 'All right, so I should have clicked my tongue to make her stop. I can't be perfect all the time!'

Mishaal's smaller mount sank smoothly to the sand, so that she had no fear of being unseated. Gracefully she alighted, with Drew's help, thankful to feel the solid, crunchy grit of the sand beneath her feet.

Soon they were picking out the sand from their food and sipping the sun-warmed water out of the flasks. Dates had rapidly become monotonous, too sickly-sweet and thirst-creating. Mishaal thought of the nomads of the desert who existed on little else at times.

Drew was preoccupied. Staring across the undulating land, his eyes narrowed, he chewed slowly, not seeming to taste his food.

'Can you see the temple still?' she asked, wanting his attention, his eyes on her so that she would feel loved again.

'It hasn't walked.' He gritted his jaw. 'Or has it? Goddamit, what if the blazing thing's a mirage?' Flinging down his food, he jumped up, cursing. Clenching his fists, he stood facing in the direction of the temple as if goading it to move towards him.

Mishaal did not know what to say or do. Sometimes this man of hers mystified her completely, but then men were not renowned for their open natures. They kept their secrets, reflected seriously on God and the problems of the world, and were not troubled by petty complaints. That was what Rhikia had said when she was telling Mishaal about marriage.

'How can you tolerate this blasted wilderness?' Drew growled suddenly, turning fierce-eyed towards her. 'You've never whined once, you don't pester or whimper or beg for help every few yards! Are you made of iron, woman?'

Heat flowed up her neck and into her cheeks. She had never told anyone about her origins. What little she knew was a secret to hold to her breast. One day she had planned to tell Drew, but not yet, not yet. Would it dampen his anger if he knew? Swallowing, breathing shakily, she considered.

'I – my mother was a Beduin, one of the Sulubba tribe.' Reaching her eyes, the heat burned in a stinging strip across her temples. 'Perhaps I took to the desert life so easily because of her blood . . . Her family had stopped wandering and made their home in Abeesha, but they say, once a Beduin, always a Beduin.'

'So you prefer the desert to America, eh?' His eyes were passionless as obsidian, shadowed with emotions and complexities that she could never hope to understand in such a brief time of knowing him. 'Would you rather stay here? Have you changed your mind about coming with me?'

His hands were clamping her shoulders, biting deep and making them ache.

'Whither thou goest,' she whispered, scouring his eyes for some hint of warmth, but there was none. 'Whither thou goest I shall go. My destiny is to be with you, my Drew. I have no doubts of that. Allah has willed it.'

'*God* has willed it,' he corrected sharply, cupping her jaw in his palm. 'You have forgotten Allah, remember? You are Christian now, leaving behind all that barbaric heathen nonsense and taking on a new life, a new religion – and a new husband.'

How could she explain to him that she had never been one of the heathen, not the heathen of whom he spoke with such derision. Did he class her as a pagan idolator, the name he had used for the ones who worshipped before the days of the Prophet? How could he do that? The Prophet had cast out all false idols.

'Yes, my Drew.'

'When we are in New Jersey, you will soon forget your origins and the land where you were born. Whatever land one came from, America is the loved one, the new life, the new beginning. People have come from all over the world to make a new start there: English, French, Irish, Europeans, Scots, Welsh, all colours and all creeds. You'll never feel out of place, not as you would in the drawing-rooms of England.'

'Why should I feel out of place?'

'I was thinking of . . .' He faltered.

'The colour of my skin? But you like it, you said.'

'Yes, I do, honey, indeed I do. It is just that . . . well, there are slaves in my land whose colour is bordering on yours, half-castes, bred from dark and light-coloured negro stock.'

'But you will tell people that I am half-English!'

'Some of the negroes are half-English, too, honey! Or rather half-American. You see, because their masters want to breed light-skinned slaves they lie with their negresses. It is a matter of economy, very practical and logical when you think about it.'

'So you will tell people that I am half-Arabian and half-English!'

'I wonder . . . I wonder what they will think of you?'

'I do not care! I care only what you think of me, my Drew. As your wife, I can face anything, believe me, I can! The women of the Sulubba tribe are used to insults and anger: they are the poorest tribe and must exist by doing work for the richer ones.'

'I know. The tinkers and hunters. Had I not known that, I would have said you were proud Rif or even Berber with that arrogant stance . . .' His eyes were twinkling now, to her relief.

'The Berbers are warring, and the Rif, too. When you are poor you do not have the energy to do battle. My mother was a great beauty . . . She sang in the city and there she met my father, a traveller from America, just like you, Drew. He too was handsome and they fell in love.' Her lip quivered. 'Soon, my mother was with child and then my father fled, not wishing to be burdened with her and an infant. She could not return to her family for the shame of it, so she stayed with my foster mother, Rhikia, until the child, myself, was born, and then she fled to take her life because she could not live without my father.'

'How much of that is true and how much did you make up, my pretty little poetess?'

'It is all true!' Mishaal said indignantly.

'Intolerably romantic and awash with gush. I am sure that the truth was far less attractive.'

'Love is the bringer of great pain as well as great happiness. We learn by it; who would wish to lead a dull and passionless life without love? I would rather love like my mother did, then die young, than never love at all! It is not what you call gush!'

Suddenly his arms were round her and her little trembling body was crushed to his.

'Do not say any more about dying, honey! No more!'

They stood there, tightly clasped, and the light changed, the sky becoming a full-blooded blue behind them, the sun a glowing topaz from the diadem of some great and eternal god. Peace filled them both, the peace of love and companionship and the knowledge that they were meant for one another.

That night they lay tightly in one another's arms, knowing that on the morrow they would reach the ruined temple: the temple of dreams and long-lost hopes and wishes. His readers would love to hear of the ruins, Drew said. They relished descriptions of ancient buildings lost to time, now rediscovered. It fired their imaginations, and ensured that he would have a best-selling volume on his hands. His employer's books in similar vein had been enormously successful.

'The legends about this place . . . They will relish those, too. Have you heard them?'

'I? But I do not even know the name of this temple, my Drew, or why it is out here so alone, with no dwellings near it.'

'It did have once.' His voice was relaxed and yet Mishaal sensed his excitement. 'There was a city round it, but time has swept it away with the winds and the dust and heat of the desert. Probably the houses were simple, made of mud and straws, unable to withstand storms, the *simûm* and so on, but the temple itself was built of solid marble. They built for eternity, you see, not knowing how history would alter things ineradicably. Honey, you know that map I showed you?'

Mishaal remembered a crumpled, ragged scrap of ancient parchment on which there were scrawls and scribbles; she had not understood why Drew handled it with such reverence.

'It is a treasure map, the key to our fortunes, our great future! Many hundreds of years ago, jewels were buried in that very temple and they have remained there ever since. My employer, Lord Tavenish, first got scent of them when he was here just before you were born, honey, but illness took him back home. This country's climate is murderous for Westerners. But he never forgot that old legend. Now that he's in bad health, and won't live much longer, so the physicians say, he'd like to see the jewels before he dies. It's only natural.'

'Yes, only natural,' Mishaal echoed, her mind spinning. That old legend about the Jewels of Destiny . . . Rhikia's favourite, the one she had been raised on, like a fairytale, and he, her Drew, had the map that pinpointed them. It sounded unbelievable. Strangely, she felt unaccountably sad at this talk of jewels. It brought back Rhikia and her childhood, and something else, a sensation of loss and grief, of ruined plans and a woman weeping; the sound came eerily to her ears, causing her to shiver, yet she could see that Drew heard nothing. His eyes were still glowing with the thought of his treasure. The weeping continued, filled with heartbreak and tragedy. Clamping her hands to her ears, she cried out, 'Stop! Stop!'

Drew looked shocked. 'Am I boring you, honey?'

'I heard a sound . . . the – the wind sweeping through the rocks. It was frightening, like someone sobbing.' Trembling, she flung herself into his arms, only to find that there was no comfort there for her that night.

Her eyes flicked open. It was black and chilly. She had heard the thudding of hooves in the sand. Someone was stealing their mounts! Nudging Drew, she flung back her covers and watched from the tent opening as he rushed outside, a gun in each hand.

Through the opening, she saw their camels where they had left them, their feet hobbled so that they could not escape. A spear of ice sliced between her shoulder blades. The thudding hooves were not thieves running away, but men coming towards them!

'*Ya Allah*, protect him, oh God of the Christians, watch over him!' she babbled, fingers curled into fists. Then she remembered the knives he carried, and she searched wildly beneath the bedding. She felt the coldness of death in her palm and loathed it. This knife had killed; she could feel it; there had been blood and agony on its blade.

Rushing out, she saw the riders looming, six or eight, then more, so that their little camp was girdled. Beduin . . . nomads whose intent they could not gauge. They might be friendly or violent; how could she tell?

'We are friends!' she called out in Arabic. 'We come as friends, we mean no harm! If we are in your territory, we mean no harm and we shall leave without causing you any harm. Allah be merciful, Allah the one true and exalted god! *Billâh 'ailak!* For God's sake, I implore you!'

The girdle of dark riders on their dark horses closed in,

moving so rapidly that she could not run, nor even reach Drew's arms in time . . . Swiftly, like the closing of an eye, they dismounted and ringed Drew.

Wildly he fired. He was still firing into their dark throng when they took him, grasping his arms so that he struggled in vain to free himself. One of the men clasped the front of his shirt, bunching it in his fist, and, with his other hand, raised his curved dagger, thrusting it firmly against Drew's throat.

Screaming, Mishaal tried to reach him. It is not happening, it is not happening! she had thought as she watched him being encircled, but it *was* happening and he was a prisoner about to be killed. Oh God, she must save him! She must! The curved dagger was pressing closer, deeper, blood was beginning to flow.

Suddenly, her feet left the ground as she was hoisted roughly into the air by a powerful arm, and flung across a horse. Its rider was silent and, twisting, she turned to see his face. Screaming and struggling, she hit out with her bunched fists, smashing at his arms and chest and neck, as high as she could reach in her ungainly position.

Tears blinding her, she could see nothing but the shadowy shape of a man in Arab clothes, a dark face half-concealed by his flowing headdress, then, as her tears increased, he became a great bubble-covered figure, then a blur. She felt a powerful hand stilling her, clamping her face-down into the saddle so that she could not move. Her legs hanging down, she felt the strain on her spine, and her fingers clawed at the saddle, trying to gain a hold so that she could fight back. But the horse gathered speed, moving as if carried by the *simûm*, undulating across the night-black sand, faster and faster so that she thought it might take wing.

'*Daheelek!* For the mercy of God, let me go!' she screamed. 'What have you done to my Drew? You *shaîtan*, you *shaîtan*, you black demon, *jinn* of a thousand evils, killer of men! Take me back, *daheelek*! *Daheelek!*'

'Be silent, wolverine,' was his reply. 'Be silent or I shall bind thy mouth.'

Then she knew that she was in the hands of one who was

merciless and foul, and that she could expect no compassion. They had killed her beloved Drew and now she could expect the worst that could befall a woman in such circumstances . . .

It did not mean that she need accept in humble silence. Struggling, kicking and lashing out with her fists, she continued to scream curses and abuse at the man who had captured her. Unaffected by her fulgent tirade, he rode on silently, carrying her away from her love and her destiny and her great future with Drew in the New World across the seas.

Chapter Nine

She was unconscious when the horse came to a halt at the nomads' camp. It was not yet dawn, the time when the first call to prayer would rouse the sleepers.

The rider looked down at the inert body hanging over his horse. He had no intention of assaulting an unconscious woman; he must put her somewhere until she had recovered from her ordeal. He carried her into a tent, the smell of goatskin strong and thick in the air, and placed her down on a pallet, covering her with a goatskin. He did not want her fevered, so that she would be useless for his purpose. Now she would sleep, and, when she woke, all would become plain to her. Women with stubborn minds like this one must learn that man was master, that all their blandishments and abuse would fall on unhearing ears. She would soon learn; all the others had learned. Eventually, she would accept her fate and blend into the life of his tribe as the others had done and this scene would be forgotten.

Had she thought that life as her Westerner's harlot would be sweet? More fool she. It would have been hell on earth; she would have been scorned and treated with contempt wherever he took her. Fleetingly, he thought of his cousin, Alamma, who had fallen in love with a *nasrani*. No Beduin girl was ever forced into a marriage that she did not want, although marriage to one's own kin was of paramount importance. Alamma had followed her *nasrani*, only to find that he had a wife already in his own land, where men had but one wife by the laws of that place.

Poor Alamma. She would have been his bride and the mother of his sons by now, but she was dead: she had taken her own life rather than endure the shame and humiliation of being a fallen woman. If only she had come back to him, he would have forgiven her, taken her to his tent and treated her with tenderness. How he had loved her, his brown-skinned Alamma: the heart of his life until she had set eyes on the *nasrani* in the city.

The girl was sleeping. It had alarmed him that she was of mixed blood. He had thought her all Arab, in the shadows of the night, for the moon was small, until she had turned those bright-green eyes on him and emerald fire had streamed from them. Her skin was fair compared to Alamma's, yet her hair was basalt silk.

He knelt at her side, reaching out to touch the skeins of tumbled hair, unable to see how they gleamed in the darkness of the tent, yet knowing that they did. He could feel their cool, shimmering life beneath his fingers as he stroked a few skeins between forefinger and thumb. She was arrogant; he thought that she might well have Berber or Rif blood, in which case he must return her to her people: Allah's warmongers par excellence.

The scent of her body rose to his nostrils. Jasmine, frankincense and myrrh, roses. She smelt like an offering in the temple. A woman of roses, honey and frankincense: an offering *to* him, or *from* him? His jaw clenched. Life in the black tents: did she know anything of it or was she some byblow born in the city of a bittersweet and tragic love such as Alamma's? His heart contracted. He had known of the man whom he and his men had dealt with tonight, but nothing of this girl, not even her name.

He strode out of the tent, into the star-jewelled night. Dawn was near; the camels were snorting and easing their stringy limbs. Soon there would be the call to prayer. He would set one of the women to care for the girl until she was strong enough to do what he wished; no, on second thoughts, perhaps two women would be better, for she was a girl of unparalleled angers.

Smiling to himself, he strode away, his mind intent on the coming day's events.

Mishaal woke from a shade-filled dream. Gaunt, stalking giants had been surrounding her, closing in, death-threatening, vicious. She was to die, a sacrifice, her blood was to be strewn on the earth to propitiate the gods . . .

Waking, she thought herself still asleep. It was dark; there was an animal scent in the air. There was no sound save for the rustle of dried grasses as a beast grazed. She was damp with sweat, her limbs droning with pain, her back strained and bruised. When she tried to move her head, it was to see a pantheon of stars flashing across the darkness, acid-bright.

Her moan brought someone close. She could not see their face.

'My Drew?' she whispered in a strangled voice. 'Is that you?'

A woman's voice answered, in Arabic, the straightforward speech of the desert, with none of the city affectations.

'You are safe, daughter of strangeness. Do you wish anything? You have but to ask and Nur shall obtain it for you.'

The smell of goats was overpowering now, for Nur was one of the goat-herding women, famed for her ability to sit alone in the desert with her beasts and say nothing, want for nothing and expect nothing. She was old now and others had taken her place, yet she still considered her patience to exceed that of any of the others of her tribe, especially the men.

'Where's Drew?' More stars sped across her vision as she struggled to sit up. 'Where is he? What have you done with him? Allah, my head . . . Tell me, woman, where is he? *Bring him to me now!*'

The woman shrugged, looked away, then played with the tassel on her bernouse.

'Answer me, Nur, you said anything I wanted you would obtain! Where is he, where is my Drew?'

Tears of frustration filled her eyes and a dull, pounding headache was thrusting its way up from her shoulders.

Nur shrugged again, splaying her henna-patterned hands. They looked like dried leather gloves, brown and parched and crinkled. Bracelets jangled on her bony wrists.

'Fetch Drew to me now!' Mishaal croaked, unable to summon her anger to fire point. 'Fetch me that man . . . The one who brought me here!'

Nur got up, walked to the tent entrance, paused, then stepped outside.

Alone, Mishaal recalled the night before. The nomads surrounding them, the men attacking Drew, the knife pressing into his throat. She began to scream, over and over, knowing that he was dead and that she had been abducted as he was dying. He had died alone, without her arms around him. Oh merciful God, which paradise would he go to, hers or his? She did not even know if the God-Allah had the same one! They would never meet again, never kiss and love and ride together beneath the star-jewelled skies, never marry in the New World and watch their children grow . . .

She wanted to die, too, to join him now, take his hand and go with him on his journey to the land beyond, the paradise of man and woman.

Had the Beduin woman left a knife, anything sharp with which she could kill herself? Oh, for one of those glossy black guns that radiated death to the touch.

She was scrabbling through the mats and goatskins when Nur returned with a second woman, Shamim. They stood in the entrance to the tent, blocking her way. Angrily she pushed at them. She must find a death weapon outside, for none was here.

Shamim was solid for a Beduin, and her muscular arms hooked on to Mishaal so that she could not run.

'Child of angers, what is it you wish? Would you insult the Exalted One by refusing your fate?'

In her fury she thought that the Exalted One referred to the Beduin leader and that Shamim was talking of the fate that would take her, Mishaal, to his bed.

'There is no one on earth who would force me to lie with a man I do not love! Let me go, you she-camels! I am a free woman, not a prisoner! Where is that jackal who brought me here? Tell him that I shall go free . . . He cannot keep me here against my will!'

'*Jackal!*' Shamim gasped. 'You speak with the tongue of a *jinn*! How dare you insult the Amir? He will have you punished for this abuse, child of the *jinn*.'

'Amir? That bully? Never! He is tricking you all! Amirs are noble, generous princes, not devils who abduct women!'

'*Ya Allah*, but you are sunstruck! Lie down and we shall bring Zamir to you. She will fight the evil eye and free you from this possession.'

'Evil eye? I am not possessed!' Mishaal cried. 'Where is my Drew, the man I was with in the desert? If your man had been attacked before your eyes would you not be deranged? *Billâh 'alaik*, fetch me someone who has some sense in their heads!'

Nur and Shamim exchanged a glance and then Nur stepped outside the tent, recollecting the old Arab saying, 'If you meet a one-eyed person, turn over a stone.' The girl in the tent did not have an eye missing, but Nur thought that she was likely to bring them all a terrible misfortune, so she searched for a large stone and carefully reversed it in her hand while praying ardently to the one true God, Allah the all-merciful.

The Amir was with his favourite mare, Shahida. She was fevered after the night's activities and he was soothing her with herbs to bring down her fever.

Seeing the sick mare, Nur cried out, 'Allah preserve us! Already it is happening! She is bringing evil upon us! Nothing but misfortune shall be our lot, *ya saiyid*, nothing but misfortune!'

The Amir looked up in surprise.

'Who is bringing us misfortune?' he said, his tone impatient. He had no time for old-wives' gossip and superstitions. He was trying to lead his tribe out of the darkness, where they had languished for centuries due to such ignorance.

'The girl, the one you brought here last night! She has the evil eye! Her tongue is poisoned, her eyes glow like demons' . . . She is crazed; she will see us all dead!' Nur flung herself to her knees before the Amir and kissed the hem of his robe. 'Send her away, lord, send her away. In the name of Allah, I beg you! She is bewitched!'

The Amir rose to his feet, yet stayed by the side of Shahida so that she would be comforted by his presence.

'Nur, do you believe in the one true God, Allah the all-merciful and compassionate?'

'*Bîllah*, but you know that I do, lord!' Nur gasped.

'Do you not have a great reputation for saying little but knowing much, Nur?'

'That is so, lord, that is so.'

'Yet for one who believes in God and is famed for being knowledgeable while keeping her own counsel you are apparently lacking in faith, and noisy to boot. Do you think that your wisdom exceeds that of your lord and master?'

Nur's face flushed. 'Indeed no, lord. Ah, if I thought that, how overweening I would be, how unbearably proud and bloated and –'

'Yes, that is so. Now, would you return to Shamim and tell her to tend the girl, and keep her in the tent until she is fully recovered. If she behaves oddly, then it is because of her ordeal, not because of the evil eye, do you understand? Do you recall how Tarik behaved when he slipped while climbing and struck his head? That was not the evil eye but the consequences of an ordeal that upset the body.'

'I hear you, lord, I hear you.' Again Nur kissed the hem of the Amir's robe, then backed away, salaaming in the most reverent manner her aged bones could tolerate.

Returning to his horse, the Amir knelt down again and began to feed the dried herbs gently through the square white teeth, fraction by fraction, stroking the flushed neck and whispering words of affection and solace in the flickering ear. Shahida, who had been with him since he was an untried youth; she who had carried him beyond the desert to the cities, beyond the fringes of the *simûm* and the stars, his Shahida, beloved lady of a thousand journeys. What if old Nur was right and the girl had brought them misfortune? Shahida was sick, yet she had never ailed before. He could not prevent a sweep of coldness creeping along his back. How he had striven to take his tribe out of the dark ages and into the modern world.

In the city where he had been schooled, at the great university of Pashbur, there had been little talk of the evil eye and possession by *jinns*; such babble was for ignorant old women and men whose blood had clotted with age.

'Allah preserve a boy who must be a man!' The words of his tutor returned to him now as he comforted Shahida. Barely seventeen, he had returned to his dead father's tribe as Amir, stood in the blazing sun robed in simple cotton clothes edged with goldwork embroidered by his female relatives, and forced into his face an expression of strength and confidence.

Hundreds, thousands, had ridden past him in salute, giving their loyalty and acknowledgement to the new Amir, not only his father's immediate tribe but all those who were related and to whom his father had been Amir-in-chief. Now he had that title, yet he was still a boy. The tears had solidified behind his eyes like wax so that he could barely focus; his hands had trembled, his knees shaken, yet his face was impassive as ever his father's had been on such occasions.

Allah, but he had been thrown in with the most resounding splash!

Next, he must have a bride and the one who would be his, long accepted by both their families, was Alamma; she too was in the city with her sisters to buy materials for her wedding attire. He had never seen her again.

He blinked fiercely. Why weep like a boy when he had been a man for ten years? Women somehow eluded him. His mother had followed his father to the grave, for they had loved one another passionately. His sister had died of the lung fever, and then the cousin whom he might have married in place of Alamma, if only he could have brought himself to do so. Now Shahida . . . sweet one of the desert winds and the stars.

As he passed the black tent where the green-eyed one was incarcerated, he heard shouts and curses. She was fierce as the desert sun and as uncontrollable. What in the name of Allah would he do with her? His men had brought her baggage to him, and it was waiting in his tent when he entered. Slowly he unfastened the soft pouch and looked inside.

Such colours, glittering and gleaming like a mirage, blues and greens, silver and gold, amethyst and indigo . . . Feathers, he saw, as he lifted out the robe. Was this the attire of a *jinn* who transformed herself into a great feathered bird? Nur might well think so and for a moment he too agreed. He had never seen anything like it before. Was it perhaps the marriage attire of a Western woman? The veil which they were said to wear on their heads? A ceremonial gown for some ancient, secret rites? No, he did not think so. His ignorance was like a barb; it sent him back to his seventeenth birthday when he was untried and hesitant yet none must know, for hundreds looked to him for their every need. He would never know unless he asked the one whose robe this was.

Beneath the robe, he found dainty anklet bells, bracelets and rings, and then he threw back his head and laughed out loud at his own stupidity. She was a dancer, a girl who flaunted her body before men and then no doubt sold herself to the ones who could pay her fee. How could he have been so unbelievably dense? A *bintilkha'ta*, a fallen woman, that was what she was and he had imagined her to be different, special . . .

His teeth gritted. Yes, women had played a significant part in his life by their very absence. No one had ever said it to his face but he felt inside that he was not as other men. Had he been thus he would have married long ago and been the father of many sons. That was his duty: his destiny. What other chieftain would have allowed mourning to affect him so deeply that he could not love another woman after Alamma? He had brought a girl to his camp and he had been stirred by her ethereal beauty, the purity that glowed in her face even though she railed at him like a *jinn*, only to find that she was a dancer, the lowest of the low, a pleasure girl from the city where immorality bloomed like the palms.

Cursing, he flung the costume across the tent and strode outside into the midday sun where all thought of tenderness and mercy was scoured from his mind.

Chapter Ten

Day followed tedious day and Mishaal did not see the Amir, although she demanded many times that he visit her. Shamim and Nur were with her night and day, leaving her alone only for the intimate necessities of the body; she began to fear that she would die in this fusty black tent.

The dawn call to prayer would wake her every morning. They would bring her dates and *laban*, or goat's milk and dried figs, and she would wish that she could sleep for another half day. Soon she was expected to participate in the simpler activities of the women, mending animal skins, scouring dishes with sand, mixing ointments and unguents, shaking out the bedding and mats from the tent and replacing them tidily.

Acute boredom set in on the fifth day. She had recovered from her desire to take her own life. Now all she wanted to know was Drew's fate. The two dotty old women knew nothing except women's tasks. They brought her a necklet of talismans, blue beads and charms against the evil eye, which she was forced to wear daily for, if she left it off, they screeched and berated her. They, too, were heavily decorated with such charms against the evil eye, she noticed, and they seemed to add more each day. She did not know whether to laugh or cry.

Her dreams were haunted by Drew and that bestial scene in their camp, the monstrous figures attacking him and the blade cutting into his throat. Again and again she tried to recall the scene in accurate detail. But her emotional reaction had turned it into a caricature, the black shadows, the dagger at Drew's throat, the impatient horses pawing the sand and whinnying like mythical beasts of legend. Was the hand gripping the dagger moving, or was it being held as a threat? If only she could remember! There was only one who could answer her questions and her requests to see him were greeted with derision.

'*Ya saiyid* does not speak to *nasrani*,' Nur would say, folding her arms and sniffing.

'*Ya saiyid* tolerated me long enough to bring me here!' Mishaal would retort. 'Tell him I am of Arab birth like him, tell him, I order you!'

'Phah! Green eyes, you have not the dark Arab eyes, and your skin is white.'

'That is my concern. I was born in Abeesha! Tell *ya saiyid* that I was born near here, on the city which borders on the Land of Mirages, tell him that! Tell him that I know about the Jewels of Destiny!'

Tourmaline eyes glittering, Mishaal stood with hands on hips facing the old woman, who would shrug, then raise her eyes heavenwards, only to shrug again.

'Tell your lord and master the Amir that I know where the Jewels of Destiny are!' Mishaal cried, her face scarlet with frustration.

Did she imagine it or was there a look of alarm in the old woman's eyes? It vanished at once and Nur did not move, nor did she reply. She seemed to be dozing, her snores growing louder, her fingers clutching the conglomeration of blue beads and charms hanging at her shrivelled neck.

Mishaal threw up her arms in despair. How could she escape from this hideous tent? Scrabbling amongst the bedding to find her comb, she tried to torture her long hair into tidiness. She had wanted to wash it until she learned what the Beduin women washed their hair in: camel's urine. She had gagged at the mere mention and decided that her hair must stay dirty.

'Camel's urine saves the water,' Nur explained. 'Water is scarce, and getting scarcer. The wells are running dry all over the land. It is the will of Allah: He wishes to punish us. We can do nothing about it. The legend speaks true.'

Legend or no, Mishaal was not going to wash her hair in the bodily excretions of those irritable, ugly and snorting beasts who roamed the camp as if they were lords. She often heard them snorting and belching and sometimes the younger ones would thud up and down outside the tent. She was told that her own mount was being safely tended. The Beduin were tender and nurturing towards their beasts, unless privation forced them to be otherwise.

Having combed her hair and straightened her russet-coloured robe, Mishaal made for the tent entrance, thrusting aside the flaps with determination. Nothing would stop her from seeing the Amir now: nothing!

Outside, the sun was like a blow in the eyes and she staggered, narrowing her eyes and trying to focus. Everything was limned with a dazzling orange glow so that people, tents and animals shone luminously. Faces turned in her direction to stare; people stopped what they were doing and stood watching her. Even the two young camels nearby appeared curious, craning their rubbery necks to peer at her.

'The Amir! Take me to the Amir!' she cried, rushing forward, heedless of the sunlight cutting her vision. 'Where is he?' she appealed to a woman stirring a pot by a fire. 'Where is the Amir?'

The woman flinched as if bitten, muttering prayers of protection. Mishaal felt like screaming loud and long.

Children came towards her, but only to stare boldly. She repeated her question to them but they giggled and ran off. Two returned, braver than the others, and tried to tug at her skirts with their grubby brown hands.

'White face, you have a white face!' they cried. 'Your eyes are the green colour! Why are your eyes the green colour?'

'Your Amir will tell you if you will only take me to him!' Mishaal said impatiently.

'He is not here. He hunts,' a boy said, lifting his wrist to show where a bird of prey would be resting on the Amir's arm.

'How long do his hunting trips take?'

'As long as *ya saiyid* wishes it, oh green-eyed one. A day, two, three, who knows?' The boy shrugged.

Slowly Mishaal's eyes searched the crowd of Beduin who were now watching her with ill-feigned curiosity. She felt as if she were on stage.

She turned as she recognised Nur's voice howling and wailing as if she had seen a *jinn* marching towards her with fiery eyes and hooked nails.

Mishaal was disgusted with these half-witted people. She did not have to stay here like a prisoner! Turning on her heel, she headed for the nearest camel, then, realising that the Beduin could easily pull her off before the animal had effected its languorous ritual of getting to its feet, she scanned the camp for a horse. There were two grazing on the far side. Ignoring Nur, she tore towards them.

Hers were dancer's muscles and they needed exercise; now they were soft. Nonetheless she reached the horses before the stunned nomads had stirred themselves into a plan of action. Next minute she was thundering away from the camp.

How difficult it was to ride bareback and without reins! She bounced around the horse's back, slithering up and down in an odd jerking movement which rattled her teeth and pinched her breath. Soon the camp was behind them and Mishaal was heading out into the wilderness.

Ahead lay a mount of sand, a golden, glittering dune. When she reached its far side she would be safe.

The rider came out at her like a great dark eagle, frightening her mare so that she reared up, screeching in terror. Losing her grip on the mare's mane, Mishaal slid down the horse's spine, over her rump, and thudded to the sand. She had bitten her tongue and blood filled her mouth. One elbow was bleeding from a graze.

The breath smacked from her lungs, she looked up into the face of the rider who had caused her fall.

He stood over her with a proprietorial air, slim, strong tanned hands on narrow hips, his obsidian eyes glittering with open enjoyment at her fate. His face was the colour of rich dark honey, his eyes bright jet almonds fringed with ebony lashes, his nose strong and lean, the bone jutting proudly above a grinning mouth and teeth that looked as if they had been bleached white by the desert sun. He wore a bernouse of flowing black, and on his head the *kuffayia* and *aighal* of the Arab lord. For a few moments she forgot her anger and pain, and gazed at him open-mouthed. She had imagined him to be a fiend, twisted, hideous, sneering and lecherous, but he was . . . She searched for the right word, then found it: noble.

Matiya had professed to be able to tell a man's nature by the shape of his nose and lips, the colour of his hair and eyes. Dark eyes for passion and energy, she would say; lighter brown eyes for the traveller and the man who will jest at anything. Those with a hooked nose were fierce in their desires and coveted money, and those with thin lips had such powers of energy that they rarely tired.

Her mind still shaken from the fall, Mishaal tried to see the Amir through Matiya's eyes. If his arched nose did not mean that he coveted money, then it meant that his passions were fierce and unbridled. Those thin lips were energy, the dark eyes stood for yet more passion and ferocity. A man to be feared and avoided; yet he did not appear savage. He was looking at her with something like covetousness yet it was an admiring gaze, respectful, even, and she found herself blushing.

'The lady *jinn* has decided that she would rather walk back to her home?'

Gritting her teeth, Mishaal tried to rise. It needed dignity and composure and above all a disregard of pain. Blood was streaming down her arm and staining her skirts, and filled her mouth with its bitter iron taste. She staggered, but he did not move to help her. She was glad, yet annoyed – why, she did not know. She wanted no savage handling and yet it was ungallant to let a lady struggle and not assist her, so Drew had told her many times.

Drew!

'Where is my husband?' she cried. 'What have you done to him, you fiend?'

'Your husband?' The Amir arched one slender black brow. 'So he is your husband, is he? I had not thought it.'

'And how would you know, you savage? I doubt that you

can write your own name? Do you make a cross?' she sneered.

'A cross is for the *nasrani*, little demon, not for a Muslim.'

'Where is my husband?' she cried again, wanting to slap his face and wrench out his hair in clumps and bite him until he yelled for mercy.

'He fought my men in honourable combat.'

'And?' Mishaal's heart was battering against her ribs so that her lungs could not take in air.

'He lost.' The Amir shrugged.

'You mean . . . You mean . . .' Mishaal felt the blood leaving her head. The scene before her was changing colour from gold to grey then to black, thick, shadowy black.

'He is dead. He died with honour.'

She did not remember fainting, unconscious until she came round in his arms. He was staring into her face with concern. She would have gouged out his eyes if she could have moved her leaden arms. She cried out to him to get away from her but he did not move, and then she began to weep, such rending tears that she was ashamed of showing such a force of emotion before her enemy. Tears rained down her cheeks and soaked her neck and breast and she could not stop them.

'Allah, the wells would never run dry if you wept like this more often, little one!' he said.

'So you will be cruel to me every day then?' she hissed. 'What does it matter if your wells run dry? I hope that they do, all of them, and that you and your people all die of thirst! I want you to die horribly, like my Drew! But for you, we would be at the temple now and Drew would have got what he came here for. Then we were going home, to his home, America! You have ruined all that, you have taken my man from me and my home, my future, everything! Because of you I am alone and destitute, and you talk of wells running dry!'

'I heard you mention Allah, the name of the one true God, when you were angered at being brought to my camp. I thought you a Muslim; is that not so? And do you not recall what the Prophet said when he was asked by one of his followers what was the greatest thing that they could bestow? Water, he said, water to the thirsty.'

'You do not look thirsty to me! You look disgustingly healthy and strong!'

Mishaal was trying to struggle into a sitting position away from the direct and raking gaze of those powerful, percipient eyes, but her head was spinning, and tiny, dazzling stars were flashing past the corner of her vision. Feeling nauseous, she clamped a hand to her mouth.

'It is the shock of the fall,' he said, palming her head with one supporting hand. 'It will pass if you lie still.'

'And provide dinner for the carrion birds? Is that what you want?' she managed to snarl through gritted teeth.

'I shall be here with you to protect you, do not fear.'

'I am not afraid. I have never been afraid of anything!' she hissed, feeling a second wave of nausea flood through her breast.

'Lie still and breathe calmly.' Before she knew it, his hands were feeling along her limbs. She plunged her legs at him to stop the embraces, but they were not the preparations for love-making: he was feeling if she had broken a bone in her fall.

'I am intact!' she snarled.

'Yes, your bones are, I see, and what of the rest of you?'

For a moment she did not understand what he meant and then when realisation arrived, she thought: no, he cannot mean that! He would not dare to question me about my virginity. He would not dare! But it seemed that he would . . .

She was scarlet when he repeated his question. He was taking advantage of her shocked condition to pry into her personal affairs, the jackal!

'That is none of your business! Who do you think you are?'

'I am lord and master of my peoples, keeper and protector of their safety and guardian of their souls. They do my bidding and I ensure that they want for nothing, unless Allah should decree that the rains do not come.'

'I am not one of your people! I had – have – an American father and an American husband, I am free, do you hear? I am a free woman and you have no right to add me to your, your harem!'

'What harem is this? Do you see one? I do not. Have women

bathed you and robed you in silks for my bed, scented you with oils and unguents and washed your hair in essence of roses? No, you have not seen any harem. A gaggle of old women, old men, wild youngsters untrained as *kaffirs*, and devoted mothers . . . These you have seen, not concubines.' He surveyed her with a quizzical expression, his arms folded as he waited for her reaction.

'Why else would you bring me here? I – I was not interfering with you and your people and you fetched me out of my own camp and took me from my husband.' Her mouth trembled; she had forgotten her nausea.

'I had good reason. I thought you were a Beduin girl, abducted by a *nasrani*.'

'You thought *what*?' She could not believe what he was saying.

'Yes, and I thought that you would be undyingly grateful to me for rescuing you.' His thoughts flashed to Alamma. Had he been so overwrought when his eyes fell on this wild damsel that he had thought it was Alamma he was saving?

'You are bewitched by the sun and possessed by *jinns*! What arrogance, what presumption! I do not care if you are the Sultan of Constantinople, you have no right to abduct women and add them to your tribe as if they are slave girls. I want to go back now, you will take me back to my home and return my belongings to me, and, and . . .' She stopped, her throat swelling. She wanted to cry, 'And return my Drew to me!' but she could not voice the words.

Drew was gone for ever; she had lost her darling, golden-haired American, and all his kisses and loving had died with him. Plunging her face into her hands, she wept.

Her buttocks were too bruised to sit astride a horse so she had to return to the nomads' camp on her stomach, hanging over the Amir's saddle. She felt the greatest fool in Arabia and no doubt everyone else shared her opinion.

It did not do her stomach any good and she felt sick again and dizzy when the Amir helped her down. The sandy, rocky earth felt as if it were wobbling.

Nur and Shamim were there, babbling and screeching, and Nur tried to kiss the hem of the Amir's robe, begging his forgiveness for being so witless as to let the girl go. The Amir said that all was forgiven; in future any beast that could be ridden must be firmly tethered and watched.

'Prepare as if for battle with the Koreish,' he announced to all those who were standing close by. There were grins and nods. During the life of the Prophet, the people who gave endless trouble, and who tried to woo the Prophet's followers from him and corrupt Mohammed himself, were the Koreish. Intolerant and zealous, they had several times come near to murdering him. 'Remember what the Prophet said: the unbeliever is he who kindleth a fire and when it hath thrown its light on all around him, God taketh away the light and leaveth him in darkness and he cannot see. Deaf, dumb, blind, therefore they shall not retrace their steps. As to the infidels, their works are like the *Sarâb* mirages in the desert, which the parched traveller imagines will be water, only to find that it is nothing when he approaches . . .'

Barbarous ebony eyes stared into peridot ones. The green eyes fell first.

Mishaal watched the Amir stride away, his loose, white robe swinging round his glossy leather knee boots. His back was that of a zealot: a man who believes and will never change his beliefs; how could he criticise the Koreish when he was the same as they?

'You pagans are all the same!' she screamed after his receding back. 'You have no mercy, no compassion! I am a *nasrani* now, do you hear me? *Do you hear me?*'

Nur and Shamim looked at one another with shocked faces and loose mouths, while a ruffle of noise spread round those who were watching. They were taken aback by her rage, which she found satisfying. She would make these dull and stupid, superstitious nomads think again if it took her every smattering of energy. What did they know about the world, about truth and destiny and reality? She would tell them. They would never be able to stop her mouth. Never.

PART THREE

The Arabian Prince

Contentment is reached by such perilous paths one could well go astray;
And I, worse the luck, have no comforting guide my misgivings to quell.

Fuzûlî

Chapter Eleven

Faith and no-faith are both engaged in Thy search.

Mohammed is the lord of the two worlds and of mankind and the Spirits
And of the two nations, the Arabs and the 'Ajam *(non-Arabs).*

Two Islamic mottoes

The days dragged on and Mishaal watched eagerly for another chance to escape. It was not to be so easy this time. His people obeyed their Amir as if he were a god, and, as he had ordained, every animal and beast was tethered firmly, leather thongs coiled round their ankles, or reins so intricately knotted that she would have needed endless patience and time to unravel them. Even the children were put to watch any beast that could move, even the oldest and least energetic camel. Mishaal gritted her teeth and clenched her fingers with frustration.

As the weeks passed, she yearned to be alone so that she could dance, knowing that it would ease her soul and calm her tortured spirit. She had asked the Amir about her dancing robe. Did he know where it was? He had not replied. She would not beseech, so she had to remain without it. Perhaps it was decorating the body of one of his concubines – surely he had them hidden away somewhere? All the Muslims were lecherous, obsessed with sexuality and the females who would bear them sons. 'The sex act, for pleasure and for progeny', how often ZouZou had said those words.

Life in the Beduin camp was arduous. She would never have believed that so much work was of vital importance. Washing and weaving material, cooking and grinding cereals for the unleavened bread and couscous, mending goatskins, picking out leaves and other debris from dates so that they could be stored in sacks of leather, the eternal grinding of coffee beans for the ceremonial drink that played so important a role in the nomadic day, and the pouring of goat and camel milk into leathern bags to hang at the tent entrance until they thickened into yoghourt.

The day began at dawn with the call to prayer, which Mishaal pointedly ignored. The men would step out of their tents into the still chilly morning air and kneel together in the sand to say their devotions, while the women stayed inside to pray before lighting the fires round which they would cluster. Then it was tea the Arabian way, disgustingly sweet and taken black without milk. How sickening this was compared to the way that Drew had liked it . . .

The sounds of the animals would have woken her had the prayer call not. Cocks crowed, hens squawked, sheep bleated, and the birds carolled as they swooped down to snatch left-over crumbs and grains.

She was not allowed to gather brushwood which would have given her some exercise, so she had to put all her exertions into grinding coffee beans and cereal grains, smacking the pestle into the mortar with gusto and driving it into the base, round and round, then smack again, all the while imagining that it was the Amir's face. He would never be found on his knees undertaking such menial tasks, not with all these devoted and reverent females to wait on him. A taste of these simple, repetitive tasks would be the making of his character, she knew, but he would never be called upon to carry them out. Even a poor Muslim was treated like a pasha by his wife, and this one, whatever his name was, did not appear over-endowed with gold and riches. But he was important and all-powerful, that much she had gauged. Old men flung themselves on their knees before him and kissed the hem of his robe; even proud young men from other tribes, who wore the *kuffayia* and *aighal* of a chieftain. The Amir was an overlord, a king in all but name, and it was just her misfortune that he had been her captor. Had he been poorer or without importance, she would have been able to escape.

She was given rough, straw-like balls of goat's, sheep and camel hair and shown how to weave them into long strips to be sewn together firmly. Eventually, a tent could be made from the joined sections, which was weatherproof, sheltering and resistant to rain. In amongst these balls of hair, as she found to her horror, were fleas and lice that leapt and wriggled out of their tangled nest. Mishaal slapped and smacked at them, crushing them between her sandals and gasping in disgust at the tiny bloodstains. Nur appeared with a censer made from a cheap and tinny metal inside which was camphor to purify the air and kill the bugs.

The sight of the incense burner brought a wrench to Mishaal's heart. Matiya; Rhikia's house; all that she had left behind her and now missed so much! While the camphor burned, filling the air and making her lungs feel light, she mended black cloths for the two women whose tent she shared. These cloths were worn over the head, and had slits for the eyes. However, not all of the Beduin wore the black veils.

In the city, only women of the bordellos went unveiled and Mishaal found this comparison strange. These wild, free women married young and were faithful; they were usually happily married and stayed with their husbands until death, so Nur told her. Yet in the city, the naked face was considered indecent and an open invitation from the fallen woman to her client . . .

Nur did not wear kohl, the eye paint made of antimony from Sidi Kacem but Shamim did, decorating her eyes with a pointed stick so that the thick black lines edged her lashes like black ointment. Both women dyed their waist-length hair with henna, a laborious and messy business which filled the small tent with a smell like freshly mown hay.

It was during one of these sessions that Mishaal, much to her own surprise, took pity on Nur, who was trying to paint her feet as she had done when young. Now her aim was inept and she could no longer reconstruct the zigzag pattern. Taking the utensils, Mishaal began to paint the old woman's feet. An arthritic arm raised to push her away, then dropped. Looking up, Mishaal found a pair of wrinkle-framed dark eyes looking at her with the shock and amazement of a wild bird trapped in the hand. Smiling to herself, she went on painting the thin brown feet.

Later, when the design had dried, Nur brought Mishaal a dish of *laban*, her favourite milk, and a handful of succulent dates. When Mishaal insisted that the old woman share them with her, it seemed that a great hurdle had been leapt, a cautious friendship begun.

Milk warm from the goat was heavenly, and Mishaal often stole a mugful before mixing it with a little of yesterday's yoghourt and then gently heating it over the fire so that it could be left to thicken in its leathern pouch. One day she was sipping her stolen milk when a shadow fell across her. Looking up, she saw the Amir standing, feet apart in their shiny black knee boots, a quizzical expression on his autocratic features.

'I deserve it!' she defended herself. 'It is mine by right!'

'Who said otherwise? It is well known that the *nasrani* is never happier than when he or she is thieving.'

'That is exactly the opposite of the Christian creed! The Christians say that Muslims are thieves, did you know that? They say that the hard life of Islam turns even saints into sinners . . .' she challenged, tossing her head.

'But did the Lord Jesus Christ not live in similar conditions? I had thought that it was so. In fact, did He not exist in the wilderness without food and water? Did that hardship turn Him into a sinner, then?'

'I – No, He was, was, the Son of God!'

'Why then did He need that challenge? Did He have doubts about Himself and His mission, perhaps even about His own purity of soul and thus a need to test Himself? Would that be it?'

'Yes, I . . . yes, that would be it.' Mishaal tore her eyes away. How little she really knew about Christianity. She realised now that she had taken that religion upon herself with eagerness: and thoughtlessness. How could one defend something about which one knew so very little?

'And all of the Christian world is dependent on a man with such powerful self doubts? Is that not unwise?'

'He did not have them any more after the ordeal in the wilderness! After that He was strong, invincible!'

'Yet Mohammed was always strong, even when He first had the call. He was invincible. Nothing ever altered His course even when at first others reviled or ignored him.'

'Nor did Jesus Christ! He was never in doubt for one moment: He knew what He must do, *all* of it!'

'And what was it that He came to do?' The Amir's voice was deep and velvety; she could feel herself falling under his spell. Perhaps it was not the Amir at all but a *jinn* who had stolen his form? No, she must not think like the superstitious and ignorant Beduin women!

'He – He came to – to teach about loving one another and being good to those who live near. He said that no one must kill, or worship false idols. He said that alms must be given to the poor and that He came to call the sinners not the saints . . .'

'Then you are a sinner?' How overwhelming was that basalt gaze; she could not resist it, nor could she tolerate it. Colour swamped her cheeks and the dish of milk in her hands tipped to one side and spilled on to her knee unheeded.

'No, no, I am not,' she managed to gasp in a strangled voice.

'Then why did you wish to become a *nasrani*, child of Islam?'

'My father was, was a *nasrani*!'

'But your mother was of Arabia, so you told me? What of her? Will you forget her name and her family and take upon yourself nothing but your father's religion?'

'If my mother had lived, she would have taken my father's

name. She would have forfeited her family name on marriage. If she had married a Muslim it would have been the same. Why then is it wrong for me to do this?'

'Clinging to memories can be harmful and interfere with living. Old Nur dreams of the days she spent in the wilderness with her sheep, when she was a legend for her fortitude and never suffered from loneliness. That is a sustaining memory. It excludes nothing of her race or lineage, but rejoices in the best of it all. Do you have any proof that your unknown father was of excellent birth and reputation? What if he were a felon, a man who did not heed the word of Christ?'

'All men of the West are Christians and practise their religion faithfully!'

'Have you never met a villainous Muslim? There are men of all creeds and races who would be saints or sinners; belonging to a particular faith does not preclude sin. That is for the individual to battle with himself.'

'Why do you hound me like this? How can it be proved that my father was lacking in faith? How can anyone know?'

'Then how can you know that he was not?' The Amir squatted beside her in the sand, taking her trembling hand in his. As warmth, comfort and solace flowed from his palm into hers, her rigours died away. She knew that he was being sensible and logical, and probably correct, yet she did not want to take heed.

'Why do you pull your hands away, child of Islam? Am I evil, would I harm you?'

'If you mean me well, then take me back to the city and my foster mother!'

'Are you promised to any man?'

His question took her by surprise.

'Promised? How can I be when I was married?' she retorted, shaking her head so that her thick black hair swept to one shoulder, taking with it the veil that was concealing her head.

'You were not married to that *nasrani*.'

'I was! He was my husband! Why should I lie?'

'Why indeed? I tell you that you were not married to that man. Were you promised to any other?'

'Why do you want to know? What business is it of yours? Are *you* promised to anyone? Are *you* married? How many wives do you have and what of your concubines? You see, I can ask questions too!'

His gaze was on the crown of her head where her hair gleamed glossily in the sunlight, and there was a tender delight in his eyes that shook her. Beduin women frequently left their faces unveiled but they always covered their heads. Did the sight of her unveiled head move him to sexual thoughts? Irritated and angered, she tugged her head cloth back in place, pulling it forward so that her cheeks were concealed.

Slowly, as if in a dream, his hand came closer to her face, the fingers gripping the cloth and then sweeping it away so that she had no concealment at all.

'*Ya Allah,* but you are beautiful of spirit, a bright and gleaming torch of light like your name.'

His voice was sensual, deeper, softer, and it eddied along her veins like aphrodisiac.

'Why do you want to know if I am married or have concubines?' He gripped her little pointed chin in his hand so that she was forced to look at him. 'Do you desire me, my bright little flame, is that it? You shout and curse at me to hide your true feelings?'

'*Bîllah!* But that is not it!' Mishaal leapt to her feet, kicking out at the Amir who leapt back, his boots narrowly missing being showered with sand. 'You are more arrogant than the Grand Turk, more conceited than any pasha! I ask you why you hound me and you talk of my desiring you. Have I hounded you except in the cause of justice? No Beduin girl would be restrained like this, so why do you think that you can keep me a prisoner, *why*?'

He opened his mouth and she thought that he was going to tell her everything; a great yearning for the truth seemed to shine in his eyes. Then, taking a breath as if aware that silence was the prerequisite on this matter, he left her, striding off in his boots, great powerful strides that cut through the expanse of sand as if it were child size.

Mishaal looked down at the spilled milk and found that

she was shaking in the silliest way, like a child scared of its angry father. Such heat emanated from the Amir that he should spend his time turning milk into *laban*. Moving to the tripod of branches on which hung the leathern sack filled with milk, she began to jerk it backwards and forwards furiously, not caring that she might well have butter instead of yoghourt after this show of emotion.

Guests were due to arrive from another tribe and the women were scuttling about making preparations. A sheep was caught and pinioned to the ground by two of the men. Mishaal watched in silence as the sharp knife cut deep into the animal's throat, its body jerking and juddering as the nerves were severed. The head was cut off and taken away so that the eyes could be cooked for honoured guests.

A beautiful rug was unrolled, its rich emerald, scarlet and sapphire colours glowing brightly. On this the guests would sit while they were served with their coffee. First they would be handed small dishes of tea brewed the Arab way. While they were sipping, the major preparations would be under way for freshly ground and heated coffee. Twice now Mishaal had watched visitors being served, but had been forced to stay behind a curtain and remain silent. This time she was to be one of the servers, a great honour in the Beduin household. The guests were to be received in the Amir's tent which she had not yet entered.

Nur had given her a piece of blue material to sew into a robe for herself and on her head she would wear the black cloth of the nomad woman, round which would be twisted any piece of coloured material that she cared to use for anchorage. She decided on one streaked with blue and scarlet, twining it round her head like a many-hued plait. Her hair beneath was loose and freshly washed, combed until silky and rippling. If she wished she could veil herself, said Nur, for no one would expect her to behave as a Beduin when she had been with them for so short a time.

Mishaal considered the piece of indigo calico which these Beduin women wore to hide their faces. Should she wear it or should she not? Until now, she had veiled herself to maintain the privacy she yearned for, or at least a pretence of it. While the veil could be a prison, it could also be a protection.

Many of the older women would retire as soon as the guests arrived, as was the custom, a blanket being hung as a dividing wall behind which they would watch and listen and sometimes peer over the top, but not emerge. The bold among them would sit on the perimeters, their behaviour impeccable.

Mishaal had peered out through the entrance of Nur's tent a dozen times, watching for the sand cloud that would announce their guests. She had been told the name of the man who was coming with his sons and his followers, Shaikh Ashraf Ajmal, a distant cousin by marriage to the Amir.

Shouts were heard. The guests were near, their camels could be seen. Youths and boys ran to greet them, to take their camels and feed and tether them while the Amir would greet the Shaikh in the exuberant, filial way of the Arab. Then Mishaal would rush to the Amir's tent and begin her work.

She had decided to go unveiled but as she rushed into the Amir's tent for the very first time, she caught up the head cloth and tucked it across her nose and behind one ear for much-needed protection. His eyes would be upon her, she knew it, searching, enquiring, demanding answers that she could never give. Allah be praised, for creating the *litām*, the veil.

The interior of the great tent caught her by surprise. A sultan's palace, richly furnished and blooming with sumptuous colours, carpets of crimson and indigo, enormous woven cushions of blue and scarlet, gold and apple-green, woven hangings on the tent walls, censers and urns of what looked like pure gold, and the dizzying odours of frankincense, myrrh, ambergris and jasmine, taking her back to Rhikia and Matiya and her young days of sheltered innocence.

She hovered at the entrance, her gaze taking in all the comforts, while the wafting incense filled her lungs and swept her away, far, far back in time to she knew not where:

another age, ancient, gorged with religion and strange, exotic rituals. Her heart was stirring, waking, triumphing over the physical limitations of her body. Her bones were melting, her spirit flying: she must dance, she must!

Only with enormous effort did she force her quarrelsome legs to the corner where she must kneel to prepare the guests' coffee. Ah, how she yearned for her peacock robe and the music of the tabor and drum, so that she could transport herself out of the prison of man-made time and float back to the ancient age when the Earth Goddess reigned.

Shaking her head, she sank to her knees and gathered the utensils towards her. She tore open the leather bag containing coffee beans, lifted out the required number. Then she dropped them in the long-handled skillet, its iron weight heavy and unwieldy. These would be lightly roasted, while she stirred them now and again to brown them evenly. She sat looking down at the steaming beans, smelling their rich and choking scent, resenting it for covering up the mystical odours of frankincense and myrrh. The beans ready, she tipped them into a carved wooden dish to cool before she ground them into a gritty brown dust ready for boiling. When the copper coffee pot had boiled over the fire, she tipped in the grounds, and the moment that the water came to the boil again, she removed it from the flame to repeat this process twice.

Where were the cardamom seeds that must be placed in the bottom of the pot before she added the water? Heat washed over her face and neck. There was the empty coffee pot waiting, and there was the steaming dark fluid ready to be poured, but where were the seeds?

She had searched beneath everything, even the scarlet and blue carpet on which she was kneeling, when the tent flap was flung back and the Amir stood before her, his face dark with disapproval. Every instinct in her shrieked that she must be the submissive woman of Islam and beg his forgiveness, crouch at his feet and kiss the hem of his robe. Muslim men were gods, to be humoured, pampered and revered, yet had not Mohammed himself said that false idols must not be worshipped?

Summoning her courage, she even managed a tiny smile, straightening her spine and staring her oppressor right between the eyes. He was gloriously dressed to greet his guests, wearing a loose robe of spotless white, over which was a flowing cloak of fine black wool edged with elaborate gold thread, and on his head the snowy *kuffayia* secured with the *aighal* that denoted his rank.

She had never seen him look more beautiful or more proud.

Her heart gave the most unnerving leap, as if she had received a fearsome shock; drawing back, she forced herself not to run to him and kneel for forgiveness at his feet. Allah, she had been here such a short time and already she was thinking like a humble nomad woman! Did the desert sun leech the brains and take away the wits?

'Mishaal.' His voice was the coolest dew on parched cactus flowers, manna falling from heaven itself. It shivered along the flesh so that she could not divorce her thoughts from knowledge of him: he was in that moment the universe to her, great, fathomless, infinite, human only because he had human form and voice.

'The cardamom seeds, I cannot find them,' she whispered, refusing to kneel, refusing to say, '*Ya saiyid*', yet conscious that close behind him came the guests, ears flapping, eyes dilated to see her lack of respect. Even had she been his favoured concubine she would have called him by his title before others.

'Then we shall drink the coffee without them,' he said simply.

'Yes, of course, without them.' Turning, Mishaal poured the steaming liquid into the coffee pot and then sat cross-legged waiting for the guests to settle themselves on the cushions.

The coffee dishes were minute, made of delicate porcelain hemmed with gold leaf. They did not have handles. Nur had said that they were very old, from the days when the Amir's family had possessed unending wealth and great riches brought to them from across the seas. Now, nearly all of that was gone. She had not explained further.

One by one, Mishaal filled the tiny dishes and passed them to every guest in turn, averting her eyes and salaaming before each man before pouring out the next cup of greenish-dark liquid. She found the coffee very bitter but these men seemed to be relishing their helpings. It was the custom that guests' cups were filled repeatedly until they held out their cup in their right hand, shaking it between forefinger and thumb to signify that they had sufficient.

It was also the custom that the preparation and serving of the drink be carried out in the most ritualistic and graceful fashion as a mark of great respect for one's guests. The desert host could not do enough for his visitors; even if he were destitute, he would kill his one and only sheep to roast for them, pour out his last *laban*, share his last figs or dates.

But drink his coffee bitter without cardamom seeds . . .?

Mishaal was tautly waiting for unfavourable responses, sure that there would be criticism and complaint, but the Amir downed his coffee, beamed, and said: 'It is good this way, wihout the flavouring. Such flavouring is for the tongues of children.'

To her surprise, Mishaal saw all heads nod in agreement. Hurrying, she proceeded to refill the dishes, going through the same elaborate ritual of pouring, salaaming, pouring and salaaming, while keeping her eyes averted.

The sheep was being roasted outside the tent and the succulent scent wafted in now and again. Mishaal, unobserved, looked from one guest to the next. Who would be the most important one, he who would be given the eyes of the sheep, that immense honour reserved for chieftains and grandees? The men were jovial, dark-skinned, richly clothed yet none of them was lithe and youthful. One only had an air of vigour not exceeded by his companions. He was about twenty, his eyes soft and brown, his clothes of the finest material; he had tried twice to catch Mishaal's eye. Whoever he was, shaikh or shaikh's son, she would not acknowledge him, and in that moment she understood what power the concealment of the veil could give to a woman. Purdah placed in the hands of woman all the decisions that mattered: whether to reveal herself, whether to flirt or smile or seduce whether to remain concealed so that none could guess her true thoughts. Had she been unveiled then she would have spent all her time keeping her expression fixed and dreading that she would blush hotly.

The men were now exchanging family news, not a little of which was gossip. She studied the Amir's face to see if he relished the indiscretions that followed, the childish babble about infidelity and children born out of wedlock, the scandal of a woman who had fled with the husband of another. No, there was no glint of prurient enjoyment in the Amir's eyes, nothing but polite and courteous attention.

She was far away, thinking of the temple she had seen with her darling Drew, visualising it in her mind's eye, the soaring opalescent beauty of the deserted yet elegant building, shimmering like polished alabaster in the savage desert sun. Taboo, he had said that the temple was taboo, and now, recalling his words, she seemed to remember that she had heard a legend concerning just such a forbidden temple in the wilderness. She was scouring her memory when she heard the Amir's voice calling her name.

Salaaming, she went to kneel before him.

'I found your baggage,' the Amir said, without apology. 'There was a robe of feathers and a glittering material . . . I presume that it is yours?'

Heart thumping, she nodded.

'You wear it to dance?'

'Yes,' she croaked, heat assaulting her cheeks.

'Will you wear it now and dance for us? You would be honouring us greatly.'

'Dance now, here, for *you*?'

'If you will. We would be delighted. We have no form of entertainment here and these gentlemen would relish the opportunity to enjoy what I believe was one of the most famed sights in the city.'

'You – you have heard that I, that I was a dancer?'

'I have. Will you dance for us, Mishaal, and brighten our days?'

She was puzzled. He had claimed that her baggage was lost. He had made no mention of her former life, nor questioned her about it, yet now he seemed to know all. Would she dance for them? She looked at the brown faces all politely averted as the Amir spoke to her in low tones. What would these desert nomads know or understand of the greatest art ever born, the dance? She would be lowering herself to perform for them; she was out of practice; the Amir was insolent asking her on impulse like this. All these reasons for refusing came into her mind and then vanished. She would dance. She needed to dance.

'Nur has your costume in her tent. We await your return.' The Amir smiled, a gentle, patient curving of his sensual lips. Bowing her head, Mishaal took to her heels.

Nur's tent was empty except for the peacock robe which had been spread out over a cushion. What arrogance! He had assumed that she would agree! Impetuously she wanted to flee the tent, abandon the peacock robe, attempt another escape while the Amir and his guests were gossiping in the main tent.

Ah, how she wished that she could flee. Instead, tears in her eyes, she snatched up the peacock robe and held it to her face and breasts in joyful reunion. Her spirit, life, joy, enthusiasms were all in this beloved costume. Oh, delight to have it back!

She donned the peacock robe in haste, her hands trembling. Bliss to be wearing it again, bliss to know that she could dance again . . .

Rushing back to the main tent, she knew that she could not appear from behind a scented curtain as she had at Rhikia's. The tent flap would have to do. She caught sight of Nur.

'Nur, please would you tell the musicians to play this piece of music: the temple dance from Ushuar?'

'What if they do not know it?' Nur said, always ready with what she believed to be helpful warnings.

'They will. The notes are very like those of a song which is popular, the Song of Mariam. Tell them that . . . Please Nur, His Highness has asked me to dance. He is waiting.'

The old woman's eyes took in the anxious face, the extraordinary costume of multi-hued and glittering feathers, th unexpectedness of the situation, and then, much to Mishaal's relief, she hastened as fast as her old legs would take her into the Amir's tent to instruct the musicians.

Minutes passed. Mishaal paced up and down biting on her lips. What if he had changed his mind? He seemed a man of strange impulses. What if he jeered at her performance? Allah, why had she not run away when she had the chance?

The first notes of the temple dance of Ushuar floated out to her, weaving towards her like slivers of hoar frost waking her from a spiritual sleep. It did not matter that one or two wrong notes were struck; she was so enraptured to hear her music again that she wanted to fall down on her knees and thank God. She would dance her gratitude instead, for only in the performance of one's art can one truly thank God for the gift He has given.

The tent flap was slowly being pulled aside, and there they were, expectant sun-browned faces all turned in her direction, and there was the Amir, eyes wide, watching, waiting.

Across the thick carpets Mishaal moved as if swirling an inch above the luxuriant texture. The scent of incense was overpowering, as if someone had just lit a dozen tapers for this moment. Jasmine and honey, ambergris and roses ... Sweet and intoxicating, initiating her into the most ancient, forgotten rites when dance was sacred to the Goddess ...

Round and round she whirled, feathers shimmering, hair flying, feet slender and weightless, joy filling her veins as the musicians played the temple dance of Ushuar. Time flowed and then ceased to exist; the month, year, place, all were as dust to be brushed aside with the sweep of a jewelled hand; centuries formed and were evaporated as swiftly; the hand of the magician was in her performance. No, more than the hand: she *was* the magician.

Oblivious of the effect on her audience, Mishaal danced, a moonbeam of light, a rainbow of dazzling colour and movement, as mesmerising and astonishing to these desert-bred men as if she were a living peacock dancing only for them. Lilting, swaying, swirling, she lost herself in the steps she loved, the music enchanting her so that she in her turn might enchant those who watched her. As the final notes faded, her spinning slowed, and she came to rest, arms crossed across her breasts, head lowered. There was an uncanny silence in the tent. It did not dismay her . . . There was often silence as she finished her performance! Long seconds passed and then the Amir began to applaud enthusiastically, followed by his guests who shouted and roared their approval. Slowly she raised her head, seeing only a blur of faces before her; she was still in the other world.

'A prize, you have found a prize!' she heard a man cry, and the Amir replied: 'It was given to me by Allah,' and then she was fleeing the tent, out into the desert air that greeted her like a curtain of heat. She absorbed the aridity, the restive movements of the camels and donkeys, the children's shouts and the clanking of cooking vessels, a woman humming as she wove.

Which was real, this, or the world she entered when she danced, the world of phantoms and ethereal beauty?

Dimly she remembered asking for the music of the Temple of Ushuar yet she had never heard of it before. The Song of Mariam, sad, sweet and haunting, was the music that she had made her own, and it was to this that she had danced today, and yet, she had known all the time that it was originally the temple music of Ushuar, its origins lost in antiquity and yet real to her, so very real that she had been in that very temple while she danced . . .

Hearing a footfall behind her, she turned as if in a dream. It was the Amir, his eyes dark with concern.

'Are you all right, Mishaal? You danced like . . . I have never seen anyone dance as you did just now. Are you truly of this earth, or a beautiful *jinn* come to torment?' His eyes were twinkling, yet she could see that he was deeply moved; disturbed too. He was in awe of her for the first time. Just as well, she thought, just as well.

'I am quite well, *ya saiyid*,' she said, her voice cool.

'I am very grateful to you for dancing for us. My guests have never seen such perfection, they say. They will never forget your performance.'

'That is kind of them. Now I must rest.' She turned away, but he caught her arm.

'Mishaal, forgive me . . . You think me arrogant and heartless, I know, and I have done much for which I should ask your forgiveness, yet you must remember that I am only a man, puffed up in my ignorance and stupidly self-seeking at times. What is the arrogance of man when faced with the mystery and depths of woman? Nothing, I do assure you. Against that I have no weapons. I am helpless.

'Mishaal, tonight I decided that I want you for my wife. Will you be my bride?'

She gasped. She could not have heard correctly and yet she had, for he spoke again.

'Your life will be one of happiness, I promise. I shall not intrude on you. I know that you were raised in the ways of the city and every allowance will be made for that. Mishaal, tonight I knew that I must have you for my wife.'

'*Must?* Always you have what you desire, *saiyid*, and it would appear that no one has ever said no to you. This is one woman who will never say yes, I vow it now before the one true God! Never would I marry you, not even if there was nothing but amity between us. You have destroyed my life and all my dreams, caused the death of the only man I have ever loved, and broken my heart. I long for the day when I am free of you and your peoples and can return to my own home and forget you. I danced tonight only for my own delight and not for you or your guests. It is over now, and I shall speak no more of this. I ask but to be left alone.'

Gritting her jaw she glared up at him, not melting even when she saw the anguish in his eyes, the way his face lost its glow of hopefulness. When he reached out to pull her close to him, she twisted away from his arms and took to her heels, disappearing into Nur's tent and fastening the tent flap behind her with shaking hands.

Chapter Twelve

He that leadeth into captivity shall go into captivity.
Apocalypse, 13:10

Sweet, sweet, sweet as honey in the mouth,
His kisses on my lips, my breast, my hair;
But now my heart is as the sun-scorched South,
Where lie the fields deserted, grey and bare.
Ancient Egyptian love song

The visitors had other news to impart. Even those who lived at the farthest perimeters of the Land of Mirages spoke of the same frightening phenomenon, that of the wells running dry. At first it had been a single well, and then another, and then two becoming arid together, even those that had gushed for centuries. It was a wearisome and exhausting business fetching water from a far-off place. No longer was the fetching of water women's work; now men had to travel in search of it with camels to carry the water skins back to their camps.

Hearing Nur and Shamim discussing this in anxious whispers, Mishaal tilted her head to one side the better to absorb their words.

'*Bîllah,* it is the legend!' Nur wailed in a low throaty voice, pressing her palms together in a salaam as if invoking Allah's mercy. 'All my years, and they have been many, thanks to the one true God, I have thought upon that legend and its meaning. Out in the wilderness with the goats, I thought upon God and His ways and came to many conclusions about many things, yet never did I understand what was meant by that legend.'

Mishaal quirked a brow at this amazing statement.

'It says, "Should any non-believer's hand remove the Jewels of Destiny from their hiding place then the wells of the Land of Mirages will run dry unto the Day of Judgement and starvation and famine shall be a fatal visitation upon the peoples." Oh, how I raged at my dull mind for not knowing what were the Jewels of Destiny and who would be the non-believer!' Nur shook her head from side to side, adjusting her veil as it slid down her shoulders.

'As you say, Nur, what are these jewels and who is this *kaffir* who finds them and taints them with his heathen hands? Yes, if these jewels are precious to Allah, the one true God, then the tainting by a *kaffir*'s hand might so enrage Him that He dries our wells as retribution. Yes, I see that might be so,' Shamim mused.

Nur sighed impatiently. 'But who has seen these jewels *if* they exist? None! And if no one has found them, believer or *kaffir*, then why are our wells running dry, by God!'

Mishaal had been stitching slowly until they spoke, her thoughts on her lost lover. To hear that the old legend was coming true, to hear them mention the Jewels of Destiny of which Drew had spoken with such fervour and longing, sent a frisson of dismay and excitement through her body. It was as if a curtain were lifting and she was looking into a shining pool of water in the depths of which were figures moving like manikins, the ancient ruined temple that was taboo standing behind them, guarding its ancient treasure.

'Mishaal! Did you not hear me, you dreamer? You have stitched that veil to your skirt!'

Heat rushed into Mishaal's cheeks as she saw what she had done. So much for the disturbing visions that had plagued her lately. Or did they plague her? She was not so sure that she did not relish them, feeling as if they had belonged to her of old and were dear and familiar, a part of another life, long ago . . .

Cutting the stitches with a knife, she began to sew again, stabbing the cloth as if she wished to wound it.

*

Ashraf had never penetrated the city before. Until now he had only been as far as its outskirts to collect fresh dates or olive oil, salt or spices for his master.

It was a handsome city in its way. Born and reared in the desert wilderness, Ashraf would always prefer that to the clamour, stench and commotion of town life. The desert below, the stars above, that was his idea of paradise. There was something about stones and walls that sent a shiver of apprehension down his spine. Nonetheless, he was not lacking in eagerness for the quest he was about to undertake at his master's command. He was single, having not yet selected a bride, so he could behave as he wished during his search without suffering from guilt. He would begin his quest in the Street of Abdullah, where immorality reigned (but not as predominantly as in the Street of the *Jijims*).

Secretly, he believed that his master was befuddled to think that the girl was a dancer. Everyone knew what their proclivities were, and he had seen the girl with his own eyes: she was not of the fallen woman variety, he would stake his life upon it. Yet the *saiyid* had insisted that she was a dancing girl from this city and that her relatives must be found, or her friends, if she had no living kin.

Just occasionally his master was given to unsettling fancies. Normally, he was a man of iron will and stubborn as a she-camel when he set his mind upon something. It was only what Allah willed, however, his master descending from a great line; in fact, so Ashraf believed, from one of the desert kings of the time of the Prophet, or was it one of the queens? Ashraf scratched his stubbly head trying to remember. Alas, he was not blessed with the faultless memory of his grandmother, Nur, the old one. Now, why was he here? Ah yes, the dancing girl. He had to find her kin, or her friends. The Amir wished to know everything about her, where she was born, of what parentage, and how she had spent her early years. Once, Ashraf had lain with a girl from the *Ouled Nail*, and he had only just survived the experience. Ever since, the faintest thought of her glossy, sinuous body, slanting, kohl-rimmed eyes and heaving breasts was enough to launch him into the most embarrassing state of tumescence.

The women of the *Ouled Nail* were trained from childhood to dance and provide unforgettable hours of sexual satisfaction for their customers. Heavily painted and robed in glittering gowns with collars and headdresses sewn with gold coins, the gifts of grateful clients, they could be compared with the *houris* of paradise, so Ashraf believed. If one such girl was waiting for him in the after-life then he would not complain. Now, why had he been recalling that lusty night? See what effect it had wrought upon his body. Flinging his cloak across his thighs, he hid the erection jutting there.

This was the street he sought, named after Abdullah the eunuch. Even though castrated, Abdullah had been able to sustain an erection twice as large and more lasting than any normal man. Men of that inclination had travelled here in hordes to buy him for an hour, or two hours, or whatever they could afford. For ten years, the eunuch had been Pasha of Passion, and then he had died suddenly and painlessly, while kissing a woman.

'He should have known better!' went up the cry. 'Women are not to be trusted!'

The street was long and straight, resembling Abdullah's famous organ, so the legend went, and down it Ashraf sauntered, regaining his equilibrium. The doors were painted different colours, bright and attractive, with names painted on their panels, or on strips of sun-parched wood. 'Queen Farida', acclaimed one, and another stated, 'Parveen, Lady of the Night'. Ashraf's mouth twisted into a grin as he read the signs, especially the one saying, 'Zaida, Princess', for out of the window of that narrow house leaned a young boy with a luridly painted face and a veil which he proceeded to raise to show carmine lips and decaying teeth.

Suddenly the street fanned out into a tiny square with a fountain and battered barrels jammed with exotic blooms streaming wildly in every direction. No loving gardener tended these blossoms; they were neglected and spreading without hindrance, like the occupants of the houses. He stopped at a door proclaiming 'Salida, the Great One', and raised his hand to knock.

*

'You cannot lie to him!' the girl cried, her face stormy with disbelief. 'It is a sin against Allah! He has come all this way to find out the truth and he is paying you generously for your time, yet you will deceive him. Why, in the name of Allah, *why*?'

The girl she was addressing pouted sulkily and turned her head away.

'You do not understand, Kausar. You are too young and ignorant. One day when you are older you will realise what I have suffered and then you will realise why I do this.'

'There is never any good reason for lying!' Kausar flung out her arms, palms uppermost.

'Huh, suddenly you are the righteous one, free of sin and purified like a saint, is that it? Who are you to criticise me? Where are the infants you strangled at birth, where are they, tell me? If the authorities knew!'

Kausar clenched her teeth, circles of pink searing her cheeks.

'We all have secrets in this house, Salida, and most of all you. What of the lover you helped to die with a pillow? How the authorities would love to hear of that!'

'So we are agreed that none of us is perfect,' Salida sneered. 'Why then this false desire for honesty? Do you love the man? Is that it? You have lost your heart to him?'

'Phah! There is no man on this earth worthy of my heart!' Kausar smacked her fist against her thigh.

'Kausar, I asked you a question, you dim-wit. Answer me!' Salida was on her feet, shoulders hunched, staring into Kausar's face. Salida was on the heavy side, no waist to speak of, broad hips and heavy thighs and fat, ugly feet, but men did not feel that fat was a barrier. The more there was of a woman, the more they had for their money.

'What did you want to know?' Kausar planted her feet some way apart and faced Salida as she would an advancing bull.

'For every whore there is a time when love enters. Always they say that it never will and they harden their hearts and seal their bodies against passion, yet love will come one day. It has come to you, Kausar, I can see it in your eyes.'

When every man who lies with me is my incestuous father? Kausar thought.

'You are wrong, Salida. I have only seen the man twice, and that was briefly. Besides, his face is scarred.'

'Then you did not watch while he lay with me? I am sure that I heard a rustle behind the screen.' Salida had not in fact yet bedded Ashraf, but it was her custom to brag that no man had evaded her bed.

Salida gripped Kausar's thin shoulders and moved closer, so that the scent of jasmine filled Kausar's nostrils.

'No, I did not watch, Salida. You imagine things. If we were in the desert I would say that the sun had robbed you of your wits.'

'So you sneer at me, is that it? Always you jibe and insult. You are the witless one, Kausar, and I rue the day that I let you share my home. Allah, but I would give anything to see the back of you!'

'The feeling is not only on your side, Salida,' Kausar said through gritted teeth. 'Have you any notion of what it is like sharing a roof with a murderess?'

'Bitch!' Salida launched her bulk at Kausar, stabbing her nails into the girl's neck and shoulders, raking and cursing as she did so. Kausar raised a bunched fist, arrow-like with fury, and smashed it into Salida's face, right on the end of her nose so that the blood gushed out in an arc.

As Salida's screams rioted through the house, a serving girl came to the door, eyes wide, to say that Ashraf of the Beduin was waiting downstairs and that he wished to question her mistress.

Ashraf sat in the waiting room with his head down. He was uneasy in case he was seen by someone who knew him, slim though the chances were. The Beduin were happy family men; they married for love and were faithful partners. But Ashraf was different. His intended bride had died of a fever and he had delayed choosing another. Only now as he sat in this house of ill repute, waiting to question a *bintilkha'ta*, a fallen woman, did he realise how rootless he felt. It was not the way of the Beduin to remain unmarried and without sons. When he returned to his master he must make all haste and choose a girl to share his bed. He would like sons, six or seven of them . . .

'*Ya m'allmi, ya sitt* cannot see you for the moment. If you will be waiting I shall bring you refreshment.'

'Thank you.' Ashraf bowed his head lower still and swallowed. Upstairs was the woman whom he had come to question. It was she who was the sister of the one they called Mishaal whom his master desired to marry. This was the house to which his enquiries had led him after three days of false trails. 'Salida, the Great One' . . . Was she the woman who had been screaming as he stepped into the building? If so, he would have preferred to leave hastily, but he could not without first satisfying his master's wishes.

An hour later, he had been fed honey fingers, orange sherbet, lemon sherbet, sugared candied peel and honeyed dates and he felt decidedly nauseous and still Salida had not sent for him.

Pacing up and down the threadbare waiting room he longed to be back in the desert. Camels did not argue and answer back, nor did they scream and have tantrums. The stars illuminated the sky, while here smells and smoke dulled his perceptions, befuddling him as if he were drunk. How did city dwellers exist on their sticky diet of sweetmeats and sherbets? There was nothing more divine to him than a fresh fig picked from its tree, brown and curving like a woman's breast, with a natural sweetness that refreshed without nauseating.

'*Ya m'allmi, ya sitt* is awaiting.' The small serving girl was salaaming reverently as if he were a god. No doubt the men who paid the bills here were considered as such.

Salida was sitting on a massive scarlet silk cushion tasselled with gold and silver fringes, this having been placed on a bright-coloured Turkey carpet so that the worn sections were almost covered. A tiny monkey on a chain cowered in a corner, its back bent, its face taut with misery. Poor sad little orphan.

'*Assalamu Alaikam!*' he said, salaaming as if in respect

when all he wished to do was compose his features. '*Peace be on you, sitt.*'

'And upon you, Ashraf. Here, come and sit beside me and share my wine.'

'Wine?' Ashraf's heart turned a somersault. Wine was forbidden.

'You are a faithful Muslim?' Salida's mouth twisted a little but she sought to control its movement for she knew that it made her ugly. Had not Kausar told her so often enough, the bitch?

'I am.'

'How tedious for you. Can my servant bring you anything else?'

'No thank you. I have eaten of my fill while here. You are a generous lady.'

Were they in the desert, the fact that he had eaten under her roof would commit her to his safety and protection. He knew that he must remind himself such was not the case here in the city. He did not like Salida; he could not pinpoint what it was that made his skin creep and the tiny hairs on the base of his neck agitate like magnetised filaments. The room had an unpleasant atmosphere; he longed to leave.

'You wanted to hear more of my sister, I believe?' The woman's eyes narrowed. 'I do not usually speak of her: it grieves me too much, but if it will aid her . . .' She lifted a finger to her nose as if about to weep.

'Just the truth, *ya sitt*, just the truth, that is all I wish to know, nothing more. You shared the same mother?'

'But of course! How else could we be sisters!' Salida tossed her dark head. 'I was the eldest, born before her.'

'I had thought that she was an only child, and that her mother had not borne a child before.'

'You were wrong. It was concealed because of . . . well, my father. He was married, you see, very respectable and unwilling to admit that he had been whoring.' Salida paused, eager to see the effects of her bold words on this naïve desert nomad. 'Sad, but I am only one of thousands of bastards in the world.' She affected an insouciant smile.

Ashraf did not respond. He sensed that she was predatory

and that she delighted in another's discomfiture, but he was determined that she would not feast on his.

'Tell me more of your mother, *ya sitt*.'

He was studying Salida's colouring. It was not unlike that of his master's loved one: long black hair, as dense as ebony hidden from the sun, eyes a lighter brown than usual. Could they be said to come from the same mother as she who had given his master's beloved those unforgettable and extraordinary green eyes? Or was that the work of her father? This woman was large-boned and bulky. She had no grace, no composure. He could see her mind working, like a scuttling beetle against the stones.

'My mother was very beautiful, very graceful and slender. She had the brightest and most unusual eyes . . .'

'Green?' Ashraf flushed with fury the moment that he had interjected that word. Now he had given her information that she should have given him, *if* she knew it.

'Yes, the loveliest green, so that she was famous for her eyes. The green-eyed one, they called her. That was why my father fell in love with her when she was very young. He was a big man, raw-boned, very strong, very healthy. In my build I take after him.' Safe ground there, for how could this dim-wit know otherwise?

'Her name, can you tell me her name?'

Ashraf held his breath. This was the moment of truth. If she could not supply the proper name, then he would go, and with gladness.

'Maryam, of course, but you knew that did you not?'

'I knew it, yes.' With all his heart he had wanted this woman to give herself away so that he would know she could not possibly be related to the lovely creature who was his master's beloved. He felt sick, and not just from excess of sugar. This raw-boned, swollen, immoral woman for his master's sister-in-law? Allah, but he would die if he could prevent it!

'Did you live with your sister as she grew?'

'I did. She was a small infant and needed constant tending. I loved her dearly and she loved me. Our mother was distraught after that . . . distressed and unable to settle happily because she had been so much in love with my sister's father, the *kaffir*. It was very sad and there was nothing that I could do, being so young.' Salida shrugged her beefy shoulders. 'My little *jijim* vanished one night, taken away by my mother I know not where, and I never saw either of them again. I searched but I was only young and I had no money, no home. Friends took me in and raised me or I would have been on the streets.'

And now you are, thought Ashraf silently.

'Can you recall your sister's name?' He sat back, his face like marble, determined that he would reveal nothing. If she did not know this name, then the charade was finished.

'But of course! Mishaal, that was her name: she who shall be as a torch unto her peoples. Not that I know what that means, but I was told it later.'

Ashraf slumped on his cushion, a great sob welling in his bosom. He was seeing himself returning to his master to tell him of this. '*Ya saiyid*,' he would say, 'your future sister-in-law is a whore, a woman of great immorality and low repute. She is feared and loathed by many and I beg you not to attach yourself to the one you have chosen because it will bring this dreadful woman into your family!'

Dare he say all that? He would wish to, with every particle of his being. How would the Amir take it? Badly, very badly.

'Dear one, come and sit closer to me and talk. It is the will of Allah that you came here, is it not? Let us now be friends, and more, if it is your wish?' Salida leaned forward to reach for Ashraf, her capacious breasts bulging from her robe. They were rouged, spangles stuck to the swollen half moons. Round each nipple was a circlet of bright red. Despite himself, he was fascinated. Could one be repelled and attracted at the same time? He was about to find out.

'Come, sit here.' Before he knew it, his robe was flung back and her hand was squeezing at his manhood; instantly, it was erect and throbbing. Gently she stroked it, while thrusting her breasts against him. He felt an uncontrollable whirling sensation and then her breasts were enveloping his manhood and she was panting and gasping as she crushed him. He was at danger point when she drew back, her face burning. Next moment, she was pulling him on top of her and knotting her legs round his back and he was diving, deeper and deeper, into the moist satin depths. He shuddered, wailed, and lay limply, loathing himself, loathing her for entrapping him. He had failed everyone. He had lain with his master's future sister-in-law, God forgive him. It was no consolation to know that so had every other man in Abeesha.

He tried to pull away from her but she flung herself across him, her tongue in his groin, licking, darting, sucking. He could not believe what was happening to him: he was hard again. Allah, how could he get away from this demon?

Bucking, he thrashed around as she aroused him and then he was emptying himself into her again, groaning, wrenched in two with ecstasy and revulsion. After, they lay gasping, Ashraf shaking as if he had been pursued by devils, sweat streaming down his neck and back.

He opened his eyes to find that Salida was observing him intently.

'You may come here every night that you are in the city. I welcome you. It will take me three days only to prepare for my journey to the desert with you. I have a few business items that I must conclude.' She tossed her head, eyes flickering.

'You return with me?' he squeaked.

'But of course. The Amir will want to meet me, will he not? Allah, there is to be a wedding, is there not, and I wish to be among the guests in my rightful place, to see my beloved sister become Amira. Is that not the custom?'

'Yes, it is, of course.' He nodded, feeling stupid. After a few moments he had gathered sufficient strength to rise to his feet. Gathering his bernouse around him, he attempted a jaunty walk to the door.

'Oy! You have not paid me!' Salida called after him, her voice rasping.

Ashraf turned, blinking. Pay her? Why? She was almost family: one did not pay one's master's relatives for the use of their bodies.

'I will return tomorrow,' he grinned nonchalantly while the pit of his stomach shivered. 'I will pay you then.'

She seemed content, for she waved to him, blowing him a

kiss which he did not return. Soon he was galloping down the stairs and out into the street where he gulped at the night air as if it were the elixir of life.

The farther he left the street, the more his sense of reality returned. What had he been thinking of, in the name of Allah? She had bewitched him! He was as helpless as tissue in her scheming hands.

He thought of entering a mosque then decided that he could not face it: he was tainted, soiled. Whoever claimed that visits to whores were thrilling and exciting was insane! It was an ordeal of the most hellish proportions, and even more grisly in that he had gained sexual enjoyment from it, while his soul and heart had been chilled and repulsed.

He did not see the small boy following him to his lodgings, the boy paid by Salida to keep track of him. Her network of spies and gossips was excellent; she knew everything, everyone's private business. She was not going to lose this opportunity to become the sister of an Amira; no, most certainly not. Her whole life would be changed by it; she would be rich and revered; the Amir would find her a wealthy and titled husband as he was bound to do as her only male relative, even if only by marriage, and then she would live in comfort for the rest of her days. Ashraf would do what she urged; he would not reveal that she was a whore; no one would ever know of her past. She would never speak of it again. The new life beckoned her; she was filled with a heady delirium, biting on her fingers and sighing as if she had just fallen in love.

First there was the matter of Kausar. Her body would have to be buried somewhere deep where it would never be found. Getting to her feet, she went to the rear of her room and pulled aside the curtain. There lay Kausar, her mouth stretched in a grimace, her tongue protruding. She looked uglier than she ever had in life, the bitch. That was one blabber-tongue safely out of the way.

Chapter Thirteen

To her surprise, Mishaal was to be given her own tent. One morning Nur and Shamim woke her with a dish of dates and a drink of camel's milk and told her the news.

At first she felt delight and relief, and then dismay. What if it were a device to get her alone so that the Amir could intrude upon her privacy? At the moment he would have to give good explanations to these two old women as to why he wished to visit Mishaal in their tent. He might be their revered and beloved master but she was a young unmarried girl and if he truly wished to marry her – Allah forbid it! – then he would not desire to blacken her reputation.

The tent was of modest size, black like all the others, but inside it was generously furnished with rugs and pillows and even a low divan which was the first that she had seen in the camp, an ornate bronze table with jug and bowl to match, gleaming bronze lamps to burn oil and incense, and, in one corner, her travelling bag. Rushing to it, she opened it to find that everything was inside just as she had left it.

'Now the city lady will complain no longer.' Shamim folded her arms.

'It is not for material goods that I long,' Mishaal retorted.

'It is good to have the belongings of one's own body, the personal implements and so on.'

'It is. However they cannot compensate for one's lack of freedom!' Mishaal glared at the woman, who shrugged.

'You have your own tent. What better freedom is there? You are honoured. See how *ya saiyid* has lavished comforts upon you, the things that he has brought for your happiness.'

Shamim pointed to the lamps and the table.

'It is no kindness to give someone the last thing that they want, when their first need is ignored.'

'Allah, but city dwellers are cracked in the head!' Shamim snorted. 'Would you have rags and tatters in place of this?'

'If I were free, yes!' Mishaal rose to her feet. She had a presentiment that the Amir would be along soon to see how she liked her new home. She was right.

'I wish to show you that you are free as the air,' the Amir said as he stepped inside the tent a little later. 'Now you have your very own home, where you can do as you will, and you cannot say that we have imprisoned you.'

'So I am free to leave here now?' Mishaal's face flamed. What hypocrisy he showed; she could not bear him anywhere near her! 'I may have a camel and return to my home? Is that what you are saying?'

'Your home? Which home is that, Mishaal? The brothel?'

'*You know?*' Allah, how had he found that out? Was he a magician who could see the truth in glass?

'Yes, I know.'

'But you will never understand, never! Why should I explain to you, my gaoler? What business is it of yours where I grew up or with whom?'

'You think that I will condemn you, but you are wrong.' He stepped closer.

'No man condemns the woman he wishes to bed, but after, oh after, he will not see her in the same light!'

'You show your origins by saying that. The hardness of the whore is in your tone.'

'And the lust of the male is in yours!' Mishaal gritted her teeth.

'Is this lust?' In one spinning second, he had caged her in his arms so firmly and so expertly that she could not retreat, and his mouth was on hers, scintillating and blessed, stimulating her down to her toes with a springing joy that she had never felt before. She could not move. She did not wish to move. Suddenly, and much to her alarm, because of this kiss the Amir's nearness had become her world. All else was oblivion.

'The stars glitter in your eyes when you rage at me and your cheeks flush like desert flowers,' he told her, freeing her mouth momentarily.

'You – you – cannot sway me like this! I am determined!'

'Determined to escape into the desert wilderness? How long do you think you would last, little *fáhd*? All you would find out there are your brothers and sisters, the brindled wildcats. They would bring you down as they would a gazelle. Did you know that if you had been a Beduin child and were sickly, we would have given you the name of a hardy animal, the *fáhd*, the brindled wildcat, to imbue you with its strength so that you would grow tall and strong?'

'So do not call me that or I shall become stronger and more ferocious than ever you could be!'

'But are you not a woman?' His nigrescent eyes glittered so that she fought to be free of his arms, pushing and twisting. 'Why behave like this, little *fáhd*? It will weaken you, not make you sturdier, and you will not have the power to resist me.'

'You will only be one of the hundreds that I have resisted!' Mishaal spat. 'Men, what are they? Muscles in the head as well as in the arms, greedy bellies and even greedier senses . . . I despise them all, especially you, whatever your name is!'

She believed that she had scored a great point against him but he was laughing delightedly, feet apart, arms folded.

'So you do not know my name, eh?'

'I can make up one for you . . . How about Demon of all Lusts, or Devil of Passion?' Her fingers curved, itching to strip the skin from his cheeks.

'Husain, that is my name. A popular Arab name, nothing odd about that, would you say? Husain ibn Rashid ibn Yussuf ibn Husain, in the direct line since the time of the Prophet Mohammed.'

'Do you taunt me with your family heritage when you know that I have none, that I do not even know the name of my father?'

'But what if one with such ancient lineage loves one who has nothing but herself to offer him, and thus, because of love, he will take her to be his bride without dowry, what then, my heart?' His voice was soft, coaxing, tender against her ears, but she knew that she must not trust. How often had she seen the tragic results of trusting a man at Rhikia's house?

'No man would do that, certainly not a great prince like yourself, Hussein ibn the Universe! Use me, yes, but never take me to wife! I was the wife of a man whose nobility and honour far excelled any that you have ever practised and he overlooked my origins completely: they meant nothing to him whatsoever!'

'It is no use persisting in that silly story that you were married. Your American used you, and would have gone on using you, a little comfort in the desert night, until he took ship for home. Do you think that he would have presented a brown woman of exotic origins and infidel religion to those white-skinned *nasrani* women in the New World? Do you think they would have accepted you as his wife? No, the ordeal would have annihilated you, little *fáhd*, for all the spirit that you show here. Any man who truly loved you would never have dreamed of putting you through such an ordeal. Allah, the man was a fool!'

'You are sick with jealousy and you wish to damage all that is dearest to me, but you shall not. I am *nasrani* now, I took my husband's religion, and no one shall take it from me!'

'"*What's the use? I look for roses but the thornbed's all I find!*"' He was quoting verse to her, that of Ahmet Paşa, and her eyes must have shown her surprise. She could respond in kind!

'"*Would I knew the spells to change my heart to solid stone like yours!*"' she riposted, exultant at the shocked expression in his dark eyes.

'"*If it's only with the stars you're destined to be in accord, Ah, my moon, I'll star the world with tear drops day and night combined . . .*"' he continued.

'"*Like a flute the age would wail, the earth would moan most mournfully, Did I once let what is in my nature be divined.*" Do you want more, O Great Prince? What of the verses of Cem Sultan, Kadi Burhanettin, or Şeyhî, perhaps, or Daî, what of Daî? There are more if these do not please the noble Amir . . .'

'For a whore you have a sharp memory for names. Where did you hear those? Was one of your clients a learned man?'

Turning slowly, Mishaal went to the bronze table and, as if about to admire it, she took its matching vase and, twisting with the speed and grace of the dancer that she was, she flung it straight at the Amir's face.

Ashraf had a fever. Examining his organs in a fearful fury, he could find no sign of spots or blemishes, yet who knew what he might have caught from that hussy? Slapping his hands to his ears, he remonstrated with himself. No, not hussy, but his master's future sister-in-law, Allah forbid!

'Oh beneficent, all-merciful Lord, let it not come to that! Let it not be so, that hussy in my master's family! I should die of it.' Was it possible for the taint of evil to cause sickness, for she had that taint about her, he would swear to it.

The lodging-keeper came in with *pilaf* and water for him. Could he stomach the greasy mess of the badly cooked *pilaf*? No, the mere sight revolted him. Allah, but he longed for freshly picked figs and buttermilk fresh from the goat!

'Do you have any fruit?' he croaked.

'For extra. It will cost you extra, *ya m'allmi.*' The man salaamed.

Oh, for the desert where a poor man would give his last food to a guest in his tent!

'Then please bring me fruit, as much as you can carry.'

'It shall be so, *ya m'allmi.*' The man salaamed again, then retreated, eyes glowing. His was a humble residence and at this time of year he had many rooms to let. This man was a desert dweller, miserable beneath a roof and caged by four stout walls, ignorant of city ways and prices; he would make a small fortune from him before he left.

Outside, the boy was leaning against the wall, picking his nose. He had not moved for two days. The lodging-keeper barely glanced at him as he thrust past.

The boy was bored, yet the harlot had paid him generously. The Beduin had not shown his face for nearly three days now. Perhaps they would bring him out feet first when next he ventured into the street? The boy had been paid a week in advance and he hoped that he would get at least one more week's pay out of this, for he had a mother and five sisters to support. Had the man inside looked the sort, he would have brought one of his sisters to him now and forced him to pay her generously to keep her mouth shut. It was a useful tale, that of a young girl sobbing that a man had tried to rape her.

The night would be here soon, and the boy would be ashen with cold. He had no cloak, only a thin and tattered bernouse and sandals with broken straps. He thought yearningly of his pad of rags at home, where he could curl up in the middle of his sisters and mother and glow with warmth from them.

Ashraf fell on the fruit when it came, tearing at the flesh and sucking out the juice with desperate excitement. How did these city dwellers survive their stodgy, plain and boring diet? Everywhere he went, it was greasy *pilaf*, lumpy couscous and leathery meat, the vegetables, when they appeared, cooked to a tasteless mush. No wonder these people looked so pasty and hunched. Of course, if fruit were so expensive, then few would be able to afford it.

Next morning he felt his old vigorous self, waking to a bright dawn and the sound of the muezzin's call to prayer. His fellow Beduin would be rising and assembling for the first prayers. Did all desert dwellers feel like this away from their home, empty and desolate and tortured with the longing to return? He fancied that it must be so.

Breakfast was dried figs like little leather pouches, so resistant to the teeth that he had to chew them and soften them in his mouth for some time before being able to taste what remained of their flavour, served with slightly sour milk, cold, dry couscous from the previous night, and a slab of exhausted goat's cheese which lay miserably on the plate as if begging for release.

No excuse now for Ashraf not to complete his business. He must hire a camel and return to his master to break the grim news. While he travelled, he would have to wrack his brains to think of ways in which to decorate the truth so that it became palatable, although he knew, deep in his heart, that it could be as appetising as the rocky figs and weary, mould-flecked cheese.

The boy reported straight to Salida, telling her that the man was departing into the desert. She had been in a state of readiness for hours, her bags packed, the donkey ready to take her to the city's edge where a camel awaited her. She knew what lay ahead of her; she was well equipped with water, dates and yoghourt, and the boy would be coming with her as extra support. With good fortune, she need never return to this hellish city. She would be the sister-in-law of an Amir, the half-sister of an Amira, what more could she desire?

The heat blasted down, parching her face and tightening the skin on her nose and cheeks so that she could not move her lips without grimacing. She had lost her veil during a flurry of wind and now had to tear a piece from her under-robe to wind round her head. She ached to be back in her own comfortable home with her feet on a padded stool and servants bringing her sherbets and fresh fruits, round and succulent.

'*Sitt,* take care or you will fall!' The boy's sharp voice roused her. She was slumping in the seat, slipping into sleep, her mind blanking out into a welcome, cajoling blackness. Jolted back into reality (or was this heat and glare the illusion?) she struggled to summon her wits.

'Allah, I will tell the truth, all of it, if you spare me! I will turn back and forget my hope for a new life if you spare me from this, Lord God!'

'*Sitt,* you will fall!' The boy's sharp voice sailed into her ears but she could not respond. Slowly, she swooned from the camel's back, landing with a heavy thump on the sandy terrain.

Bashir, the boy, ran to her, his eyes bulging. She was dead and he would be blamed for her murder! *Ya Allah*, what could he do now?'

But she was not dead, only stunned and bemused by the

heat. Helping her to sip from his water flask, he shielded her from the sun. There was no break in the scouring heat of the day. Bashir sat beside the woman's head, his back to the sun, his upper body blocking out some of its glare while she rested and sipped water.

He wished that he had never come with her. How would he get her bulk back up on the camel? If she did not recover, he would have to ride back into the city for aid, and what would become of her out here in the merciless wilderness with the carrion birds circling overhead?

'Bashir, I wanted to be sister to the Amira . . .' Her wits were wandering with the heat. 'I have the right, yes, I have the right. I have earned it, oh yes, indeed I have! Years of struggle and poverty while *she* lives in splendour . . .'

'Rest, *sitt*, or you will overtax yourself and we shall be stuck here unto eternity,' Bashir groaned.

Salida caught at his ragged sleeve, tugging him close.

'You do not understand what I have endured, no one does! My friends have turned against me, despite all that I have done for them. People owe me money which they refuse to repay . . . Years ago, I was carrying a child but I was too poor to give birth . . . I had to lose my baby, do you understand what I went through? *Ya Allah*, how can you, a mere boy, know what it was like for me?'

'My mother and sisters are poor, too, *sitt*, very poor. They suffer too.'

'But not like me, oh, not like me! No one has suffered like me!' Tears filled Salida's eyes and swept down her cheeks. 'It will be different when I am with my sister again. I shall never have to worry about money then, all blessings to the one true God!'

'So now you must get up, *sitt*, and we must continue before the buzzards get us. If you want that money, you must ride, *sitt*, and not lie there weeping.'

Salida looked up at him with pain-racked eyes. Boys, selfish, cold, they grew up into men who were even colder and more self-indulgent. She had little interest in any male who was too young or too old to be a customer, and to her, Bashir was a prop, a slave to do her bidding, nothing more.

'You will have to help me up. I cannot do it alone. My back hurts and I think I have wrenched a shoulder. Oh, the glare of that sun, it strikes like a flame. Allah, why must we depend upon camels? When will man invent some easier mode of travel?'

'They say that in *nasrani* countries there are metal camels with flaming bellies which speed along tracks within an hour or two.'

'That sounds like sorcery, the work of evil *jinns*. Who would turn a camel into metal and set it on fire unless they were devils themselves?' Salida tried to heave herself up on to one elbow.

'That is so, *sitt*. That is how I think too, but I have heard of these flaming camels and they make fast speed, very fast.'

'What's the use of gibbering about them now? We don't have one here, so we're marooned.'

'If the *sitt* can get back on her camel then we shall be able to travel again.

'Get me up, then! Come on, boy, help me.' Salida held out her hands to Bashir, who, gritting his jaw, took them tightly in his and tried to haul her to her feet.

Husain was agile too and the vase missed him by an inch. He felt the ornament fly past his face and the cool air of its passing, and then he turned to face Mishaal, his eyes sad.

Folding his arms, he stood surveying her for some moments in silence. 'Poetess, learned lady, dancer *par excellence*, and now firer of dangerous missiles. What my ancestors would have done to have had you when besieging fortresses and in need of someone to fire their catapults! Would you have laughed as you jettisoned stones and flaming pitch into the faces of your enemies?'

'Only if they deserved it,' Mishaal retorted.

'How would you know, if you had never met them? There is always a distance, a barrier, between enemies, so they never gauge the truth about one another. In the end they hate everything about one another, loathe every hair, every gesture, and are full of mistrust and suspicion. Is that how it will be with us, Mishaal?'

'I do not waste my time thinking about you!'

'So you know nothing about me, just the façade which is for everyone to see? What do you truly care about my heart or my soul, my needs or my happiness?'

He had moved closer. She could smell the desert on him, sandy, primeval, all-powerful. Suddenly, she was frightened. He had been raised here in this place; he knew everything about this wilderness, she knew nothing. Here, his power was absolute; he was like a god, one of the ancient ones, omnipotent, awe-inspiring, and yet she had a strange and unsettling sensation that he was no stranger to her; somewhere, somehow, she felt that she had known him before.

'Why are you silent, little *fáhd*? I am accustomed to you shrieking and brawling. Are you angry because you did not damage me?' His eyes twinkled.

'Yes, I wanted to break your skull!' she cried, yet she did not mean those words.

'Then it was not Allah's wish that you should, or I would be lying on the ground now.'

'Are you trying to claim that you have Allah's protection above all? Oh, you bigoted Muslims!' Mishaal tossed her head.

'So you still consider yourself *nasrani*, little *fáhd?* You worship the man who died on the cross, and revere Him as the Son of God?'

'That is what Christians do, as you obviously know.'

'What of Mohammed and the one true God? What do you think of them?'

'Mohammed was a good man. He meant to bring peace and justice to his people. He made laws which work just as well now as they did in his lifetime. He gave us a code of behaviour which is beyond criticism . . . I think that he – he had much in common with the Christ. He wanted his people to be generous to the poor and live good lives. He wanted them to learn as much as they could, even if they had to travel the world to do so . . .' Mishaal halted, uneasy. How those dark eyes had the ability to unnerve her! She did not know whether he was approving or angry. She preferred him to lose his temper rather than to watch her in silence.

'Yes, Mishaal. How close were their creeds. Mohammed said, "Shall I tell you the worst amongst you? Those who eat alone, and whip the servants and give to nobody," and "He who kills even a sparrow needlessly is accountable to God on the Day of Judgement." What have you read in the Christian Holy Book, anything?'

'My – my husband read to me from it, but mostly he told me about the Christ and what He did.'

'Were you not struck by the similarities between the two creeds? Jesus told his followers to love one another and give alms to the poor, and the first of the Christian commandments is "Thou shalt not kill". Is there so much difference between the two religions?'

'I – I it is not for me to say. I am no mullah.' Mishaal's cheeks were growing rosy. What were his intentions in this conversation? To make her look and feel a fool? He did not have to do much to make her feel like that.

'But *I* can say, for I am leader of my peoples and my line travels directly from that of the Prophet Mohammed. Yes, there are similarities in the creeds. Only one whose mind is bigoted could disagree on that point. So what is it about Christianity that attracted you, Mishaal? Tell me.'

'I found it difficult to – to accept the idea of a man dying on the cross to save souls, I admit that.'

'That notion is totally alien to Islam, so it is not surprising that you found it unacceptable. We see God as all-powerful, all-seeing and omniscient, without any son of His having to die for our souls.'

'Yet you accept the Christ as one of the prophets of Allah!'

'Oh yes, but that is because His teachings were so similar to those of Mohammed. In many ways, they were of one mind, but we of Islam are equally sure that Jesus Christ was not the Son of God but that His story was the retelling of the legends of the older pagan religions.'

'How do you know so much? What have you learned here in the desert? The Beduin know nothing, *nothing*, they are beggars struggling to find food and water . . . How do they have time to study?'

'Yet you can quote the poets of Islam, Mishaal. How did

you find time to learn their words in between entertaining the men who came to your bed?'

She had thrown the vase; there was nothing else nearby. He stood taut as a panther, waiting for her reaction. He loved goading her, yet she could not hold back her immediate reactions to such insults.

'I was a dancer! No man ever came near me! I spent all my spare time studying. From the age of four, I was tutored by a man of learning. My foster mother would not have me grow up unable to write my name as so many girls do.'

'What does it matter whether a *bintilkha'ta* can write her name? Who would be interested in her mind?'

'No one was, except myself. They came to see me dance. You have seen me dance, too. Would you not say that I had some skill in that field?'

'Yes, for filling men with a passionate desire to take you in their arms. It is a dance of seduction, Mishaal. That is what you planned it to be, a method of seducing men so that they would pay highly for your charms.'

'You sound like ZouZou! That is what she wanted me to do, but my foster mother would never have allowed it. Nor would I. You judge me, so you condemn me, but that is your opinion only and you do not know the truth. If you did, would you accept it?'

'I know what it is like being poor and reaching the stage where you will do anything for money to buy food . . . I do not condemn you, Mishaal, far from it.'

'You have never known what it is to be poor! You have all these people at your feet, you have tents and camels and livestock. Your tent is filled with riches such as I have never seen before. What can you know of destitution?'

'I lived amongst the poor as a student, Mishaal. How can you know about me, either? My family were wealthy for centuries. Great traders in the days of the Caliphs and merchants, they gathered fabulous treasures. A Beduin can be a nomad and carry nothing but his tent, or he can become a travelling merchant and that is what my ancestors did, until they had acquired great wealth. Then, for seven hundred years, they ruled here in this wilderness that you despise so intensely, until it came to the day when I was born. By then, there was very little left of the treasures. They had been sold over the decades to ensure the survival of my people. Drought came and animals died by the hundred. The wells kept us going, yet now they too are running dry. If we want water, we have to transport it, sometimes many back-breaking miles. Every day there is news of another well drying up. I have only one thing left worth selling, my mother's marriage jewels, the jewels that my future bride should wear for her wedding day. Then it is destitution for me and my people, too.' His eyes were bright with misery.

Mishaal hung her head, filled with shame. One moment he made her feel like hitting him, the next, he had moved her so deeply that she wanted to weep.

'There was no money to pay for my education, yet it was unthinkable that my father and grandfather's son, the Amir of the Land of Mirages, should remain illiterate, so I lived like a beggar while I studied, then my father sold a gem which had been in our family for generations, the Diamond of Mirages, and with that I finished my education and travelled the world to see what it was that other men set such great store by.'

'*Nasrani* men, you mean?'

'But of course. I wanted to see how this Christian creed had evolved. After all, it is older than the Mohammedan teachings. If Christians could uphold their beliefs and live as their disciples taught all those centuries ago, then I felt that our own religion would also survive. If they could not, then I knew that we of Islam may well have a fierce fight ahead to maintain our beliefs.'

'Why maintain them? The Muslim religion is cold and barren. Where is the place for women? They are treated as servants and used by men as packhorses or – or for pleasure.' She could not meet his eyes.

'Ah, little *fáhd*, you have not been gently raised, that I can see. Where amongst my peoples have you seen women treated as packhorses? They share equal partnership with their men. Beduin women are never forced into marriage against their will; they are allowed to choose the man they want, and

Beduin marriages are happy. They marry for love and love alone and rarely do they part before the end.

'In London, England, where the Queen is called Defender of the Faith, I heard of young heiresses forced into marriages with men whom they feared and loathed. In that land, everything that a woman possesses becomes her husband's upon her wedding day and he can use it as he wishes. If he be dissolute and drunken, he can waste her fortune and she has no redress in law. Yet if she should err, even in the slightest degree, her children are taken from her and she will never see them again, nor will any champion her cause.'

'I have only your word for this!'

'I speak the truth. Why should I not? I was also treated to the contempt and revulsion which is felt by these so-called Christians for those who are not of their creed or colour. Some were kind, it is true, and many were interested in my life, but only as an exotic curiosity. That is all I was to them. I had a title, yet no fortune to pay my way, so I lived amongst the poor and suffered with them. I wanted to see for myself what men could be subjected to by their fellows; what was the worst that a man could endure.'

'I can tell you what that is!' Mishaal burst out. 'It is being half-caste! Having a *nasrani* father and a Muslim mother, so that you do not know who is your kin and what line is truly yours! Then, along with that, make your sufferer one who is born in sin, her mother so disgraced that she takes her own life, disowned and dishonoured. Have that sufferer raised by the dearest and most devoted foster mother, but in a place where all are knowledgeable in the ways of the world, knowing everything about man and woman, while she, your poor sufferer, remains apart from them all, never knowing whether it is because she is half-caste, born in sin, or innocent of – of man, or all three, but mostly believing it is because of all three, so she has felt like – like a leper all her days, yes, a leper!'

His arms were round her as the tears began to flow, and it was there, in the tent which was her new home, that she experienced the joy of being comforted by a man who knew all of her story, her inner agony, and her shame, yet who did not shrink from her, nor turn away.

In his embrace, she was revived as she had never been before. She did not wish to thrust him away or repel his tender kisses as they caressed her cheeks and forehead, so gentle, so caring, that she could not be affronted by his intimacy. She was a stranger to this sensation, safe, relaxed, secure. As she recognised its source, she felt only fear: fear of this man who had caused the death of Drew, and then made her his prisoner. She must not weaken; if she did, she should be his helpless minion like all the others here who revered and made obeisance to him.

Stiffening, she tried to push him away, her face white. But his mouth was on hers, sweet and reviving as dew, and a long, unsettling shudder coursed through her body so that the fear began to fade. The kiss was fresh water in the wilderness, manna for the starving, *drâhim* for the poor, a soft pallet to protect against the rocky desert earth, the breath of God filling her with delight and new-found happiness.

What had she felt with Drew if not love? This feeling was deeper, it contained a spirituality and a blessing which Drew's kisses had not roused in her. If she were sick, then this kiss would revive her; if she were distraught, then this kiss would calm her soul . . .

The arms that cradled her were the strongest and most blessed that she had ever known; here was the father whom she had never known, the brother whom she might have had; and also her stalwart rock; she could sense the implacable strength in him, that same power and authority which made him so beloved by his peoples.

Yet how could a murderer and abductor be her saviour?

Nonetheless, the kiss was paradise and extraordinary sensations were breaking over her skin. She wanted to revere him, too, and call him '*Ya saiyid*' and kneel at his feet, knowing that she would be safer there than anywhere else on earth. How warm was his body, and how perfectly it moulded against her own; she could curve into him and become as one, so close, so united did she feel with him, and after just one kiss, one only . . .

Realising that she was offering him her heart, she gasped, pushing away, standing back to thrust off the drugged sensation flooding her limbs. He had enchanted her; she was too weak to resist. Her mind was alive with dread, her thoughts perplexed; she must be alone to untangle her true belief from wild assumptions. Turning her back to him, she retrieved her veil to preserve her modesty. Struggling for composure, she was all too aware of him standing behind her, waiting for her to speak. She wanted to, but could not. He must go; she must be alone; she had nothing to say to him at this moment; she could not trust herself.

Chapter Fourteen

Salida had lost track of the days; at first she had counted them assiduously but soon the heat had so benumbed her brain that she could not remember the total. Was it four, or five? Seven? Soon she discovered why this was called the Land of Mirages, for, on what she calculated as the fifth day, she saw walking towards her the most heart-wrenchingly handsome man. How tall he was and straight-backed, striding as if he were in the city on a balmy spring morning. He smiled at her, salaamed with great courtesy and then from his belt he unfastened a money bag, soft, round and brown. How clearly she perceived its colour and texture. Into her outstretched palm he put the bag, so that she could feel against her skin the heavy, rumbling, clinking of the coins. She was rich, enormously rich! They were gold; she knew that they were gold, a lifetime's hoarded treasure and all hers.

Then the boy spoke, his voice piping through her head and

the smiling, generous-hearted man shivered and vanished, like ectoplasm whisked away by the wind.

'*Sitt*, we must go on. Why are you staring like that? Why is your arm held out? Hold on to your camel else he will tumble you down again. You must put your mind to it, *sitt*, and not dream.'

'Dream?' Salida looked around her, bemused. 'Did you see that man? The one who gave me the bag of gold?'

'What man? What gold, *sitt*? You have seen a mirage, that is what it is. Now you must collect yourself for we must reach shelter by nightfall. The oasis of Bir is just ahead of us. Can you not see the walls of the dwelling?'

The boy had come this way before, thank God for that. But for him she would have perished long ago. Nothing could have prepared her for the vastness and harshness of the wilderness, for its arid terrain and unrelenting heat. In her foolishness, she had imagined that the journey to the Amir's camp would be short; instead, here they were, heading for the third oasis and apparently no nearer to their destination.

The oasis of Bir was famous for its well. For as long as man and his forebears could recall, the well had provided sweet, cool water for all its visitors and for those who wished to trek there from the surrounding camps and dwellings.

Salida could barely wait for her mount to flounder to its knees so that she could stand on firm ground once more. Breathing, thinking, even her state of mind seemed different once she was earthbound again, and off that lurching, belching monster. Not waiting for Bashir, she lumbered towards the door of the whitewashed house. It looked clean and fresh, well cared for, inviting. If they had a pallet, she would sleep straight away, and not care if she ever woke again, but first she must have fresh water!

Her agitated hammering at the door was answered at last by a small, forlorn child who peeped round the jamb and gaped up at Salida, thumb in mouth.

'Where is your father? Tell him that he has guests!' Salida announced imperiously.

The child continued to stare, but did not speak.

'Have you had your tongue cut out, child? Fetch your father now!'

From the innards of the house came a man in swinging white robes. He wore a tiny calico cap on his head, its edge embroidered with blue and scarlet threads, and his feet were encased in buff-coloured leather slippers. A black sash was tied round his scrawny waist and his face was that of an anxious, strained and disbelieving man.

'You have guests!' Salida repeated, eddying into the house in her accustomed leaden-footed fashion, almost knocking down the child and caring for nothing but the sight of a table and a real chair and food, a platter of figs!

'*Sitt*, we no longer house visitors, sad as it is for us to refuse them. Allah forgive me for this grave and foolish error! But we would, ah yes, we would, if we could, but we have no water. The Lord Allah has chosen to dry our well, the famous well of Bir that has gushed since man's memory was created by the one true, noble and merciful God! Now there is no water. We can offer nothing to travellers and we shall suffer agonies for this injustice on our part, but what can we do? We have fruit and *pilaf*, but only a bucket of water each day, then the well is dry again until the next day. There is my wife and my eight children, and our beasts, all of whom must relieve their thirsts with this miserly morsel . . . But eat you must. Come in, come in, and share our supper!'

Salida was already at the table, her cheeks bulging with figs. Often enough she had complained about fig seeds sticking in her teeth but she would never do that again. Figs tasted of paradise after two days of munching on husks and roots.

Early on, Bashir had tried to warn her that she would eat up all their food, but she would not listen. She was accustomed to gorging and gorge she would. Thus they soon had no food left and were forced to search for dry and twisted twigs, pull them out of the resisting sand and suck the roots for moisture.

The table and chair, European in style, had been left at the oasis by a merchant who had paid for his lodging in this way. They were the landlord's delight and even as he pushed more food towards Salida, his ears were straining to hear the ominous creaks from the chair as she rested her bulk on it, twisting this way and that to reach out for a variety of foods.

Round the door at the other side peeped the faces of more children, four boys and a girl, all small, thin in build and with tangled greasy black hair and pinched faces.

'Do you have no date juice, no pressed fruit to drink?' Salida asked, her mouth crammed. 'Sherbet, perhaps?'

'I am sorry. Allah forgive me, but I do not. We await fresh stores but we never know when they will arrive. Already they are very late. Alas, our land is in desperate straits. Never have we been over-provided for, yet always we had enough. See how thin and wasted are my children. These past months matters have grown worse, far worse than anyone could have known. Regularly I hear of more wells running dry. Once we had more wells than any other land, and now, we still have more, but few provide water any more.'

'Then dig new wells,' Salida said, irritated that this man's aimless chatter was interfering with her eating.

'If only we could, *sitt*, but the wells we have were dug in the places where there is ample water, and the places remaining do not have that blessing. It was Allah's will that deserts should be arid.'

'If that is so, then why grumble when the wells run dry?'

It was unacceptable that a host, even a landlord of a caravanserai, should be rude to his guest for it would offend all that was most important in Islamic courtesy, so the man licked his lips and racked his brains for a polite answer.

Bashir was chewing *pilaf* as if it were the first food he had ever tasted. He did not wish to listen to this crazy gluttonous woman. He wished that she would be struck dumb.

How subdued were the children who peeped at him from round the door. Curious they were, yet silent and devoid of spirits. Did the lack of water drain the energy? How important was it to life? His mother and sisters needed it for taking in washing, and for giving to their animals, but he usually drank sticky sweet sherbet or honey-laced date juice, semi-fermented so that it was not truly alcoholic and so would not offend against the Prophet's teachings.

Sated, Salida slumped on the table and began to snore, while Bashir looked apologetically at the landlord. How quiet it was now that the virago slept. He would leave her there, for he had no desire to try and get her to a pallet. Everything to do with this woman was backbreaking.

Thanking the keeper of the caravanserai, Bashir strolled to the door as nonchalantly as he could manage. The sky was oozing colour, streaming ribbons of blood-pink, tangerine and ochre; the sun was glowing itself to bed. He was consumed by homesickness and the longing to be tucked into bed with his mother and sisters. The feeling gripped him just beneath his heart and swept away any responsibility that he felt towards Salida.

When next the inn-keeper looked up, the boy had gone, leaving the door slightly ajar. All that was left of his presence was a small pile of date stones at the place where he had been sitting.

Salida woke with an aching back and chilled feet. Someone had thrown a coarse rug over her shoulders but it had not kept her warm. The room was dark and she looked about her with bewilderment. Where was she? Where was the boy?

Stumbling to her feet, she lumbered into the table's edge, unaccustomed to such sharp pieces of furniture. When the pain in her thigh had eased, she cried out to Bashir but there was no answer. After a time, the keeper of the caravanserai appeared, his robe flung over his head, the hem at the back caught up in his belt so that when he turned he revealed scraggy and fleshless thighs and a small portion of olive-coloured and hirsute buttocks.

'Great *sitt*, if you would please to retire to the sleeping room . . .'

'Where is he? Where is the boy?'

'Gone, *sitt*. I thought you knew. I thought that he was meant to bring you so far and then return. Is it not so? Has he deserted you? Allah forgive him! He has not stolen your property, Allah prevent it?'

'There is nothing to take, unless he desires to dress as a woman,' Salida growled, then recalled that the boy had spoken of his mother and sisters. What if he had stolen the best robes in which she planned to meet her long-lost sister? Letting out a wail, she crashed across the room to the bag in which she had packed her belongings. Red-faced and gasping, she unfastened it and probed inside, feeling the soft silky material of her festive robes, the satiny orbs of her beads, the suede of her embroidered slippers. Relief took her strength. There was a little bubbling in her throat as she collapsed against the inn-keeper, almost crushing him to the floor.

Beduin women, by custom and tradition, received elaborate jewellery on their marriage day, boldly designed and brightly coloured. Its possession was an essential part of the wearer's position in life. Bells were popular, and chains, silver beads in single or multiple links, garnet, carnelian, amber, pearl, coral and also glass stones set in silver, brass or gold. One of the oldest traditional designs, so Nur had told Mishaal, was a design of cylindrical pendants which were containers for Koranic charms and which were called *hirz*. These *hirz* were never set with gems or stones but were of great religious significance. Usually, jewellery was destroyed on the death of its owner, so there were few antique pieces, but the old woman spoke in awe-filled tones of the jewellery that had been handed down through the Amir's family, brought from one of the most distant lands in ancient times, the city of the Caliph.

Shamim herself wore a religious pendant known as a *maskah*, with two cylindrical *hirz* on either side of it, inside which were sealed Koranic verses. The *maskah* had an inscription, *Mashallah*, which meant 'As Allah wills it, so it will be', and from this dangled five silver bells. When Nur spoke of the jewellery that had once belonged to the Amir's mother, she touched the inscription on her own pendant.

'Once, our people were enfolded in riches and our tents were lined with silk, our women wore gold filigree about their necks, and then misfortune came and the land took back its wealth from us. In ancient times, when frankincense and myrrh were needed in great amounts to embalm the dead, then did we trade in these and make our fortunes, and then religions changed and the incense was no longer needed in such amounts and our forefathers no longer prospered. Some continued thus, there were one or two who dominated the incense routes . . . one they called Lord of the Incense Road, a man much feared and dreaded called Adem Ali. He died young, at the height of his powers, poisoned by one of his own concubines, so they say. A girl who had been brought from Cathay as his bride. She loved him too much, and when he lost interest in her, she secretly fed him poison.'

'And what became of her, the girl from Cathay?' Mishaal asked.

'I know no more.' Nur sniffed. 'Ask *ya saiyid* if you wish to learn the rest of the tale.'

At that time, Mishaal and the Amir were not speaking, for she had decided that only by ignoring him could she fight the insidious attraction she felt for him. Besides, she must not allow herself to forget how she came to be here, and that she was a prisoner of this man.

Nur and she were polishing jugs and vases and jewellery, sitting cross-legged on cushions at the entrance to the Amir's tent. The sun was glaring down in its usual merciless fashion, and the women wore their head veils pulled over their faces to screen them. The jugs and vases were from the Amir's tent, and it was Nur's turn to clean them, which she considered an immense honour. The jewellery was to be a gift for the Amir's cousin who was soon to be married. There were six pieces, one the *hirz* with a *maskah*, as a protection and a pronouncement of faith, one a choker necklace, called *kirdala*, which fastened tightly round the throat and from which was suspended gold pendant beads studded with garnets. The *kirdala* fastened at the back with a simple hook clasp. There were small nose ornaments, *shaf* or *khizama*, earrings called *halaq*, and finger rings called *khatim*, of gold and silver with cabochon turquoises, one for the forefinger called *al shahid*, with an especially large stone, a design worn only by rich Beduin, and another a bezel design of gold set with garnets and amber. Although rings were not given to Beduin girls as a sign of their betrothal, the women usually received most of their jewellery on marriage, and there would be a special finger ring as a first gift.

Mishaal had heard that the young bride who would receive these gifts from her cousin was nearly seventeen, and that she was called Marjan, which meant coral. Mishaal could not help but feel a twist of pain as she cleaned the rings. She had dreamed of her handsome young saviour and of how he would love her, as she would love him, but where was he now, the one she had adored? But for the Amir, she and Drew would have been husband and wife in law now, and not just in her yearning imagination.

'If the Amir is as poor as you say, where did he get the money to buy this fine jewellery?' Mishaal suddenly snapped, suffering a burst of envy for Marjan, the bride-to-be.

'We have an old custom, strange as it may sound to one reared in the towns, but we destroy a woman's jewellery when she dies, unless she wills otherwise. This was the jewellery of Hilal, who died a few weeks ago and left all her possessions for the Amir to use in this way.'

'How very noble of Hilal!'

'No, not noble. Hilal loved the Amir as do we all, and she wished to leave him some gift, a sign of her feeling for him.'

'Very touching.' Mishaal's mouth twisted. She renewed her vow to escape. It would be madness to go on foot, but all the animals were tethered and guarded, so that she could not steal one. Outside the perimeters of the sprawling camp, lay the scorching, ruthless desert, arid, unfriendly and lacking the sustenance she would need for her long journey. She would be dead within a few days if she attempted to escape but now she knew that she must go, whether she survived or not. Whatever happened to her in the iron wilderness would be the will of God . . .

'Girl, you are not concentrating. Look, you have missed all this dust . . . How can a bride wear dirty rings on her marriage day?'

'What about the bride who has no rings and no husband, either!' Mishaal cried, leaping to her feet, the rings cascading on to Nur. 'What about her?'

But she did not wait for the astonished Nur to reply. Knowing that she would be stopped if she tried to mount one of the camels, she headed for her own tent, tears threatening, and it was then, as she was about to step inside, that one of the young boys came up to her and tugged at her sleeve.

'*Sitt*, you have a visitor. Look yonder, there she is, your sister who has come to attend your marriage ceremonies.'

Following the boy's pointing finger, Mishaal saw a large, heavily decorated woman bearing down upon her with arms outstretched.

'Mishaal, oh, dear sister, Mishaal, Mishaal! Allah be praised, but it is you after all these long years!'

Mishaal sat grimly in her tent listening to the woman called Salida who claimed to be her sister.

The heat and the ordeal of her journey had evaporated the worst of Salida's heavy paint, and for probably the first time in her life her complexion glowed.

Rhikia had never led Mishaal to believe that she had a sister. As far as she knew, she was her mother's only child, and yet this heavy, persistent woman seemed to know so much about her past: her mother's name, the colour of her eyes, her hair; the misfortunes that had attended her early life.

Mishaal could not find her tongue. She sat in silence while the woman babbled on, telling of her arduous travels, how her guide had deserted her and she had been forced to hire a youth who had charged her more than three times Bashir's price. On went Salida's tale, full of struggles and fears, hardships, sufferings and semi-starvation, all so that she could see her dear, dear, long-lost sister and congratulate her on her marriage.

This did startle Mishaal. Marriage? What did this unpleasant, unwelcome woman mean?

'Why, I was told that His Gloriousness the Amir was to take you as his bride,' Salida simpered.

Mishaal began to laugh. Here she was, planning her escape from an intolerable existence, and now here was a stranger, claiming to be her sister, bearing tidings of her marriage to her gaoler!

'How have I amused you, sister? What is funny about this

marriage?' Salida asked, panting a little as the clammy heat of the tent settled around her. How did these people survive in tents in this heat? They must have leather skins. Sweat was dribbling down her spine and coiling into a pool between her breasts. The backs of her knees felt slippery with moisture.

'Who told you that I was to marry the Amir?' Mishaal asked.

'Why, his servant Ashraf. He came to the city and told me so, for he had learned who I was. The Amir sent him to find me, you see. He knew that I was truly your sister and that you would be joyful to see me after all these years. It was the will of Allah,' Salida added importantly.

'I see. Then I have much to thank His Highness for.' Mishaal's mouth turned down at the corners.

'When is the wedding? Oh, 'tis years since there was a wedding in the family! How glorious, how splendid!'

'If it were so, yes, it would be splendid and glorious, but it is not, I am afraid. You have been misled, alas, and I am afraid that your journey has been wasted.'

Mishaal sat back, observing the woman's reaction, positive that this bloated, undignified and sweating woman could never be her sister. Yet, how had she found out the details of her life if she was not her blood kin? Could Rhikia have told her? No, Rhikia would never have disclosed such information to a woman like this. How then?

A scuttling sound outside the tent announced one of the Amir's body servants.

'It is the wish of His Highness that he meets the visitor who arrived here today,' the man said, salaaming deeply, face carefully composed.

'Of course he may meet her,' Mishaal said brightly, keen to hand over her problem. While the Amir was talking to the newcomer, she could think. Oh how she needed time to think!

But the Amir wanted to see them both, and so Mishaal had to accompany the claimant to the Amir's tent and there sit with her on one of the cushions before the Amir. He was sitting cross-legged, looking every inch the great lord and master. Suddenly she was glad of it. He would know whether this woman was genuine; he would deal with her and all the weight of decision would be removed from Mishaal's shoulders. As she realised this, she felt a wave of relief, comparable to a cool breeze blowing over her clammy body.

Salida began to babble her story all over again, with much bowing of her head and reverent salaaming, interspersed with many, 'Your Gloriousnesses' and 'Your Powerfulnesses', while the Amir appeared to be considering her every word with concentration, his forefinger resting on his upper lip, his thumb beneath his chin. Once, his eyes met Mishaal's but she could not read the expression there; it might have been humour, or revulsion; how could she decipher this man's features? He was an enigma.

An hour passed and coffee was served on brass trays inlaid with bright blue and scarlet. Sweetmeats were offered, tiny honey and nut cakes, and squares of sugary jelly sprinkled with nuts. How quickly they disappeared down the throat of Mishaal's would-be sister; Salida gobbled her food and belched in a very crude manner. She had the air of a woman of low morals; yes, that was it. Mishaal was shocked. This woman was a daughter of sin: she had neither the dignity nor the composure of the lovely girls with whom Mishaal had grown up at Rhikia's.

Mishaal held herself rigidly. She had revered the memory of her mother, visualising her as beautiful, gentle and badly wronged. How then could that same sad and lovely mother have given birth to this raw and large-boned creature?

'Tell me more of your childhood,' the Amir said, leaning forward, watching the stranger's reaction closely.

That very question had been in Mishaal's mind, and so, silently, blessing him, she waited to hear the woman's reply.

'It – it was a time which brought me little but pain and anguish, Your Powerfulness . . . I – I am loathe to recall those years. I went from foster mother to foster mother. I had no possessions, no proper home; my heart was heavy.' Salida affected a tremulous mouth and damp eyes.

Normally, Mishaal's heart would have gone out to such a person and she would have been moved on her behalf, but Salida's words left her cold.

'Tell me of my – of our mother,' Mishaal said, her voice a whisper.

'She was lovely, radiant like the stars and the moon, beloved by all who knew her. She had so many admirers, dozens of them all wishing for her hand in marriage, but she could not decide between them. Had one been richer than the others, then she might have found it easier.'

Salida was speaking from her own viewpoint, not that of Mishaal's mother, and Mishaal knew this instinctively.

'My father loved her most, of course, but he was very poor and had no property and so our mother could not consider him as a husband. But she loved him, ah yes, how she loved him!' Salida heaved a loud and emotional sigh. 'And so I was brought into the world, a child of love you may say, but my birth brought such disgrace on to our mother that she was shut away by her father and no one was allowed to visit her. Nonetheless, she plotted her escape: what else could she do? She was a woman of spirit. It was your father who helped her escape, Mishaal. He was a wealthy traveller, a foreigner from a far-off land. He heard of our mother's plight and visited her house pretending that he wished to study an Arabian family for the book that he was writing. Looking up in the courtyard, he saw our mother at her window and fell passionately in love with her!'

Salida clasped her hands together in front of her enormous bosom and sighed again.

Mishaal did not know what to believe. All this could so easily be true. The acute difference in her looks and those of Salida might well be due to their different fathers, and yet . . . Biting on her lower lip she told herself that if this appalling woman really was her sister, then it was her duty to welcome and accept her as such, to treat her kindly for the sake of their poor dead mother.

Glancing sideways at the Amir, she tried to gauge what he was thinking. He was glancing at her, so their eyes met, his dark and rich as *kahwe*, hers cat's-eye emerald in the light from the brass lamp. Colour poured into her cheeks and her mouth went dry. He was staring deep into her very soul, reading her thoughts, her emotions; nothing was concealed from him when he looked at her like that. He was lord of all that he surveyed and that included her; she was his minion.

Watching enviously, Salida half-closed her eyes and clamped her fists shut. She could read men's minds: this man, this omnipotent and wealthy prince, was beside himself with desire for this gullible and naïve girl whom she must now call sister. Ah, what she, Salida, would give to have this man looking at her in that same devouring, soulful way! This girl was witless, for she looked away and blushed when he gazed at her instead of encouraging him as she ought. She would make a cold and unwelcoming bride and the Amir would soon take more wives to satisfy his desires.

Salida knew that the Amir was a man of intense passion, and that no ordinary woman would keep him happy for long. Arabian men were renowned for their lustiness, but she sensed that this one would be exceptional in every way, not only ardent but tender and solicitous. Her envy increased, and in that moment she resolved to seduce him as soon as the right moment arrived. It would not be the first time that a man had married two sisters.

The audience was over, and the Amir's servant came to lead them out of the tent. It was dusk, balmy with the indigo veil of approaching night. Mishaal paused, not sure what to do with the unexpected visitor, but Salida, turning to her, smiled and clutched her hand.

'Sister, I am overjoyed to find you after all these years. It was the will of Allah that we should meet as if by some angelic plan. Riding here, I sometimes thought that I might be wrong, that what I heard would not lead me to my own dear sister, but now I have seen you I am so sure, oh so sure that we shared the same mother! Those eyes of yours – exactly the colour of hers! Praise be to Allah, we are of the same blood!'

Chapter Fifteen

Ashraf had failed to return from the city. The Amir knew that he had few more faithful followers than the good and solid Ashraf, so if the man had not come back, something must have happened to him. He was a strong and well-built man, skilled with weapons. The Amir did not think that he could have been ambushed. Where, then, was the man who had been by his side for thirteen years?

As the days passed without Ashraf's return, the Amir knew that he must send more men to find his old friend and servant. Instructing them to ride post haste, he watched them head out of the camp. If anything had happened to Ashraf, then there would be bloody vengeance on the one who had caused it.

The Amir's hand curled on his gleaming dagger. It did not matter if a man or woman was the very least of his peoples, if they were destitute or of the humblest stock, he would avenge them if they were within his jurisdiction. It was his duty, but more than that: he cared for them, every one. Any of his people could come to him with their troubles, their losses and griefs, and he would do all that he could to make amends. His personal fortune would have lasted far longer had he not given it away so freely to those who had suffered hardships, to brides who needed a dowry, to penniless widows.

A Beduin expected his ruler to maintain the law at all times, to protect and guard those who could not defend themselves, and to ensure the safety of their grazing lands. Now that water was even scarcer, the camels must survive for even greater periods without it, and so must they, the hardy desert nomads. There was only one advantage to their wells drying up and that was that raiders thought twice about encroaching on their grazing lands. Who but a fool would herd his camels on to land so parched that the deepest wells had dried to dust?

Princes did not continue to hold power if they should fail their people's needs, and of this Husain was well aware. Despite his family's long and ancient heritage, he would deserve to be stripped of his authority and another ruler elevated in his place if he proved to be a feeble suzerain.

There were rulers who had been murdered in their beds for their cruelty or weakness, for although a desert chieftain possessed the power of life or death over those he governed, they possessed the same power over him. The savagery and hardship of the desert could ask no less. Better for one man to die than all.

Not only must an Arab chieftain earn and deserve his people's love and respect; he must be accessible to them at all times. Any man who wished to come to him with their troubles, and a desire for justice, need only enter his tent and say his first name and they would receive his attention. It was the custom to bestow upon visitors a token of some kind, money, trinkets for the visitors' wives or sisters, woven rugs, daggers, swords, a cloak or bernouse, perhaps. Now that there was little left to give in the way of trinkets and weapons, he was acutely aware that the moment was approaching when he would have no recourse but to break that ancient custom.

A certain amount of opulence must be maintained by the ruler of the Land of Mirages, for his people expected it, but he displayed it with reluctance, aware that he was merely delaying the day that he dreaded with all his heart.

There was another consideration. Only a few days ago a man had entered his tent, sat at his feet and looked him squarely in the eyes.

'Husain,' the man had said, his voice reproachful. 'There is talk amongst your peoples. Those who are proud to have you as their prince are asking why it is that you remain unmarried. What of the line of your father and his father before him, they ask. It is the bounden desire of those who look to you as their leader that you sire a son to carry on your name. It is against the will of Allah that you lie alone in your bed.'

To his astonishment, Husain had felt a flood of heat weave across his body, and his tongue attain the texture and immobility of wood.

'If I have offended *ya saiyid* then I beg his forgiveness.' The man had made a deep obeisance before Husain before continuing. 'But this has to be said by one who loves and reveres you as he loved and revered your father before you. In your son we shall derive hope and faith for the future. We do not wish to be reminded of the ending of things, of the finality and the barrenness which is with us desert dwellers night and day.'

Husain found his tongue.

'I plan to marry . . . Tell those who are concerned that I shall take a bride in the very near future. Tell them . . . tell them that Allah sent me one who will make them a fitting Amira, but that she is one who must be gently wooed. Tell them also that I wish to be like them: and by that I mean that I wish to marry for love. I would not force any of my people to marry one whom they did not love, and I ask that same indulgence for myself.'

'Dare I request the name of the future Amira, Allah guard and preserve her?'

'The negotiations are at too delicate a stage, I fear. Soon, I promise you, the name shall be given and you shall be one of the first outside my household to know.'

And then, because he could not send the man away without a gift, for it would signify that he, Husain, was angered with him, the Amir unhooked his own cloak, draped it across his outstretched arms and gave it to the man, who flung himself down again, kissing the hem of his robe and showering blessings upon him, before going on his way, his Amir's cloak proudly decorating his shoulders.

But what of the truth? Ashraf had vanished. He was no nearer to winning the affections of the woman he loved, and now she had acquired a noisome sister, a creature whom he had disliked on sight. If only Ashraf had returned with the information that he had been despatched to find!

'What will you wear on your wedding day? Is your robe prepared? Shall you have jewels? I would consider green-toned gems of some kind to set off the colour of your eyes. Would you not agree?'

Salida's persistent questions were wearing Mishaal down. Again and again she had told the woman that she had no plans to marry the Amir, but Salida only laughed and shrugged and said that this was carrying maidenly modesty too far.

'This handsome man is wishing to marry you . . . This great Amir who reigns over the Land of Mirages and who yearns to make you his Amira, and you refuse to agree? How can that be? How could any woman in her right mind say no to him? He is so glorious, so beautiful and desirable! Why, if he were to ask me, then I should agree at once to become his wife!'

'And you have my full permission!' Mishaal retorted impatiently. 'Not that it is needed. You may do whatever you please and so may he. I shall not marry him.'

Salida struggled to control her temper, but the back of her neck flushed a deep, threatening puce.

'If you ask me, then I would say that your mind has been dried by the desert sun and your wits have fled. How could you say no to this Sultan? They say he has great wealth!' She leaned forward, eyes narrowed, shoulders hunched across her extensive bosom.

'Do they? I have not heard it. All I hear is of poverty and wells drying out, and the struggles to find water for the herds.'

'And that is why you turn him down, eh? Well, if it were true then I would say that you were wise, but it is not, is it? His wealth is fabled. There is a legend about it, surely you heard it?'

'A legend?' Mishaal assumed nonchalant disinterest. This woman had not stopped speaking about money and wealth since her arrival five days ago, and she was heartily weary of

'Yes, you must have heard it, although perhaps you led a very sheltered life at Rhikia's? If it is true that you only danced and did not mingle with the customers then you would be starved of gossip.'

'It is true,' Mishaal gritted her jaw.

'Of course, of course,' Salida soothed. 'But I cannot believe that you did not hear it, all the same. Surely they have spoken of it here? No? That truly surprises me. Such a famed legend, so ancient and renowned. They say that the Amir only feigns poverty to conceal the truth, that he is fabulously rich since finding the legendary Jewels of Destiny. Naturally, he would not wish to be besieged by raiders who want his treasure, so he pretends this destitution. Very clever, very clever indeed, but there is no need for you to hide the truth from me, your own loving sister,' Salida smirked.

Mishaal felt herself grow cold. A tiny nerve flickered in her cheek. This woman could not be her sister; she was sure of it.

'I am afraid that you are wrong. The Amir is as he appears to be; he has no secret treasure and no secret wealth. As for the Jewels of Destiny . . . they are nothing but a fable, an old story which has never proven to contain any truth.'

'Aha! So you do know about them!' Salida's face darkened.

'Yes. Have you not just said that everyone knows the tale about them, so why should I not have heard it?'

Salida jutted her jaw, sucking in her upper lip.

'When he makes you his bride then you will be told the truth about his secret wealth, I swear it in the name of Allah!'

'Then I shall never know, shall I?' Mishaal replied coolly.

The moment had been exactly timed. Salida had arrived at the lodging house just as the landlord was about to carry the platter of fruit to his guest.

Smiling lecherously, she had taken the platter from the man's hands.

'This is for Ashraf? Ah, blessings be upon you. Now I have the way to let him know how I love him! He was not well when I saw him last; he had a fearful pain in his belly and feared for his health. Now I can take him these and make him a happy man.'

The landlord had gaped, but soon entered into the spirit of the occasion, as Salida heaved herself up the narrow, crumbling stairway, halting halfway to catch her breath, and to make the tiny hole in one of the oranges into which she dropped a venomous poison from a tiny phial.

If Ashraf believed in her and would tell the Amir that she was indeed the sister of his future bride, then the orange would be abandoned, and no harm done. If, however, he admitted that he was not convinced and would not support her claim, then she would beg for one last love-making session after which she would feed him the fruit with the sweetest smile that she could contrive.

She tapped on his door and called Ashraf's name in honeyed tones. When the door opened, she stepped inside, smiling broadly, hearing Ashraf speak her name in astonishment.

Ashraf was truly startled to see Salida at his door. Why was she here? The platter of fruit that she carried looked deliciously appealing; that large orange in particular, round and juicy, how he wished that he could sink his teeth into it right now. But it did not take much to offend this strange and quixotic woman, he reminded himself. Difficult as it was, she was the sister of his master's future bride, and he must placate her.

Salida sank down on to Ashraf's narrow bed and beamed up at him.

'It is so good to see you again, Ashraf. Can you guess why I am here?'

'No, indeed I cannot, but now you are, would you wish to have some light refreshment?'

'No, no, I want nothing like that, I am here to see you, Ashraf. The truth is that I have found myself desperate for your company. Oh, you look shocked, but that is why I am here. I knew that you were returning to the desert shortly and I would not see you again for some time, and I could not bear it!'

She encircled his hand with her thick fingers, and before he knew what was happening, he was sitting beside her, her head on his shoulder.

'*Sitt,* this cannot be. I must go back to my master and tell him what I have discovered and then you will come to the wedding and we shall meet again at that time.'

'Oh, but I cannot wait! Allah has kindled a great fire in my bosom for you, Ashraf!' Salida tugged at him to bring his face down to hers. 'I shall die if you wander off into the desert without me, I shall die!'

'But there will not be long to wait until the marriage ceremony. Then you will live with my master's family and we shall see one another regularly.'

'Ashraf, have you forgotten what we did in my house?' Salida kissed him on the cheek and then the neck, before she slid her hand across his knee and found his stirring manhood. Artfully, she fondled it until it was erect and then she lowered her head and began to lap at the stiffening flesh.

'You do trust me, do you not, Ashraf? You know that I long to see my sister?'

'Yes, I trust you,' he said thickly, his heart palpitating frantically.

'You know that I am the future Amira's sister?'

'Oh yes, indeed I do!'

'Then swear it in the name of the one true God, swear it!'

'I swear it in the name of the one true God!' Ashraf groaned, and then she was climbing astride his thighs and jerking up and down on him until he thought that his mind and his body would erupt.

'*Saiyid,* I wish to speak to you.' Mishaal stood before the Amir, her face veiled.

'What do you wish to speak to me about?' he said, his voice deep and velvety.

'I – that woman, the one who calls herself my sister, I do not believe that she is, *Saiyid.*'

Then at last we agree on something! Husain thought, before saying, 'What makes you doubt her?'

'She behaves oddly. She – she talks of money all the time she is obsessed with it. This morning she said that you had found the Jewels of Destiny and that everyone knew it, and that your poverty was nothing but a sham, to protect you from those who would rob you of your treasure. Forgive me for my directness, but I thought that you should know.'

Husain narrowed his eyes, his face reflective. So he was a secret Caliph, languishing in fabulous treasures while his people went hungry and were sick with thirst? How good this vicious lie would sound to them! Where had that obnoxious woman heard this lie?

'Did you ever hear this tale?'

'No, *Saiyid*, never. Salida is a great gossip. She could have heard it anywhere, probably in the city.' Mishaal was watching his face, trying to divine his thoughts. She might as easily have tried to read the thoughts of a mountain lion. That dark, panther-like gaze would tell her nothing. He was inscrutable and yet there had been a time, before the woman came with her story of kinship, when he had showed Mishaal what was going on in his mind – and his heart. Suddenly, hungrily, she yearned for that time again.

'Have you told the woman that there is no foundation for this lie she has heard?'

'I have, *Saiyid*, but she laughs. She thinks that I am hiding the truth, that I am in league with you.'

How thankful she was that she had worn her veil so that he could see nothing but the peridot arrows of her black-fringed eyes.

'Allah, the woman is possessed of *jinns*! How dare she come here as my guest and spread these lies about me!'

'*Saiyid*, I – I do not like her. Everything about her is horrible, her manner, her greed, her outlook. Can we not investigate her claim? Must we accept her as my sister?'

Suddenly he was on his feet, standing before her, very close, tenderness making his gaze limpid; his hands embracing hers.

'Little *fáhd*, did you think that I would force you to accept this woman when you do not wish it? Allah, do you take me for a despot? I am making more enquiries . . . my men are in the city even now, and I have ordered that they return on the instant. Some weeks ago I sent out one of my followers to investigate but he has not returned and I fear for his life. If my men bring me news that this woman is an impostor then we shall evict her immediately.'

'Ah, if we could do it now! She is a fortune hunter. I know it, I am sure of it!'

'All the same, for your mother's sake would you not wish to be right about your actions? If she truly is your sister, then there must be some semblance of kinship towards her, some offering to placate her, some gift or annuity.'

'That is all she came for, I am sure of it. She came because she believed that you were rich and that she would gain great wealth as my sister. She has no love for me, not even the slightest affection. There is nothing but an acquisitiveness of the most rapacious sort.'

Conscious of the Amir's hands enclosing hers still, Mishaal blushed behind her veil, her breath blowing hotly against the thin cloth so that it clung to her lips.

'Mishaal, have you thought any more about becoming my bride?'

His question fell into the electric silence between them so that the words seemed to possess a life of their own, dancing and vibrant, startling enough to make her skin prickle and her heart pound.

Swallowing painfully, she opened her mouth to reply but could not resurrect her voice. It had died, along with her tranquillity.

'Please, answer me, my heart, answer me!'

'I – I cannot,' she managed to croak. 'Do not ask it of me!'

Tearing her hands from his, she turned and fled, out of the calm gloom of his tent and into the stabbing sunlight beyond.

Reassured that Ashraf would support her story in every detail Salida allowed herself a few moments of relaxation. Beside the bed, on the rickety stool, sat the platter piled high with fruit. Parched as she was she wished that she could bite into a fresh and succulent date, or one of those juicy oranges. Gazing longingly at the platter, she realised sleepily that she could not remember which side held the poisoned orange.

A little while later, Ashraf woke, his throat rough and

contracted with thirst. Reaching out with difficulty, for Salida's bulk half-trapped his arm, his fingers closed round an orange and, raising it to his lips, he bit deep.

Chapter Sixteen

It was Mishaal's first sight of the jewels which would be worn by the Amir's bride when she married him.

Evading Salida, Mishaal had joined some of the women in cleaning and refurbishing the Amir's tent while he was absent. Word had been brought to him of three more wells running dry and the people were so distraught and bemused that only his presence would placate them. There had been riots and a woman had been injured by a flying stone. Her eye had been put out. Mishaal shuddered when she heard. What would become of them without the water which was vital to life?

It was then that she had realised something so startling that she was moved into silence. What would become of them? she had thought, identifying herself with these unhappy nomads. How many weeks had she been with them? Nine, ten, eleven? She could not be sure. Time was different in the desert. They woke to the muezzin's call to prayer and slept when darkness prevented further activity. The very essence of time was unique here: she could have been living in another age.

She and the women had watched the Amir ride out with his followers. How noble he looked on horseback, Caliph and Sultan of them all, his proud Arab stallion prancing and snorting. Prophet was beautiful, sleek, graceful, proud, and of the purest blood, his flanks gleaming ruby-brown in the sunlight, yet it was obvious from the expressions in the eyes of the women that they barely noticed the stallion. It was their master on whom their gaze was fixed.

The Amir wore formal attire as befitted a visit to another part of his amirate, and hanging from his saddle was a leather pouch containing the dates with which he would feed Prophet during the journey. As his companions rode on camels there would be camels' milk for them all, Prophet, too, for it was unlikely that they would see any grass or water pool.

Caressing the Amir's family jewels in her fingers, Mishaal recalled the story of the young colt who had been so viciously gelded to tame him. Prophet would let no one approach him save his master and for that he had been brutally cut, his siring abilities destroyed, when he had been stolen in a raid. Ashraf and the Amir had bravely ridden out to recover him, after a fierce fight with the enemy raiders.

'Make sure that the man does not emulate the horse,' the Amir had quoted at her, his fathomless, desert-dark eyes searing into hers. How she had blushed, knowing what he meant, knowing what track he was pursuing. She had stepped back, alarmed that he would try to embrace her, and she had cried, 'No!' and fled.

The heat came back into her face as she remembered. If she stayed here, she would never be free of his attentions. He wanted her; he had made that plain. But why? What other Arabian that she knew would have paid court to one whose origins were mysterious and doubtful, whose upbringing had been in a house of ill repute, and who was one of the infamous dancing girls who were usually prostitutes. Was it guilt because he had killed the only man she would ever love?

Dreaming over the jewels, mesmerised by their gleaming, pearly brightness, she pictured Drew as she had last seen him, when they had made love in his tent. Wind-blown, gilded hair dark in the dim interior, his features sweetly carved so that she could never forget them; those eyes of his which haunted her with their tenderness and ardour, the passionate mouth that she had yearned to feel on hers.

A tear splashed on to the pale gems in her hands, but she did not heed it. White opals from some distant and glorious land where emperors reigned like gods, their heavy gold setting bringing to mind the Byzantine Empire, or so the Amir had told her. Once a great Empress had owned these opals and now they were all that remained of his family's fortunes.

Another tear fell. If she could have been Drew's bride, she would not have cared had she worn tatters! Suddenly, standing there, holding ancient history in her hands, she was stricken with a grief that she had believed was fading.

Tonight, while the Amir was away, she would escape. What other chance would she have? She had hidden a sharp dagger in her tent with which to cut the cords hobbling one of the camels. If she could encourage the beast to accept her on its back and let her mount in silence, then there would be hope.

'*Sitt!*' It was one of the nomad women looking closely into her face. 'Are you fevered? How long you have been standing there!'

The opals almost fell from her hands. Bemused, she tried to resurrect a logical train of thought. Escape. The word rang in her ears. Tonight she must do it. There was nothing to keep her here except her own physical and mental weakness, her inability to summon sufficient courage to flee into the night.

Salida's mouth was watering as she watched the opals flowing like miniature moons in Mishaal's hands. This witless imbecile had everything that she wanted yet was willing to take none of it. She, Salida, would do anything for those gems, kill, torture, spy, seduce, and that was when her mood was amiable. At the moment, it was ferocious. Overhearing the Amir talking with Mishaal, she had clenched her fists as the ignoramus repeated that she would never, ever, marry him, that she would sooner die.

Murder had volted through Salida's mind, spearing her to her fingertips so that she yearned to execute it now and grip that stupid creature's neck, crushing it until the bones snapped and burst out through the flesh. The compulsion was so powerful that she could barely control herself. Fiery stars dazzled her vision and a haze of vermilion blocked her sight, loud thundering filling her ears as blood pulsed through her savagely.

What was she going to do about this milksop bitch who stood between her and the position and power she desired? She could not tolerate the waiting much longer; it tantalised her, tearing her nerves into fragments. She had begged Mishaal to accept the Amir's proposal but the girl had said no, she would never marry him, adding that it would be better if Salida returned to her home because she was wasting her time here.

'Why wasting my time? Would you marry without blood kin to prepare you and celebrate with you?'

'I am *not* marrying the Amir!' Mishaal raised her voice, her jaw jutting. 'I shall never marry him! It would be better if you returned to your home.'

'So you want to send me away, your own mother's daughter, the sister of your own flesh, your own blood and bone!' Salida's voice quavered.

'It is obvious to everyone that you detest desert life and the black tents are not for you. You are a creature of comforts and luxuries, not hardship.'

'For my only dear sister I would endure all this!' Salida clutched her hands to her heart.

'I could not ask it of you. There is nothing here for you. I am sorry, but that is the truth. I shall not marry the Amir, and that is that.'

'Why shall you not?' Salida fought for control of her temper, employing a rare patience, but her face was puce, her eyes bulging.

'That is my business,' Mishaal said firmly, facing the inquisitive woman and wishing that she had never set eyes on her.

'As your sister, your *elder* sister, it is my business!' Salida screeched, stepping threateningly close, her mouth a snarl.

Reaching out, Mishaal pushed at the vast bosom so that Salida was forced to step back, startled.

'I am afraid that you are misinformed,' Mishaal replied with the coolest dignity and calm that she could muster. 'If I were you I would pack my belongings and ask one of the men to loan you a camel so that you may return to the city.'

'How can you do this to your sister?' Salida whined, sinking to her knees and scrabbling at the hem of Mishaal's robe, but the latter had no intention of relenting. She was free of the parasite at long last, although it had taken her days to summon the courage to tell her to go. Relief was pouring into her already; she would not slap it away by changing her mind.

When it was dark, Salida heaved her bulk out of Mishaal's tent and tiptoed towards that of the Amir. She would have her revenge on the cold-hearted bitch who thought that she was queen without needing to marry a king. Salida, despite her muscular bulk, had always been able to creep around silently. It was essential in a whore who wished to steal from her clients while they slept. How dark and shadowy was the camp at night, and how eerie, for it was the last phase of the moon and there was no light. Her eyes took time to accustom themselves to the pitch, but she sliced her ankle on a tent hook, clamping her lips on a noisy squawk.

There was the Amir's tent just ahead. Her heart clattered in her breast, jerking to left and right so that she thought she would choke. A man sat before the entrance, nodding in sleep. Smirking, she crept round to the rear of the tent and got down on to her hands and knees, grimacing at the stony ground biting into her legs. These nomads were the biggest fools she had ever met, and she was going to have her sweet, sweet revenge.

Creeping under the black skin, she entered the dark, coffee-scented interior, carefully making her way towards the casket where Mishaal had placed the opals after polishing them that afternoon. Narrowly missing a footstool, she edged round cushions and boxes and the great, ornate camel saddle which the Amir leaned against on formal occasions, as was the custom.

There was the casket. Suddenly her heart was thrusting so sharply into her throat that she thought that she might faint. Sinking down, she gasped for breath, tearing open her gown to free her neck from pressure.

Recovered, her fingers clutched the casket and edged round the lid, searching for the catch. When she found it and tweaked it to see if it was locked, she felt as if she were on the verge of discovering a treasure that would alter her life.

Pushing back the lid, her fingertips touched the opals and emotion invaded her flesh, fierce, hot and strong. Allah, but if she could escape with this treasure! But she loved her own neck too much. There would be no possibility of her escaping from these Beduin. They knew the desert in its darkest and most perplexing moods; they would find her before dawn and she would have her hand hacked off for thieving. Far better to do what she planned and see another lose their hand . . .

Smirking, she scooped up the long opal necklace, its three tiers heavier than she would have thought, and the dozen matching bangles, the rings, one for every finger, the enormous earrings, fan-shaped, that reached to the shoulder, the brooches, anklets, and toe rings, the nose ring, and the ceremonial collar set with forty perfect white opals clasped in richest gold. Into the waiting pouch at her waist they went, banging against her belly and thigh as she made her way out of the tent.

Circling the snoring guard, she thought, So much for the hawk-eye of the Beduin! Creeping back into Mishaal's tent, she halted, barely breathing, staring into the gloom to see if the girl slept. Yes, there was the curve of her shoulder beneath the goatskin, and one outflung arm, pale in the shadows.

Salida almost let out a screech of triumphant delight. Soon, soon the bitch who had played her along and tormented her by refusing to marry the Amir would know what it was to insult Salida the Great Whore, the greatest daughter of sin who had ever lived!

Stepping to the leathern bag Salida had seen Mishaal packing before they slept, she felt inside it, making a hollow with her broad hand into which she slid the pouch full of opals, tucking it in well and packing cloth around it so that the gems would not make any sound when the bag was picked up. She could hardly control the uproarious, snorting laughter that she ached to release. It swelled in her chest and throat, moving up like a fist, growing larger and more choking so that her vision blurred.

Stumbling to her bed, she lay down, the breath somehow torn from her lungs so that she gasped for it in vain. She thought of Kausar suddenly, Kausar who had come to her for help when she was with child and homeless. How she had regretted taking in that feeble girl! For a time she had loved her and shared her bed, but she had finally revealed her terrible temper and they had fought, oh how they had fought. She had strangled Kausar. What was strangling a lover after strangling so many of one's own infants? If you could destroy your own flesh and blood then you could destroy anyone.

The pictures went on in Salida's mind, the faces of the tiny dying children, scarlet, their mouths distended, eyes rigid and jutting, the cracking snap of their minute bones, and then suddenly it was her face, scarlet and bloated, her eyes popping, her mouth sagging, and the pain was in her breast, jagged, twisting, as death claimed her.

Mishaal woke with a jolt. She had meant to slip away soon after midnight, when everyone would be in their deepest sleep. Now she guessed that it was dangerously near dawn so she had not a moment to spare.

She glanced at Salida's spreading bulk upon her bed. She was sleeping as she always did, mouth gaping. Soon, Mishaal would be free of this intolerable situation, the haranguing virago who had made the past few days hellish, the Beduin with their hospitable but stifling attitude towards her. Slipping on a flowing, light wool robe, she picked up her leathern bag, the one that held all her possessions in the world, for what they were worth: her spare sandals, a gown, bangles given to her by the nomad women, packets of food, rice, herbs, goat's cheese, dates and figs, a pouch of fermented milk, its neck tightly fastened so that it would not leak on to her clothes, and, of course, the peacock costume.

She glanced back once, shrugging off the suffocation that she felt in that tent, and the frustration that this so-called nomadic life had brought her. Here, she would never be her own mistress, but only his.

Running lightly, she made for the she-camel who had brought her there, with whom she had remained friendly, giving her tidbits and talking to her when she passed. Only this camel did she dare mount without help, for others could be mean, disgruntled and snappish. In her mind, she had practised over and over this moment of mounting the beast, but she bit her lip when she approached it. What if it snorted loudly, rousing the entire camp? Allah, but she would be a prisoner again!

The beast was couched, as if waiting for her, its eyes strangely limpid as she stroked its rough nose, avoiding the great rubbery mouth. There were the saddles, piled in a heap nearby. They were heavier to lift than she had expected, for Drew had always dealt with this part, and pain sang along her shoulders as she heaved one up on to the animal's back. She could not hold it in place and fasten it at the same time; she did not have the strength. Gritting her teeth she struggled to join the straps and hold them tight with one hand while sliding the leather through the buckle. Muscles groaning, she pulled the buckle tight only to feel her strength give way. To her horror, the saddle slipped loose and thudded to the sand. Tears in her eyes she began to manoeuvre the bulky object into place and then recalled that she had seen cloths beneath the saddles to prevent the beasts from becoming sore. She could not hurt any animal, even an ungainly camel, so raising her eyes heavenwards she ran for one of the soft gazelle-skin saddle cloths to fix beneath it.

'*Dhalul*, be still,' Mishaal whispered as the beast stamped impatiently.

She took out her little dagger and cut the beast's hobbling cords, rubbing at the animal's ankles to make the blood flow. Then she slipped the head halter over the protuberant nose. That was easy enough, praise be! She might as well have one more attempt with the saddle. She heaved it into place and the straps secured with comparative ease.

'*Dhalul*, sweet *dhalul*, please let me mount you!' she begged, and, to her relief the she-camel obeyed.

The beast began to raise itself, lurching forward and backward so energetically that she had to cling on desperately, clamping her knees round the rough, coarse-haired hump and praying for a safe leave taking. Now that she was seated, the camel seemed exhilarated and she did not have to say one word to make it lumber into movement. Off they went, the camel's rolling gait dizzying as she tried to steer it in the right direction. Only with difficulty did she turn the beast towards the correct route.

While the ground was even, the rolling and belching contraption was not too alarming but when they hit a dip, Mishaal felt the beast's body apparently divide into two, her body seeming to hang between the front and back parts. She tried to keep her mind on her major aim, escape, to get as far from the camp as she could before daybreak when the muezzin's call woke the nomads.

When they found her gone, they would babble to the Amir and he would rage and stamp his feet, but there would be nothing that he could do. She was a free woman, after all.

Chapter Seventeen

Shamim found the body of Salida the next morning.

Touching the body of the woman whom they had all disliked, but whom they would have continued to treat as an honoured guest, in the Beduin fashion, Shamim felt the coldness first, and then the strangely stiff feel of the flesh. Dead animals felt like this, however glossy and luxuriant their fur; beneath it, the flesh would be taut and lifeless, the gentle contours rigid, the muscles flaccid.

'Allah!' she cried out, leaping back from the corpse. 'Allah! *Allah!*' and then she was running out of the tent and shouting for help. Not until she halted, heat flaming her cheeks, did she recall that Mishaal had not been in her bed.

They all searched, women, children, men, but no one could find her; nor could they find the she-camel that should have been tethered by Saud's tent.

Without the Amir to instruct them they were not easily organised; they wasted time in blaming one another and haranguing Saud when he crept out of his lover's tent shame-faced.

Bodies must be buried quickly in the heat of the desert and so it was with Salida's. The men dug while the women robed the enormous hulk in its white shroud. The nomads bore it to the grave and placed it deep, facing Mecca as was the custom. Women were buried more deeply than men because it would be indecent if, on Judgement Day when they rose, their breasts thrust out immodestly. Having piled back the earth and settled rocks above it to keep out the hyenas and carrion eaters, the Beduin returned to their camp. There was no female relative to weep for the dead woman and no one else was authorised to do so. Secretly none would have wished to mourn her death.

They considered what their master would say when he returned and found that his beloved had vanished. Nur was making poor work of concealing her tears. Those who had known her for many years were disbelieving at the sight of her wet eyes. Nur the stoic, she who guarded goats and sheep in the loneliest places of the desert, now sobbing and wailing as if her only son had died?

They were like children without their Amir, yet they grieved for Mishaal as if she were already their Amira.

'Strange that it should be so,' Nur thought between her gasping sobs. 'One young girl . . . so recently a stranger to us but she won our hearts, and now she is gone! Allah protect her wherever she has gone!' In the Amir's eyes when he looked at the young city girl Nur had seen such fervour, such aching longing, love and desire that she had trembled. Before she, Nur, died, she wanted to see the young lord married to one whom he loved; and even more she wanted to see his sons toddling amongst the black tents. Sons meant eternity and heritage; they meant all the centuries from the past merging with those of the future so that time would never stop and the name of Husain and his family would endure for ever.

'What will he say when he finds that she is gone?' asked Belza, Nur's granddaughter.

'He will be angry, raging, his eyes will be like stone, his voice harsh as the noonday sun.'

'Allah protect us!' Belza gasped.

'We should not seek forgiveness for our own stupidity, child of my daughter, or else we shall never learn by our mistakes. We had relaxed our guard over the *sitt*, and had so taken her to our hearts that we believed she had taken us to hers. Now we know otherwise. It is the will of Allah!'

'What is, grandmother? That we know otherwise or that she should escape?'

'Do not call her, the *sitt*, she! The *sitt* is not a camel, she is our future Amira!'

'Was our future Amira,' Belza said in mournful tones, her shoulders sagging.

'What makes you think that our lord will not bring her back? Do not underestimate him. If he wishes still to make her his bride then he will go after her and bring her back.'

'If I were a man I would not pursue a woman who ran away from me,' Belza humphed.

Nur looked at her granddaughter with steely eyes. 'You have much to learn, childling, much to learn.'

The scream was heard just as dusk unrolled its soothing carpet of mauve and blue and indigo. A woman came hurtling out of the Amir's tent, an empty casket in her hands, her face streaked with red and white from shock, beads of sweat standing out like crystals on her forehead.

'Allah have mercy on us, she took the gems, she took the gems!' the woman wailed, holding out the casket for everyone to see that it no longer contained the bridal opals.

The last treasure of their peoples, the ancient opals that were their barrier against destitution. Always, whatever poverty befell them they had known that they could sell these gems. Their prince had told them that it would be thus should that time come. Now they had nothing; the girl whom they had taken to their hearts had been a thief, a cunning hypocrite, that sweet face and those innocent dreamy eyes the mask for one who was ruthless and greedy.

'A girl who could refuse to marry our prince could do anything!' Belza said to her young friends, who nodded their heads in agreement.

'I would have been *ya saiyid*'s bride if he had asked me!' exclaimed Yasmin, Belza's cousin.

'Why should he ask you, Yasmin? He does not want to wait four years before he has his first son! He does not marry children!' Belza snapped.

'Then why has he not hastened his marriage to Mishaal the dancer? If he is so eager for sons why did he not take her?' Yasmin snapped back.

'Perhaps he knew; perhaps all along he knew that she was untrustworthy; that she would turn out to be a thief and betray him.'

'Yes, look at that creature who claimed to be her sister . . . If they were blood kin, then what does it say about Mishaal? Her blood must be tainted too. She did not even know who her father was, so Shamim told me.'

'It is true that the *saiyid* is the wisest and most perceptive man among us, but if he believed that the dancer would turn out to be a thief, would he have pursued her so ardently? Why, we all knew that he loved her and wished to make her his bride! Shamim said that he had asked her twice, perhaps three times, but each time the dancer said no. Was it because she was here only to steal the opals?' Belza pinched upper and lower lips together with her thumb and forefinger.

'But the *saiyid* brought her here himself! She did not ask to come!'

'Then perhaps she stole them out of revenge because he would not free her . . .' Yasmin offered.

'Maybe, and yet she did not look the sort who would stoop to such revenge.'

'Nor did she look the sort to thieve and yet she has done!' put in Aliyah.

At that they were silent. Aliyah's words were irrefutable; all of them felt soiled somehow, as if evil had touched them, penetrating their camp and fingering them, leaving oily stains upon their clothes, their skin. With all the good-heartedness and open charity of the Beduin they had taken the girl into their midst and come to look on her as a sister; they had fed and clothed her and taught her their ways and prayed to Allah that she would soon marry their prince, so that his eyes would sparkle and his step be lighter, and instead she had betrayed them all, each one of them.

How would the *saiyid* react when he knew that the woman he loved had stolen his gems and fled? The law of the desert was harsh: it was imperative that it be so or men would run wild and banditry would flourish. The *saiyid* was the source of justice, employing the laws which Mohammed himself had ordained in the seventh century. For theft, a foot or a hand would be hacked off in public and suspended where everyone could see it, as preventive medicine. Murder demanded execution, or the payment of what was called blood money, the dead man or woman's relatives having the right to choose which they wanted. Should they decide that the murderer must die, then they also had the right to execute him, employing the same method to end his life as he had employed to kill his victim. In practice, it was considered that the relative of the victim would be more likely to shoot the murderer or to spare his life at the final moment.

The justice dispensed by their Amir was firm and wise, without any fanciful modern embellishments. In many centuries, the Beduin had not changed, so why should their laws?

'What will he do when he captures her?' Nur said to herself as she prepared to grind the coffee beans in readiness for the arrival of the Amir. Tonight, the heavy, exotic scent did not alleviate her tension as the beans roasted in the long-handled skillet. As she tipped the roasted beans to cool in the decorated wooden bowl, she heard the sound of shouts outside the tent. The *saiyid* was coming! Leaping up, she placed her hands together, palms pressed one upon the other, as if in prayer, and watched as the Amir's horse came into sight.

Allah be praised, their prince was returned safely to them! Her heart settled now that he was back; the old feeling of contentment flourishing deep within her.

Why did it have to be like this for him? He loved her, that green-eyed girl from the city, and he deserved to be loved back, and to have many healthy sons. She had loved the *saiyid* from the moment that he had toddled around the camp at his father's heels. There had been rumours then; the old seer who had died the previous year claimed to have been given a message by a hawk that had appeared to him in a dream.

'The *saiyid*'s line is ending. He will be the last. There shall be no tomorrow for this line.'

Nur had turned cold when she heard that. How could such a tragedy take place? Surely Allah did not wish the great and ancient line to die out? Why should He? Husain's ancestors had served the one true God with their hearts and souls for centuries.

She had pressed the old seer with questions but he would not move from his original story. Nur decided that the old man's mind had been addled by the sun, yet in secret she had wept for the sadness that might come to pass, if indeed Allah willed it.

Tears drowned Nur's vision. She felt as if happiness and peace were being swept from her life to be replaced by unease and the knowledge that more tragedy might be imminent.

The wells were bone dry. The royal opals had been stolen. A woman had died. Another woman had fled from love and betrayed them all . . .

Nur bent over the steaming coffee pot, the ache in her spine travelling through her limbs and making them tremble. She had never felt older than on that day; old and grief-stricken. In her mind's eyes she saw Mishaal, that sweet, tranquil face, the wide peridot eyes like the green that glimmered deep within the stolen opals, and the gentle, shapely hands as they learned how to grind the coffee beans and make the drink that the Amir loved so much. The girl had never complained about such menial tasks, yet it was plain from her soft pale hands that she had never had to scrub or clean in her life. She had raged at being captive, but she had never expected others to pamper her or take the weight of her tasks from her shoulders. Loving the Amir as she did, how could Nur blame him for wanting to keep the girl here, safe in his keeping?

'Nur.' The Amir stood before her, his face haggard with the news he had just been given.

'Saiyid!' she cried, her voice trembling, flinging herself

down before him to kiss the hem of his cloak. '*Saiyid*, it was the will of Allah!'

'Yes, of that I have no doubt.' His deep rich voice was dry and hoarse, as if his throat contained no blood to enrich it. 'Always it is the will of Allah.'

'Forgive her, *Saiyid*, forgive her!' To her astonishment, Nur found herself begging for Mishaal's life.

'Do not speak of it tonight, woman. I must come to terms with my fate. The wells have run dry, but how could I live without love, whether or no I had water?'

'You – you will go after her?'

'When I have eaten.'

Hands shaking, Nur placed the coffee cup into her master's fingers and watched him as he drank deeply.

Oh, how she yearned to be young and comely as the girl who had broken her lord's heart! How she could comfort him, cradling his head in her arms and raining kisses on his face; she would tell him that she loved him more deeply than any mother or sister could, and that she, Nur, would be his bride and bear his sons and shield him from loneliness and the terrible poverty of being without heirs!

The Amir rose to his feet, his eyes tortured.

'If the old seer were here now, what would he say, woman?'

'That we cannot change our destinies, *Saiyid*; that our destinies are decided at the moment of our birth, when we take our first breath and become separate from our mothers. Allah has preordained our every movement, our every word. That is what the seer used to say to us.'

'And did you heed him?' The ebony eyes were watchful, eager for her answer and yet dreading it.

Nur sucked in her breath. Now she could say: What choice do we have? or, He was a wise and inspired man, so we knew that what he said was truth, yet she paused. Her lord did not want to hear platitudes nor a repetition of the old seer's oft-repeated phrases. At this moment, he needed counselling of the most shrewd and perceptive kind, and the weight of knowing this fell upon her shoulders like the crushing hands of a *jinn*. What did she know, old and ague-ridden as she was a wild one. The *saiyid*, with his strength and perception, could guide their prince in his darkest hour? There was nothing she could say, no lofty wisdom, no intellectual solace, and yet . . . She could speak from the heart; she had endured a lifetime of emotions. Yes, if grief and anguish bred wisdom, then she would be the wisest woman in the land, but would that be enough to counsel her lord on this terrible night?

Gripping her hands together, she licked her lips, opened her mouth, began to speak, felt her heart jolt and pound at speed and then, to her astonishment, discovered that she knew exactly what she must say.

'*Saiyid*, there will be many who will tell you that the girl was evil, that *jinns* sent her to you so that she could steal the gems and bring ruin down about our heads, but do not listen to them, I beg of you! You loved her as you have never loved before; I saw such feeling in your eyes that I longed to be a girl again. I never knew such affection as you offered Mishaal: she was blessed, not evil; blessed by your love, by the enduring strength of it and the resistance of it against her own doubts and her rejection of you. If she has taken the opals then it was the will of Allah, and that you cannot deny, *Saiyid*, and yet . . . Deep in my heart I cannot suspect her; she was gentle and caring; different from us, it is true, but like us because she felt and breathed and was stirred by the same griefs and joys as are we . . .' Nur licked her lips again. How dry they were; she felt that they would never be moist again. She continued.

'If it was Allah's will that you love one who would betray you, then think of the lesson that Allah wishes you to learn from it, and do not deny that agony that you must surely be feeling, for, if you do, then you will deny the lesson, too. Accept and be thankful that you were allowed the joy of loving such a one, even if you lost her in the end.'

Nur's heart was twisting, and sweat dewed her face and neck. For a long time her lord was silent, his lids lowered as if rejecting her words, and she thought that she had failed, and cursed herself most strongly, then he looked up at her and there was that tender sparkle back in his eyes and her heart leapt.

'Do I go after her in hate or love?' he asked and she knew that all their destinies revolved upon her answer.

'After a thief who has taken your treasures, you go in hate, but after the girl who won your heart you go in love.'

'And if they are one and the same?'

'If you still love her, then you will believe her innocent even if you have seen her stealing your treasure with your own eyes. It is your place to believe that the one whom you love is innocent and above evil, for if you do not believe that of her, then you do not love her; any man can revile and condemn but the true lover will see only the good.'

The Amir laughed, a short, cruel burst of sound.

'My people will want justice. They will ask for her to be punished, they will say that she took the last bread from our mouths at a time when we had no water to ease our thirst. She would let us starve . . .'

'That is what the people may say, but not the man who loves her.'

'As dispenser of justice, how can I favour such a one? If I let her go free, then there will be a great rejoicing amongst all the thieves and brigands in the Land of Mirages and no one will be safe . . . No, I must find her and punish her, according to the law.'

Nur clenched her fists. She had not thought of the consequences of letting Mishaal go free. It was true that their land was a wild one. The *saiyid*, with his strength and perception, and in the way that he inspired unequalled love and devotion, had tamed the land, but not at the expense of justice. Miscreants must be punished, according to the ancient Koranic laws, for man – and woman – must endure the consequences of their actions.

Chapter Eighteen

Riding a camel at speed was not something that Mishaal would ever voluntarily do again. The lurchings and swayings, the belchings and grunts that punctuated the dizzying movement, were enough to turn her stomach.

Why had she done it? From the first moment that the pleached dawn light canopied the desert and she realised that she had entered infinity, she felt bitter regret for her departure. Hours had passed and she had not seen a *wadi* where she could rest from the skewering sun. Her bernouse was limp and heavy with sweat and her back and buttocks felt as if they had been rudely beaten. Soon her flask of water was empty, and she had no idea where she could find more. She was hungry but her throat was too parched to swallow food. The *dhalul* was happy enough, chomping on wild vegetation and tiny, dull-coloured herbs. Mishaal tried imitating her, only to find that the herbs were bitter as aloes. Spitting them out, she coughed until her throat was raw, then kneeled on the gritty desert floor and tried to recover herself. Her eyes were streaming, her tongue burning; she was sure that she had all but poisoned herself and yet the *dhalul* chomped placidly on, unperturbed.

Noon passed, and she spent it huddled in a dip in the sand, her bernouse tugged tightly round her to exclude the scoring heat. Sweat poured from her skin and her mouth became more and more taut, so that even when she slipped her tongue round her lips, it did not wet them. She thought longingly of cool well water, newly drawn from the chilled stone depths of the earth, and of milk from the goat, warm, musky and sweet, trickling down into her belly, a delicious invitation to contentment.

She got to her feet late in the afternoon, pulled the *dhalul* towards her by its rein and began again the riotous ceremony of mounting it. Once elevated, some seven or eight feet above the ground, she clung to the pommel of the wooden saddle with her left hand and a clump of coarse hump hair with the other as the beast swayed into its lolloping trot.

She had believed that she would be able to pilot herself. She knew something of the stars. Had she not observed them often enough from the window of her room at Rhikia's? Travellers could navigate themselves by the stars, and she had expected the same of herself, but it was not quite so simple. Searching for the north star, she found its twin, and then could not decide which was which. Following the wrong one would take her miles away from the city to which she was heading.

By the luminous eerie light of the waxing moon she travelled until exhaustion claimed her. Nodding sleepily, she forgot her thirst and the ache in her back, but she also forgot where she was, and nearly fell off the back of the *dhalul*. Crying out, she caught at the pommel and the tufts of coarse hump hair and clung frantically to them, her face flushing scarlet, a pain whipping through her right shoulder.

'Oh, daughter of the city, pampered and gently raised, this is not the life for you!' she cried as she dismounted and led the camel along by its rein. She could dimly make out some greenery ahead; the *dhalul* had scented it too for she began to lope, Mishaal running along beside her.

Mishaal fell asleep to the sound of crunching and gulping as the animal devoured every spurt of vegetation in sight, from tufted twigs to sandy roots and tiny, hairy leaves. Mishaal was so exhausted that nothing could have roused her. She remembered to twine the beast's rein round her ankle so that it could not wander, for when it slumped to the earth to rest, she did not feel the tug at her leg, nor hear the raucous and uninhibited sounds of a camel preparing itself for the night.

She woke with a start, wondering why there was no tent above her head. Wheeling in the pallid desert sky were two or three large birds, inspecting her with interest. Buzzards! And there hovering nearby was *el-ágab*, the miniature black eagle. They thought she might be their breakfast!

Jumping to her feet, she shouted and yelled, running up and down, waving her arms.

'You can go away, carrion eaters!' she warned. 'I am not ready to be eaten!'

The camel, shocked into consciousness, made an ear-cracking baying sound and began to lurch to its feet. Mishaal sped to its side and slipped the rein round its ankles. The last thing she needed was to be left without a mount.

For breakfast she choked down some of the goat's cheese she had brought with her. She had to choke it down, for there was no water nearby, not even a bubble of liquid from the meanest hole in the sand, not a cactus nor a succulent berry. Holding out her palm she fed the camel some dates and watched with amusement as its eyes rolled with pleasure as it devoured them.

She shivered, looking around her. The air was clear, and she could see far into the distance. She had hoped that by now she would have seen one of the landmarks passed during her journey to the Beduin camp. It was true that she had been conveyed there during the night, but surely she would soon see the twisted, sun-blackened tree or the crumbling shepherd's hut that had caught her eye the day before the Amir had ridden into her life . . .?

Drew. Squatting in the sandy hollow, the taste of goat's cheese lingering in her mouth, she tried to visualise his face, the bright, silky hair, the humorous gaze. Drew, her beloved, her darling *nasrani*. Tears welled in her eyes and she found herself filled with an aching futility, the sensation of being alive yet without purpose, without hope. When she had been loved by Drew, she had been the happiest woman on earth, willing to travel anywhere and do anything for her man. Now, she had only her own skin to save and suddenly, puzzlingly, she did not care whether it was saved or not.

Dashing the tears from her eyes, she tried to imagine Drew coming towards her. He was running, his face alight at seeing her, his arms extended to scoop her up and hug her close.

Laughing, she felt her heart jerk, the pain snipping into her lungs so that her breath escaped.

'Drew!' She stood up, legs shaking, and started to run to meet him. The ground was uneven and she tripped into dips that shook her limbs, then clambered up little hills that snatched her energy in the effort, and all the time that she ran, she came no closer to him nor he to her. On, on, she ran, crying out his name and yearning for his arms, but he was fading from her vision, vanishing like a *jinn* being sucked back into its magical bottle . . .

Flinging her head into her arms she sobbed. All these weeks she had not wept; somehow she had trapped her tears within her out of pride and scorn and hatred, and now they were determined to be free. After a time, she realised that tears were water and could ease her thirst and she began to push them into her mouth with eager fingers.

Nur, watching her lord ride out, felt her heart turn to bronze, heavy as the skillet on which she roasted the Amir's coffee beans. She did not envy her master. This day he must decide on a course of action which would haunt him for the rest of his years. Whether he punished the girl for her thieving, or let her go back to her people in the city, he would have lost her for ever.

She would pray for a miracle, but in her heart she knew that this was *Mashallah*, the will of Allah. He, the one true God was building a fortress of faith in the *saiyid* and that could not be achieved without great personal suffering and sorrow. The way would not be easy for one who was already a legend in his own young lifetime; his way must be scattered with thorns and the thirst of the just.

Husain, not knowing how far he would have to travel, rode on camel's back. When his followers spoke of their dismay at his journeying alone, he told them that the one true God would be with him, and if any guessed why he desired to find the girl on his own, then they did not say.

Generously supplied with water and food, he rode swiftly, his camel famed for its speed. He knew the desert, every bush and branch and hollow.

The Amir had no fears that he would lose his way or not find the girl whom he sought, for he could track down the smallest creature's markings in the sand, and a *dhalul* was far from small. Within moments he had found the tracks of a single camel and was heading after them at speed.

Had she not been a thief, then his heart would have been considerably lighter. He had seen old Nur's face as he rode out. She had looked as glum as if she had been told that her favourite son was going to work in the city. Poor woman. Her life had been sad in many ways. And his? He was nearing twenty-seven, an unheard-of age for an Arab to be unmarried.

This was not only the day when he would lose Mishaal, but the day when he knew that he must make the serious decision to take a wife. It would have to be very soon and love need not enter into it. For the sake of his peoples, he would have to behave like the city man and select the first healthy girl available. All that would be necessary was that she be sturdy, truthful and physically appealing, and that she loved him a little; he would never force a female to his bed. If Allah was merciful then his own love for her would grow, but love was not imperative. Sons could be and were sired in the bitterest of circumstances.

He swallowed, emotion filling his throat. All his life he had known that one day he would rule his father's amirate, and never once had he resented the burden – until now. Suddenly he saw the truth of the situation: on one side, the many tribes over whom he had jurisdiction, and on the other, the girl whom he loved but could now never marry because of her betrayal. She had brought light and sweetness into his life, a radiance that he had not believed could exist. She had entered his heart and soul within minutes of his first seeing her, and yet she was a thief, a common thief. First she had stolen his heart and then his senses; then his family's treasure . . .

He remembered how, one night, he had gone to the box where the peacock robe was stored, the robe that she loved so deeply, the costume that transformed her into an ethereal and magical being. He knew how she loved that costume and there it was, an empty husk without her sweet warmth to fill it. The feathers were lifeless and limp without her, the colours anaemic. Clasping the robe in his arms he had yearned for it to be filled with her gentle voluptuous body, but no amount of yearning and aching could have changed events. He should have known that a dancer from a house of sin would prove to be little better than a common criminal. Yet he knew that he would still take her as his bride, if it were not for his peoples. They would not accept her now, nor any sons she bore. She had been a guest in the black tents and she had deceived them all . . .

Bitterness grasping his heart, he rode on, eyes narrowed against the decimating sun.

How swiftly night fell in the desert. One minute it was balmy evening and then suddenly blackness clung to her shoulders. She knew that she must rest and eat, although the cheese would choke her. She had found a plump cactus late that afternoon and torn open its spiky leaves with trembling hands. Inside was a juicy pulp that she crushed against her tongue. It helped to slake her thirst, but the taste was acrid and unwholesome.

The *dhalul* seemed almost gay; she was munching happily and tossing her head now and again; the lack of water did not trouble her at this time of year, for she was *jezzin*, 'not drinking'. At this time the beasts devoured all the vegetation they could find and put on fat in readiness for the months ahead.

Watching the big dark shape of her in the gloom, Mishaal wondered if the Beduin would consider her a thief for taking a *dhalul*. She had no intention of keeping the beast. Once she was safely back with Rhikia, she would pay a boy to return the camel to them.

What would Rhikia say when she went back? Would she be angry and berate her for running away, or would she take her into her arms and weep, saying, Oh daughter of mine, how I missed thee and longed for thee . . .?

Mishaal bent her head. How wretchedly her dreams had turned out. She had lost the man she loved and been pursued by another, whom she loathed for what he had done to her, and now, here she was, lost in the desert with a camel and no water. Perhaps it was Allah's intention that she die of thirst for her sins? She gave a harsh little laugh. Would that be the rough justice that Drew had talked of when he told her about the new land across the seas? That was a place of rough justice where men received all that they deserved, and where the evil were punished in the end, despite their convictions of triumph.

'Oh Drew!' If she died here now, tonight, would she be with him again in the Christian heaven? But she had not had the chance to be Christened and hadn't Drew said that no one could enter the kingdom of heaven without having received that sacrament? Would she, dying, find herself beating at the gates of heaven and see Drew through them, but not be able to join him? It was a terrible thought and she tried to shut her mind to it.

Tiredness claiming her, she curled up in a tight little ball, the *dhalul*'s rein twisted round her ankle. The ground was lumpy and hard and rocks sliced into her spine, so when the *dhalul* had finally finished chewing, and lumbered down to sleep, Mishaal leaned against its coarse, warm side and closed her eyes.

It is not easy to sleep when thirst strangles you, however exhausted your body. Half-dreams flitted behind her lids, yet she was more than a little awake and imagined the moving figures and shapes to be real. Twice she jolted into full wakefulness, convinced that something black and nasty was leaning over her. Eventually she scrabbled in the shadows to find some greenery to chew, hoping that its sap would soothe her throat. The sharp taste on her tongue, she fell asleep at last, oblivious of the rumbling snores of the *dhalul*.

In her dream, Drew was leading her by the hand to a glorious waterfall, crashing in a silvered glistening sheen down a mountain side. She could not wait for the icy crystal torrent to flood over her head and shoulders and into her mouth, but first he insisted that she undress. Carefully, he removed her clothes, first the worn and sandy slippers, easing them off her hot and aching feet. Gently he kissed each bare foot, looking up at her in between, his eyes alight with love. Then he unfastened her cloak and flung it to one side, then her robe, crushed and travel-worn, so that she stood before him quite naked.

Slowly, he kissed her legs, kiss after kiss from her ankles up to her thighs, so that she shivered with delight, the roar of the waterfall sounding like the drums of destiny in her ears. Caressingly, his mouth touched her upper thighs and the ebony half-diamond between them, and she moaned out his name. His mouth was warm honey on her belly and waist, then against her breasts, circling them, kissing the nipples which stood out in greeting. Now he was standing before her, naked himself, and she could see all that beautiful, gold-muscled body of the pale Western man, so sturdy and taut and yet soft as velvet to the touch.

'Now,' he was saying. '*Now!*' and then he was taking her by the hand and stepping beneath the waterfall with her, so that the noise was deafening in her head, thundering, pounding, shouting out to her that this was what she had wanted all her life, this man, this darling man, and water . . . Water . . .

'Water, water . . .' She woke up croaking the word over and over. She was wet with sweat and the base of her spine was throbbing. That sound of thunder . . . she could hear it approaching. She shrank into herself, eyes wide in terror, trying to huddle out of sight behind the camel. She had recognised the dark shape of a rider coming towards her, blocking out the twist of moonlight spearing between the clouds. It was a *jinn*, a great black evil *jinn*!

Chapter Nineteen

Arms closed round her, gripping, tightening, so that she was a prisoner. Screaming, she kicked out, left leg, then right, crying out to Allah to save her.

'So, when your life is at stake, it is Allah whom you call . . . You are a little Muslim after all.'

It was the Amir's voice, richly taunting, yet there was an inflexion in it that she had not heard before.

'Allah and the God of the *nasrani*, are they not one and the same?' she snarled, struggling to free herself of his shackling embrace. Did he want to cage her until she weakened? He had followed her tracks. She was his prisoner again. Her face was scarlet with fury and disappointment.

Suddenly he spun her away from him, yet kept his restricting hold on her wrists. The moon had ventured out from behind a cloud and they were illumined in an aureole of bleak white light. The Amir's eyes were cruelly black, hard and forgiving as basalt, his mouth compressed as if he wished to shout a thousand insults at her yet could not trust himself to speak. There were pale lines of stress running down each side of his nose.

'I am not coming back with you!' she cried. 'I am no African to be turned into a slave!'

'No, you are not coming back with me,' he said, almost on a sigh.

'Then you will free me?' Her face lit up.

'No, not that, either.'

'Then what? Why have you chased after me? I was going to send the camel back to you . . . If that is all you wanted, then take her now. She is yours, after all.' Her mouth pursed.

'I did not come for the beast.'

'Then what? Why are you looking at me like that?' His gaze was sending chills along her back. Did this arrogant man have another, darker side? Allah, who would help her now?

'Where are they?' he rasped.

'Where are what?'

'The opals.'

'What opals? I do not know what you mean!'

'The opals that you stole from my tent in my absence.'

'Those? But –'

'Yes, those! Where are they?' His eyes narrowed, sending more chills along her flesh.

'How would I know that? In your tent, most probably. Go back and look again.'

His grip was burning, lacerating her skin.

'Tell me where they are! It is no secret any more. What you have done is known by everyone.'

'I have done nothing except try to escape from an intolerable imprisonment! You had no right to keep me! I am free now and you cannot make me go back!'

'I told you that I do not want you to come back with me. You are no longer welcome by me or my peoples. We took you in as an honoured guest and you betrayed us.'

'Honoured guest! Since when do you imprison your guests!'

'So you stole them to have your revenge on me, is that it?' His voice sounded choked.

'*Revenge?* What a stupid thing to say! I want my freedom, nothing more: the freedom that I am entitled to! I have stolen nothing!'

'It is no good lying like this, Mishaal, you just make yourself sound worse, a thief who will say anything when cornered.'

'Look, I have not stolen anything from you – not even the *dhalul* who would have been returned to you very soon! You think that you can make me beg and plead with you if you accuse me of stealing, and then I shall be your slave . . . Well, it is not so. I shall not humble myself. I am not your slave, nor am I one of your Beduin to be bullied and forced. I shall do whatever I want from now on, and you can go back home!'

'Show me where they are, Mishaal. Allah, if only it could have been different!' he groaned, gritting his teeth, raising his eyes heavenwards. She could feel the rush of emotion through his body, making his hands tremble momentarily.

'I cannot show you where they are, whatever you mean by *they*. I have nothing with me save a bag of food. Even my water is gone.'

'You know the penalty for stealing, Mishaal?'

'I know it.'

'Did you think of it when you took the opals or did you truly imagine that you could find your way in the desert all alone, when you have so little knowledge of the wilderness?'

'I have not taken the opals, you thick-witted savage!' Mishaal cried, rage tearing through her. Then, before he knew what she was doing, she was biting deep into his wrist until she tasted the bitter-iron flavour of blood.

Shouting with anger, he slapped her so hard across her cheek that she was thrown off balance, trillions of minuscule platinum stars whisking across her vision. Wailing, she fell to her knees and stayed there, too stunned to move.

'I always said you were a wildcat, and a vixen, too. Stay there and do not try to run away.'

Mishaal could not have run if she had tried. Her legs were feeble as paper, her heart aching. The place where his palm had rested in fury was scorching hot and splitting pains were searing down into her neck and across her eyes. What was he doing? Dizzily, she twisted round to see. He was turning out her bags. More fool him; he would find nothing save some dried food and a few clothes and her sandals.

She saw his hand go into her bag and pull out her clothes; then she heard the clink of metal against the stony ground. He roared out loud, shocking her to the soul, and then strings of gleaming white opals set in thick gold were hanging from his fingers, and he was turning to her, his face a mask of fury and contempt.

'No!' she cried, staggering to her feet. 'No! I did not take them! It was not me! I brought nothing away with me but my own belongings, nothing, do you hear? *I did not steal*

them! I did not!' Sobbing out, she ran to him, kneeling at his feet and staring up at his pale and merciless face.

Then, to her horror, she saw his hand go to his sword, and slowly draw it from its scabbard. She could not believe what she was seeing. The world grew silent, the desert vanished and was still, the birdsong died and a wild, whistling wind filled her ears, increasing in sound until it was deafening.

She saw the sword rise high above her beseeching hands in readiness to sweep down and slice them from her arms.

Rhikia would help anyone who had lost a daughter. Women would come to her and tell her how their daughters had died, or married evil men who would not let them see their families, or run off with unsuitable youths, and they could always be sure that Rhikia would listen with the greatest empathy. She would offer them coffee and almond cakes, or *halva* made with sesame seeds and honey, taken from a Turkish recipe, and they would sit back and reminisce abour their lost daughters, sighing and rolling their heads in misery. As the women left, Rhikia would kiss them on the cheek and insist that they keep her informed as to their lost child's whereabouts. Sometimes a daughter would return of her own accord and then Rhikia would organise rejoicings in which she would participate as if the girl were her own.

None of this would have been possible had she not sold the house of pleasure. ZouZou had raged and thrown pots and physically attacked her on two occasions. Despite this tirade, Rhikia had persevered. She felt that her involvement with the flesh trade had caused the loss of her beloved foster child; that she was being punished for making money out of sin.

ZouZou did not care. She wanted money, as many gold dinars as possible, and she would attach herself to whoever could help her make her fortune. Within weeks she was living in another house of pleasure in the Street of the Amber Eye. Rhikia had given ZouZou a share of the sale money when the house was finally sold, and she had also given shares to the girls. How different was their leave-taking! Weeping and kissing her, they had begged to stay with her, but she could not allow it. From now on, she would spend her days in prayer and humble penitence.

Her new home was small and modest, tucked away in a corner of the courtyard of Atahib where the other residents would spend most of their days, gossiping and watching their children romp, or fetching water from the circular well in the centre of the court, heaving up the battered old leathern bucket, righting it as it reached the top so that only a little of the liquid was spilled, and then emptying the contents into their own jars or buckets.

Day after day, from her small upper window, Rhikia would watch life going on outside as if nothing had happened, seeing happy children's faces and chubby toddling infants, women veiled and robed, whispering to one another and drawing their daily water from the old well.

Sometimes, one or two would look up at her window and she could tell that they were talking about her. What would they be saying? That the infamous Rhikia was living in that house? That women of sin never profited for in the end they were always brought down? Would that be what they were saying?

Once or twice, she had almost called out to them to ask if they would join her in refreshments, but her courage had failed, and so her solitary existence had continued for nearly three months. Then one day she heard a tapping at her front door. Astonished, she hurried to answer it.

Outside stood a sobbing woman, her veil drenched with tears and sagging down almost to her chin. Crying out, she fell into Rhikia's arms.

For a second or two, Rhikia's heart jolted in the most painful and unsteadying manner. It was not her darling Mishaal returned to her. When the drenched veil was removed, she saw a woman of some thirty years whose eyes were bulging and red-rimmed with tears, whose lips were chapped and flaked from all the salt that had trickled on to them in the past weeks.

'Allah, what am I to do? My daughter has left me! She is my only child. I had four sons but all have died . . . Rhikia, do you not remember me? It is Jasmina . . . I was one of the girls who left you after only a few months. Do you not recognise me?'

'Jasmina!' she whispered. 'You left to marry a merchant. You said that you would let me know how you fared.'

'Yes, I know and Allah forgive me for not sending you a message, but I was so happy, so very happy. And then my husband died, Allah preserve and protect his soul! And then my sons, one after the other, as if they were cursed, and I had only my sweet daughter left to me. She was to marry her cousin Rajim. He is a good boy, generous and wealthy, but she said that she would rather die than marry him for he has a disfigurement . . . He lost an eye many years ago and she could not bear to look at the empty socket. I said, What matter that he has one eye missing if he has all of his heart? But she was young and stupidly romantic as girls are at fourteen and she – she slipped out one night . . . She took all her money with her, and all her most precious possessions, and I have not heard from her in two moons. Everyone is searching for her, but there is no trail. She has vanished. Aiyee, she has been taken by devils, I know it!' Jasmina beat her clenched fists against her breasts.

This woman was in dire need of help and advice. Rhikia had a role to play again.

'Jasmina, most important is that you stop weeping, for tears speak of lack of faith and lack of hope. You weep because you believe that something terrible has happened, but how do you know that it has? Your daughter may be content and happy wherever she is.'

'May be, *may* be!' Jasmina wailed.

'You must pray and beseech your relatives and friends to pray for her return. Light candles and incense for her . . .' Rhikia halted. If only Matiya were here. She knew all the concoctions for burning incense for all manner of trials and tribulations. 'I am sure that she will come home eventually. You are her only close relative. She will realise that she has been very cruel deserting you and she will return and fling herself into your arms. I am sure of it.'

Jasmina blinked and looked at her with dazed eyes. 'You truly think that she will come back to me?' Rhikia nodded.

'I heard that – that your foster daughter eloped with a *nasrani* . . .' Jasmina began, then stopped, chewing at her lower lip. 'I am sorry. I know I should not have mentioned that. It is brash gossip.'

'But true nonetheless. She did do just that, many months ago.'

'You have heard nothing from her?'

'Nothing.'

'Do you feel that she will come back to you?'

'What I can feel for another, such as you, I cannot always feel for myself. How would I separate longing and yearning from the ability to perceive the future in clarity?'

'So you cannot predict for yourself?'

'Sometimes, sometimes not, usually not.'

'Yet you feel that my child will come back?'

'Yes, I feel that strongly. In a very short time, she will be eating and sleeping under your roof again.'

Jasmina fell to her knees and taking up the hem of Rhikia's robe, kissed it fervently, as if Rhikia were a great princess. Shaking her head, Rhikia pulled the woman to her feet.

'Tell me when you hear from her, won't you? I shall rejoice with you.'

'God be with you,' Jasmina said, stepping out into the sunny courtyard.

And that was how it had begun. Jasmina's daughter had appeared within the week and whether it was coincidence or she had truly predicted as accurately as any seer, others thought that Rhikia had the gift and mothers began to knock on her door at all times of the day and night.

When daughters returned, as some eventually did, Rhikia would be invited to the celebrations, her past forgotten, her sins, apparently, forgiven.

Yet not a day passed without her praying that her own Mishaal would return. Preparing for bed was her loneliest time. After nine in the evening, the house was as good as empty, echoing with Rhikia's memories, her days with Mishaal and the raising of her beloved foster daughter. How chill and gaunt the house seemed at night, as if shadows had fallen across it, removing it from the courtyard and the bustle of life, and flying it to some isolated spot on the map where other human beings did not linger. By day she might be forgiven for her sins, but by night she was just as guilty and self-reproachful as ever.

In the solace and comfort of her true friends Rhikia put aside the warped viewpoints and the derision of those who saw her only as immoral. Strange how men who viewed themselves as profoundly religious and close to God could be so vicious-tongued where fallen women were concerned, yet often they were first in line to bed those women out of sight of their wives.

But she was her own woman and would remain so. She had not missed a man in her life for many, many years, and never in a physical or material way.

There was only one thing that she lacked, and without which her life could never be normal again. Mishaal. Mishaal, the brightly lit torch who had illuminated her life and without whom life was dull and miserable and empty.

Chapter Twenty

He had shackled her ankles with ropes painfully knotted so that she could not have unfastened them in hours of struggle, and he had removed her little dagger far from her reach.

She lay on her back staring up at the night sky, seeing the multiplicity of stars throbbing and spangling against the indigo eternity, and she felt as if her heart had been taken away. Oh, the operation had been painless; she had not felt the blade slicing into her flesh nor the heart being cut out, the vacant gaping wound exposed to every breeze and rain of dust. No, she had felt nothing of the operation itself, just the after-effects, the hollow, empty misery and the disbelief.

A few yards away the Amir slept beneath a goatskin. He knew that she could not escape, any more than could the *dhalul* who was snoring and sighing close by, its ankles hobbled too. Was that not the way with females? Shackle them until they do your bidding? Allah, and all her life she had thought that she was free!

How had the opals got into her bag? Racking her brains could provide no answer. She had not taken them, nor would she ever have contemplated doing so, yet the Amir in his mighty omnipotence believed that she had, that she was a lowly thief who had plotted her revenge on him for killing Drew and taking her prisoner. All the same, he had not been able to bring himself to cut off her hands.

He had stood over her, his suntanned face pallid and haggard with emotion.

'Why did you do it, Mishaal? You could have had those opals placed round your neck by me on your marriage day, yet you chose to steal them. Why would anyone choose such a course of action when a pleasurable and amiable one was open to them?'

'Pleasurable in your eyes maybe, but not in mine, no, never in mine!' Her eyes still rested uneasily on his sword. It was back in its scabbard now, but how close it had come to maiming her!

'I would not have forced myself on you. You could have married me and I would have waited months, years, for you to come round to loving me.'

'That arrogance of yours is boundless. Still you think that I would love you in time; that it is inevitable, while *I* think that it is inevitable that I shall loathe and hate you for ever more after this!'

Flinching from her acid tongue, he was silent for a few moments, then he said, his voice rasping, 'Was it the legendary treasure, the Jewels of Destiny, that you resented losing? Oh Mishaal, little *fâhd*, all this time I did not comprehend. I did not realise why you were out in the wilderness with him . . . But now I see it. You wanted the Jewels of Destiny, wanted them for yourself, and he was your pathway to them, and you were his. "Should any non-believer's hand remove the Jewels of Destiny from their hiding place then the wells of the Land of Mirages will run dry unto the Day of Judgement and starvation and famine will be a fatal visitation upon the peoples",' he quoted as if those words were frequently on his tongue. 'He thought that you would be able to take the jewels out of their hiding place because you are a Muslim, and there would be no repercussions on him for what he had done. He knew only too well that he would have been summarily executed for causing famine and thirst in this land . . .'

'You hear only what you want to hear!' Mishaal cried. 'You are misguided, you invent all manner of stupidity and then throw accusations at me!'

'Little *fáhd*, I loved you as I have never loved before!' he sighed, his eyes bleaker than she had ever seen them, bleak and sad and devoid of hope. 'You would have been my wife, my only wife, until God parted us.'

Despite herself, tears threatened, but only because his words brought back all her sweet memories of Drew. Tossing her head to one side, she fought back the tears, hoping that he would not misunderstand again.

'Tell me why you did it, Mishaal, tell me. Did you hate me so much? If I could change what lay between us, then you know that I would, surely you know that?' His eyes were beseeching.

'Yes, you would change things so that you could make me your willing slave, yet you have more than enough of those amongst your people. Never have I seen any man so worshipped and pampered as you, O Great Amir!'

'You think that is all that is necessary? Ah, how little you understand me, Mishaal. You see only the façade but not the man behind it. He has a heart and feelings just like you, that man, but he has spent his lifetime concealing them for the good of his people.'

'You have concealed them so well that you became a despot, cruel and ruthless, thinking that you could steal anything you wanted . . .' Too late she realised that she should not have said 'steal'.

'Then we have much in common, would you not say? You

with your craving for jewels, and me with my one-time craving to make you my bride, but believe me, that is over now, over for both of us. You shall not have your jewels and I – I shall not have my wife.'

His voice had broken on that word, but he had turned from her so abruptly that she could not see his expression. Strangely, she felt queasy, as if she had been deprived of something more beautiful than she knew. For months now she had resisted this charismatic man, spurning his advances; they had squabbled and argued and she had even thrown a vase at his head, she recalled with a pang of unease. Did she not have the right to resist when he had destroyed her happiness with Drew and taken her lover's life? He thought that he could force her into marrying him, so that she would be his legal slave and servant, waiting upon him, attending to his every need, sewing his clothes and grinding his coffee beans, baking his bread and making his meals, day after day, month after month, with the bearing of sons at regular intervals until she was old and bent and wrinkled like Nur . . . But long before that, she was sure he would have taken another wife, if not two or three, as Muslim men were wont to do. She knew that the Beduin sometimes kept to one, and made devoted husbands, but great, all-powerful princes were different from the ordinary nomad whose life revolved around his goats.

She did not trust him, and he did not trust her; yet he had no cause to doubt her until this terrible day when he had found the opals in her bag. Who could have put them there? Who had wanted her to be punished as a thief, and maimed for life – if she survived the wounds.

Night was clasping her but she could not sleep. Wretchedness made her jumpy and restless, yet she could not move her shackled legs to find an easier sleeping position. Listening to the sonorous snores of the *dhalul* she wished that she were a camel, bland and dull, without the intensity of emotions that made life such a torment. Men loved more ardently than the animals but they also hated more and took their revenge in more terrible ways . . .

It was nearly dawn when she slept at last, so exhausted that she could do little else, and then something hot and wet was nuzzling at her cheek and she opened her eyes with alarm to find the camel's nose thrusting at hers, and, in the background, the Amir, his face grim, holding up a water flask to drink the flowing crystal liquid.

She could not help it, she cried out at the sight of the water and when he knelt beside her to place the flask in her hands, she almost sobbed with relief. Last night, on his arrival, he had only had an empty flask. Now it was full. How had this miracle happened?

'You hid that water from me last night when I was desperate with thirst!' Mishaal accused.

'See that twisting *qaradh* tree over there,' the Amir pointed. 'Just a few feet beneath its roots was water, a small natural spring.'

'How did you know?'

'See how lush and green the leaves are, when all around is parched and sere. That told me that water was reaching its roots. Now give me your water bottles and I will fill them.'

The camel was still attending to her face, so Mishaal gently brushed her away.

'Go and eat, *dhalul*, go and find some shoots and leaves. I am not your dinner!'

'It is the salt that she is after,' the Amir explained. 'Your skin is covered with it after a day or two of trekking in the heat.'

'Salt?' Mishaal gasped as a great long tongue lapped across her face again. 'So that is what it is all about.' At any other time she would have laughed at being a camel's savoury treat.

Mishaal drank in great, throat-aching gulps, almost choking towards the end, then lay back feeling so bloated that she could not move. Soon there was the urgency of a call of nature and she requested of the Amir that he untie her ankles, but he did not seem to hear. He was feeding his camel with dates and patting its neck.

'Please, would you untie my legs. I need to – I need to . . .' How could she put that into words? Blushing, she awaited his response.

What a great age he took to walk over to her, then he stood, hand on dagger, looking down at her ankles. They were red and sore from the thongs, but he seemed in no hurry to cut her free.

'I do not think that it would be a good idea for you to be cut loose.'

'Do you think that I shall take wing and fly off like a *jinn*? Let me free so that I can attend to the call of nature. Would you torture and humiliate me, O Great and Wondrous Prince?'

'If I had wanted to do that, then I have had ample opportunity, would you not say? Allah, but you are suspicious!'

'I, suspicious? What about you, Wondrous Prince? *You* think I am a thief!'

'Only because I find my jewels in your baggage and you taking flight with it. Surely no accident?'

'There will be an accident indeed in a moment if you do not untie me!' Mishaal cried, threshing around on the sand and kicking out her feet.

Sighing, the Amir cut the thongs and glorious life flowed back into her limbs, but leaping to her feet, she found that her legs would not hold her. Shocked, she fell against the man she hated and he caught her expertly before she collapsed to the stony ground. While stabbing pains lunged through her calves and thighs, making it impossible for her to move, the Amir's arms encased her with a firmness that frightened her. Looking up into his eyes, she saw a myriad emotions flocking there, desire and passion, tenderness, empathy – and contempt.

Her heart banging painfully, she could do little but rest her head against his chest to try to ease the weight from her legs, while her arms went round his waist. Oh, if this had been Drew, how delirious with joy she would have been, but it was not, it was not!

'You have wanted to torture me from the first second our eyes met, little *fáhd*. Admit it! You have held me at arm's length though you knew my heart was aching for you. Did I not place my heart in your keeping and bare my soul to you? Why did you repay me like this? Why?'

Tilting her chin, he gazed down into her bright peridot

eyes, now even more brilliant against her sunburnt face. Then, to her astonishment, his mouth was on hers.

'No! You followed me because you thought I was a thief! You came to punish me, to cut off my hand as a warning to others and now you want to kiss me! It is not right! It is not right!' Pushing him away, she headed for the nearest clump of rocks and spiky bushes and there squatted out of sight, her heart thumping at the immodesty of the situation. When she returned, he was waiting for her, his eyes glittering.

'So take your choice. Which is it to be? You kiss me, or you lose a hand. Do not think that you are safe because I spared you once.'

She gasped at his brutality, but did it truly surprise her? He wanted her so much that he would not punish her if she went to him willingly, for that was what it amounted to . . . He wanted to possess her body on any terms, even knowing that he could no longer marry her now that she had proven herself to be a criminal . . .

'You are a devil, Husain ibn Rashid, a devil! If you lay a hand on me then Allah will bring down His judgement upon your head!'

'*If* I lay a hand on you? But have you forgotten that I administer Allah's justice in this land and if I decide that you must be punished then punished you shall be, and by my own hand, but first I wish to taste those delights denied to me before. I have waited months for this!'

Before she could resist, he had scooped her up into his arms and carried her to a sandy hollow, a small *wadi*, dried now, where once a river had flowed. It was sheltered from the sight of any desert travellers and from the winds that swirled high and wildly into the air, tossing sand and grit as they travelled.

There, on the goatskin, he placed her, standing astride her like a conquering Tartar, his face stretched with exultation at her submission, and then he was caging her body, pinning back her hands and kissing her neck and throat and cheeks as if his life would be in danger if he paused.

She cried out, screaming at him to leave her alone, but he did not see why he should listen to the wailings of a female thief. Kiss upon kiss seared her mouth and face; she had never been kissed like this before, but then she had only had one lover . . . This man was fashioned of desert fire and scorching sun; he was tough and invincible as the ancient rocks and paleolithic stones that rose out of the arid earth like terracotta giants. Born and raised in the sun-parched wilderness, resistant to all weathers and hardships, famine, drought, the scouring *simûm*, the wind that tore up everything in its path and replaced it in surreal formation, nothing reached his heart or his soul – if he had one – and she doubted it. What hope did she have now that he was revealing his true self, out here where she had no one to aid her, no one to heed her screams?

'Little *fáhd*, why do you look at me with such loathing? Have I not cared for you all these months and seen that you had food and your own tent? Why do you despise me still?'

'Is it demanded of me that I love the man who will cut off my hand? Love one's own executioner, is that what you ask of me? Allah, but you are crazed!'

'Had you not guessed that I could not summon the ruthlessness to maim you? One attempt was more than enough.'

'But it is your right as the owner of the jewels that were stolen, and you are a man who believes in taking what is rightfully his, are you not, Husain ibn Rashid?' Her voice was steely cold.

'Until now . . . But you, Mishaal, have driven sense and caution from me. I lived a lonely life until you entered it, and then it was like the sun rising at dawn to bathe me in light . . .'

'Yes, that same sun that parches the earth and dries your wells, do not forget. Amir of a thousand dried-out wells, that is what they will call you.'

'If I make love to you, will it make more wells arid? Is that what you mean? I doubt it.'

A thought was swirling round in her head, but she could not pin it down. Why should there be this terrible drought at this time? That old legend. She had heard it regularly during her growing years. Rhikia was fond of local tales and whenever she recounted any, along would come the legend of the wells drying out and the Jewels of Destiny. No one knew what they were or where they were hidden, and many dismissed the whole story as an old wives' tale, but there were others who believed. Drew had believed. She had seen his map, the map showing where the Jewels of Destiny were concealed, but she had been so besotted with him that the jewels had meant nothing; she had barely taken in their meaning. All she had wanted was to be with him wherever he went, to follow where he led . . .

The map. She could see it now in her mind's eye with that keen memory which had made her such a successful pupil and capable of memorising pages of verse as well as the *Qu'ran*. Marked with a smudged black cross was the ancient ruined temple, the one that had long been taboo to the desert people. No one would willingly venture there; it was a place of *jinns* and demons, and ancient evil, a place where men and women had worshipped idols forbidden by the Mohammedan creed.

Drew had said that the Mother Goddess was the one for whom the temple had been built. She had found that difficult to comprehend: a woman in place of God? How could that be? Yet Drew had said that it was so, that many hundreds of years ago, heathen pagans had idolised a female goddess who had gone under many names, Innana, Asherah, Astarte, Artemis, depending on the country in which the female idol was being worshipped. She was an evil entity who drove her followers into terrible depravities of which he could not speak, he told her, for they were too hideous and sickening. The women followers sold their bodies to men, prostituting themselves in the name of religion. His mouth had curled with revulsion at mention of them.

Then Christianity had swept away that dark sickness, bringing in the light which had burned so fiercely ever since.

'"The Dark Mother," she was called, and she demanded human sacrifice and the spilling of blood on the earth and repugnant fertility rites more vile and unsavoury than anything before or since.'

Drew's words rang in her head. She could almost hear his voice as if he spoke in her ear. The Amir was looking at her strangely. His kissing halted, and she dropped her eyes.

'What are you thinking, Mishaal? That you hate and loathe me? Do I not deserve more than your contempt? Allah, if you have ever been true to yourself, then be true to me also!'

She could not believe her ears. First, he accused her of theft and threatened her with maiming as a punishment, and then he wanted her respect and affection!

'I have always been true to myself, *Saiyid*, because I know no other way to be. Allah, do you think that I deceive myself by hating you? In your pride and hauteur, do you imagine that I must love you because that is what you demand of me? Has no one ever said no to you, Husain ibn Rashid? Love cannot be forced, nor can it be produced to order; it must be earned by those who want it. Perhaps you have not earned it.' Her voice shook.

'I have the love of my people. They are generous with their devotion,' he reminded her.

'Then let that be enough for you. For any other man, it would be more than enough.'

'Mishaal, we can argue until the next full moon and never come to any solution,' he groaned.

Coldly she faced him. 'Solution? What solution could you want now? You have accused me of theft, you have said that you will punish me, you have decided that I am no longer fitted to be your wife because I am a low criminal, and yet you seek a solution. There is none, I do assure you. Punish me and then let me go free. I want nothing else but my freedom.'

She had not meant to weaken before him but suddenly tears welled in her eyes and she was thrashing out at him with her clenched fists, striking wildly, not caring where she hit.

Her flailing arms were caught and trapped, and she was caged against him, crushed so that she could not move while his mouth conquered hers. She could not breathe or think or find words; she was mute and bemused, captured, and yet given her freedom in the strangest and most inexplicable way.

'Mishaal, I pursued you to punish you, yet all the while in my heart I think that I knew the truth. I could never punish you, whatever you did to me. I love you too much. How could I stop loving you even if you stole my greatest treasure?' His eyes were tender with emotion.

'I did not steal it,' Mishaal protested. 'I did not!'

'Though everything points against it, I believe you. Do not ask me why, but I do. Allah, if I do not think you are innocent, then who will? What manner of man would I be if I accused you when you needed me most?'

'So you do not think I took the opals?' Her voice was a faint and startled whisper.

'May Allah stand as my witness, but I do not. I was angry, overcome with rage that you had run away from me, and that after all these months you still reject me. That was at the bottom of it. I prayed that the opals would not be with you. I prayed with all my heart and soul.'

'But they were with me. Someone put them in my bag to incriminate me, because I certainly did not!'

'I have said that I believe you. Do not look at me with those blazing-star eyes! Mishaal . . .' He took her gently by the hands. 'I want you to love me. I need you to love me. Do you understand what I am saying? I want you to love me more than your own life, more than the stars and the air you breathe, and your dancing and the music that you love, more than your freedom . . .'

Stunned, she absorbed what he was saying, realisation slow to clarify. She could not take it in, this passionate intensity of feeling from the man she considered callous of heart, arrogant and aloof, yet his eyes were blazing with what could only be a frank devotion. He was sincere; he meant what he said. Overwhelmed, she turned her head away from his compelling gaze and stared unseeingly at the low-slung blaze of distant gold and terracotta hills.

PART FOUR

Lovers in the Desert

And then the Christian girl whom he had loved
Dreamed in her sleep; a shaft of sunlight moved
Before her eyes, and from the dazzling ray
A voice said: 'Rise, follow your lost shaikh's way;
Accept his faith, beneath his feet be dust;
You tricked him once, be pure to him and just,
And, as he took your path without pretence,
Take his path now in truth and innocence.
Follow his lead; you once led him astray –
Be his companion as he points the Way.

Farid ud-din Attar

Here with a Loaf of Bread beneath the Bough,
A Flask of Wine, a Book of Verse –
And Thou
Beside me singing in the Wilderness –
And wilderness is Paradise enow.

Omar Khayyam

Chapter Twenty-One

A gabble of sound woke Rhikia from her sleep. Outside in the courtyard women were standing round the well pointing and staring at one another, then breaking out into babbles of hysterical chatter. One woman was on her knees as if beseeching God, and soon others were following suit. Alarmed, Rhikia flung on her clothes and hurried to join them.

'Only yesterday my cousin told me that four wells have run dry in Akbar, yet that is three days' journey away. How can this well run dry also? How can it happen?' Old Farida was tugging at Rhikia's sleeve and demanding answers that she could not give.

'Farida, what is it? You say the well has run dry? Is it the weather? It has been dry lately. The rains are very late.'

'No, no, not the weather!' Farida shook her head in agitation. 'This well has given water since the time of the Prophet himself. It is one of the oldest wells in the land. They say that Mohammed himself drank from it on one of his journeys, and that He blessed it because its waters were so sweet.'

'Well, if He blessed it, then it should never run dry.'

'But it has.' Farida jutted her lower lip. 'Last night little Yusuf fetched water for his mother who is ill, and he had no trouble in filling his jug. This morning, there is nothing, not a drop!'

'Yusuf must have had a very big jug!' Rhikia tried to make a jest, but the faces around her were twisted with shock.

Leaning over the edge of the well, she stared down into its

dark and chilly depths. She reached down to pick up one of the small pebbles that had come loose from the stonework and dropped it into the void. For some moments there was silence until the sound of the pebble clattering against dry stone as it landed. There was no reassuring plop.

'You see, you see!' cried the women encircling her.

'Yes . . .' Rhikia drew in her breath, a sudden chill flowing through her heart. She felt cold and stiff, as if she had spent the night in that icy hole; there was something fearfully wrong; she could sense it. Much more than this well being empty, far more. The legend . . . Suddenly, she thought of the old legend and the warning that if any non-believer touched the Jewels of Destiny then all the wells would run dry in the Land of Mirages . . . But she knew nothing of the jewels, nor did anyone else, so why think of the legend now, except that it had always been her favourite because it reminded her of Mishaal . . .

Maryam had said, *Call my daughter Mishaal, for she shall be a torch to light the way for her people.*

Gripping the chilly edge of the well, Rhikia remembered and tears flooded her eyes.

'Bîllah 'alaik,' she whispered hoarsely, '*Bîllah 'alaik*,' imploring God to bring Mishaal back to her and make her world right again.

'So my would-be half-sister is dead.' Mishaal digested the news without any sensation of grief.

'You never felt that she was of your blood?'

'Never. Oh, I may have idealised my image of my dead mother, but I could never see that ugly-spirited Salida as my kin. I did not take to her . . . there was something unsavoury about her. She repulsed me.'

'While I was in Akbar, I heard a story about this Salida. It was not very pleasant, unrepeatable in fact.' The Amir lowered his eyes. 'It seems that she had a bad reputation. She was infamous for being willing to do anything for gold, and I mean anything.'

'That does not concern me. She was not my half-sister.' Mishaal jutted her lip.

'I did not mean to criticise you, little *fáhd*, do not be so sensitive.' Husain went to touch her hand but she pulled it away sharply. They were having a very uneasy truce. 'I spoke to a woman who knew her quite well, she was some sort of distant cousin, I believe. This woman said that Salida had heard of you through a friend at Rhikia's . . . That was where you lived, was it not?' Mishaal nodded. 'When you disappeared, Rhikia made extensive enquiries, sending out her girls to try and find you. One spoke to Salida, telling her what had happened and Salida said that she would try to find you. She took money towards this end, but I do not think that she had any intention of stirring herself. Much later, she heard through one of her nomadic clients that you were to marry a wealthy Amir, and she devised her plan to pretend that you were her long-lost sister.'

'She was crazed! If Rhikia knew, she would have stopped it immediately.'

'Yes, but she did not know, did she? You were out in the wilderness and only Salida knew where you were because her client spilled it all to her.'

'Do you know who he was?'

'No. I wish I did.'

'So that dreadful creature travelled all this way on camel's back in the blazing heat to claim me as her relative, so that she could live in state for the rest of her days. If only she had known!'

'That I was a pauper? That I have no treasure left but the opals? Yes, if only she had known.' Husain's face was shadowed with a poignant sadness that stabbed at Mishaal's heart, not that she intended to let him know.

'If she had discovered the truth, then her nature would have coerced her into some kind of petty revenge. She was always on the watch for slights, usually imagined,' Mishaal mused.

'Stealing the opals, you mean? Perhaps in the darkness she thought that she had put them in her bag, and was planning to sneak away but was halted by her seizure? Some would say that it was Allah, the all-watchful, who struck her down.'

'Yet He knew that I carried the opals but He did not touch me.'

'He knew that you were innocent, little *fáhd*. He also knew that I would come after you for sure if I thought that you had stolen them.'

'Maybe.' Mishaal's voice was husky, her cheeks softly tinged with rose.

'Allah! I'm sure that I would have come after you anyway!'

Mishaal did not reply and looked away. Since he had kissed her that day, matters had changed between them. She could not explain what had happened, other than that her loathing of him had dissipated, yet she was determined that she would not be swayed by this new, tender, solicitous prince who was attempting to woo her by persuasion rather than by force. If she weakened, then she would look at his sword, that brutal weapon that did not judge, flatter or caution but condemned outright, without trial. Had the Amir been able to summon enough courage, then that blade would have hacked off her hand, summarily, and without benefit of any defence.

Why did men have need of such brutal guns and swords? Why did they call them arms, as if even their very own limbs must be capable of slaughtering?

She had never seen the Amir hurt anyone, with or without a weapon, yet he carried that sword with such pride; Shamim said that it had been in his family, handed down, for nearly 400 years, so that in its time it must have been responsible for many deaths. Mishaal had shuddered and said that she did not wish to hear any more. For some reason, men needed the reassurance of killing before they felt secure.

While one half of the world was occupied with creating life, the other half was occupied with its slaughter. Perhaps woman had been created to readjust the imbalance caused by man, but how much easier it all would have been if man were as peaceable as she.

'Mishaal, where are your thoughts?' His velvet-dark voice interrupted her reverie. 'Why are you always so distant from me? If you loved me, my troubles would fade. I would not care if the entire land ran dry, if the grazing lands scorched to dust and the opals were lost to me for ever!'

Mishaal's cheeks burning, she looked away from his fierce black gaze.

'Would you have me disloyal and faithless to the memory of my first love, the one whom you killed with your own hand?'

'No, not with my own hand, Mishaal. *I* did not kill him, I promise you that.'

'Faithful wives are the best, would you not agree? Would you want me to spurn *your* memory within months of your – your . . .' She could not say that word, 'death'. The thought of his dying was too awful. Flushing even more, she jumped to her feet.

'Mishaal!' he called after her, but she was running from him, wishing that there were somewhere safe and shaded to hide, but there was only brilliant, scorching desert and the bright light that seemed to cut through one's bones.

He caught her within a few yards, gripping her arms and pulling her round to face him, willing her to droop into his embrace. Glaring up at him, she struck away his hands.

'If you truly love me, you will not touch me!' she cried, urning before she could see the hurt in his eyes.

Before they had covered many miles, the sky began to darken, he air to cool. Mishaal's back was scored by the sun, her ace only kept from searing by the veil pulled down over her nose.

Her camel seemed indignant. Hurrumphing and snorting, t had been tossing its head every now and again, and now it ooked as if it were preparing to halt.

'There is a wind getting up. We'll have to stop. See those *amra* over there, we'll head for them and see if there's any helter.'

As Husain spoke, the wind began to roar around their ars, slapping into their backs with threatening punches that lmost unseated Mishaal. Turning her camel, she followed he Amir towards the rocks.

There was little shelter there for it was but one low strip of rock, too low to crouch behind. If they lay flat, then their heads would just be protected. Dismounting, Mishaal ran to the *samra*, saw how low they were and bit her lip in consternation. Now the wind was out for the kill, lashing, shrieking and whirling along the desert, and as Mishaal looked in the direction of its approach, she saw a massive curtain of bronze coming towards them.

'Down!' Husain cried, tugging her to the ground beside him, and seconds later the wall of wind-whirled sand broke over them.

Crushed into Husain's chest, she pulled her head veil over them both, while the screeching, venomous sandstorm reared its monstrous head above them. Sand was everywhere, despite their covering, in their mouths and ears and noses, their hair and nails, ingratiated beneath their clothes. Mishaal could feel the gritty uncomfortable texture of it pressing against her flesh under her robe. It felt as if she had some prickly skin disease.

'Don't be afraid, little *fáhd*, the storm will not last too long. Allah has decided that He did not like his housemat over that side of the desert so He has arranged to fly it over here. There is always a logical reason for even the most extraordinary desert weather.'

'You make Allah sound like a discontented housewife!'

'And would you not be if your house was filled with human beings like us? How He must hate that serpent for upsetting His plans!'

'Changing the mat will not get rid of the sinners . . .'

'No, but it will take His mind off them for a few moments,' Husain grinned.

Despite the savagery of the *simûm*, Mishaal found that she was happy. Now she had a perfectly valid reason for clinging to the Amir, her arms round him as if for safety, so that she did not need to battle with her conscience. How powerful his body felt beneath the thin cotton of his desert clothes; there was not a particle of excess fat on his frame and yet he was not bony or frail. Muscles flourished beneath his skin, strong, healthy and reassuring. His shoulders were broad from years of hunting, riding and duelling, his waist lean and narrow, his hips sturdy. As for what lay below, of that she dared not think, for she found herself possessed with the most urgent desire to lower her hands so that she could explore this marvellous and stimulating male body.

The *simûm* seemed to go on for hours. Mishaal wished that she could shake out her veil to rid it of the weight of sand, but she knew that she would be buried in flying grit and debris if she did so. The dark, steamy hollow in which they lay so closely together was hatching the most unexpected feelings inside her . . . Coughing to free her throat of sand, she pretended to be in discomfort so that she could try and shake away the longings that were overpowering her, but it was useless. It was more than the steamy heat of their enforced hide-out that was making her robe cling to her so damply; she was aching with desire; she wanted Husain to kiss her again, claiming her mouth for himself, closing her heart to all other men, all other memories, even those of Drew. She was quite desperate to have this happen, yet she dared not instigate it: what would he think of her?

'You are trembling, little *fáhd*. There is no need to be afraid. It is only sand. Soon, it will stop.'

'You are not afraid?'

'What sort of man would I be if a little whirling sand frightened me? Come closer and try to sleep until it passes. It will not be long now.'

Mishaal nestled closer, but felt many miles away from sleep. She could feel his heart beating, a steady rhythmic sound that reassured her that life and a future still beckoned. Clamping her arms more tightly round his waist, she experienced a happiness which had eluded her for many months, an elevation of spirit that made her mouth tilt into a smile.

Even in the dark, steamy cave, he felt her happiness.

'Why are you smiling, Mishaal? One minute you tremble, then you smile. You are the most baffling of women.'

'I did not, that is, I was not . . .' she caught her lips between her teeth. What could she say, in truth? 'I tremble for you, *Saiyid*'? That would be the most open invitation for him to make love to her. Heat flooded her face and neck;

the desert temperature must have risen ten degrees at least. Sweat trickled down her cheeks and forehead in rivulets.

'Now you tremble again! You do not have a fever?'

'How could I when I am wearing the Koranic charm that Shamim gave to me?' she said, her tones cynical, for the Beduin belief in the all-encompassing protection of their charms was one that she felt she would never be able to share.

To her surprise, the Amir was laughing, taking the chance of an even larger mouthful of sand as his body rocked with delight.

'Mishaal, you should be teaching Beduin children, not wandering around the desert looking for your *nasîb*.'

'But it is not my fate for which I search!' she protested.

'Then you are not like me, for all my life I have been in pursuit of *nasîb* . . . Sometimes it seemed to be in my grasp, then at others it would recede and I would feel that I would never possess it. That is how I felt about you, little *fáhd*.'

She could barely see his face in the sandy, steamy gloom, but she knew that his eyes were overflowing with tenderness. Suddenly she could not swallow; her throat was tight, her heart banging crazily. She tried to speak but only an undignified croak arrived.

'There is a far better way of keeping sand out of the mouth,' he said. 'Here, let me show you.'

It did not matter that their faces were drenched with sweat and burning hot, nor their mouths dew-wet, their bodies sticky and gritty, for when Husain's lips met hers, the world became glorious, the sun glowed with a pleasant, balmy heat, the sun-parched flowers, their white, red and violet petals shrivelled, burst into riotous, swelling bloom, herbs became scented again, rich chamomile and sage, and the *sumr* tree, the dainty and fern-like acacia, sprang from the scorched earth as if by an act of God. The *qaradh* tree bellied out as if there were no wind, its parasol-shaped branches a welcoming shade, and the shiny green *dhodar* bush, native to the *wadi*, gleamed as if freshly lacquered, pride and delight sending the sap soaring through their stems.

In Akbar, a man who had been staring gloomily down one of the dried-out wells, suddenly saw the sparkle of water in the dim interior below. Crying out, he flung up his arms, rushed to tell his neighbours, tripped on his *kuftan* and crashed to the earth, picked himself up, his heart banging crazily, and ran shouting and screaming that the water was back, that Allah had heard their prayers, *the water was back*!

In the courtyard of Rhikia's house, the well remained arid, but one woman, old and nearly blind, swore on the Name of the One True God that she had seen a movement in the depths as if the water was returning.

'No, Faitama,' the others cautioned. 'You see nothing but hope down in the darkness. There is no water. Allah has forsaken us.'

Leaning out of her upper casement window, elbows resting on the baked-earth ledge, Rhikia heard Faitama's claim and the other women quite rightly denouncing it and tears welled in her eyes.

One by one the water sources in the city were failing. Although there had been no rains for months, there had always been the underground streams or the river to supply them. Now the wells that stood over those sources were barren, too. Crops had shrivelled and twisted to charred black fronds; she had seen Mortam-ibn-Ali, the inn-keeper, weeping as he tried to sustain his beloved lemon trees with fermented date juice rather than see them die.

People knew that he stored casks of *nabidh* in his cellar, and that was why there had been a raid on the inn only two nights ago. The city dwellers were terrified that they were going to die of thirst, so Mortam and his wife had been knocked to the ground and all their stores stolen. No one had touched their day's takings.

'Look, Faitama, you were wrong! You saw what you wanted to see!' a woman was crying. 'There is nothing in the well, nothing! Allah has forsaken us. All we can do is pray.'

Aware of nothing save their feelings for one another, Husain and Mishaal kissed a second and third time, clinging close like lost babes in the wilderness, but in finding each other, far from lost.

'My love, you don't know how I've ached for you! I thought you would spurn me for ever, that I would die without having heirs . . . After you, I could not have chosen another bride: I would not have had the heart for it. I want only you, little torch that lights my way . . . I saw you as my beautiful Amira, shining and radiant, beloved by all our people, lighting their way for them, a shining torch . . . Who gave you that name?'

'My mother before she died.' Mishaal's voice was hoarse. She was remembering Maryam's prophecy: the one that Rhikia had so often repeated to her. 'One day, my daughter will light the way for the people of the Land of Mirages.' That was what she had said, and Mishaal had dismissed it as typical of a mother's doting and optimistic fondness. Until now. Her heart seemed to have forgotten how to beat. It was bumping and leaping, knocking against her ribs as if it must escape. She did not know whether to laugh out loud or weep.

'Was your mother a seer?'

'I – I think she must have been. She said what you have just said now, but I did not believe it. I thought nothing of it.'

'From the first moment I saw you I knew that you were different, Mishaal. You could so easily have been coarse and vulgar, intent upon seducing men and enriching yourself, but you're not. You are, well, it seems to me that you're somehow starlit from within. You shine, you glow with sweetness and goodness. You care so much for people . . . everyone from the highest to the low.'

'How can you say that when I was running away? What care was I showing then?'

'But what care was I showing in trying to keep you against your will? You have shown me a side to my nature which I do not like, Mishaal, and it was right that I should discover that I am not as almighty as I thought.' He gave a lopsided grin, revealing sandy white teeth.

'Such modesty from His Highness the Amir of the Land

of Mirages!' Mishaal teased, only to find that she was being caged so fiercely that she could not breathe, and his mouth was on hers, seeking, devouring, branding. She was helpless now, frail and malleable in his arms, but oh so willing.

There, while Allah rearranged his sandy carpet, Mishaal came to understand the true meaning of love, enchanted by kisses that were honeyed moonbeams dancing on her lips, and by words of loving adoration that made her heart beat again. Battened down by the sandy covering, hot and sweltering and gritty, they might have been in Eden, about to discover that knowledge is more stimulating than ignorance, or paradise itself, where man and woman achieve all that is denied them on earth.

How closely and agreeably their bodies moulded, as if fashioned for one another's delight, curve into hollow, muscle against velvet flesh, sinew against satin, hardness against tenderness, eyes dark and mysterious as a desert night gazing into ones as bright and crystalline as newborn ferns; nature's truths and nature's secrets commingling blissfully, a revelation of love.

They did not hear the wind lose heart and crumble away into penitent silence, nor realise that they could throw back the sandy covering and inhale the clear, sharp air that had been purified by the *simûm*; all they knew or cared about was there for them, the man and woman celebrating the ancient primordial rites of love, mouth upon mouth, heart upon heart, thigh upon thigh.

'He did not know himself; in sudden fire
He knelt abjectly as the flames beat higher;
In that sad instant all he had been fled
And passion's smoke obscured his heart and head.
Love sacked his heart; the girl's bewitching hair
Twined round his faith impiety's smooth snare.
The shaikh exchanged religion's wealth for shame,
A hopeless heart submitted to love's fame.
"I have no faith," he cried. "The heart I gave
Is useless now; I am the Christian's slave . . ."'

Husain's words rang in her ears but when she looked at him, his eyes were glittering with humour.

'Is that one poet that Madame Scholar is not familiar with? His name is Farid ud-Din Attar, and he was a Persian mystic of the twelfth century. His birthplace was Neishapour, where Omar Khayyam was also born.'

'Why do you quote those lines, Husain? Do you think that you will lose your religion if you lie with me?'

'I, lose the wealth of Islam? Never!' he grinned. 'We are bound close together, Islam and I. If religion were endangered by lying with those of foreign creeds, then there would be no Muslim Sultans left. All those in their harems were or are of different faiths.'

Nonetheless, his words had made Mishaal uneasy, and she knew why. She, a Christian? Yes, she had boldly declared herself so many times – in the past. But what of now? What of these wilderness days in the company of the *saiyid*? In truth, she no longer knew what she was, Christian or Muslim, but she knew that the uncertainty disturbed her deeply.

'Why do you frown? Have I not shown you that I care for you very much? Do you doubt me?'

'No, I – I doubt myself, *Saiyid*,' she whispered.

'That title is not for my future bride . . . She may call me Husain. Will she do that?' Gently he tilted her chin with his forefinger.

'She – your bride – will, will do that when she is wedded to you, whoever she will be.'

'So you still resist me? Yet you will lie in my arms and let me kiss you as I would my wife . . .'

'In your arms I am happy, perhaps happier than I have been for months, and that is all I know,' Mishaal sighed, 'but I shall never agree to marry you.'

'You ask too much!' Suddenly the raging hauteur of the Rashid dynasty stamped Husain's features and he drew away from her, throwing back the sand-weighted covering so that the sky's light dazzled into her eyes, filling them with sharp, aching tears. Before she knew what he intended, he was striding away from her into the wind-torn desert, leaving her alone and stricken with a piercing misery.

Chapter Twenty-Two

Night shrouded them suddenly, one moment bright day, the next, cavernous dark. Mishaal was caught unawares; perhaps this early night was caused by the *simûm*?

She could not get out of her mind that time, only an hour or so before, when the wind had raged, the sand had flown, and she was in the *saiyid*'s arms. She was shaken and confused at what had happened. He had made love to her so blessedly, and if she died that night, she would die happy because of his kisses, yet he had not taken her: that last, sweet, final joining was omitted. Something had stopped him, yet she knew that he had burned to do so.

And she had burned to be taken by him. Biting on her dry lips, she scanned the horizon, knowing that he would not be far from her and yet terrified that he might have gone. After she had angered him, he had leapt on his camel's back with a grace and competence that she did not think she could ever emulate, and then, from on high, he had shouted to her to follow him.

She had obeyed. What else could she do? She had no food, no water, and her flight of the past two days had shown her how merciless was the desert to those who entered it unprepared. As usual, she had difficulty mounting her camel. First, it would not sink to the ground so that she could stride it, and then it would not get up despite her increasingly angry commands.

From the distance she could sense the *saiyid* watching her blunderings and her face flushed hotly. What did he care? Would he not rush to help her if he loved her as he insisted?

Hot, with sweat pouring down her back and sand rough in the back of her throat, she begged and pleaded with her *dhalul* to rise. It would not. It had closed its eyes, the great drooping lids were down, the long stubby lashes jutting out. During the storm the two beasts had huddled together, heads lowered, eyes closed, accustomed to such weather; it was the times of peace and calm that showed them at their worst, Mishaal mused.

Finally, she shouted: 'The storm is over, idiot *dhalul*, the storm is over! You are safe now, d'you hear me? Allah will protect you, so move, move!'

Nothing happened. Tears pressed behind her eyelids. In a minute she was going to break down and sob in front of that arrogant man who sat astride his camel as if he were Emperor of the World. She would weep with sorrow in front of him, but never with weakness. Blinking, she turned away to spit out sand. However much she rubbed from her ears, nose and eyes, there was always more.

And then, to her chagrin, he called one word, so faint that she could barely catch its sense, and her camel began to rise, lurching forward and backwards in its characteristic way so that she had to cling on desperately with hands and knees. Trust him to know all the animal-training tricks!

She had never seen a camel obey anyone so eagerly. Of course, the Amir Husain ibn Rashid would expect total obedience from the beasts of his kingdom, would he not? Clamping her lips in a thin line, but keeping her face averted as if the scenery to her right was not to be missed, she followed the Amir.

That night they camped near a dried-out *wadi* where once there had been shining green *dhodar* and grey *deni* bushes, and the dainty *sumr* tree, long-thorned and splay-branched, clumps of sweet herbs mingling with the unexpected blossoms of rich yellow and scarlet. Now there were only sharp round stones coating the dip where water would run when the rain came, and on one side a gleaming snail's trail where decades of camel trains had wended their way after drinking.

Dinner was *laban*, scented with leather from its pouch, chunks of goat's cheese, and the interminable dates. Mishaal longed for fresh fruit oozing juice but knew that she ought to be thankful for food at all.

In moments the Amir had made a camp fire and was sitting before it enjoying his repast. It was going to be a cold night and he had thrown a goatskin around his broad shoulders. With the falling darkness and the leaping, lunging flame of the fire, he looked almost primeval, time slipping away so that he might have been an ancient warrior dining with his family after a victorious battle.

Mishaal glowered into her food. He had not spoken to her all that day, yet he would coax and cajole the two camels as if they were dear to him. It was obvious that the track they were following led away from the Beduin camp. The position of the stars had changed considerably. All the same, she refused to be the first to speak after their silly tiff, although she found herself reliving those blissful moments during the sandstorm, growing warm at the memory of his mouth on hers, his body moulded to hers. How foolish she had been to think that such intimacies could alter their disastrous relationship!

If only it were Drew here with her, his laughing eyes kindled by the reflection of the flames, his arms reaching out to pull her close. There was no more honourable man in the world than her Drew. Sadly she corrected herself. *Had* been no more honourable man.

Having eaten all that he required, the Amir ensured that the fire would not die during the night, before curling up beneath his goatskin. It was obvious that he cared more for the camels and the reassurance of his own comforts than he did for hers, or he would have seen her clamp her lips on a cry as she plonked herself down on a stubby, spiny little plant that stabbed her leg. Rubbing at the injury fiercely, Mishaal fought back the words she yearned to shriek at him.

Tomorrow, she would insist that he told her where they were going.

*

The roar woke her with a horrified jolt. For long seconds she could not recall where she was. She could see the stars but there was no reassurance in their infinity. A primordial growl sounded. Tugging the goatskin closer, she tried to shrink into a little ball and peep out from under its shaggy edge to see if the Amir had heard the sound.

The place where he had been sleeping was empty!

She pushed her hand into her mouth to stop herself from crying out. He had left her . . . run off in the night and she was going to be devoured alive by wild desert beasts! She had never heard a growling roar like that, so ferocious, so loud and powerful. Her skin seemed to tighten and shrink, the hairs on the nape of her neck standing out as if chilled by an iced wind.

She heard a crunching sound: a wild beast coming along the shiny stones of the *wadi* to eat her! Now she could not help but scream, hating herself for her cowardice. Then came the roar. Masterful, commanding, it announced: I am the King of the Desert!

'*Saiyid, saiyid!*' she called out, her voice cracking like a child's, but there was no reply.

He had deserted her, vanishing into the wilderness leaving her alone to be horribly, brutally slaughtered by some savage creature with great, sharp fangs.

'Mishaal, why do you sob like an infant?'

The Amir's voice was a miracle coming out of the basalt darkness. Crying his name, she leapt to her feet and flung herself into his arms.

'I thought you had left me! Where were you?'

'I heard the same sound that woke you. I was keeping guard, just over there. Allah, did you think I would leave you here alone?'

'Yes – yes, I did,' she admitted, shamefaced.

'It is a lion. Have you not heard of them? There are not as many as there were years ago in our forefathers' time, but there are still families of them here and there. They are having a hard time of it with no water and many of the animals they would normally feed on are dying of thirst. He is restive that one, do you hear him? Something has disturbed his sleep, but he won't attack us.'

'How can you be so sure?'

'We are not to his liking. We are too sinewy and stringy for his taste. You see, he will go off in another direction very soon.'

'And if he comes our way?'

'Then I will defend us, but only if I have to. I do not willingly destroy those whom Allah created.'

'You killed my Drew!'

The words were out before she could bite them back. She felt his body stiffen, his head fly up.

'No, I did not kill your Drew,' he said, his jaw clenched.

'But you let your men do it! Perhaps this affectation of yours not to kill those whom Allah has created is only tenable because you have men to do your dirty work for you?'

His arm fell away. She felt as if the Ice Age had returned, that ancient time when they said the rocks and the sand and the hills were turned to great, glistening chunks of ice. He was shunning her and she could not bear it. Yet what she said was true. How could he deny it?

'Your Drew was a thief. He planned to steal the Jewels of Destiny which are rightly mine and my people's!'

'Oh, you and your jewels and your destiny! You're obsessed with them! All I ever hear is jewels and gems and opals and – and – how you want to marry me – and –'

The lion's roar came again, just a few yards away, loud, insistent and blood-freezing. Yelping, Mishaal threw herself back into the Amir's arms, clinging to him with a desperation that would have cheered him enormously had it not been because she feared that she would become a lion's dinner.

They clung together in the darkness while the lion circled them, snuffling now and again as if trying to get their scent, and scuffling at the rocks with thick-padded paws.

'He is after something more succulent than us,' the Amir whispered. 'A jerboa or something bigger.'

'If he attacks us, will, will you use your sword to kill him?' Mishaal whispered hoarsely, her calves trembling.

'No, my bare hands, of course. Why should I bother with a weapon?' The Amir's eyes glittered dangerously.

'You would not!' she gasped.

'Does the thought of my wrestling with a lion touch your heart? Would you weep if I were killed?'

'No, I would, would . . .' Gulping, she plunged her head into his shoulder, squeezing her eyes tight as if by doing so she could shut out the image of him being mauled and savaged.

'Little *fáhd*, you do have a heart!'

Tilting her chin, he looked down lovingly into her eyes, and in the next glorious moment she had flung her arms round his neck and he was hugging her so passionately that her feet left the ground.

'Oh, my little rebel . . . my wild one, what are we to do with you? Allah, if only I had been able to school myself in the ways of a woman's mind before I met you, but I did not have ten years to spare for such study,' he teased, while she craved for him to kiss her, over and over, until her heart sang.

The lion was going in the opposite direction, concentrating on his kill. Moments later came the agonised, piercing scream of the creature he had trapped. Unearthly, the screech tingled along Mishaal's spine like cold, barbed fingers.

'He will sleep now, in his den,' the Amir comforted. 'We shall be safe.'

'I might have been his dinner but for you,' Mishaal whispered huskily.

Laughing, Husain caught her up in his arms, swinging her into the air with barely an effort, and carrying her to their little camp where he placed her gently on her goatskin.

'Even the lion is of Islam. His meat must be bled before he eats,' Husain reflected aloud.

'Do not speak of it. It is horrible!' Mishaal entreated.

'Have you never eaten meat then?'

'Yes, but no longer.'

'You are surely not telling me the truth? How would it be possible to survive without it?'

'Many poor Beduin do so for months on end.'

'That is true, but they are bred to it. You are not.'

'How do you know? My tutor never touched meat. He said that one became the same as what one ate, and if meat must be bloodless, as ordained by the Prophet, then he would become bloodless from eating it.'

'A novel notion, but it does not hold water. There is still strength in the lion.'

'How do we know that he might not be even stronger without meat?' Mishaal tossed her head, seeing that she was on the way to losing the argument. 'Camels and goats live on greenery and see how tough they are!'

'That is so, but then Allah willed it that they should be eaters of grass and herbs. It is in His scheme of things.'

'And what of us? Did Allah ordain that we should be eaters of herbs, grass and meat? How do you know?'

'Because we have His words in the holy book, his instructions and advice on every aspect of life.'

'Yes, I know. "Three things only has He forbidden you: carrion, blood, the flesh of swine, what has been hallowed to other than God, the beast strangled, the beast beaten down, the beast fallen to death, the beast gored, and that devoured by beasts of prey – excepting that you have sacrificed duly – as also things sacrificed to idols, and partition by the divining arrows; that is ungodliness,"' Mishaal quoted the *Qu'ran* to perfection.

'I continue to be astonished that a dancing girl has any education,' Husain retorted, stung at her incisive and knowledgeable recital. However modern-thinking and enlightened he believed himself to be, it was at moments such as this that the overbearing masculinity of his forefathers surfaced, white-hot and intractable. There was a place for woman, and it was not above man.

'When the Prophet said that he who goes out in search of knowledge is in God's path until he returns, he did not put any bar on the sex of those who learn!' Mishaal reminded.

'But he did say that "Righteous women are obedient, and those who are rebellious should be admonished, banished to their couches and beaten"!'

'Ah yes, of course, pick on those who are smaller and weaker and treat them with cruelty!'

'Have I ever been cruel to you?' The Amir's cheeks were dark bronze with emotion, his eyes flint-bright and accusing. Stepping close, he gripped her by the shoulders, shaking her furiously so that her veil fell to the ground and the bones clicked in her neck.

Undaunted, she cried: 'There is time yet! I have not known you that long!'

'I think that my true nature would have revealed itself by now,' he growled, keeping that imprisoning grip on her shoulders.

'But it is! At this very minute! You are hurting me, you are trapping me, so that you can do what you want with me . . . I will not bend to your will, so you use force! How can you deny it?'

'*Bîllah 'alaik,* woman! For God's sake! You will drive my senses from me.'

Nonetheless, he dropped his hands from her so suddenly that she reeled, blaming the paralysing chill upon the blustering wind that gushed past them seconds later. She felt lost without his touch, but she would blame it on that wind until the day she died, she swore it!

They stood there, avoiding one another's glance, feeling stupid at the paroxysm they had bred with their unaccountable antagonism, while the unbidden wind danced around their feet in a twisting, lurching carousel, as if to say, 'Notice me, in the Name of Allah, notice me!'

Chapter Twenty-Three

Love's conflagration fills my heart and head;
All patience, reason, strength have turned and fled!
Renew your courage, put aside your fear
And in love's fire let reason disappear.

Farid ud-din Attar

'Why is there such a secret about where we are going?'

Mishaal was squatting on her goatskin eating dates and trying to imagine that they were bright, scented fruits pouring with juices. They had been travelling for three days and, with each passing hour, they journeyed farther and farther from the Amir's camp and the city where Mishaal had grown up. She was saddle sore, sick of dates and fermented milk, and yearning for fresh, cool sweet water. She dreamed of it trickling over her body as she lay in the gentle, soothing hollow of a *wadi*, with lulling velvet rain dewing her face and calming her senses.

Once, she had fallen asleep in the saddle, her dreams filled with sparkling rain and rushing, healing waters, only to wake in alarm as she lurched forward in the saddle.

'Are you all right?' the Amir cried, and, furious at herself, she snapped back that she was perfectly all right! She did not meet his eyes so failed to see the look of loving concern welling in his own.

Now he was searching for sweet herbs to feed the camels, digging with his hands into the rough and stony earth, regardless of his nails breaking. Looking up at her question, his face dissolved into the most radiant, shining smile, its force so stunning that she felt her heart jolt. Then suspicion clouded her reaction. Why did he smile in that mysterious way, yet remain silent? What was he keeping from her?

'Will you not tell me where we are heading? Why will you not tell me? You vow that you are never cruel and yet what is this if not cruelty?'

He squatted down beside her, his eyes glittering and unfathomable as ever. There was no water to wash the gritty earth stains from his hands and so he rubbed at them with the inner corner of his cloak, while Mishaal waited for an answer.

'You would not come with me if you knew where I was heading,' he said at last.

'Why not? What choice do I have? Do you mean you would let me go home if I chose it? Let me go home then! Let me go now!' Her voice rose sharply.

'There is no choice about it, not for either of us.' Having

spoken, the Amir clamped his mouth shut as if he would never speak again, while Mishaal clenched her fists and visualised leaping at him to box his ears.

As the silence lengthened, she sighed, staring up at the skies and back down again in exasperation.

'If you do not tell me where we are going, I shall refuse to move from here!'

Amazingly, he roared with laughter.

'Will you chain yourself to the rocks over there? Do you think you are so heavy that I could not pick you up with one arm and fling you over my camel?'

'Ah yes, the he-man tactics again . . . Always force and muscle, but never gentle persuasion!'

'Only where a woman is so witless and stubborn that she will not *see* reason!'

'How quickly the insults fly when you fail to get your own way, Amir. What a great disservice the world has done you by agreeing with your every word until now,' she taunted, salaaming deeply towards him with mock reverence, her eyes scathing. 'Anyone who fails to support the Amir's view is witless and stubborn and should be banished to their couches and beaten!'

'Yes, I should beat you until some sense permeated that hard little head of yours.' He flexed his hands. 'And banishment sounds like the best idea you've had yet.'

'Banish me then! I am willing . . . Let me go back to my home and you shall never hear from me again. Would that not suit you, O Great Majestic Highness?'

'No, wild one, it would not. What of your destiny? Only a coward would skulk away now . . .'

'My destiny? What do you mean? You talk in riddles all the time!'

'"The torch that lights the way for her peoples . . ." There is little sign of that glowing light now, is there?' His mouth curled.

'*My* peoples?' You make me sound like some great queen or sultana . . . I am no one, Husain ibn Rashid, no one!' she cried, bunching her fists and sweeping them through the air in fury.

For response, he turned his face away muttering something

beneath his breath and she tried to quell her noisy breathing so that she could catch his words. But she did not succeed, and she refused to ask him to repeat it. Once a woman showed curiosity about a man, she was lost.

He began to gather up their belongings, throwing parched grit and soil on the fire to quench it. He studiously avoided looking in her direction, while she longed to attract his attention in some way, any way, and see his beautiful, old-gold eyes lighten as he gazed on her, his mouth widening into that heart-shaking smile.

She flung her possessions together, tying them in a clumsily knotted scarf, not seeing that she had forgotten a package of dates and a slab of the delicious yet thirst-makingly-sweet confection that he had brought with him. Made of nuts, honey and chocolate, it was pleasant only when there was plenty to drink.

Seeing what she had overlooked, the Amir picked up the packages and followed her to her camel where he took the untidy baggage from her hand, pushing in the dates and the *halva* whereupon the entire flimsily tied fabrication slipped open, its contents cascading to the ground.

'Look what you've done, you stupid, clumsy, interfering man!' Mishaal cried, her face flushing. She had no doubt that he had done it on purpose for the delight of seeing her having to assume a grovelling position to retrieve her possessions.

'It is never your fault is it, little *fáhd*, always mine . . . If you wrap your food with the artlessness of a two-year-old, then that is my fault, and if it falls in the dust, then that is my fault also . . .' He arched one ebony brow.

'Yes, of course, of course!' Mishaal lashed out furiously, feeling her nail nick his cheek as her hands flew, and seeing a scarlet plume of blood form on his skin.

Slowly, he touched his face, then looked down at the blood on his hand. She stepped back, mortified at what she had done. She had never meant to fetch blood.

'If you had young to defend I could understand your behaviour, but you do not . . .' he said, almost as if speaking to himself.

His eyes were bright with hurt, and she was ashamed. Looking down, she bit on her mouth and wished herself far from there. No one was more surprised than she when his arms came out to draw her close, and the taste of his blood was salt on her lips as he kissed her emphatically, with a finesse and circumspection that moved her despite herself. No, not despite herself: because of herself.

'I could not love you more if I tried for a thousand decades,' he whispered against her cheek. 'I thought when the *simûm* came that we had found one another, and I was so deliriously happy, yet now we fight like bitter enemies again. Why, little *fáhd*, why?'

'You shut me out of your thoughts . . . You tell me nothing! I might be a slave in bondage dragged through the desert for all you care!' Mishaal burst out.

'Let Allah be my witness, I love you, and always shall. You must remember that I have led my people for many years and I am unaccustomed to explaining my actions, especially to a woman.' As she began to push him angrily away, he said, 'No, forgive me for saying that, I know it sounds arrogant, but it is true! I am willing to change, or try to change, my heart of hearts, believe me, I am . . .'

Peridot eyes stared deeply into mysterious, basalt ones searching for the veracity of his words. Did he mean what he said, or was it yet more lies to make her lower her defences?

Again his head came down, and she could not resist, nor draw back as his mouth claimed hers so sweetly, so confidently, reassuringly. Her heart felt as if it were swelling, aching with joy as she responded, the delight of his embrace reaching far beyond anything she had ever experienced. Within the sweet circle of his arms she was transformed, no longer a bewildered orphan who had spent her years trying to conceal the bruises on her heart, the deep inner conflict about her origins. Here, with this man, she was a queen, wrapped with love, veiled in sweet joy, trembling from brow to toe at his nearness.

They were brought back down to earth by her camel belching, and suddenly they were both laughing, still clinging tightly as if they would drown if they broke apart.

Mishaal gazed up at him in wonderment as if seeing him for the first time. His hair was wildly black, its curving strands blown into antagonism by the winds, specks of dust and sand flecking his face, his skin darkened by exposure to the sun so that his eyes looked even more like glossy black pearls, their lashes far too long for a man and gleaming like silk. There were no lines upon his face, save for those bred by laughter, and she knew deep in her heart that there could not be a better sign if she were looking for a cherishing companion. Why had she fought against his love? This was the man she wanted and needed, the only man in the world for her. There would never be another whom she loved and adored so profoundly, so heart-stoppingly, as this.

Her heart seemed to judder to a halt, lurching so that she had to swallow to calm its rapid movement. Had she been asked, she could not have said whether it was night or day, whether the sky was denizened with stars or rich rose-gold with sunlight. Nothing existed for her but his face, his beloved face and the brilliant, reverent tenderness filling his eyes.

Unbelieving, she reached out to trace his lips, those nobly delineated lips that bedazzled her senses. How handsome was his mouth; there was no meanness there, no petulant curl or avaricious tightness, nothing but the most generous, open and valorous curves, such strength and yet such sensitivity. Her fingertips tingled as she traced them across the upper lip and then the lower, then moved on to his jaw where the bold, fearless lines left no room for any hint of weakness. He loved her; he truly loved her; and she loved him . . .

'Heart of my hearts, my desert rose,' he whispered and she caught and savoured his words so that they sang their way directly to her heart, carolling and bright as the silver-tongued song of mythical birds. 'I would give up all I have for you, my little lioness, all. I want to make you my Amira and crown you with gold and rubies, and dress you in the rarest silks the world can offer . . . But I cannot. All I have to give you is my love, my unchanging love, and the promise that you will always be my one and only wife, for I shall never take another.'

'Husain,' she sighed his name, her head dropping to his chest. In her mind's eye she had seen his hands rising above her head, and in them was a glittering gold coronal studded with gems so brightly dazzling that they eclipsed the sunlight's beams pouring down on them through swirling motes of dust. Blinking, the vision was gone, but it left its aura, one that stayed with her for some time. No doubt her imagination had created that coronal as a symbol of the weight of the responsibilities that she would have as his bride . . . Perhaps that was what she feared most, and what had kept her from admitting that she loved him? Gone would be her hope of freedom, her youthful, carefree days, the peace of solitude when she wished, the hours of daydreaming that were such sweet balm. Yet she had not thought herself cowardly . . .

'Say that you will marry me!' he pressed, holding her so close that it was as if they had been forged into one being that no one could ever put asunder. 'Say it now, my heart, before you change your mind!'

'I – will . . .' she halted, seeing the carefree days slipping away, knowing that her life would never be the same after this, and that he would have won: she would be his slave and he could do with her as he willed. 'I fear the – the loss of my freedom,' she whispered. 'Marriage is slavery . . . I do not want to be a slave!'

'Slavery? You, my slave? Mishaal, my beloved, I am *your* slave, can you not see that? I am your slave!' Gently he tilted her little pointed chin, and looked so deeply into her eyes that she could not stop herself from trembling.

She felt a choking in her throat as if it could not take any more emotion, and she hid her face again, her arms wrapped round his narrow waist so that he became her anchor, and in that moment she knew that she would never founder again, that he would always be beside her, and, in knowing that, she could lay all her ghosts to rest.

'Mishaal, answer me: have pity on me!'

'I – I, yes, I – may say yes, one day soon, but do not

press me now!' Pink-cheeked, she felt a surge of heat weave through her body. She had wanted to say yes, was going to say yes, but she could not find the necessary courage, although her heart told her otherwise.

'Must I be satisfied with that answer for now?'

'Y-yes,' she stammered, sad that she had failed him, and yet knowing that she could not have done otherwise at this point.

'Then it shall be so.'

With his words, she knew such a rising of joy that she wanted to cry out, 'I shall be your wife! Yes, yes, I shall be your wife!' but this time he put his lips to her mouth and their kisses said everything that needed to be said.

That night, they made camp with lighter hearts than they had known for months, and while Husain lit the fire and gathered their goatskins round it, Mishaal put out their food, the sweetmeats, the dates and figs, the fermented milk, and a few dried herbs that would crush in the tongue with a heady, lilting fragrance that went straight to her head when she was thirsty.

The camels were chomping on the brittle grass, making their usual greedy and unschooled noises. The night was starry and piercingly clear and the heavens had never seemed closer or more miraculous. If Mishaal reached up, she was sure that she could touch those sparkling silver stars and bring them down to look at them more closely, for were they not one of Allah's greatest creations?

Allah. His name still sounded foreign on her tongue. She knew that she had given her heart to the Christian God, wanting Him and needing Him because of Drew, because she had believed that Drew and his God were her destiny. To turn her back on that Christian God was not easy. She told herself repeatedly that it was the same God and that a change of name did not change the truth, but still she felt as if they were separate, as if entire universes stood between them, with no possibility of their being united.

A little rain had fallen, saluting them with its sudden

military descent, sharp and hard on their heads and backs. It was nowhere near enough to moisten a land that was parched as stone, but it succeeded in filling a *wadi* so that they could refill their water flasks. When they had done so, and drunk their fill, Mishaal leapt into the rushing stream that was now cascading along the *wadi* bed. It came up to her calves, its blessed coolness a heavenly libation. She was ready in that moment to believe in every god who had ever been worshipped.

Splashing around triumphantly, she forgot the trials of the past few days and all that had gone before, remembering nothing save for this miracle.

Watching, a few yards away, his face ready to display interest in the cactus-like plants that he was cutting open for their succulent pulp, Husain felt a thrill surge through his body. She was like a sprite leaping and jumping in the fleeing water, her face illumined with a childlike glow that twisted at his heart. He had never known a woman like her; she was the embodiment of perfection to him, so lithe and graceful, her nature generous and noble. With a pang of cold horror he recalled how he had stood over her, his sword in readiness to hack off her hand. How could he have considered such a vile act, even if she had stolen his jewels?

What would *his* crime have been if he had maimed her for life, or left her to bleed to death in the desert wilderness? Would Allah have forgiven him? Maybe, but he would never have forgiven himself. Relentlessly he had pursued her these past months, wanting her beyond belief, and at the end of that pursuit, he would have given her a thief's death . . .

Shame struck at him, so that his hand trembled, and the sword that had been in his family for generations slipped from his damp palm.

As it lay there on the sand, he found himself staring at it, the sword that had literally fallen from heaven . . .

He had not heard her come up behind him, for her feet were bare and clogged with sand that was now plastering their wetness. The hem of her robe was dark with water; her face was shining.

'Why do you look at your sword in that way?'

'I remembered something from long ago. Do you know how long this sword has been in my family?' She shook her head. 'Seven hundred years. Seven hundred years! My ancestors were grazing their camels in a place where they had never rested before. It was a time of drought, just as it is now, and the desert dwellers were suffering great hardship. They were forced to travel farther and farther into the wilderness in search of grazing land, just as we have been doing this year. The old ones fought against making camp in this new place . . . they said that it was taboo, that man had worshipped a false and hideous idol there, a woman god. Can you imagine what anathema that notion was to the sturdy old Beduin?' Husain's eyes twinkled mischievously. 'There was a *haikal*, an ancient temple where all these heresies had been committed, but because of its idolatry, the place was taboo. No man must approach or enter, for fear of losing his soul and offending Allah so deeply that he would be cast out from his people for all time.'

'But your ancestors did camp there, because of the drought?'

'Yes, yet all the while the elders threatened disaster and damnation. And then as they sat around their evening fire, they heard the most fearful and blood-chilling sound, a great, ear-cracking roaring, rushing noise . . . It was like thunder yet without the storm, an earthquake without the quake. High above them they saw a blinding white light of such brilliance that they thought they would be blinded; stronger grew the light until it equalled the sun's brightness at noon, and the heat from it was so intense that they feared they would be roasted.

'The animals screamed and fell. Men hid their faces and awaited death. Then there was a terrifying shuddering as if the ground would gape and suck them into its depths, and the sound was transformed from a roaring into a whining hiss that pitched towards them. Then they heard the crashing impact as something hit the earth, and the air became thick with the smell of sulphur.

'By morning, some were dead, mangled and scorched in a way never seen before. Close by, there was a deep gouge in the sand, a crater, and in its centre was buried what proved to be a meteorite.'

'What is that?' Mishaal asked, her expression rapt.

'Those mysterious bodies high above us in the skies, the ones that can be seen when the air is very clear, those are the planets. Some of them are older than time itself and very sturdy; they will always be there; others, smaller and more fragile can be split and broken up by whatever forces prey on them. Sometimes, one of those fragments will fall to earth.'

'I see, and what happened then?' Mishaal was trying to imagine what a meteorite would look like, would it be ferociously hot, and scalding to the touch, as she imagined the sun would be, or cold as the icily-glittering stars?

'Some men died, along with their camels, buried beneath the rubble of stones and sand erupted by the collision. Men could not wait to get away from that spot. Now, even more than ever, it was taboo. There was talk of the pagan god's fury and her revenge on Islam. At that time, my father's ancestor was seven years old, and he never forgot that night, although he was forbidden to speak of it because he had narrowly missed death and his mother wept whenever the story was raised. He was her only son.'

'What of his father?'

'His father had died when he was five . . . in a plague epidemic brought to the desert dwellers by travellers from the city. It is not uncommon for the men of my family to become tribal leaders at an early age.'

'And what happened when he grew up? Was he allowed to speak of the meteorite then?'

'He did more than speak of it. He went back to the place that was taboo, and searched until he found the crater in the earth. It was exactly as he remembered it from childhood. He and his followers cleared the crater, removing all the rocks and stones, and in the process finding the skeletons of the men and camels that had died on that terrible night. After giving them proper burial, they returned to the crater to find that it had begun to fill with water, and so they named it *Bir er-Ra'ad*, the Fountain of Thunder. Along with the stones and debris cleared from the hole came fragments of the meteorite itself, bluish-coloured, streaked with silver and extraordinarily light in weight. My ancestor, Hamid ibn Husain, decided that it would make a magnificent sword for then he could say in truth that he ruled by the highest laws of the land. And so it was fashioned into a weapon some two and a half feet in length, and it needed little polishing because it gleamed constantly, and still gleams until today, all these centuries after. Ornamentation was added, as befitted an Amir's sword, a hilt was made for it by a silversmith in Damascus, and a gold-embossed scabbard, and the greatest artist of his day designed a *Qu'ranic* charm to be engraved into the blade. From that day, the sword has been called "the Sword of God" and is given to the heir when he becomes ruler of the tribes.'

Mishaal's eyes were on the scabbard hanging from Husain's belt. Could this be for the Sword of God itself? Eagerly she reached out to touch, caressing the embossing. It looked like new; she did not think that it could be all those hundreds of years old.

'This is not that same sword is it? Found in the place that was taboo?' Her eyes were growing dreamy, the peridot seeming to change into a misty *eau-de-nil* with a sparkling silver sheen; her face had relaxed, her mouth drooping a little, her head dropping down into her neck. Before he answered, she knew that it was, for she was reliving the tremors of the earth and the heavens as the meteorite disgorged its particles towards the unsuspecting Beduin below. Wielded as by the very hand of Allah, this fragment had caused a man's death as it crashed to the sands. She even knew his name.

'There was a man called Ali ibn Hassid in your tribe at that time?'

'Yes, how did you know? He was Hamid's uncle and protector, a good man who –'

'He was an evil man. He was planning to murder Hamid and take his place as Amir. This very fragment of heaven rock which was made into this sword was the same that struck Hassid on the temple and killed him outright. It was the Will of the one true God . . .' Mishaal's voice fading, she closed her eyes, then opened them as if someone had placed a cold hand on her neck.

Husain was holding her in his arms, astonished at what she had said. Even if she had been wrong about Hassid, how had she known his name, and that he had died in the meteorite disaster? Now she was clinging to him as if petrified, her slender body quivering, and he was showering her with kisses and caresses to soothe her. Yet all the while he was asking himself, 'How did she know? *How?*'

Chapter Twenty-Four

Would it be the same place, the very same temple of the Mother Goddess? If it were, then it would be like returning to his roots, for the Sword of God had been lifted out of the depths of the earth. He wondered if the Fountain of Thunder would still be flowing? If they ever got there, he would know.

He had told her their destination; curled in his arms, by the light of their camp fire the previous night, he had spoken of the Jewels of Destiny, feeling her grow taut in his embrace as she tried to move away from him.

'Jewels! Is that all men think of?' she had cried, her cheeks flushing.

'Not *any* jewels, but the legendary Jewels of Destiny. You cannot deny that you know of them . . . you and your American were in search of them when we found you.' He spoke in a matter-of-fact voice, forcing himself not to reveal even the slightest tremor of emotion. Oh, if she guessed the rigours of jealousy that he had suffered thinking of her with that fortune hunter! He could not risk speaking of it for fear that all his true feelings would erupt. Every time he thought of her with that brigand, he wanted to explode in a searing fury that would equal any meteorite. How dared that *nasrani* invade his lands and try to steal his woman?

He could not visualise life without his little *fáhd*. He had never known how piercingly lonely he was until he looked deep into her bright-green eyes and fell in love with her. From then on, his life had been complete, and the half of him that he had not realised was empty, was filled, a holy grail overflowing with love.

'Why are they different from any others?' There was a strange uneasy light in Mishaal's eyes, or was it the reflection of the fire? He could almost imagine that the flames were inside her eyes, and that the reflection was real and the reality reflection. 'You have the opals.'

'They would feed my peoples for a day and then there would be nothing – if I sold them. By tradition, the bride of the chieftain wears them on her marriage day.'

'If I ever agreed to be your bride, do you think that I would put vanity before the needs of your people?' She sounded astonished that he could think so.

'No, but it would be a matter of pride to me that you could wear them.'

'Oh, pride! Put that aside with vanity; they are of no use!' Impatiently, she pushed at his hands when they sought to enclose her again.

'So you would marry me in rags, without a jewel to proclaim your status?'

She was warned by his sleepy expression; he thought that he could trick her into replying, 'Yes, of course!' Smiling gently, she arched her brows.

'If I ever married, it would be for love, not for gems and status. Now tell me why I had to come along on this quest? Why was it necessary?'

'I was sure that you would refuse if you knew where we were heading. It would revive unhappy memories for you, I thought, and so you would say no.'

'Only partly right.' She tossed her head.

He sighed. Why did she have to be so intransigent? If only

she could have had Nur's docile nature . . . but then of course he would not have loved her so ardently. Who would love a mouse when they can love a lioness?

'I needed you with me, little *fáhd*. Until I found the opals gone, I had planned to set out on this journey within a week or two. The drying wells in Akbar and the problem of finding water delayed me. I planned to take a party of companions, plenty of provisions, and you.'

'Why me?'

'Sometimes you can be very obtuse, Mishaal! Because I love you, because I need and want you with me, because I did not know how long the search would take. Also . . .'

'Yes?' Now would come the true reason.

'You saw the treasure map.'

'Ah, now it is out! You need me because you think that I know where the jewels are!' Outraged, she leapt to her feet, almost stepping into the fire in her fury. Lurching inelegantly, she could feel her heel catch in the hem of her robe. Cursing beneath her breath, she struggled for balance, maintained it, and stalked off into the blackness of the desert night.

'Mishaal!' She heard his voice, keen with urgency but she refused to turn back. She was not scared of lions or wolves or anything else that lurked in the blackness. There had been plenty to drink that day and she was refreshed, her exhaustion lifted. She would walk and walk and walk and he was not going to catch her.

'Mishaal!'

She heard his footsteps thudding in the sand as he ran to catch up with her, and then to her amazement he was smacking at her ankles, hard enough to make them sting. Furious, she slapped back at him and then, feeling the cold air on the backs of her legs, she gave a little gasp of horror. Somehow she had set her robe on fire when she stumbled, and he had run after her and beaten out the flames with his bare hands.

The pungent smell of burning cloth rose to her nostrils as he pulled her into his arms and kissed the anger from her soul. What an idiot she could be; he had saved her from a terrible death. He could have laughed at her and watched her burning; she had insulted him yet again. Why was he so patient with her?

'Is – is it truly because you think I saw the map?'

'Of course, what else?' he lied. 'And if you tell me that you didn't see it and have no idea where the treasure is, then I shall push you over the first cliff that we come to!' Grinning, he clamped her tightly to him so that her feet left the ground.

'I – I did see it,' she whispered.

'You did?' He held her at arm's length, conscious that his palms were beginning to burn where they had quenched the flames.

'Yes.'

'Can you remember any of it?' He could not keep the glint of excitement from his eyes.

'You said you did not want me for that, but only because you loved me! If you loved me you would not ask!'

And with that, she stormed back to their little camp and curled up tightly in her goatskin, refusing to speak to him again that night.

She woke to the ear-cracking sound of the desert birds. How fulsome was their song when there was no wall or tent to take the brunt of it.

Hearing the crackle of the fire, she opened her eyes carefully so that he would not see she was awake. He was squatting beside the flames, roasting a small creature that he must have caught while she slept. The tantalising aroma of meat rose to her nostrils and made her stomach gurgle so loudly that she was sure he would hear, but he seemed preoccupied with what he was doing. Then she saw the rags bound round his palms and her heart lurched. She had forgotten about his burned hands; she had not cared one jot for his discomfort. How dare she speak to him of pride? She was the proud one!

'Will you eat some meat?'

He knew she was awake. How had he guessed?

Despite the loud rumblings in her stomach, she said, 'No! Find me some herbs if there are any . . . please.'

'A little meat wouldn't hurt you, or your principles, I'm

sure. Allah would forgive you for weakening under such circumstances.'

It was a figure of speech, but it was also a red rag to the bull to suggest that she might weaken.

'No, thank you. There are still plenty of dates left,' she said primly.

The *laban* was improving with age and heat and could now be scooped out in large, solid white chunks which were tartly refreshing and cooling. Mishaal devoured her share without looking at Husain who was chewing on his roasted meat with enjoyment. *Laban* was very filling and she never felt hungry after eating it. It was also very soothing on sunburnt skin and she gently patted it into her face, especially her nose, every day. When she finished, she looked up to see Husain watching her quizzically, his mouth in readiness to give that wide grin that broke her heart up into a trillion shining pieces.

She was angry with herself for behaving selfishly. But, so that he would not suspect how much she wanted to grin back, she tossed her head and compressed her lips tightly.

She started to pack up their belongings, with a little more care than last time, and prepared to mount her camel for the day's journey. While she worked, he did not speak. She was sure that he was desperate to question her about the treasure map, but if he did, she would ignore him. To think that she might have believed him when he said he loved her and it had all been so that she would tell him what she knew about the map! What deceit and trickery, and he dared to accuse her of taking his wretched opals!

As they rode, she pondered over their destination. She had little trouble recalling the details of Drew's map, but understanding it was another matter. She had seen the place marked with a star, and Drew had commented that that was his lucky star, but, other than that, she had not known the name of the area. No one would go near it, he said, more fool them, because his employer, Lord Tavenish, had come across this map while he was in the Land of Mirages and it clearly showed that there was ancient and very precious treasure hidden there.

'How does it tell you that?' she had wanted to know, poring

over the map but unable to recognise anything out of the ordinary except for the blotchy ink of the hastily-scrawled star.

'There were papers with the map. My employer lived here for some time, he explored, he travelled. He was planning a series of books on the Arab way of life.'

'Why did he not come himself this time?' Mishaal had asked.

'Illness, alas. He has everything that a man could wish, respect, esteem, great wealth, a title – he is the Earl of Tavenish – but his health has caused him unending anxiety. The intense heat affected him while he was here, and he went down with a fever from which he never really recovered.'

'That is sad. Does he not have a wife to love him?

'A wife? He has buried three wives, and now lives alone. He is too old to consider remarriage, so he says, and besides, a wife would view him solely for his property and title, would she not? One must beware of fortune hunters.'

'Would it not be better to marry someone who stayed with you because of your money rather than live a lonely old age?'

Laughing, Drew had ruffled her hair.

'What a little romantic you are,' he had said.

Mishaal and Husain halted at a small deserted oasis, where once there had been water and date palms. Now there was nothing but parched sand and rocks, a small hard hole where once there had been water, and the twisted stumps of long-dead trees, their life juices scorched away by the sun.

Remembering the brief rainfall and the streaming *wadi*, Mishaal dreamed of leaping into cool, rushing water that would swirl past her hot and dusty ankles and revive her. They were now deep in the Land of Mirages, a place where travellers had enjoyed – or suffered – mirages of such beauty and such horror that some had lost their minds.

What a glorious ebullient moon there had been the night before. It had hung over them like an omen of favoured bliss, a sign from the one true God that He approved, the roundest and most opulent pearl ever seen in all eternity. Behind it, the sky had been dark as jet and mysteriously empty; somehow, the stars had vanished.

'They have eloped,' Husain said, grinning, his fingers caressing her little pointed chin as if it were precious crystal. 'They wish to emulate us.'

His fingers were charmed, they stirred such a multitude of passions and emotions deep within her. If his hands could arouse her like that, what would his kisses do beneath that ebullient moon.

Their eyes caught and held, and she blushed while he adored her openly, whispering her name beneath his breath as if it were a prayer, which, to him, it was.

Sighing, she went willingly into his arms, clasping him closely and knowing that if she died at that moment then she would die the happiest and most blessed woman in Arabia. His lean, muscular body against hers composed a sweet and heady music that serenaded her senses until her eyes and ears and mouth could see and hear and speak nothing else but him, the beloved.

In the distance wild beasts howled at the pearldrop moon, their hearts gorged with longing and desire, yet they would never know why they were suffering, or be able to sate their unnamed cravings, while she knew it all, everything, from the first beginnings when man went into woman's arms and they kissed for the first time and the world stood still and silent in salutation. As knowledge swarmed in her veins, she envisioned time receding, into the misty ancient past when man and woman had draped themselves in animal skins and hunted for their food. Then, they had worshipped the Mother Goddess, Mother Earth herself, fashioning clay images that were rotund and voluptuous, the stomachs swelling to honour the miraculous birth of the child, emerging from that warm, cushioned haven, and bringing with it continuity and perpetuity; a future, and the reassurance and comfort of hope.

Fecund mother goddess . . . How they had revered her, with worship and sacrifice, in the deep, dark places of the earth itself, the low, eerie caves that represented her childhaven, and into which the snakes slipped and vanished, returning to their Mistress, so that they too were revered because they lived so close to Her.

And as the decades went by, she became taller and fairer,

goddess of love and grace, and fertility, mother of the crops and flowers, the begetter of the earth itself, creator of all things, honoured in every part of the world; Artemis and Inanna, Venus, Demeter; and the greatest mystery of all: that she not only gave birth to infants in her own image, but in man's image also . . .

'Where are you, Mishaal?' His beloved voice brought her out of her reverie. 'When I kiss you, your eyes cloud over as if you are seeing images invisible to me, and your spirit flies . . .'

Nuzzling into his neck, she sighed. 'There is something about this place . . . I sense hidden things here, more strongly than I ever did in the city.'

'So you are a seer, and you never let me know!'

'I do not see things, they see me . . . Oh, how can I explain? The images come to me of their own accord: I cannot summon them.'

'What were you seeing then?'

'This place hundreds, thousands, of years ago, when the Mother Goddess reigned, before man interfered, before the male gods came into being . . .' She pressed a hand to her temple.

'There were hundreds of gods before Mohammed spread the word of the one true God, then all the others were banished, only Allah remaining.'

'Yes, my tutor told me of that, but this is long before all that multitude came into being. At first a woman ruled and she was earth and seas and heavens incarnate.'

'That is not what the *Qu'ran* says . . .'

'No, but that is what I saw. I am not insisting that my vision is the truth, only telling you what I saw . . .'

He felt her tremble, heard her swallow as if her throat had tightened and was parched from insufficient water, but it was not water that she needed, he knew. It was love.

And so he had tilted her dark head and dropped tender, nourishing kisses on her face, first her forehead, smooth and creamy bronze, then her eyelids which were soft and as velvety as rose petals, then her nose, petite yet strong and sculpted with character and determination, her curving mouth with its tip-tilted corners and the little hollow above her top lip, which demanded to be kissed a million times, and then each rounded cheek where the proud bones arched so magnificently, and finally that small, pointed chin where the tiniest dimple hid away until she smiled.

Next her throat, shielded from the sun and so paler, a camellia-pallor, and such silken skin that desire flared through him almost uncontrollably. With an effort, he held back. She was very young; she was to be his bride. Whatever reasons she had for refusing him now, he would not take advantage of her. Such honourable intentions, and yet where love is concerned, honour somehow has a way of incorporating what, outside of love, would be the basest behaviour . . .

She did not draw back when his lips reached her breasts, nor when his tongue slid across her nipples, encircling and rousing them. Her mouth opened in a silent gasp and her lashes fluttered. He was aching now, aflame between his thighs, so hard that he was throbbing; he knew that he could not hold out much longer. Years of driving himself on, of fighting or ignoring the demands of the flesh had steeled him to resist and resist again, yet now he was passionately, surgingly desperate to be united with this radiant, fey creature who had stolen his heart.

He wanted to drive into her body, entering as the conqueror, and marking her as his territory, see her body swelling with his sons . . . But first the cataclysm of love, the ancient ripe, sweet arts, the holding and kissing, the forging together and moving as one, the clinging, and the loosing of the fires . . .

Out of half-closed lids, Mishaal saw the moon directly above, even larger and more opaline. Then she forgot the moon and all that nature offered and held up her arms as Husain came down to her, his eyes dark as antimony, his expression one of rapture. She almost laughed out loud as his weight covered her, it was so right, so joyous. She could do little else but revel in his closeness, his caging embrace and commanding masculinity. Her knees curved up and round his narrow hips, her skirts falling back as he sank down into the warm, moist heat of her, that throbbing male hardness piercing and entering into a pool of liquid silk.

She felt strangely moved, dizzy and disbelieving. How bitterly she had fought him all these months and now she was so willing, so eager to be one with him. Piercing sparks of fire were dancing along her veins in celebration, heat turning her flesh to flame. Her throat was tight and raw, her eyes hot; the air did not seem to be reaching her lungs. Then there was nothing but the hard, tender yet aggressive thrusting between her legs, filling her with desires and longings that only he could satisfy.

With Drew it had never been like this. Now she could laugh at herself and think what a fool she had been in her ignorance. Drew had known none of the arts of love, or, if he had, he had not troubled to use them. With him, it had been fierce and fast and over in moments and, knowing no better, she had believed it to be bliss. With her Amir, it was a prolonged, heavenly satisfaction, so that she had time to relax and relish, to be filled with wonder and exultation. Why had she resisted him for so long? How could she have suspected him of being ruthless and unloving? It was obvious that his feelings for her were surgingly deep, and that however deeply he thrust into her, he could never be as close as he wished.

Heat swept through her, fragmented flame that darted and nipped at her nerve endings so that she became insatiable for him. She wanted to be filled and devoured, conquered, overwhelmed. When they were roused, they were equal partners in sexuality, both possessing the same raw, powerful desire. In his arms she lost that fey expression and became woman incarnate, fleshed out, voluptuous and ardent, aware that every craving she would ever experience would be answered in his embrace.

'How could you think that I had base designs on you, my beloved? All I ever wanted was you.' Momentarily he rested on his elbow, looking into the eyes he adored.

'I never did think that! Well, perhaps just a little,' she dimpled. 'You could not blame me, could you?'

'If all I wanted was your memory of the burned map then I could have asked you months ago, and insisted that you told me. Were I the villain you make out, I could have had you tortured until you told me. Instead, I asked you to be my bride.'

'I know.'

'Did that not tell you of my good intentions?' he persisted.

'I might have thought that you were besieged with guilt for causing the death of my – my lover, and, in true Islamic fashion, wished to make amends by becoming my protector yourself. That has been the way of things since the days of the Prophet, hasn't it?'

'Yes, and that might have been true had I not loved you, but I do love you. You have my heart in your keeping, Mishaal.'

'Perhaps I am not ready for such a great responsibility? You were raised in readiness for your amirate. I had a sheltered childhood in many ways.'

'I am capable of empathy, beloved. It is the custom for many Arabs to have slaves, especially chieftains. When I became Amir, I freed all my father's slaves because the thought of anyone being in bondage on my behalf sickens me.'

'But I have seen slaves in your camp!'

'Yes, some two dozen of them refused to be freed. They elected to stay with my people, even though they are free men and can leave at any time. Shamim is one of them.'

'*Shamim!* But she is the most Arabic looking of women, a true Beduin born and bred I would have said.'

'Her grandparents were slaves, whatever their origins. They came from the Gold Coast, and they were partly white themselves, of European stock mixed with African. Her mother was quite dark-skinned, but her father was half-Arabic and half-French, so she is paler.'

'So she is a half-caste like me . . . Why did she never mention it?'

'I cannot say. She acepts; she is content.'

'Meaning that I am discontented?'

'I would never criticise on that score. We each have our destiny and how we react to it is a personal matter.'

Somehow the passion had faded from their loving. Even though it had been avid only minutes before, now there was a rapidly cooling distance.

Reluctantly, he turned away so that she could not see the exasperation darkening his eyes, but he heard her intake of breath and knew that she was about to rail at him.

'It all goes back to your ideal of womanhood, doesn't it? However much you disclaim that, you were raised to believe that woman should worship and revere, and when she is not on her knees before her man, she should be on her back beneath him. That is the truth of it, is it not? Even slaves wish to remain in bondage to you, they revere you so greatly, and I should be humbly grateful for the merest glance from your eye! I cannot help it that being a half-breed brought me inestimable suffering as I grew up. Which way should I turn, was I Western or Eastern? Did men come to see me dance because of my talents as a dancer or because I was some kind of freak, green-eyed, black-haired, pale-skinned? Some days I would look in the mirror and see a Western girl with pale face and combed hair; other days I was oriental, my hair loose and wild, my homage all to Allah . . . Perhaps Shamim never had a mirror to look in; perhaps she is less sensitive; perhaps no one ever taunted her about her origins? People were suspicious of me because of my *nasrani* blood . . . They thought that I could not be a true believer, that I would cause troubles to be cast down upon them because of my evil foreign taint . . .'

'The ones who suggested that would be uneducated and superstitious; they cannot help their ignorance.'

'You see, you do not understand!' Mishaal cried, splaying her fingers and raising them impatiently. 'You are on the side of those who taunted and accused me. You say that *I* should have been the tolerant and patient one with them . . . How could I when I was a child?'

'Because you knew better. Because your foster mother saw that you were educated.'

'And what a furore that caused! I was educated despite everything, all the arguments and rages of ZouZou who wanted me to be sold from the age of nine! She thought that my fair skin would command a high price! And how do you think the others I lived with responded to my tutor's presence and the books he brought for me to read? "Putting on airs and graces, aren't we?" they would sneer, when Rhikia was out of hearing. "No one less than the Sultan of Turkey would satisfy this high and mighty one! She is too good for us!"'

'Did you remind them that Mohammed said "He who goes out in search of knowledge is in God's path until he returns"?'

'What good would it have done? They would have thought that I was elevating myself above them even more and pointing out that they were not in God's path!'

'Yes, of course, you are right.' Husain rested his arms on his knees, his ragged glossy black hair falling across his cheeks like spiked dark fingers delineating his cheekbones.

'You would not think of that, would you, when you have been high above all others all your life, and they humble, obliging and obsequious to the great *saiyid*! Who has ever told you that you were arrogant and supercilious?' she challenged.

'You,' he replied, his eyes glittering enigmatically, 'and on more than one occasion, if I recall.'

Deflated, she opened her mouth to snap a retort and then closed it. Where was this getting them? To think that only minutes ago she had been lying beneath him in the most obsequious and lowly position of all, allowing him to see into her heart . . .

Gritting her jaw, she turned her back on him, reached for her goatskin and curled beneath it in readiness for sleep.

PART FIVE

Village of the Skeletons

God nourished you in love and holy pride,
But ignorance detains you from his side.

When love has pitched his tent in someone's breast,
That man despairs of life and knows no rest.
Love's pain will murder him, then blandly ask
A surgeon's fee for managing the task –
The water that he drinks brings pain, his bread
Is turned to blood immediately shed;
Though he is weak, faint, feebler than an ant,
Love forces him to be her combatant;
He cannot take one mouthful unaware
That he is floundering in a sea of care.

Farid ud-din Attar

Chapter Twenty-Five

Rhikia's old servant opened the door to Hamid thinking that it was Jasmina come for her weekly gossip, and her mistress's cousin strutted into the little house as if he were its master.

Hearing his thickly resonant voice, Rhikia's heart plummeted. She could not bear him. Gross, with a protuberant, bulging belly that pronounced decades of dedicated self-indulgence, he was deaf to any views but his own.

Entering the little front room, Rhikia stood her ground before her cousin, her feet planted firmly on the woven blue and crimson rug. His face when he turned to greet her was swollen and the colour of ox blood; he looked as if he might be on the verge of apoplexy. Before she could speak, he launched into a tirade, all subtleties abandoned.

'I have with me a letter from the Imam of this city. I doubt that you will have met him, for he does not mingle with your sort. But for your past life, he would have come here with me, but he declined to do so. Nonetheless, he has commanded in the name of Allah, the one true and compassionate God, that you marry me. I will read out the letter to you.'

With a flourish, Hamid drew out the rolled parchment, began to unroll it and opened his large, gap-toothed mouth to recite its contents.

Shaking with rage, Rhikia snatched the parchment from his hands.

'I can read!' she growled, and began to study the letter. After a few seconds, and despite the rosy haze dancing before her eyes, she realised that the letter was genuine, and that the Imam was indeed ordering her in the name of Allah to agree to marry her cousin Hamid, for it was 'ungodly and impious that a woman should be living alone without a male protector and her behaviour was an offence and crime in the eyes of God, besides being a wretched example to all womankind'.

Rhikia would have laughed out loud had the letter not been so pompous – and so serious. Gritting her teeth, she stepped to the little oil lamp on the carved rosewood table in the corner and, having rolled up the letter tightly, tipped its edge into the flame.

Hamid, who had thought she sought a better light to read by, gave a guffaw of fury and lumbered across the room to retrieve the missive from the flames. He did not care how he wrenched Rhikia's arm while struggling to take the letter from her.

Rhikia sank to a seat, tears of mortification threatening. She, weeping? She had wept for no one but Mishaal in twenty years and she was not going to weaken now before this bull elephant of a man. She caught her breath as he sank down beside her on the little carved bench so that it shuddered beneath his ominous bulk. Next moment, his questing hands were on her shoulders and his greasy, sweating face thrust into hers. His eyes were glazed, squinting with what at first she took to be ungovernable anger and then realised, to her dismay, was lust.

'If you will not heed the words of Allah, then you will be shown what is good for you, woman! I have had enough of your stupidity . . . You know that my business is in trouble and selfishly you refuse to support me. Well, I shall not leave here until you are mine!'

Then she remembered. Hamid was a fruit grower: all those sweet, succulent fruits that could not exist without water. He believed that she was wealthy now and that her money could go towards bringing water from a great distance so that his crop would not die . . . Allah, but he was a dolt and she was in great danger!

When his bulging, sweat-drenched face pressed against hers it was like being crushed by a pulpy fruit that had split from its rotted skin. Nausea engulfed her, but with a sharp reaction she brought up her hands and thrust him away with all her force. Unfortunately, he was prepared, and he reeled back towards her almost immediately, a cunning grin fixed on his blubbery mouth. She tried to back away, slip out of his grasp and escape, but he flung his knees over hers and pressed them so hard into the bench that she thought they would be cut off. Crying out, she slapped her palms across his face repeatedly but all that ugly fat was a protection against pain. Hamid only grinned the more.

Lunging close, he clamped his lips on hers and pressed and sucked, sucked and pressed so that she could barely breathe. As if from an age away, she heard a shuffling sound outside the door and knew that her old servant had seen what was happening and was sobbing pitifully before fleeing to her room.

Rhikia could not move, nor could she retreat sufficiently to escape those suffocating lips, reeking of garlic, spices and rancid butter. Now his ox-like fist was gripping one of her breasts and twisting so that she screamed out, and, having trapped one of her hands, he was pressing it between his enormous thighs so that she was forced to feel the tiny little stave sticking up hard and rigid. How small it was, her palm barely covering it . . . Maybe Hamid behaved like a bull elephant because of his poor endowment? Whether that was the case or no, she could still conceive a child if that ridiculous little pennywhistle entered her body. She was not that old.

That thought gave her strength and so when she found her palm clamped to the upthrust quill, she did what she had instructed her girls to do with men who had difficulty in their erections. A sharp, deft movement and Hamid was finished, shock and disbelief in his eyes as he slumped over her hand.

Well, at least the worst of it was over; if fury drove him to strike out, she would simply have to bear the brunt of it as she had borne so many things in life: alone, and bravely.

He seemed bemused. She held her breath, not wanting to goad him. Eventually, comprehension filled his eyes and, snorting, he slapped her savagely across the cheek.

She swayed like a rag doll, her face ashen save for the crimson handprint lacquering it, saliva edging out of the corner of her mouth, and then blood from where she had bitten her inner cheek. Straightening her spine, she stared Hamid straight in the eye.

'This will get you nowhere, cousin. I shall never marry you. My life is my own to do with as I will, and *no* one is going to persecute me, least of all you.'

'You are a stupid, brainless bitch, the most stupid, brainless bitch who ever crossed my path.'

'Then why is it that you are so eager to marry me?' Rhikia said thickly through bruised and swelling lips.

'You are my kinswoman and it is my duty and my right to take you in marriage, however vicious you are. I promise that your wilfulness will be cured within a very short time. You will be happier then, I assure you; a woman needs to know her place before she can be content.'

If it had not been so tragic it would have been laughable. She, the independent and self-sufficient business woman being harassed and assaulted by this rude old lecher! But there was no doubt what was behind it: avarice.

'I shall never agree to marry you, Hamid, and no one will support you in forcing me against my will. I am a free woman, not a slave or a *nasrani* captured on some foreign shore. If you want another wife, go to Rais Ali Abul, the Turk who brings his shiploads of concubines to the market.'

'They will not be kinswomen of mine,' Hamid retorted sulkily.

'Nor will they bring you a fortune to help you buy water for your fruit growing, will they?'

Hamid could not conceal the dark vermilion that flooded his face and neck.

'That is utter rubbish, woman! I am a rich man, very rich. I will give you everything you desire –'

'I *have* everything I desire, save for one thing: my missing foster child. I shall *not* become your wife, Hamid.'

She heard him swallow squeakily as if he might not succeed, as if he might choke on his own spittle, and then he said hoarsely:

'I shall return with my kinsmen, and the Imam . . . We shall not leave here until you have seen how ignorant and blind you are being. You will be my bride within the month, Rhikia, I swear it on my dead mother's life! and in the name of Allah!'

When he had gone, Rhikia sank to a stool, her head in her hands. How was it that life could be so tranquil and rewarding, with new friends and so many hopes for the future, and then overnight it could all change and become a waking nightmare?

Rubbing a trembling hand across her mouth, she tried to calm her thoughts so that she could design a plan of escape, but nothing would come except fear and a tight, suffocating panic.

He would be back; he had sworn it. When men gathered together, there was no escape. They made the law, they were the law. It was the custom for widows and divorced women to be taken under the roof of their nearest male relative: that had been instituted in the days of the Prophet when frequent wars and skirmishes meant that men died in large numbers, leaving penniless families. Then, in the seventh century, it had been an excellent plan, but now it was distinctly outmoded. The nomadic people of the desert never forced an unwilling woman into marriage, so why should the people of the cities? It was barbaric and open to every wrongdoing known to man.

The Prophet had said, 'Marry such women as seem good to you, two, three, four; but if you fear you will be unable to treat them equally, then only one . . . and give the women their dowries as a gift spontaneous; but if they are pleased to offer you any of it, consume it with wholesome appetite. But do not give to fools their property that God has assigned to you to manage . . .'

So it was left to the unscrupulous to decide who were the fools. Did a Muslim woman who wished to live alone and resist her cousin's advances come into that bracket? Already Hamid had called her stupid and ignorant, would fool be the next on his list?

*

They came to the *Béled mât*, the dead village, in wonderment. Husain was positive that there had never been a settlement this far into the wilderness. How would the inhabitants have survived, year in year out, with the nearest well five days' fast ride away? One hand tucked in his sword belt, the other resting on the pommel of the Sword of God, he surveyed the small adobe dwellings made from earth caked with water, so small that he had to bend double to enter through the low doorways. Inside were the remains of living, bleached ashes where once there had been a fire, a low-rigged rough-wood bench, a woven mat that crumbled to dust when he touched it, an ancient, rusty cooking pot hanging on a hook over the place where the fire would have been lit.

In one corner was a heap of fragile rags, their colours long since blanched by age and the arid heat. Hoping to find some clue amongst them, he picked them up, only to find cobwebs of cloth in his hand as they fragmented to festoon the air with choking slivers of dusty cotton. In his palm there remained only a medal engraved with Islamic runes of some kind.

Outside in the sun he read what was written on the medal. To his perplexity, it was the old legend about the wells running dry and how only the hand of a believer could find the Jewels of Destiny or else disaster would erupt. How unaccountable that it should be this legend . . . For a few moments he felt the hairs on the base of his head stir and move, as if a chill breeze had risen.

Mishaal, curious, took the medal from his hand and read the legend for herself.

'See how bright and new the metal is, as if it has just been forged and yet the village is in ruins.'

She and the Amir were grudgingly on speaking terms again, subject to the occasional fiery tirade. She had still not told him what she could recall of the treasure map, only that they were heading in the right direction. She had known that for sure as soon as they had seen the *Béled mât*, for that had been represented on the map by one or two roofless huts, and the words that now made sense to her: The Died-out Place. And in her hand was the medal with its mysterious legend, the words dancing on the glowing metal as if illuminated by an inner sun. Was it her imagination or did the metal feel hot, scorching a circle in her palm? Frowning, she returned it to the Amir.

'I had no idea this place was here . . . I have never heard anyone speak about it. But then this whole area has been taboo for so many centuries, it's not surprising, I suppose.'

Despite herself, Mishaal spoke in a rush of words. 'This place was on the treasure map! *Bélad mât*, the Died-out Place, that was what it said, and I could not see what it could mean. Now it all makes sense, of course: a ruined village deserted by its residents long ago.'

'So we are definitely on the right route?' Enigmatic eyes scrutinised her face.

'Yes . . .' Clenching her lips, she turned away. Why had she blurted that out? There were moments quite beyond her comprehension with this infuriating, bombastic and adorable man, during which she seemed to temporarily lose her wits and do and say things that betrayed her true feelings.

Cursing beneath her breath, she stalked towards one of the little huts and poked her head through the low door. Inside, after the glaring afternoon sun, it was thickly-velvet black, ebony as the grave, and there was a smell that repulsed her. Sniffing, she tried to identify it, but could not, although the thought of death and decay came into her mind.

She entered the hut, bending low and waiting until her eyes could perceive through the gloom.

Her screams brought Husain to her in seconds and yet it seemed a lifetime before his arms were round her.

There was a low, Western-style table in the centre of the hut, and round it sat seven people, or what had once been people.

Now they were devoid of flesh, nothing left but the stark, scaring framework beneath, jutting, blanched bones and imbecilic grinning skulls set eternally in the rictus of death.

One who looked as if he might have been the leader of the group, wore rotting headgear, a *kuffayia* and *aighal*, the desert kerchief with its corded band to keep it in place, and dangling from his osseous neck was a medal which, on closer inspection, proved to be a larger version of the one Husain had found in the first hut.

'Why have they all died together like that?' Mishaal croaked, her knees shaking. 'Was it some terrible plague?'

'I don't think so . . . What plague has such sudden symptoms? They look as if they've been . . .' he broke off, mindful of the sensitivities of the young woman clinging to him.

'As if what?'

'As if they've been shocked to death. As if something so terrible and unimaginable happened that their hearts gave out. See how their mouths gape open, and their arms are twisted back as if they were fending off some oppressor.'

'How dreadful. No wonder it's called the Died-out Place!' Tugging at his arm, Mishaal urged him outside where she rested her head on his muscular chest for long moments while she recovered. 'They – they looked like some sort of secret clan, or priesthood . . . as if they had met for some vital reason.'

'Did you notice that the elder wore a larger version of the medallion?'

'How odd. How long do you think they've been sitting in there like that?'

'Some decades, I would say, judging by the state of the huts. Dry desert heat can preserve bodies for some time, but they have no flesh left. They weren't mummified by the climate.'

'The room is so quiet, so still . . . Everything in its place as they left it . . .'

'The same in the other hut.'

'Why did they build homes here in this waterless spot? Surely even Beduin would have difficulty surviving here for long?'

'Yes, they would. I wish that I could answer your questions, Mishaal, but I cannot. Now shall we eat?'

Husain soon had a fire burning merrily and had found a selection of berries. These were waiting for her along with the ubiquitous *laban*, now coming to an end. What would she eat then? Husain was roasting a small bird that he had killed with a stone catapulted from a sling. Her mouth watered as she smelled the meat cooking, but she would have none of it, even when he pressed her. What need did live flesh have with dead flesh? Her conversion was complete.

'Your *laban* won't last much longer. What will you eat then?' He looked at her quizzically, as if reading her thoughts.

'I'll find something.'

'After this, there won't be much greenery or berries around. If Allah smiles on us we may have a brief burst of rain, but from the look of the sky now that is the last thing on His mind.'

'Something will turn up.' Mishaal shrugged, chewing on a bitter herb, its taste redolent of decay.

'Where do you get your optimism from, little *fáhd*? Nothing ever seems to affect your serenity of mind, skeletons excepted,' he grinned winningly to take her mind off his words.

'My mother was also a great optimist.' Mishaal's tender little mouth twisted. 'She fell in love, and in doing so, believed that she would be loved in the same unstinting manner, but it was not to be.'

To her surprise, his hand came out and rested gently on hers, like a dove protecting its fledgling. Her cheeks flamed and the bitter aftertaste of the herb rose in her throat so that she wanted to cough gustily. Tears pricked her eyes. When she turned back, Husain was looking at her so piercingly that she bit on her lip. How could she support such cold-eyed scrutiny? His eyes were fierce and penetrating as those of a hawk; she felt as if he were paring away each layer of her inner self, section by section, until he could see her vulnerable heart, throbbing with its unquestionable passion for him.

How did he effect this extraordinary accomplishment? All her life she had worked at concealing her true feelings from everyone, even Rhikia, and yet this man had the ability to enter where no one else had ever done, not even Drew. Thinking back, least of all Drew. Oh, he had been convivial and attentive, but in bursts, and she would never forget the raw, dizzying sensation of cold, ruthless death that had assailed her when she touched his pistol. That weapon had killed many people, and without compunction; had it been the same for the man who had pressed its trigger?

'It is criminal that the wrongs of the past generation should affect those of the next, or that their tragedies should create such deep ripples that they wear away at the hearts of those who come after. Be an optimist, little *fáhd*, but think a while before you leap into things.'

'That is what I have been doing,' she replied, her bright-jade eyes twinkling irreverently, and then he was grinning too and finally they were laughing and hugging one another close.

It seemed important to Mishaal that they try to dispel the aura of death and despair that haunted the Died-out Place. Love was the only emotion that could survive death; the memory of it could last for centuries; suddenly she was struck by the urgent need to declare her love, and, in doing so repel death and all its fears.

And so she reached up her face to be kissed, her eyes limpid with yearning, and Husain pulled her to him, so that she could feel his heart lurch into the wildest beating, sense it thudding against her own, and she wanted to laugh out loud for joy and the sheer perfection of this hallowed moment.

It did not matter that they were Allah-alone-knew-where, wandering in the wilderness of wildernesses, with very little food and water. It did not matter that she had forced herself to hate, loathe and despise him for more than half a year, calling him murderer and rapist beneath her breath and to his face. She had known a hint of the truth all along: he was everything that she most desired in a man. His was no tinsel strength, no feeble prettiness decorating an empty jar that would ring out loud and emptily if she knocked against it. His was the steel and tenacity of centuries, handed down from father to son, over and over, so it was desert-tempered, a bright, hard burning vigour that nothing could quench.

Soft and malleable in his arms, as if she were enchanted, she was the bowstring and he the bow to stretch and tauten her until her senses were finely, sharply honed; and then would come the firing and the moment of release, yet in that release they would be for ever joined.

For ever joined.

Chapter Twenty-Six

This time, there was no hesitation. When his kisses became more urgent, his breathing heavier, she responded similarly, longing to be swept away in a rush of ardour, almost dazing in its ferocity. Nearby the camels nosed amongst the gritty, stony protuberances that had turned the sandy earth into a moon's surface, searching for twigs that contained a modicum of sap, or some more of the bitter-sweet herbs.

The sky was changing colour, from bright pellucid china blue to a deeper, aurous rose, feather-whisks of turmeric yellow spearing the rose in sweeping, imaginative arches. The afternoon breeze had lost its breath and there was an urgent silence, as if everything were waiting anxiously for what must surely come next.

His hands were gentle yet skilled, baring her pearly shoulders so that he could kiss them as he had kissed her face and throat. Never had he seen such unblemished beauty, such a smooth, achingly-lovely cream skin, the glory of it bringing his heart into his mouth and so he kissed her with his heart as well as his lips. Almost in disbelief that this could be happening, he pulled her robe lower still so that he could see her creamy breasts. Full and heavy and mellow, they swelled deliciously at his touch, and he circled them with his mouth, wishing that his kisses were bars that would make her his prisoner of love. If only he could mark her as his own in some beautiful, passionate fashion . . . Not with the veil and her marriage purdah, the curtained existence, hiding in the gloom, out of men's vision, for that was anathema to one born wild and free amongst the nomads. There must be some other way, if only he could think of it . . . Something that she would accept where she rejected becoming his bride as yet.

Below her breasts was pale silk flesh dipping down to her flat stomach and the little, almost heart-shaped bridge covered in silky ebony hairs that shielded her womanliness, the sweet, moist valley that he yearned to enter.

Running his fingers through those silky hairs made her gasp out loud, and when his fingertips pressed nearer to her womanhood and she squirmed, colour filling her cheeks, he could see a pulse beating wildly at her throat. Inside, she was liquid as sweet gold honey, tender, soft and tiny, impregnable as the youngest virgin he had ever taken. She was no experienced *'ālmah*, not that he had ever truly believed that she was, not with those dreamy, tender eyes and that sensitive, generous mouth. There was so much about her that struck a vital chord with him, apart from the physical attraction: something spiritual, almost metaphysical, strangely delicious and deeply, deeply thrilling.

She was at one and the same time possessed of all the knowledge and mysteries from the beginnings of civilisation, and all the innocence of the most sensitive child . . . But he was not going to analyse why she had captured his heart. That was beyond analysis.

Her inner thighs were firm and pale against the rivulets of ebony ringlets, and his lips could not help but gravitate to them, while his palms curved against her wide hips as if he were anchoring himself there for his own survival. One after the other, he showered kisses on her legs, down to her dimpled knees and slender ankles, and the delicate arches of her feet. When he went to kiss her toes, she giggled and kicked her feet away from him, but he won in the end.

Mishaal was watching him in wonderment. He was behaving as if she were some great Amira to whom he owed subservience and fealty, his eyes, usually as perplexing as those of a basilisk, bright with love and passion. At first, she had been convinced that she was nothing more to him than a common *bintilkha'ta* for he had pursued her as enthusiastically as if he wished only to share her bed. When a man wished to give as well as to receive, he took a little longer before making his feelings known: or so she had believed.

Where his mouth had touched her flesh, she was positive that there were fiery little marks, as if her body had responded to his fire with flame of its own, as if he were the flint and she the tinder to be ignited by him. She could feel the flames rearing inside her, feel their insistent lapping heat; she was burning, searing with delight, unable to quench the fires.

It was she who pulled him close, impatiently, flinging her arms round his neck and scooping his hips with her knees so that his iron hardness was thrusting against her most sensitive part as she surged up to meet him. For long, exquisite moments they hovered on the brink, and then, in one blessedly savage thrust, he had entered her and they were in heaven.

Both had discovered that it was easier if they did not speak, for how quickly their hasty tongues led to dispute. So, silently, save for sighs of love, they became well and truly one, so close, so perfectly forged, so inseparable that it would not have mattered if the skies had cascaded around them.

How did it happen, this glorious sensation that affected the sight and the hearing, the heart and the spirit, enclosing them in a brilliant cocoon of love? Time had halted, life was suspended, as they entered into the realms of the twice blessed, those who love and are loved in return.

Husain fitted deep inside her, touching all the most responsive parts so that she could do little more than gasp in delight and hug him close inside their world, one created by them and excluding all others. She was warm and rosy and there was a sensation dancing over her flesh which she could only describe as sparkling. Minute spears of almost unbearable electricity were radiating from where he was bedded deep inside her; there was a surge of power that she had never known before, strange, a little frightening and yet irresistible, urgently beckoning her to obey.

Her hips arched of their own volition, pressing up to meet her lover's as her knees locked round him more tightly, her nails digging into his back to make small cerise sickle-shaped indentations. He bucked against her, fiercely hard and giving his all as he took hers. Her eyes closed in ecstasy, her mouth parted, hair swirling out on the sand around her in serpentine tendrils. Surely it would happen now, quite soon, as it had with Drew? But she was wrong. This was no hasty, impetuous mating; this was patience and tender empathy, a giving as well as a taking, by a man who was concerned to find out what she wanted before he gave her what was most dear to him.

The tearing, tingling feelings were increasing; she felt as if she would explode, split apart into a thousand infinitesimal pieces; heat circled her face, scorching, so that she yearned for a cool wind to flow.

Husain's eyes were bright and black as pearls, glowing with his need for her; his dark hair tangled round his face giving him the look of a cupidinous satyr. She could hardly believe that this was happening! How beloved he was, how adorable and handsome and courageous! Now he was smiling a little and urging her on; he knew that her moment was near.

'Sweet little *fáhd*, do it just for me, let me feel you grip me tightly. There, that's it, isn't it, my heart? Isn't that beautiful?'

She heard herself crying out, her voice rising, pitching high, as the shock waves hit her, wrenching, tearing, gripping with such tremendous and ecstatic force that she was helpless to do anything but welcome them. So this was it: the great mystery of love, a god-force which every woman possessed if she found the right man to unlock it for her . . . In those all too brief moments, she was united with something divine, reaching beyond the stars.

Only then, when he was quite satisfied that she was fulfilled, did Husain release his own control, gasping out her name. She felt as if he had given her his heart in its entirety.

After, they lay cradled in one another's arms, heedless of their thirst, the dry, baking heat and their sweat-dewed bodies. As the sun began to dip in the sky, falling like some aurous topaz jewel towards the arc of the horizon, they realised that they must drink before repeating their accomplishment, but before Husain could fetch their water flasks, which were almost empty, the air began to thicken, and there came the distant, primordial growl of thunder.

'I don't want to shelter in one of the huts!' Mishaal exclaimed, but the sudden torrent of rain that smashed down on them precluded sensitivity. Husain pulled her towards the nearest hut, which, being the one he had first looked in, did not contain any ossified remains to alarm her. They stood inside for a moment, while the rain attacked the mud-baked roof so venomously that Mishaal was sure it would cave in.

When Mishaal had seen for herself that the hut contained no horrors, Husain went outside to look for containers, old drums, bowls, broken pottery shards, a cooking pot or two, and set them in the open where they would catch the rain. Glancing up, he saw that the camels were sheltering against one of the larger huts, a disgruntled look on their long-nosed faces. Grinning, he rejoined Mishaal, who exclaimed at his drenched clothing and insisted that he took it off.

Placing the bowl of rainwater on the baked earth floor, he allowed her to minister to him, removing his bernouse and the full-sleeved shirt beneath it, and then the European style breeches that he wore for riding. Of supple brown leather, they were now soaked to a darker hue.

As he stepped out of them, Mishaal felt her cheeks growing hot. How quickly intimacy grew after making love. It changed matters completely; from being antagonists they were now partners as well as lovers.

She could not help but admire his lean body. His shoulders were generous and strong, his arms muscular from years of hunting, riding and defending his lands with the Sword of God. A small waist and narrow yet powerful hips descended to legs that made her senses tingle. They were perfect, strong and sturdy, yet beautifully shaped as if formed by a master sculptor whose *pièce de résistance* was the lower limbs. To think that the owner of those marvellous legs was in love with her!

Hiding a smile, she draped his wet clothes over the back of a worm-eaten bench and took the bowl of rainwater that he offered her. The water tasted fresh and pleasant and she drank deeply until she felt bloated. The rain thundered down, and it was now so dark that they could barely see one another's faces. Squatting down, Husain beckoned to her to join him and he took from the pocket of his breeches a packet of figs and a chunk of goat's cheese.

As if they were picnicking in the most delightful place on earth, they finished their dinner, emptied the water bowl and then looked at one another. Within seconds, they were kissing, their lips sweet and sticky from the figs, and soon they were lying down on the hard, uneven floor, heedless of the dust of ages, and wanting one another more than anything else.

It followed naturally that Mishaal should soon find herself naked, her sand-stained robes flung away. Flesh on flesh was exhilarating; a sparkling, tingling delight that coruscated over her skin. Oh, they were made for one another, she knew that now with certainty. When her lover settled himself in the warm crook of her body, grinning down at her, she grinned back. Before long, he would be back where he belonged: deep inside her, and she would rejoice.

'Are you changing your mind about me now, little *fáhd*? Would you say that I am not such a villain after all?' His dark eyes twinkled.

'It isn't fair to ask me that when you are holding me prisoner!'

'Why not? Can it change your feelings? Will you call me a villain out of bed but never in it? If that's so, then we shall have a very stormy marriage, or else have to spend most of our time in bed!'

'I have not said that I shall marry you,' Mishaal reminded, but somehow her words carried little conviction when he was on top of her, his basilisk eyes, alight with passion and humour, staring straight into her own. She might have been a helpless kitten and he a desert lion for all the strength she had to resist him.

'How can you refuse me now when I have made you mine and bedded you?' He spoke with practicality and a direct logic that would have been unarguable had he not been dealing with a woman.

'Men have had their way for far too long! They think they

only have to compromise a woman and she must marry them! That is how all manner of wrongs are committed; can you not see that? A woman marries to protect her reputation, and unscrupulous males are well aware of it . . . They compromise a woman so that they can get what they want.'

'And what is it of yours that I want? Your great fortune? Your enormous lands and estates that stretch from here to here . . .?' He marked two dots in the dust of the floor, touching one another, to represent her lack of belongings – 'or is it your title? Queen of Arabia, Sultana of Islam, now which one is it, I forget?' His eyes were mocking.

Mishaal blushed furiously, pushing him away, but he refused to go.

'You want sons from me: is that not enough? I am to wear myself out bearing your heirs, and then when I am bent and wrinkled from producing infants every year, you will take a wife half my age and abandon me!'

His reply was to bellow with laughter. That loud, hearty laugh of his infuriated her.

'Mishaal, you have a vivid imagination! How many of my people did you see with more than one wife? Very few, indeed.'

'Chiefs always have more wives to display their wealth and importance!'

'Yes that is so, but all the same we Beduin marry for love and are faithful. A man can show his worth far more by having one wife and loving her as she should be loved than by any amount of show. I shall be sticking to just one: you. You have my promise on that.'

'Oh, I know men's promises! Like my father's to my mother! "I love you, I will give you anything, if you will only be mine," he said, and then he left her and went back to his foreign land, not caring what became of her. She killed herself, she killed herself because he deserted her!' Tears springing into her eyes, she buried her face in her hands.

'It will not be like that with me. Have I not shown you that my feelings are unchanging? All these months I have loved you and nothing has altered that, not even your worst tirades, not even when you threw that vase at me!'

'Why did I miss you? It should have hit you right on your head!'

'Why? Who would love you then? There would be no one, Mishaal, do you realise that? No one.'

She did not answer. She was thinking of Rhikia. If her foster mother would have her back, she would go to live with her again as soon as she convinced this man that she was not going to marry him by force. Whatever happened, she would go to Rhikia, or send for her as soon as she could. If the worst came to the worst, Rhikia could come and live with them in the black tents and have her own tent and be treated with all the honour deserving of the Amira's heart-mother . . . if she could ever be torn away from the house in the Street of the *Jijims*.

'You are wrong. There would be someone.'

'Your foster mother? You deserted her, remember. Why should she have you back now?'

'Because she loves me and I love her.

'Did you think of that when you eloped?'

'I was going to write to tell her what had happened, and, and, ask her to join us in America!'

'Would she have gone?'

'Yes, to be with me.'

Husain was silent. He had rolled to one side and was leaning on his elbow. The cataclysmic rain was coming to an end and there was a faint sighing, hissing sound in the air as if the scorched earth were simmering. What was he going to do? He, the Amir of this great land, the hardest and wildest in the world, so it was said, did not know how to woo and win the woman he adored. Had he, unknown to himself, lost his heart as a child when he assumed the burdens of his amirate, so that his tenderness and empathy were no more than façades that this perceptive and infuriating female saw through?

Mishaal was thinking, I shall not give in to him! He has had everything he desired all his life, but he shall not have me! I am not to be bartered or sold into slavery with promises and vows of love, any more than I would have let money be my master in Rhikia's house . . . We are temperamentally opposites and our marriage would be a disastrous failure . . .

Suddenly, with a low growl, he leapt to his feet and stormed outside the hut. Taken aback, she went to the door and peered out. Standing in the rain in a nimbus of mango-coloured light, his naked body irradiated as if he were limned with gold, he looked tall and dazzling as an archangel shaped and sculpted by miraculous hands, the wild ebony hair tangled round his head. Her heart twisted and thumped hard against her ribs so that she had to gulp for air, and the longer she stared at him, stupefied, almost shaken, by the tumult of her feelings for him, the more he seemed to shine and move with the confident imperious grace of an immortal.

It could have been a trick of the light, now that the rain was leashing itself and the sun surging through the reddish-gold mist created by the marriage of baking heat and dashing rain, and yet she knew instinctively that it was not. She was looking on him with the eyes of a lover.

Chapter Twenty-Seven

They had enough water for days now that the rain had left its calling cards. Seeing the containers filled to the brim, Mishaal thought instantly of bathing. How sand-stained, crumpled and sticky were her robe and cloak and how she ached to fling them away and leap into a pool up to her neck. That would not be possible, but she could sit in one of the containers, a large, round, shallow bowl, and be soaked to her hips, so she went about doing that. First she heaved the shallow container to a private place behind two of the huts, then she filled the bowl from two of the cracked rain-filled old jugs. Having checked that Husain was still some yards away searching for berries, she flung off her clothes with a satisfying sense of accomplishment.

She had no intention of feeling ungainly as she sat spread-legged in the unbalanced makeshift bath, but she longed for some scented soap to lavish on her sun-parched, dusty limbs, and then, afterwards, rich attar of roses and jasmine to massage into her neglected body. Sighing, she leaned back as far as was comfortably possible, and, closing her eyes, imagined that she was in a silver-veined marble bath, with fresh rushing water laving her into a delicious, semi-comatose restfulness. There would be soft fluffy linen to dry herself with, a silver comb to untangle her long hair, then the sweet-scented oils to nourish her face and skin, and a fragile peacock-blue robe to slip on afterwards. It would be paradise, and how she yearned for it.

If only there was some semblance of soap, but there was nothing that she could use in its place, not even the *laban*, for that was finished now. It was cool as an atheist's blessing now that the rain had gone. How swiftly the beltane-heat of the desert dried out the sopping sand and bushes, and there was a dainty little breeze ushering in the evening. Above, the sky was rich mauve streaked with sweet-william pink. Happiness was easing its way along her bones, and, half-closing her eyes, she drifted into a light doze.

The snap of a tinder-dry twig woke her in alarm. Flaring her eyes, she imagined one of the vile skeletons clanking towards her, rictus-grin distended with glee. For a moment she saw nothing in the baleful yellow light that was now glowing around her, and then, leaning against one of the huts, arms folded, mouth set in a wide, appreciative grin, she saw the Amir.

'How dare you!' she cried, shrinking down into the bowl and crossing her arms over her breasts. 'Have you no decency?'

'No,' he grinned back, moving neither his position nor the direction of his gaze.

Crying out in frustration, Mishaal scrabbled in the sand for the broken shards of pottery that were all that remained of one of the jugs that she had dropped and broken, and flung them feverishly at the Amir, who grinned even as he ducked and evaded them.

'If that is all the gratitude I get, then I'll take my soap elsewhere,' he said, turning to leave.

'*Soap!* How did you get that?' She almost leapt out of the bowl before she remembered.

'I found it in my saddle bag.'

'All this time we've had to use sand and now you discover you had soap after all! *Oh!*'

'As Allah is my judge, I did not know I had it with me.'

'May I use it then?'

'I may be too feeble to bring it to you after that crack on the head . . .'

'Then I shall come and get it!' she retorted, but the delighted expectation on his face changed her mind at once. 'No, if you would bring it to me . . .'

'If you say please.'

Swallowing her rebellion, she muttered the required word and waited.

He walked towards her casually, as if it were quite the usual thing to find nude girls bathing in pottery bowls in the iron wilderness. Blushing, she crouched forwards so that he could not see anything except her knees and her crossed arms, while she cursed for having thrown her clothes so exultantly into the distance.

Standing over her, he dropped the soap into the water. It was lye soap, so there would be no softness in it, but it would help her to feel clean again. Looking up at him, she saw the glint of wickedness in his night-dark eyes, but she did not have time to gauge what he planned to do next.

Flinging off his cloak to reveal that he was quite naked beneath it, he was soon sitting astride the bowl across her pressed-together knees and swilling water over himself as if he shared a bath with a woman every day. Reaching out, he tipped another jug of water over his legs, and, having found the blob of soap, began to lather it into his stomach and thighs.

'No one invited you to join me!' Mishaal complained, jutting her jaw, and trying to keep her eyes off what was staring her in the face.

'It is my soap,' he quirked one arched, ebony brow.

'And my bath!'

'Allah, why are women so possessive? *Ya sitti*, will you allow me to share your bath?' He salaamed obsequiously.

She opened her mouth to shout no, and then closed it again. If she argued, they would be here all evening. All she had to do was to climb out. Silently, she went to do that, only to find his hand caging her wrist.

'I think it would be more enjoyable if we did this together, don't you? I will soap you and you can soap me.'

Blushing hotly, she dared not speak for fear of revealing how hoarse her voice would sound. Slowly, tenderly, he began to soap her arms and shoulders, and her still pressed-together knees, then the tops of her breasts, paying extra attention to the nipples. His hands were rousing, stirring her senses and igniting her desires. Biting on her lips she stifled a shuddering sigh.

Then when she could bear it no longer, he handed her the soap and beckoned to her to do the same for him.

Nervously at first she soaped his arms and chest, the glossy muscles firm and powerful beneath her fingers, then lower to his flat, hard stomach, where she paused, overcome with shyness, until he took her hands and placed them a few inches lower, not low enough to offend, but only to suggest. A nervous giggle behind her lips, she continued to massage, touching the area that had brought her so much joy only a few hours ago. Curling black hairs framed the indefatigable weapon that seemed to possess a life of its own, for it sprang to power as she caressed its velvety skin. There it stood, facing her boldly, demanding her full attention, and she was suddenly so overwhelmed that she pulled back her hands and went to escape.

Tenderly he caught her again, caging her so close that she could do nothing else but kiss him, and kiss him again, her heart banging wildly, her head spinning. Smiling, he held her as close as the bowl would allow.

'Little *fáhd*, wildcat with a heart of silk, it breaks me when you are cruel to me . . . What do I have to do to convince you that I adore every inch of you and always shall? I would not part with my soap to anyone else!' His eyes twinkled.

For once she did not retaliate, nor did she make a murmur as he bent to kiss her throat and shoulders, then her breasts, his fingers circling her nipples with confident finesse. She ached for him to continue, to repeat what he had done before, yet her need disturbed her deeply. She did not want to be weak! She did not want to admit that she needed him! So she said nothing, and did not even sigh as he explored her body, dipping his fingers into the fresh-silk triangle between her thighs so that she could not quench a shudder.

Hungrily, devouringly, his lips covered hers, and she responded eagerly, clutching at him impatiently, desperate to have him deep inside her, in the secret haven that she kept for him alone. Yet she would not give him his reply; somehow, she felt that she would keep her independence if she did not commit herself in words.

His long, lean legs arched over her thighs, his arms hugging her close, he slid deep into her body, so that they were one indivisible being, heart-whole, spirit-joined, their auras linked. Mishaal lay against his chest, supported by his strength, enthralled by his sweet possession of her, silently urging him to stay where he was for ever.

High above them, a spear-bodied hawk hovered, waiting for its prey to emerge, then swooping down in noble alignment, opened its voracious beak to trap the juicy desert mouse before wheeling back up into the blue to return to its young with their dinner.

The pore-swelling heat of day was fading fast. At night the desert heat could drop many tens of degrees and turn high summer into mid-winter in a few hours. They did not notice; if snow had fallen, they would not have heeded it. Even the scathing *simûm* might have passed them by. Eyes for no one else, they sat cocooned in love.

After long moments of satisfaction, during which they kissed repeatedly and looked at one another in wonderment, Husain began to surge more deeply inside her, so deep that she could feel him touching her where she had never been touched before, and it made her flesh tingle, tiny, sparkling sensations cavorting over her skin like gossamer spiders' legs, dozens of them dancing, frisking, delighting, so that she could hardly bear it. It seemed to centre in her breasts, twisting round and round, tighter and tighter, knotting itself so forcefully that they felt as if they were on fire, soft, swelling flesh burning bright, and all the result of his skilled fingertips. Somehow the flames were searching deep beneath her skin, lower, down to the well of love, a great luminous star radiating outwards from there.

Wonderment at such sensations made her mute; she simply revelled, allowing herself to be swept away on an Eastern carpet of love, the fragrant air of paradise fanning her face, the scent of jasmine, roses and sandalwood in her nostrils. No longer was she merely human, but elevated high amongst the immortals; she could ask no more.

How had she lived all these years without this blessing? How stupid she had been, shutting herself away except when she danced; hiding her heart as thoroughly as she had her face, dreaming of the man who would rescue her. He had come, altering her life immeasurably, and in a manner that she could never have predicted. From being a naïve child, a dreamer of dreams, she had become a woman, a liver of life.

'Little wild heart, how silent you are. Do you not know that the moon is glowing just for us? Allah has willed it so.' Husain's voice was spun silk in her ears. 'The God of the Christians would not smile on you now: He would condemn. Intimacy before marriage is frowned upon by Him . . .'

'Only to protect women from being forced by men,' she whispered back, but her heart was absent of retaliation. 'That seems to me an excellent ruling.'

'And what happens when the marriage is celebrated? Does the Christian God declare that intimacy is blessed at all times then?'

'I – I do not know . . .'

'No, He says that it must only be for the procreation of children, not for pleasure.' Husain's eyes were twinkling wickedly.

'*Not* for pleasure?' Mishaal gasped in disbelief.

'Not for pleasure.'

'You are teasing me! That cannot be so!'

'Staunch Christian men would never take advantage of a lady before marriage; they keep their lusts for the women of the streets. Christian ladies are expected to be chaste and pure and not enjoy the conjunction of a man with a woman . . .'

She wanted to cry out: 'But Drew was not like that!' Yet she knew that what Husain had told her was true; she could sense its veracity. And if it were thus, then Drew had treated her as a low woman of the streets, taking her virginity and making love to her without the sacrament of marriage that was so vital to Christians.

'Do not speak of this, I beg you,' she whispered. 'Do not spoil this moment.'

Seeing her discomfited, he took pity on her, pulling her closer and lavishing kisses on her face and throat. They were still joined together, a perfect fit, Husain still hard and erect, touching the heart of her with delectable sensation. She did not believe that anyone could survive so long as he, and yet he did, on and on, allowing her more than enough scope for every erotic feeling that she could summon.

Where his fingers had touched her, they had left tingling imprints; where his lips had caressed, there were sparkling circles. She felt as if she were alight with heat and dazzle and colour; the nucleus for all the love in the world, and it was because of her Amir and only because of him.

When the culmination came, she bowed to it with reverent joy for it brought her closer to God than anything that had gone before. Whatever God she had been in search of, she had found Him now, the spiritual exultation of this union telling her so profoundly, yet she was still unsure of His name . . . Was it the God of the Christians or Allah the All-Merciful: which interpretation should she accept?

The passion tore all thoughts from her mind and she curved against Husain as he filled her body with his gift of life.

After, noticing how chilly it had become, he fetched their goatskins and they lay entwined with the skins tucked round them, watching the stars bubbling with argentine brightness and pondering over the friendly moon. How beamingly benevolent and happy he looked as he watched over them.

'I wish – I wish that this could go on for ever like this,'

Mishaal said huskily, her head on Husain's sholder, her knee across his muscular thighs.

'Why should it end?'

'The best always does.'

'That is a stern lesson to have learned so young, my heart. He put a finger under her chin. 'Sometimes, wanting something is all that's needed to keep it. Only those who take the best for granted are likely to lose it.'

'But how can it go on? You followed me to punish me for theft. Your people think I stole their birthright . . . They are not going to accept me back with open arms after I rejected them!'

'So you wish to come back with me, little *fáhd*?' His voice sounded choked.

'I – I was only telling you why I cannot do that! It would be impossible – the embarrassment for everyone . . .'

'Do you think they would not listen to their Amir? I shall tell them the truth: that it was a mistake, that an ill-wisher planted the opals upon you to blacken your name out of envy and spite, because they did not wish you to become my princess . . .'

'No, what you mean is you will order them to accept me, whatever they may be feeling in secret, however much they despise and loathe me!'

'They took you to their hearts, Mishaal, they did not feel hostile towards you. How could you think that? Allah, where do you get all these notions from?'

'They watched me night and day. I was kept a prisoner! That is hardly loving, is it?'

'On my orders they did that, because they knew I loved you and wanted you as my bride. Did you know that they had despaired of my finding the one I would marry? Deputations of men used to come to plead with me every two or three weeks . . . Beduin would journey from all over to beg me to choose a bride and have sons so that their land would be safe. Then when you arrived and they could see how I felt about you, they decided that no one was going to be the one to let you escape!' His eyes twinkled in the darkness. 'Word spread faster than a whirlwind that I was in love, that the girl in question was fair of body and sound of limb, and that one had at last been found who was worthy to wear the Theodora opals on her wedding day . . .

'You remember the men who visited me and for whom you danced? They had come to congratulate me and to inspect you to see if you were as fair as rumour would have it.' Husain's eyes twinkled more brightly.

'Inspect me!' Mishaal squeaked. 'I am not a piece of merchandise to be inspected!'

'Of course not,' he grinned, his voice soothing. 'But you must admit that they could not believe what they had heard: how could anyone be so beautiful and graceful, so fair, innocent and virtuous?'

She made a tutting sound. 'All that is silly flattery. I saw a dozen more beautiful young women in your camp, all of whom would have given their right hands for your love!'

'Yes, but I did not love them, and anyway, what would I have done with a dozen right hands? Framed them in silver?'

She tutted again, prodding him in the stomach.

'What does love have to do with producing sons to strengthen your lands? Surely you could have gone into it with the same ruthless, single-minded determination that you put to everything else? You could have closed your eyes on the wedding night, or pretended that you loved her! How suddenly you produce all these high-flown principles, *Your Highness* . . .'

'I believe that love is vital. Who would bring children into the world who were not born of love? The feeling that a mother and father have for one another affects their child's nature. I believe that most firmly. My own parents and my grandparents and my great-grandparents were all deeply in love with one another. The stars are in a different setting for a child born out of love, they are colder and more detached. I want my sons to be in control of their own destinies and not have their destinies rule them . . .'

'And what of your daughters?' Mishaal reminded.

'The same for them, of course, and that they have your unblemished complexion and long ebony hair, and those rich green eyes that seem to delve into a man's soul . . .'

'Do you approve of daughters being given into marriage for the sake of political unions?'

'Have you not listened to anything I said? I would not expect any child of mine to do something that I would refuse to do. You have my vow on that.'

Sighing, she relaxed against him. Why did she need constant proof of his integrity when she had accepted Drew at face value, never besieged him with questions and eloped with him without a second's consideration?

As night burgeoned, the Died-out Place became nerve-tinglingly eerie. Earlier that day Husain had shored up the door to the hut where the skeletons sat holding their eternal, silent discourse for Mishaal could not settle with the thought of those osseous frames so nearby, looking ready to leap out of their seats to chase her. Husain had prayed afterwards, just as he would if some of his own people were being newly buried. Watching silently, Mishaal had thought of God, religion and eternity.

Yet even with the door blocked, there were dancing shadows and movements in the dark hollows and angles of the deserted village, and all she could do was keep her eyes shut and try to sleep, Husain's arm around her. He did not have a shred of fear in his body; she doubted he would flinch if a whole *cortège* of skeletons came rattling towards him. When she thought that, she shivered at the image it conjured up. What was it about this place that reminded her of everything that it was wisest to forget?

'Sleep, little one. No one will disturb us,' her lover whispered in her ear, dotting his words with kisses on her earlobe. 'In the morning we shall leave.'

Mishaal did not know whether to be glad or sorry. They had enjoyed a loving tryst here, yet there had been shock and fear, too. They would be leaving behind one of the scariest, most disturbing experiences of her life, but also the most beautiful and moving.

Lying awake beside her, thinking of the medallion bearing its legend, Husain faced for the first time his worst fear: that a non-believer had reached the Jewels of Destiny and removed them, and that was why the wells in the Land of Mirages had been running dry. In his mind's eye he saw the American fling the treasure map into his camp fire before Husain could save it. He had thought it destroyed, but what if there were more than one?

Chapter Twenty-Eight

They left the Died-out Place in the pearly dawn light, having broken their fast with herbs, berries, and carefully rationed dates. The juicy berries were manna from heaven after so many meals of dried fruit, and Mishaal gorged on them, with Husain quirking a brow at her greediness.

'Do not blame me if your stomach aches after that,' he said gently.

Mishaal flashed tempestuous eyes at him, but said nothing. She had never been one to blame others for her own failings and foolishnesses.

The camels were snorting and pawing the ground, in excitement. Husain said that they may be scenting greenery in the distance, which would be good fortune for them all, but he was frowning as he peered towards the horizon.

Knowing what was coming now, Mishaal steeled herself.

Turning, he took her hands in his, his eyes beseeching.

'My heart, will you not tell me if we are on the right route? Remember that the Jewels of Destiny will be yours if we find them. Think of my people going thirsty and dying of famine. I know that you have a tender heart, even though you hide it carefully. Mishaal I –'

'Yes, we are on the right track.' She told him in more detail what she had seen on the treasure map, the roughly sketched huts and the words '*Béled mât*', and how she had been unable to guess what such a phrase could mean, until she had seen the old ruined dwellings.

'I think that I have always had an inkling of the area where they might be. There are so many legends attached to this land, Mishaal. It has seen a thousand battles, skirmishes and raids, warrior chiefs slaughtered in war, and once, many more than a thousand years ago, the daughter of an ancestor of mine was Zenobia, Queen of the Desert. Have you heard of her?' Mishaal shook her head.

As they moved slowly away from the Died-out Place, Husain told her the story of Zenobia.

'She was the daughter of Zabbai, a Beduin chieftain, her mother Greek and proclaimed as the greatest beauty of her day. She was a descendant of Cleopatra, Queen of Egypt. Although Zenobia began life in the black tents, moving around with her tribe in search of grazing for their cattle, just as we do today, she grew to be so strikingly beautiful and brave that it was only a matter of time before a man sought her out in marriage.'

'Who was he?' Mishaal was imagining the radiant Zenobia galloping along on camel's back, her ebony hair streaking behind her, the blood of Queen Cleopatra in her noble veins.

'Prince Odenathus, ruler of Palmyra, the wealthiest and most opulent city in the desert, everything that the Land of Mirages is not,' he added, his mouth twisting wryly. 'The wealth of Palmyra attracted the Romans, and they were planning to lay siege to it, so the Prince began secret recruitment in the desert, finding and training men to fight against them. It was there that he met Zenobia and her father. Very soon they were married, and Zenobia moved to Palmyra to exchange her camel-hair tent for a magnificent stone palace.'

'Did they love one another, or had she no choice?'

'You would ask that! They were in love and Zenobia loathed the Romans as much as her husband did. Soon she was helping to train the Arab recruits herself. Constantly in the saddle, living rough like a soldier, she eventually had the chance she wanted: to lead her men into battle. The Persians were expected to attack her city any day and so she and Odenathus attacked them first. They were resoundingly successful. Next they attacked a Roman army, and again were victorious. People spoke of Zenobia being charmed, and surrounding countries united with Palmyra.

'Then, unhappily, Odenathus was assassinated and Zenobia had no option, heartbroken though she was, but to proclaim herself absolute ruler and call herself Queen of the East . . . Remember this was roughly two hundred and fifty years after the birth of the Prophet Christ and times were dangerous and violent. She could not show any human weakness, or the Romans would have stepped in immediately, as they were always so delighted to do. By now she was a legend herself. Riding a white camel, and wearing a cloak of imperial purple, she had soon conquered Egypt. Next were Palestine, Babylon, Persia and Asia Minor, then all Arabia, and by the time Zenobia was forty, she truly was Queen of the East and Rome had been forced to relinquish almost half of its former empire to this extraordinary warrior queen.'

'You do not sound alarmed by her success. I cannot think of any other Arab man who would speak so admiringly of a female's war-like accomplishments!'

'I am a fair man, Mishaal, and give honour where it is due. Besides, she was the daughter of one of my ancestors, was she not? Her blood is in my veins,' he grinned.

'It is very old blood!' Mishaal grinned back.

'But good all the same.'

'So you can claim descent from Cleopatra and Zenobia, two great queens . . .'

'Do you find that a pleasing thought?'

'The ancients were fascinating people . . . so much of their culture and brilliance has been lost for ever.'

'Meaning that I am a dullard and a boor compared to my glittering ancestors?' His basilisk eyes twinkled.

'No, only a boor,' she replied, but she was laughing and so was he. 'What happened to Zenobia? Did she reign in peace?'

'With Rome enraged at her victories, and wanting their ill-gotten empire back? No, they planned assault and she planned defence, yet when the two armies did meet, she was victor once more . . .'

'For good?'

'No, next time they sent Aurelian, and his skilled forces beat her back into her walled fortress city where she locked herself inside, saying that she would die there but never surrender.

'The siege was long and in time the people were starving. Zenobia could not bear to see it. One night she escaped, letting herself down the city wall by ropes and mounting the camel that a spy had brought for her. They crept past the Roman guards and headed eastward towards Persia. But before leaving, Zenobia gave something to one of her spies, a man who had served her since she was an infant and with whom she could have trusted her life. He was to take a package and bury it until the Queen could return safely and reclaim it. She could not take the risk of the Romans getting their hands on it.'

'What was it?' But Mishaal felt that she already knew. Of course! Now everything was falling into place.

'Her jewels, every jewel and gem that her beloved husband had ever given to her, and booty from all the conquered cities, rubies and emeralds, black pearls, diamonds, sapphires and gold, the Crown Jewels of Palmyra and other looted cities . . . their value beyond calculation.'

'They were hidden by this man? And no one ever found out where, is that it? But the legend grew up about them, as a kind of warning?'

'Yes, that is almost what happened.' Husain gave her an admiring glance. 'The trusted servant was never seen again, although he was supposed to have followed the Queen into exile to tell her that the Jewels of Destiny were safe.'

'Was that what they were called then? It seems an odd name for a woman's jewellery.'

'Time gave them that name. You see, there were many who would say afterwards that Zenobia's love of jewellery and her determination to amass large amounts of it – including some that rightfully belonged to others – had brought about her downfall. Her tragic destiny.'

'So she did not escape into exile after all?'

'She reached the river that would take her to safety . . . she was within feet of it when the Romans caught up with her.

They killed her guards and took her prisoner. When her people heard, they surrendered the city, and a Roman garrison took it over, but the citizens rose against them, slaughtering every one. When Aurelian heard, he descended on them with his army and wiped out Palmyra as if it had never been. They destroyed everything, the cities, the temples and palaces, the beautiful columned avenues . . . Nothing was left but a dusty legend.'

'And what became of Zenobia?'

'There are two tales . . . one that she starved herself to death when she heard what had happened to her people, another that Aurelian took her to Rome and forced her to walk through the streets in chains behind his chariot, but that she was then left to live much as she preferred until she died three years after.'

'Poor Zenobia. So she left her jewels somewhere buried in the desert, in a place that came to be considered taboo after the old gods and goddesses were abandoned and Mohammed spoke out so strongly against the worshipping of idols. Why did the jewels not turn up before then? Did no one have any idea where they could be?'

'A man could search these deserts for centuries and not find what he wanted. A treasure map turned up during my great-grandfather's time, but it was stolen during an enemy raid. He told me about it when I was a boy, but he could not recall what the map said. He was an old man by then and his mind wandered. He spoke of a place of worship and said that the jewels were there, but that was all he could remember. Zenobia built many temples to her goddess and I have been to the place where Palmyra stood, and seen the ruined temples and palaces. I explored every one, although they stretch far across the desert, but there was nothing. Nothing.' The word was a sigh.

'I find it hard to believe that no one tried to find the jewels in past centuries: all that enormous wealth hidden somewhere!'

'If it was known to be hidden. Who was to know about it? Zenobia did and her close companions on that day, but who else was to suspect that she hadn't left her jewels at Palmyra and that the Romans hadn't taken them when they conquered the city?

'The desert hides many secrets. Ancient scrolls and parchments appear out of nowhere, almost as if Allah has willed it. Long-deserted caves are discovered and when they are searched, papyrus parchments are found in languages no one can understand, and pottery and tools from civilisations that died out in the mists of time. On the walls of caves are the strangest paintings, wild animals drawn in stains made from berry juices and watered clays, perfectly preserved because of the dry climate. Zenobia's treasure might have had a better chance of being found if it had been sealed into a deep cave hidden away in some *samrâ*.'

The sun was searing on their faces now and Mishaal had drawn her veil across her nose, so that only her eyes could be seen. Behind them the desert plain lay flat for dozens of miles, scorched, cracked and chapped by wind and sun for centuries. She decided to have one last look at the Died-out Place before it vanished over the horizon. Husain turned with her to share the sight.

They stared straight at the place where the ancient, deserted village had been, fully aware that their eyes should be resting on it. There was nothing there. The Died-out Place had vanished as if it had never been.

Chapter Twenty-Nine

'Whore!'

Rhikia faced her cousin with ashen cheeks and trembling legs. This was his third visit since the time that he had tried to force himself on her, and it was becoming obvious that he was hoping to beat her into submission with insults.

'Your name is befouled throughout the city . . . Even in the desert wilderness they have heard of you, Rhikia of the debauchery and depravity. You have made yourself naked before them with your infamies, and all will shun you now.' Hamid was waving a bulging, beringed finger at her. Sweat was trickling down his temples.

'Unless you make a respectable woman of me? That is what you mean, isn't it? Allah, but you nauseate me!'

Hamid croaked, the words knotting in his throat.

'I have tried kindness with you, and patience, but it has got me nowhere. You are an infamous creature, a vile hussy, and you will pay for it. The Lord Mohammed says that men are the managers of the affairs of women, for God has preferred in bounty one of them over the other, and for that they have expended of their property. Righteous women are therefore obedient! Those are the words of the Prophet, blessed be his name!'

'But did he also not say that it is unlawful for believers to inherit women against their will? Nor must men debar them so that they can steal their property, and that they must consort with them honourably?'

'Add to that, woman! Add to that! Mohammed said that a woman can be debarred and her property forfeited if she has committed a flagrant indecency! A flagrant indecency, woman, did you hear that? Would you deny that you committed such a crime?'

'I would.' Rhikia held herself rigidly.

'*Whore!*' Hamid screamed again. 'You forced young girls into a life of debauchery and abominations! You inveigled them into your house and before they knew what was happening, they had been corrupted beyond return. You, woman, *you*, were responsible for that flagrant indecency!' Hamid's rolls of fat quivered.

'I gave homes to girls who would have starved in the streets!' Rhikia retaliated.

'Ha, ha, ha! Starved in the streets? Vile nonsense! I myself contribute alms for such fallen women. They are never left in destitution.'

'Oh, but they are!'

'And you bore a child out of wedlock . . . Some would not condemn you for that, but I would. Splitting our family, making your father ill and killing him with your shameless behaviour!'

'He – he is dead?' Rhikia put a hand to her mouth.

'Three days ago. Where were you when he died? Too guilty to show your face!'

'Why did you not tell me that he was so ill?'

'He did not want to see you, woman. He feared that you would visit him and blacken his name even further. "There is Rhikia the Whore," that is what they would have said as you entered his house, Allah give him peace and joy in paradise! You killed him with your lustfulness, and by denying him grandchildren, that was what most destroyed him in the end. Selling your bastard into slavery . . . How could you have done it?'

Through her tears, Rhikia stared at him in perplexity.

'I have never had a child,' she choked. 'Never. Who told you that?'

'ZouZou, she told me all.'

'Was she there when our father died?'

'Of course. He had forgiven her and taken her to his bosom. He will leave her everything, and you will receive nothing.'

'That does not worry me at all.'

'No, but it –' Hamid pulled himself to a halt. He was wild with fury that he would get nothing from Rhikia's father because of her way of life. 'Your father wept to think of his grandchild sold into slavery. He would have raised her had you given him the chance.'

'If ZouZou told you all this nonsense, then she is lying. I have never had a child and I would never sell a child into slavery.'

'You lie, I know you lie! I know her name! She was Mishaal! Her name was Mishaal!' Hamid crowed triumphantly.

'Mishaal, daughter of Maryam, not my daughter. When Maryam could not care for her any more, I took her in as my foster daughter.'

'What manner of woman would leave her daughter with a whore?'

'A desperate one.' Rhikia threw back her head.

Hamid made a hurrumphing sound of disbelief. Coming nearer so that she could smell the garlic and the rancid butter of his breath, he reached out a clumpy fist and encircled one of her breasts, pinching hard, then harder, so that the room tilted vertiginously and nausea rose in her throat. On, on went the finger and thumb, pinching tighter and more maliciously until she could bear it no longer. In one swift and efficient movement she brought up her knee and drove it straight into Hamid's private parts with all the strength she could muster.

Towards midnight Rhikia gathered her belongings. She would not weep at having to leave her happy little home; she would be strong. Within a few hours, Hamid would be arriving with the religious leader and a diatribe of male relatives to sweep her off to Hamid's house where the marriage preparations were already under way. It seemed that despite her 'crimes', Hamid still wanted her as his wife.

She would die first!

Unfortunately, there was no way that she could refuse. Hamid had the Imam on his side, and no one would interfere with *his* wishes. No man would allow a woman to defy him. That way lay female anarchy. Women must be schooled and trained, and beaten into obedience, as Hamid had beaten her after she had struck him in the groin. She would bear the scars for the rest of her life.

No one would come to her aid now; she was wilful and disobedient and in great error. Even those women whom she had helped when their daughters were missing had deserted her since she had made it known that she would not marry her cousin despite the wishes of the Imam.

When it became plain that Hamid was not going to leave her in peace, she had made emergency plans and now she was putting them into action. One of her regular customers at the house in the Street of the *Jijims* had been Ali Ben Ali, cousin by marriage to the Amir of the Land of Mirages. How different cousins could be: Hamid so vicious, and Ali Ben Ali so benevolent. Annually, after Ramadan, he had always given her girls a little gift each, a package of spices or incense for a brazier; butter for their *pilaf*; gilded bells for their bangles or anklets; *kohl* for their eyes, the rich black antimony from Sidi Kacem; rouge for their cheeks; henna for their hair and the designs that they loved to paint on their hands and feet to protect them against evil *jinns*; lengths of brilliantly coloured silk for his favourite girls, Mejah and Kyria, and always something for Mishaal, whom he worshipped from afar. Last time, it had been a fan of silky rose-pink ostrich feathers.

More tears flooded Rhikia's eyes as she recalled those happy days when Mishaal had been with her, her beautiful, graceful girl. Allah, how she had prayed that, wherever she was now, she would be safe and content!

Into a leather saddle bag she piled dates, figs and raisins, rice, flour for making unleavened bread during the journey, butter, a flask of *laban*, three flasks of drinking water and packets of herbs and spices. Beneath the food, she had hidden her few pieces of gold jewellery, carefully acquired over the years, and the bag containing the proceeds from the sale of the house in the Street of the *Jijims*. Enough to prevent her from starving during the next few years.

It was fully expected that Hamid, as her closest male relative, would impound the little house when he found that she had gone. Ali was to pose as Rhikia's creditor, appearing, apparently in a great rage, claiming that she owed him large sums from her days in the Street of the *Jijims*, and how he had been searching for her to demand that she pay her debts. When the little house was sold, Ali would pocket the proceeds as his 'rightful payment', and take them to Rhikia at the Beduin camp where she would be hiding out.

A smile flickered through her tears as she visualised Hamid being cheated. It was all that he deserved.

A low whistle beneath her window alerted her. There was Ali Ben Ali with his two shadowy companions, fellow Beduin who would take her to their camp in the Land of Mirages. The moment of freedom was come.

Strapping the bag closed, Rhikia glanced round rapidly, memorising the little house where she had planned to spend the rest of her days praying in atonement.

'Rhikia, you are well?' Ali Ben Ali beamed at her.

'Yes, yes, come in, come in,' Rhikia whispered, popping her head out of the door to see if anyone was watching, but the courtyard was silent and dark.

'The camels are waiting on the edge of the city. My son here . . .' he gestured to a smaller version of himself, 'and his good friend will see that you reach the camp safely. I warn you, Rhikia, that the journey will be long and arduous, especially now that the wells are dry, and the oases have no water. Are you still sure that you wish to go?'

'As Allah be my judge, I cannot wait to be away from here!' Rhikia raised her eyes heavenwards.

'You are a brave woman, Rhikia. Ah, if only I did not have four wives already, then I would make you my bride!' Ali Ben Ali offered the greatest compliment of which he was capable.

Rhikia did not know whether to giggle or sob.

'I have packed plenty of food as you said, and water and flour. How long will the journey take? I have never been on a camel's back before,' she confessed.

'In the region of a week, a little more if you suffer from saddle sores and have to rest. The camp is quite far distant now, for they have been in search of water, you see. Allah, but this shortage is terrifying! I do not know of one well that has not run dry in the past few weeks. We came past an oasis and there were corpses lying nearby, men who had died of thirst only a short way from the city, Allah preserve their souls!'

'I – I shall not have to see them, shall I?'

'No, we shall bypass that place now we know it is arid. Come now, Rhikia, we must leave. We want a good headstart.'

'I do not think it is likely that my cousin will follow into the desert. He is a very lethargic man; a stranger to exertion. He is also disgustingly fat, and the heat would kill him. Besides, he would then be in another prince's domain and subject to his laws, would he not?'

'Yes. City laws end where the Land of Mirages begins. In the wilderness, the Amir is sole monarch.'

'Did you not say that he was to marry?' Rhikia whispered as she followed the men out into the street.

'Yes. He has chosen his bride at long last. Some said he never would – that he would die without having heirs. It would have meant war and bloodshed, a battle between his sole surviving male relatives, plus of course the rival tribes who wished to take his place.'

'I thought that the Beduin chose their own rulers and that they would select a suitable Amir should one not have sons?'

'That can be done, Rhikia, but in the Land of Mirages, the present Amir's line has been uninterrupted since well before the days of the Prophet, an extraordinary lineage. Who would wish to follow after that? Besides, the Amir, Allah keep him safe, is deeply beloved. His people worship him.'

'Do you know him well?'

'I have met him on some half dozen occasions.'

'What is he like?' By talking, Rhikia was trying to keep her mind off the memory of her forlorn little house, and the frightening and unknown future before her.

'He is handsome as the stars and strong as the desert lion, the sun rises and sets in him, he . . .' Ali Ben Ali flattered.

'Yes, but what is he really like? And shall I see him, do you think? Would he be willing to listen to my troubles and perhaps help me if he can?'

'Well, you are a city dweller, but he is the most generous of men. He has never turned away anyone from his tent. He sold all his family's treasures bar one to help those of his people in need.'

'He sounds a saint!'

'He is, oh, he is, but he is also a normal man with normal needs, yet he has been so altruistic about caring for his people that we despaired of his ever looking to his own desires.'

'Choosing a bride, you mean?'

'Yes, choosing a bride. But now he has. She will be called the Amira Nur: that means "The Light of Husain", you see. I have not seen the lady but I hear that she is radiant as the moon.'

'Shall I be able to attend the wedding celebrations, do you think? Oh, I would not intrude, of course. The Amir's bride will have her own relatives there to assist her before the ceremonies.'

'Apparently not, Rhikia. She has no one. There was a half-sister, I believe, but she died suddenly.'

Rhikia's eyes lit up. 'She has no one? Oh, then I shall offer my help!'

Suddenly Rhikia felt happier about having to leave her cosy little home. With all her experience of orphaned young women, she was sure that she could help and befriend the young bride. Suddenly the desert trek ahead lost much of its fear for her. At the end there would be a young girl without family, who, if Allah were in benevolent mood, might well be in need of a foster mother.

The wind had been tearing at them since midday, sandpapering them with grit and dust. Mishaal had recognised another landmark that had been on Drew's map: a long-dormant volcano called the Fiery One, and she pointed it out to Husain, excitement in her voice.

'We are close now,' she said, her throat raw from the grit and sand. 'Only a few more hours, I would say.'

Husain's face brightened. 'What is the next landmark?'

'The Oasis of the *Jinn*. It is west from here.'

'The Oasis of the *Jinn*?' Husain's eyes grew dark. 'That is one of the most dreaded places in the land. No one has been there for years.'

'There might be water . . .'

'There might, or there might be illusion and mirages of the most confusing and dangerous kind . . . or so the old stories say.'

'They might be good *jinn* . . . Why should *jinn* always be evil?'

Husain laughed. 'You are right of course, little *fáhd*, why should they be?'

The wind was shrieking, grazing the sides of the dead volcanic pyramid and lashing at them venomously. Lowering her head, Mishaal loosened her veil and shook out the collection of sand and dust embedded in its folds. When she looked up again, she saw in the distance a group of viridescent palm trees, brighter and greener than she had ever seen. She pointed them out to her lover.

Heads bent against the tumultuous blast, they made for the Oasis of the *Jinn*.

After three hours of battling with the determined zephyr, they seemed to be no closer to the oasis. There it stood ahead of them, temptingly emerald and lush, yet they were getting no nearer. The sky was black and choked, and to their left they could see an ominous dark twist on the horizon.

'A whirlwind,' Husain warned. 'What we've seen of the *jinns* so far suggests they're far from kindly! We'd better dismount and find shelter until it passes.'

To Mishaal, time seemed distorted as she obeyed her lover. She knew that she was moving rapidly, her eye on that fast-approaching menace, yet it seemed to take an age for her to get down from the camel, collect her baggage, and make her way to the jagged and uneven slope of crag that loomed behind them. Here, there were many sheltering places, hollows and caves, boulders to crouch behind. With Husain beside her, she stepped cautiously into the shadowy entrance of the nearest cave, his hand in hers, her heart thudding furiously. Ahead there was a deep, jetty blackness leading she knew not where, but all her instincts told her to stay out in the air and light, yet she could not. Closer now came the whirling devil, and soon he would be upon them. If they faced him, they would be swept to perdition.

Gripping Husain's hand even tighter, Mishaal took her first steps into the chill and silent blackness.

PART SIX

Oasis of the Jinn

And I have listened till I felt
A feeling not in words
A love that rudest moods would melt
When those sweet sounds were heard
A melancholy joy at rest
A pleasurable pain
A love, a rapture of the breast
That nothing will explain.

John Clare

Say what is Love – to live in vain
To live and die and live again
Say what is Love – is it to be
In prison still and still be free?

John Clare

Chapter Thirty

Inside the cave they could still hear the screeching and wailing of the wind as if it were following them. As their eyes adjusted to the pitchy dark, they found that the hollowed-out berg was not so forbidding as it had seemed. Having spread out their goatskins on the rocky floor, they sat down to eat what was the last of their dried fruit.

'When we get to the oasis, we'll fill up our bags,' Husain reassured, while Mishaal could not help but think of the time they had taken riding until the sun had dipped quite low from its noontime peak, with the oasis still as far distant as ever.

Husain was reluctant to rest. While Mishaal would have given anything to relax against him and gaze into his eyes as a marvellous antidote to their plight, he wanted to explore.

'Often in these caves, if you travel far enough, you find water. Even if it is just a small pool, I'm sure you won't object to bathing in it, will you, my heart?' His eyes twinkled. 'Leave me some to drink before you splash around, though . . .'

'You think there will be water?' Mishaal was on her feet instantly, catching at her lover's hand as he stepped carefully over the rocky floor into the rapidly narrowing corridor of stone.

Very soon, the passageway was so narrow that Mishaal could touch its smooth sides with each hand as she walked. They were considering turning back, thinking that nothing lay ahead, when she spotted the pinhead of candescent light ahead of them.

'Sunlight!' she cried. 'There must be a gap in the berg!'

Now the blackness did not seem half so frightening to her as they forged on, making for the light. It swelled and became rounder as they came closer to it, almost like the sun rising, its brightness increasing until the candescence changed to a vivid apricot-gold. Suddenly, they were standing in a cavern, the narrow passageway having blossomed into a massive balloon of gilded, dazzling sunlight, and there, directly in front of them, twinkling and glistening like cloth-of-gold, was a large, almost perfectly circular pool.

Grinning at one another in delight, they rushed to the water's edge to cup the cool, aurulous fluid in their palms. The waters glittered in Mishaal's hands, as if the sunlight truly were within them, and when she lifted them to her mouth, a warmth seemed to rise from them, yet it was a refreshing warmth, as if she were absorbing the sun itself. It was an illusion, of course, caused by the water rationing of the past few days.

She laughed as the golden water trickled down her throat. She could feel its passage all the way down for it tingled in the most curious way. Grinning at her lover, she saw that he was puzzled over something, too. He was staring at the water in his palms and frowning.

'It comes from God!' Mishaal cried. 'It comes from God! Do you not see? He sent us here: it is a miracle, a miracle!'

She began to sway, her face wreathed in smiles, and then she was tearing off her desert-battered clothes and flinging them away, and, before Husain could stop her, she had plunged into the pool.

'Come on, it is beautifully warm,' she cried, splashing around energetically, then she bobbed under the water's surface to wet her hair, and her eyes were enraptured by what she saw in the bottom of the pool. Brilliantly hued pebbles and stones, golden yellow, scarlet, ivory, apple-green, deep rosy pink, cornflower blue, all the colours of the flowers that bloomed in the desert after the rains had been. 'Look below you,' she called to Husain. 'Look at the colours – they are marvellous!'

Then, feeling arms clamping round her legs, her heart

twisted in a painful somersault before she realised that it was her lover pinioning her. Tossing back his shining ebony hair, he sprang to the water's surface like a merman, swirling the waters so that their aurulous glow dissipated, scattered into silver-gilt slivers, and then reformed, creating an aureole around them.

Gleeful, they kissed and hugged and kissed again, and silently blessed the wind for sending them into cover. Soon Husain was gently supporting her on his hips while her knees clamped round his back, as he slipped deep inside her so that she shuddered with ecstasy.

The pool was not very deep and the colours of the pebbles at its base were thrown up, like a kaleidoscope, singing through the waters so that the lovers were trapped in a stained-glass window of sapphire, crimson, yellow and emerald, a glorious rainbow prism.

'A million years of rain has created this pool,' Husain whispered in her ear, 'and just for us . . .'

'No, no, God made it,' she whispered back, her voice a sigh. 'It is a blessing just for us.'

'God made the rain . . .' Husain smiled in her ear, before plunging more deeply into her, so that the waters were fractured and the prism of colours temporarily disbanded. They were as close as man and woman can be, and as happy. They had sunlight, water and earth and one another, their element complete.

The water slapping tenderly against her thighs and buttocks as Husain scythed in and out of her soft, moist centre, Mishaal curled close to him, her head on his shoulder for a few moments as her delight became almost intolerable. The myriad-coloured lights increased in brilliance, sweeping and dazzling across them, so that Husain's face was jewelled in ruby and sapphire and amethyst, as if he wore the ceremonial mask of some great and ancient mythical god, becoming, for one sharp, disturbing moment, a stranger to her. Then, the colours dimming again, she sighed against him, relieved.

'This moment was destined, it is part of our *nasîb*, our fate, my heart,' he murmured, nibbling her earlobe so that tingles of excitement sang through her body. 'We did not arrive here by accident . . . We were guided here, to this *siḥr*, this enchantment, and you, little *fáhd*, are a *saḥḥāra*, a sorceress who has bewitched me.'

'Then you are my *saḥḥār*, my sorceror,' Mishaal twinkled back. 'Do you think this cave is magic? Shall we be transformed into *jinns* and live here for ever more in happiness like this?' Pulling back a little, she gazed into her lover's face. The jewelled lights were dazzling again, his eyes no longer black pearls but gentian-blue sapphires, rich and bright.

'For ever more, for ever and ever, God willing,' Husain said fervently then, staring at her, he said, 'Your eyes are purple as amethyst now . . .'

'And yours are blue as flowers!' Mishaal reached out a wondering finger to touch Husain's right temple.

Then they forgot the miraculous prism in which they were trapped as in some magician's lair, and began to mount the steps towards the most glittering prize of all. Everything seemed to be exaggerated in this multi-coloured cave, including physical responses, and as Mishaal's excitement bloomed, she felt as if she might be swept away beyond all control.

She closed her eyes, yet the variegation of colours was in her head; she could see them still as if her eyes were open, and there was a hazy warmth about them, as if they burned at an eternal fire, the leaping, twisting flames spouting cerise, and ochre, honey gold, apple-green, mauve and cerulean. She wanted to know if Husain was seeing the colours in this way, too, but she was so deliciously, slumbrously happy that she could not summon the energy to say the words out loud.

They were lying cradled in one another's arms at the edge of the pool where a soft slope of gilded sand cushioned their limbs. One moment they had been suffering all the hardships of the wilderness, and then they were basking in heavenly colours and sheltered from wind and storm in a place which must have been there from the time of Adam and Eve. It was dreamily warm, yet the air was moist – Husain said that was because of the pool – and it would have been paradise had there been food to eat, but it was expecting too much that there be fig trees flourishing there.

Slowly she opened her eyes, to find Husain watching her.

'There are jewels in your eyes,' he said, his voice husky, at which she jabbed him in the chest with a teasing finger, and retorted, 'Yes, that's what I've been complaining about all this time!'

Laughing out loud, he gathered her close.

'But you won't complain from now on, will you, my heart?'

She pretended to consider this request seriously, cocking her head to one side and sucking in her lower lip.

'It will depend on you, Husain ibn Rashid. See me for myself, see me as I truly am, and I shall not complain.'

'I always have, little sorceress, which is why I want you for my bride. Would you have me take a girl without fire in place of you? A girl who bows her head meekly and salaams whenever I speak, and flings herself to the floor at my feet? By the Prophet, how tedious that would be.'

'So you claim to prefer one who argues and crosses you? One who believes that honours should be earned and not gifted because of an accident of birth?'

'Is that what you believe?'

'Is it right that a ruler, however evil or corrupt he might be, should have dominion over his people simply because he is the heir of the ruler who went before him?'

'Mishaal, that is talk for old men, not for beautiful young women like you!'

'Why should it be for old men? Do not women have brains, too? You see, you do not accept me as I truly am! I want to dispute many things that are accepted in the world. I want to know the answers to so many problems! For years, I was a – a chrysalis, and now I have cast off my shell and I want to make up for all those cloistered years. I want to talk, and learn, and make decisions, and raise my children to be like me . . .'

'Our children.'

'Mine.'

'A daughter raised in that way would not have an easy life. It is better for the Muslim woman to –'

'Yes, I know! To be raised behind veils and shut away in the harem, never to speak unless spoken to, never to question her husband's wisdom, or lack of it, never to think for herself, to produce a healthy son every year and worship her husband out of gratitude that he spends three hours a week with her, unless of course some new favourite has taken his eye . . .'

Husain was sitting up now, his arms crossed. 'If I were that sort of man, would you be speaking so freely to me now? Would I not have chastised you and cast you out long ago? I could have forced you to marry me, Mishaal, and by now you might have been expecting my son.'

'You would not go against the word of the Prophet! "No woman must ever be forced".'

'Many men would disagree, whatever the *Qu'ran* says. Sometimes a woman is possessed and does not know what is best for herself.'

'More often that is the male failing!' Mishaal snapped back.

It was obvious that the brief honeymoon was over. Mishaal began to gather her clothes together. Her bernouse was still wet, but her robe had been draped directly below the sun's blaze and was almost dry. Shaking it out, she did not notice the scorpion until too late. It sprang out of the folds as she shook them, and struck her between her breasts. Screaming out, she leapt backwards, narrowly missing wrenching her ankle on a dislodged rock.

Husain was beside her in seconds, his sandal crushing the scorpion into oblivion, and when she turned and clung to him, he kissed the top of her head tenderly, yet a little impatiently.

'Now wasn't that rather a sign of weakness from the world's greatest virago?' he tempted. 'The scorpion would never have dared touch you. He was already off in full flight when he realised who you were!'

Mouth hanging open, Mishaal thrust him away. How dare he call her that: world's greatest virago indeed! Then the funny side of it hit her and she began to laugh, knowing full well that it was not true and he did not mean it.

'That's some insult coming from the world's greatest treasure hunter!' she retaliated, still laughing, and then, noticing that the pool was right behind him, her hands shot out and she pushed him in.

The wind was dead. Mishaal and Husain stepped out of the enchanted cave and into the blistering glare of the afternoon sun. They were hand in hand. Sand had been shored up in the strangest shapes, hiding and half-concealing, so that the landscape looked very different from a few hours ago. They both turned their heads in the direction of the Oasis of the *Jinn*. It was still there. So it was not a mirage, after all.

Then they turned to see how the camels had fared, only to find that they were not where they had left them, their ankles hobbled together, sheltered in the lee of a crag. Where could they be? They could not have escaped out of their hobbling thongs. Could they be covered by shifting sand? This was a return to reality with a vengeance, the savage reality of the deepest and most deserted centre of the Land of Mirages. They had water in plenty now, but no mounts, and the Oasis of the *Jinn* lay some hours' journey ahead.

Mishaal's hand tightened round her lover's. She refused to be daunted. Whatever had happened had been the will of God, she was sure of it, and if it were, then she must accept it.

'*Mashallah,*' she whispered, her eyes very bright. '*Mashallah*, it is the will of God.'

Husain looked at her in surprise. It was the first time that he had ever heard her say that phrase, encapsulating the piety of Islam. 'It is the will of Allah. Allah's will be done.'

They began to walk towards the Oasis of the *Jinn*.

To keep their minds off the roasting heat, they talked. Husain told her about his mother, Salima, and how she and his father had adored one another.

'They never exchanged a heated word; they were happy

as the saints in one another's presence. My father used to tell me the old tales about the Prophet, and there was one that was my mother's favourite. She said that men spent their whole lives searching for material things when the most valuable things of all were staring them in the face.'

'So what was her favourite story?'

'One of Mohammed's disciples came to him saying that his mother, Umm Sa'd, was dead, and asking what were the greatest alms he could give away for the good of her soul.

'The Prophet replied, "Water", for he was thinking of the panting aridity of the desert wilderness. "Dig a well for her, and give water to the thirsty."'

'Water! Of course!'

'Simple, isn't it, and yet how vital a truth. Without water, none of us would be here.'

They walked on, the parched heat rising in dry, baking clouds from the earth, and as evening settled around them, Husain turned to her, grinning in that heart-stopping way of his.

'If only that pool had been filled with fish, we could have caught and eaten them. They say that you can see in the dark if you eat fish from a pool.'

'They would have been so colourful, we would not have dared touch them! I would not fancy a blue fish, would you?'

'I would not mind what its colour was if I was hungry. I would give anything for some *sawîck*, indigestible though it is.'

'What is that?'

'Have you never heard of it? Green grains, toasted and pounded, then mixed with chopped dates and honey or sugar. It is carried on long journeys where cooking will be difficult.'

'Last night you cooked a poor little *dhabb* that had done you no harm whatsoever!' Mishaal accused.

'Would you rather see me eating *sawîck* then?'

'Of course. I pray that you will eat more grains and *laban* and fruits, and leave those poor little lizards and birds alone!'

'So that is a condition of our marriage, is it? I do not eat meat any more?' He quirked a black brow, his eyes brilliant whether with annoyance or humour she could not tell. 'What happens when it is time to sacrifice a goat or a sheep? Will the Amira turn up her nose and munch on a dish of dates? That would offend our people.'

'They are *your* people and no, it cannot be a condition of a marriage that will not take place, can it?'

'So you are back on that silly track again, are you? And I had thought that you had matured these last few days. They say that the desert weans the infant and makes him a man.'

'Then the longer you are in the desert, the better!' she retorted, but she was laughing.

Although on camelback, they had travelled for hours never seeming to get nearer the Oasis of the *Jinn*, there seemed no hindrance to their progress on foot. They could see the palms appearing to grow in size, and their hearts gladdened when they realised that they would reach it by the next morning. There was a striking configuration of stars over the oasis, glinting brightly, as if in welcome.

As darkness enveloped them, they made camp, thankful that they had their goatskins, and the cooking utensils. Husain went in search of another plump little *dhabb*, while she took her turn at lighting the fire.

Happiness had filled her totally, and she began to sing. It did not matter that their camels had vanished, and they had barely any food; nor did it matter that they were in the desiccated heat of the Land of Mirages. Happiness when it came would not be turned away; singing, she had her arms crammed with dried rushes and crispy branches from the *misht* tree when Husain returned, the *dhabb* in his hand.

When the fire was burning fiercely, the lizard suspended over it on a little tripod, Mishaal began to hum beneath her breath to the tune of the music that had accompanied her peacock dance. Grinning, Husain turned the little spit and watched as the *dhabb* roasted in its skin. When it was ready, he cut it open, skinned it, and removed the tiny liver and sweetbreads and the succulent part of the tail to eat first.

'Eat some, Mishaal, or you will weaken and I would not welcome having to carry you in this heat.'

'No,' she said, turning down the corners of her mouth.

'This year I took a vow that I would not harm one of God's creatures to sustain my own life.'

'A Muslim vow or a Christian one?'

'I took it this year, so it was Christian.' She tossed her head.

'Allah would not condemn you for eating an animal when you would otherwise die.'

'Why? Does He not love all his creations equally? Would He want any of them to kill another out of greed?'

'Perhaps not out of greed, but out of necessity and great hunger. Is that too bad? Allah is pleased when a calf or a goat is sacrificed so that His people will eat well and be healthy and alive to honour and worship Him.'

'I see it differently – for myself, that is. Others may think what they will. I would never try to change their minds.'

'As I am trying to change yours, you mean? You are very saintly, Mishaal.'

'No, you must not call me that! It is too great a burden. Who would want that weight upon his shoulders?'

'Or upon hers?' He cast her a wicked, twinkling glance.

A lifetime in the desert had honed Husain with power and resistance; he did not seem to suffer from dehydration, or the blast of heat that drove itself into every crevice. Looking at him, Mishaal could see no signs of the exhaustion that she was feeling. She felt as if giant hands had squeezed her savagely, wrung her out, and let her drop to the ground. She had blisters on every toe, and her heels felt as if they had been kicked and bruised. Even a deep, deep draught of water did not alleviate that sensation of being slowly mummified. She drank again, having eaten the three shrivelled and tasteless dates that were little more than sugar now, and thought yearningly of freshly drawn ewe's milk, light and nourishing, and bright, acid-yellow lemons tugged from their dark-leaved tree then cut open and pressed to her lips so that the tart and reviving juice poured down her throat.

'If Allah is watching over us, we might be fortunate enough to see a flight of locusts,' Husain said, munching on his *dhabb*.

'Locusts? But they eat everything in sight, don't they? I thought they were scavengers?'

'They are, but they are also a handy portable food.'

'Food?' Mishaal blanched at the thought of eating one of those bewinged and ugly insects.

'The Beduin catch them, dry out their bodies and save them for a savoury treat when times are hard.'

'I see.' Mishaal swallowed, thinking of the locusts being crunched by hungry nomads, those hideous long, brittle legs going down human throats.

'Would you refuse one then? Boiled, they are not unlike green vegetables. Would you consider them included in your vow?'

'God made them, too,' Mishaal said stubbornly.

'Yes, but He also made the vegetation and the berries that you eat . . . They are as much living things as animals, surely?'

'They – they do not have souls.'

'So you think that animals have souls, do you? You should have been raised in India. Sometimes, I wonder if you were!'

'Why India?'

'The Hindu are a religious sect who believe that everything and everyone, from the smallest insect to the greatest human, has a soul, so they will kill nothing, not even an ant, for fear of disturbing the balance of karma.'

'What is karma?'

'Retribution, punishment for misbehaviour and failings, and also rewards for virtues displayed in previous lives. So if an ant is killed, it cannot claim its rewards, you see.' His eyes twinkled.

'Are you teasing me? I cannot believe that!'

'That is what the Hindu believe, and other sects too. They have refuted their reward in paradise for an eternal rebirth called reincarnation.'

'What is the aim of it all?'

'To reach *moksa*, that is, release from the eternal cycle of birth and death.'

'I do not believe in perfecting the soul for material rewards.'

'I think the highest among them would not consider material rewards to be their ambition. They want to help the earth, become purified and strong in spirit.'

'I approve of that!'

'You would, little *fáhd*. The body lags far behind though, does it not?' His eyes dropped to her blistered feet.

'Would you have me physically stronger than you, then? If I were, you would not have such a thrilling time showing off your Herculean strength, would you?' Now it was her turn for her eyes to twinkle.

Laughing, he reached out and caressed her under her chin with his forefinger.

'So now I'm a vain Olympian, am I?'

'You could say that.'

'And who was it who admired their face in the waters of the underground pool? Not I.'

'I was trying to see what the colours were at the bottom!'

'Maybe, maybe not,' he said infuriatingly.

'Definitely maybe not!'

'Have it your own way then.'

'Don't I always, according to you?' she giggled.

Then they were curling up in readiness for bed, the fire banked up to scare off predators, and their goatskins tucked around them, Mishaal's stomach rumbling embarrassingly.

'There is still some of the *dhabb* left if you want it.'

'No, thank you!'

It might have been the effects of hunger but when he kissed her, she seemed to burst into flame, a searing, scorching delight that eddied voluptuously along her flesh, and what had been intended as a loving goodnight kiss became a moment of intense passion for them both. Clinging together, hip to hip, they vanquished all the terrors of the night in the sweetest and most delirious fusion, pouring out their hearts and libations to one another.

Only an hour or so's steady travel away, the Oasis of the *Jinn* waited for them, its palm trees saluting one another in the night breeze, the fibrillating leaves dark as basalt, the small, candescent pool below them shimmering like cloth-of-silver in the moonglow, and the hazy moving shadows of the *jinn* flitting across the water like windborne leaves.

Chapter Thirty-One

When once your hands are empty, then your heart
Must purify itself and move apart
From everything that is – when this is done,
The Lord's light blazes brighter than the sun,
Your heart is bathed in splendour and the quest
Expands a thousandfold within your breast.
Though fire flares up across his path, and though
A hundred monsters peer out from its glow,
The pilgrim driven on by his desire
Will like a moth rush gladly on the fire.

Farid ud-din Attar

Fear God and give glory to Him; for the hour of His judgement is come: worship Him that made Heaven and Earth, and the sea, and the fountains of waters.

14:7 *The Apocalypse*

By morning's brazen light, the Oasis of the *Jinn* rose like an Old Testament miracle out of the sand with its limpid waters, thriving palms, dainty *sumr* trees, and the green-lacquered *dhodar* bushes, brightly hued flowers round their roots, their scarlet, lemon and sapphire petals so vibrant and rich that Mishaal knew she must touch them to see if they were real.

'How can this water be here like this, so far from anywhere? Should it not have dried up in the drought?' Mishaal stared down into the pool, its surface so clear that she could see every detail of herself reflected.

'An underground river must be below. There is no other possibility.'

'Or one of your beloved Allah's many extraordinary miracles?' Mishaal cast a sideways glance at Husain.

'Why not? He created Heaven and Earth, after all. What is one small oasis after that?'

'Do you realise that this must be one of the oldest oases in the desert, if it was on that treasure map originally?'

'There must be many just as old. Rivers do not vanish overnight – they are replenished with every downpour that comes.'

'Look at those enormous date palms . . . They will be ready for picking. It's the right time of year. Do you know, I have never picked a date off a tree.'

'Are you good at climbing?'

'I have never tried.'

'Perhaps I should do the climbing and knock them down to you?'

Husain had never seen such large and succulent dates. It was a little early for expecting them to be fully ripe, yet they were perfect for eating. He looked down below him to see Mishaal laughing excitedly as she caught the rich brown fruits in her skirt. Behind her the pool sparkled and shimmered and out of the corner of his eye he was sure, just for one swift second, that he saw something looking up at him from the depths, yet when he blinked and looked again, there was only water. What had it been? He tried to recapture it mentally as he loosened more dates. A face? No, that could not be, yet there had been an expression, or features, that formed some sort of expression, even if they were not human. Perhaps the heat was affecting him for the first time.

The Sword of God was firmly in his grasp as he hacked at the fruit, so he would never know how it suddenly slipped from his hand and dropped into the pool.

Mishaal gave a little cry, turning just in time to see it disappearing into the depths with a small, ringing splash.

'No!' he ordered when she looked as if she would dive in to retrieve it. 'I will get it.'

'Can we eat first? I am ravenous.'

'My heart, how could I refuse you?' He kissed her cheeks and the tip of her nose when he reached the ground.

The dates were fresh and honey-sweet, so soft that they felt like flesh, the water from the pool nectar of the old gods, and they ate until they were ready to burst.

'You can't swim after eating,' Mishaal reminded as Husain began to take off his clothes. 'You'll have to wait awhile.'

It was not difficult to fall into a light doze as they lay on the plushly verdant edge of the pool in the gathering heat of midday, arms round one another, ankles linked. Husain had no intention of resting for too long. Without his sword, he did not feel whole.

When he opened his eyes, it was dark. Shocked, he leapt to his feet, looking around. The palms bowed eerily above him, great jetty shadows, and at his feet the pool brooded, ebony satin, unrippled. There was a scent of incense in the air; puzzling because there appeared to be no source for it. Suddenly, he knew that he must retrieve his sword before another moment passed, dark though it was. How could they have slept for so long? Mishaal was still asleep, her arms tucked beneath her cheek, her dark hair fanning out around her.

He stood at the spot where the sword had disappeared into the water, and then, before he could remind himself of what had looked up at him from the pool's depths, he lowered himself into the cool wetness.

At first, it was hip deep, then suddenly bottomless. Drawing in a deep breath, he dived down into the abyssian darkness. Feeling about with his hands he felt rubbery weed and slimy plants, rocks, pebbles, something shiny and silver that flashed past his shoulder and was gone.

Feeling something hard and thin, his heart danced. He had found the sword! Rising to the surface, he surveyed what he clutched in his hand. It was nothing more exciting than a bar of iron, yet it had felt like the Sword of God in his grasp.

He stood for a few moments gathering his breath. Mishaal had woken and was sitting with her arms round her knees, grinning at him.

'When you rose out of the water naked and gleaming, I thought *you* were the god of the sea!' she said admiringly.

'If I were, then I would be able to see in the darkness. Allah, but I wish I could!'

'Take care, my beloved,' she called as he dived again, spearing the surface so fast that he had vanished out of sight before her words had died.

This time it seemed to be even darker, the plants and weeds more obstructive. They twined round his legs and tugged like greedy hands. Out of the corner of his eye, he thought he saw the strange silvered creature, whatever it was, treading water, examining him with curious eyes, but it was not there when he turned to face it. The name of the place came back to him: Oasis of the *Jinn*, and he shuddered.

His foot found the sword, his heel turning on its blade. Gratefully, he scooped it up in his hands and bore it to the surface, his heart so glad that he knelt at once to pray.

'Will you join me, Mishaal?'

She knelt beside him and bowed her head while the sword lay in front of them, saved from its watery grave, a ribbon of slippery weed convoluting its handle. Her eyes fell on the blade in astonishment. Reaching out, she touched the engraving that had caught her attention.

'Was that there before? I do not remember it.'

Picking up the sword, Husain stared so hard at the engraving that she thought he would never speak again. Then he spoke, his voice strangled.

'No, it was not there before. Have you read it? It is the legend, the same that was on the medallions we found in the Died-out Place.' His hand went to his neck, where one of the medallions lay, and then to Mishaal's breast, where another hung, half-hidden by her robe.

'*The* legend?' A sparkling shiver flowed over her skin and down her spine. 'You mean, the legend of the wells running dry?' She ran her fingertips over the Arabic wording. How could the words have got there? It was impossible.

'You know I mean that one, Mishaal.' He cast her a basilisk look, as if she were to blame. 'How in the name of Allah did it get on the sword?'

'Perhaps the fish round here can write?' She tried levity, but he frowned at her, his jaw clenched.

Whatever they thought or said, however much they guessed or pondered, there was no answer. He stared at the lively, thread-like Arabic script, deeply and ineradicably scored into the metal, and he knew that they would never have a solution.

Time seemed distorted while they were in the oasis, yet they had no desire to leave. These were the halcyon days, the Days of Heaven, and they wanted them to last for ever. The next day, as evening ushered in the cooler air, Mishaal reached into the bottom of her bag and lifted out her peacock costume. She had not worn it since she had danced for Husain's guests. How long ago that seemed; another universe, another epoch. Sliding her fingers over the glossy coloured feathers, she felt her heart leap as if it were coming to life again; as if she had been sleeping until this moment.

Watching her, Husain smiled with pleasure. She was so beautiful, her movements so limpid, as if she moved in flowing waters, gliding through the air weightlessly. How thick and lustrous was her hair, waving silk that cried out to him to be caressed, and her sweetly curving body, her proud little neck, the small, tender yet capable hands. Not once had she complained to him as they journeyed through the blistering heat that was second nature to him, but not to her, and during the hours they had toiled on foot, she had looked so content, as if she were approaching the happiest time of her life. He had hoped that it was because of him; now he was not so sure.

Now, as she lifted out the peacock robe, he knew that he could well be wrong, and a solid, sharp and unwelcome weight blocked his chest. Her face was illumined, as if painted with a hazy gold light and when she held up the robe and hugged it to her breast, she seemed to be oblivious of him. She was remembering all that she had been without him, before they met, when her life had been reclusive, only punctuated by the times she spent before her appreciative audience, dancing in that magical, halcyon way that made men feel as if they had been living in a deep, dark cavern until they saw her. He knew from his own reactions that some would stumble away after seeing her performance to find that their lives were pallid and vacuous. She was a beacon in the wilderness, a brilliant, glowing torch that lit his land as if it had never known sunlight.

Now the weight was in his throat, a gathering of tears coagulating thickly. He had not thought himself capable of such poetic feeling, but he was; suddenly he wanted to compose verse and sing to her, praise her to the stars and call down the moon in honour of her radiance.

From nowhere, the faint and haunting music began, the drum, drum, drum of the tabor and the eerie, echoing flute. He knew that he was imagining it and yet it sang against his ears and into his consciousness as convincingly as if it were reality. Mishaal could hear it too; he knew it as soon as he saw the expression on her face. There was wonderment and exultation, and disbelief commingling with the earnest longing to believe.

As she began to dance, the transformation started, the feathers of her costume gleaming as if they were living, their fluttering softness gently lifting and falling as she swayed, so that every colour shimmered and danced in a kaleidoscope. It did not matter that the light was dimming; to the entranced Husain, there was sun brightness and a glimmering candescence that would have alarmed him were it not surrounding the woman he adored.

Gracefully, lovingly, she swayed and swirled, raising her arms so that she took on the appearance of a great, multihued bird about to take flight, and it was as if her feet had never touched the ground, and there was no weight or substance to her body, only the lilting, haunting music and the featherlight movements that brought tears to Husain's eyes they were so beautiful. If he died at that second, he would die the happiest and most grateful man on earth.

Mishaal was in her own little world, elevated by the music that was exercising a strange enchantment over her. It seemed to come to her from the desert wilderness, the basalt blackness beyond the oasis, as if an Arabian Pan were playing his pipes just for her, and a spell were being cast that raised her into the stratosphere of witchery and enchantment. She did not want to question or seek; she wanted to dance.

Dipping and whirling, gyrating and swaying, she was conscious only of the weightlessness of her body and the encompassing desire to perform her peacock dance in reverent honour of all that was most glorious and deserving in life. It was a celebration and a benediction, an offering to the God of the Muslims and of the Christians; whether His name was Allah or Jehovah, He was the same Great One who had breathed life into the earth, the sea and the skies, the One who was responsible for her own creation and that of the man watching her dance.

The lessons of her childhood filled her mind.

'Allahu akbar, Allahu akbar,
La Allah illa Allahi
Allahu akbar wa lillahi al-hamdu
Allahu akbar kabirihi wa al-hamdu
Allahu akbar lillahi kathirihi
wa subhana Allahu bukratan wa asilan.
La Allahu illa Alahi
La na'bud illa aiahu mukhlasina lahu ad-din
wa lau kariha al kafiruna
La Allahu illa Allahi wahduhu
sadaqa wa'duhu wa nasara 'abduhuh wa 'azza junduhu wa
Lazama al-ahdzab wahduhu
La Allahu illa Allahi wa Allahu akbar wa lillahi al-hamdu.'

'God is great, God is great
There is no God but God.
God is great and to God the praise.
God in His immensity is great and to God much praise.
Glorify Him in the dawn and at the fall of night.
There is no God but God.
Him alone we serve, purifying our worship to Him,
Though the unbelievers hate.
There is no God but God alone.

His word is truth, He gives victory to His servant;
He gives glory to His army and puts the sectaries to flight.
There is no God but God. To God the praise.'

She could hear the chanting voices of the Muslim *Atakbir*, the declaration that God is great which was at the very heart of the beliefs of Islam; it was as if a great multitude were encircling them, their voices somehow in tune with the eerie music. She was dancing a prayer.

She was dancing a prayer.

Husain was suddenly aware that the medallion hanging at his neck was hot against his skin, not painfully hot but warm enough for him to notice it, and enclose it in his palm. The strangeness of this did not disturb him; were they not in the Oasis of the *Jinn*, where day was night and haunting music played for them from invisible instruments? His eyes fell to his sword lying by his feet and it seemed to him that the freshly engraved legend was limned with silver, fluorescent and bright. Directing his gaze back to Mishaal he saw that the luminescence around her had increased so that she glowed like a silvery torch, a moonlight-coloured flame in the night.

Mishaal, whose name meant Torch, whose mother had said, 'She will be a light for her people.' And suddenly he knew, and the knowledge was so engulfing, so overwhelming, that he could not breathe or move. *The legend was Mishaal: she was the legend*. She was the one, the believer whose hand must lift the Jewels of Destiny from their ancient resting place in the temple of the Mother Goddess. She was the one who could invade that place of taboo and yet bring no harm to herself, or to him; she and she alone could fulfil the words of the prophecy and return his people's fortune to them . . .

Whirling, dazzling in her silver-limned aureole, Mishaal knew nothing but the glorious ecstasy of her dancing, the heartfelt delight of this spiritual terpsichore that lifted her into the ranks of the immortals so that she touched the portals of paradise, saw the colour and texture of the shimmering gates, the pearly clouds and the sapphire skies before slowly, gradually returning to earthly reality.

The music did not die; it drifted into silence, as if carried away by the wind, and Mishaal's dance ended with it, suspending her in the cold sharpness of reality, the silvered universe of illusion gone. It was painful; she needed comfort.

Holding out her arms, she ran into Husain's embrace and begged to be soothed with his kisses.

PART SEVEN

The Jewels of Destiny

I have a high purpose firmer than a rock and stronger than immovable mountains,
And a sword which, when I strike with it ever, the useless spearheads give way before it.
And a lance point which, whenever I lose my way in the night, guides me and restores me from straying,
And a mettlesome steed that never sped but that the lightning trailed behind it from the striking of its hooves.
Dark of hue, splitting the starless night with a blackness, between its eyes a blaze like the crescent moon,
Ransoming me with its own life, and I ransom it with my life, on the day of the battle, and with my wealth.
And whenever the market of the war of the tall lances is afoot, and it blazes with the polished, whetted blades,
I am the broker thereof, and my spearpoint is a merchant purchasing precious souls.
Wild beasts of the wilderness, when war breaks into flame, follow me from the empty wastes;
Follow me, and you will see the blood of the foemen streaming between the hillocks and the sands . . .

Antara Ibn Shaddad, 6th C.

Chapter Thirty-Two

Leaving the oasis was not easy; they could have stayed there for the rest of their lives. Recalling their experience as they left the Died-out Place, neither of them looked back for one last glimpse of the bowing palms and the glinting pool. If the oasis had vanished in a drift of dream dust, then they did not want to know. It was engraven in their hearts.

Neither of them, at that point, was aware how terrible the reality would be, but it was imminent, a dark, winged shadow to engulf and imprison.

The treasure route on the map was clear in Mishaal's mind; it was bright and sure, as if she had seen it only moments before. Now there was only a short way to travel, two simple, straightforward days; and then everything took a different turn, and all their plans were destroyed.

The riders were upon them in seconds, for they were on racing camels, strong and sturdy animals that lumbered down on them aggressively. Veiled, the riders looked like villainous desert bandits. Mishaal shrank against Husain, her hand to her mouth, while he stood boldly facing them, the Sword of God in his hand, the legend gleaming as if newly limned with silver. To defend the woman he loved he would fight to the death, and kill her too rather than allow her to fall into the hands of vicious bandits who would enslave her.

Ordering his camel to kneel, the leader of the bandits leapt down to the sand and headed for Mishaal, who gave a cry of horror and clung to Husain. Then, to her astonishment, she heard the bandit calling her name, over and over.

Standing before her, he tugged off the veil that was shielding him from the sand clouds and her heart turned over when she saw his face, those bright blue eyes, so beloved, the silver-gilt hair, the smiling mouth, the arms held out to embrace her.

Beside her, she was aware that Husain had gone rigid, his sword arm slowly lowering. He was speaking, but she was so stunned that the words rippled through her head and did not make sense.

Drew ignored him, taking her hands in his and looking down at her adoringly. Oh, she had not believed that a man could return from the dead! Were they still in the Oasis of the *Jinn* and was all of this a mirage, an illusion? Tears trickled down her cheeks and then she was crushed against him, half-laughing, half-weeping, and he was telling her how he had searched the Land of Mirages for her and that he would never ever let her go. 'Honey, if you only knew how good it is to see you! The trouble I've had getting finance for this expedition . . . the problems! You just wouldn't believe it. I had everything ready and then I went down with the most wretched fever and when I came round, I'd somehow lost two months of my life! Two entire months! Darn it, but it is good to see you again, honey!'

He held her at arm's length to see her properly, his face alight with exultation. She could sense Husain's withdrawal, could feel him stepping away, in silence. He would let her choose; he would never try to force her if she decided upon Drew; they had come too far together for that. She was still shocked; she had not yet found her tongue. All she knew was that a miracle had taken place, and that the man she was to have married was returned to her.

Drew led her gently away from Husain and towards the waiting riders.

'When this is over, we'll go to America, honey, just like I promised. You'll be able to dance there like you wanted. You'll be a real artiste, fêted and famous. There'll be no more of this ragged urchin life for my wife. I want to see you in silks and satins, and little kid boots for your feet, and there'll be pearls for that lovely neck . . .'

The words washed over her, little silk drops pattering into her mind so that she had no resistance. All her dreams were reviving: freedom in the New World, the freedom to live as she pleased as Drew's wife, to dance in respectable halls, not the sordid brothels of her homeland. He had said that she would be renowned, that lords and ladies would come to see her perform and she believed him.

There was a footfall behind them. This time it was Drew who stiffened, anger darkening his face. Turning to Husain, he growled,

'The little lady goes with me. You're outnumbered, six to one, so I wouldn't try anything foolhardly if I were you.'

Mishaal had turned too, and now she could see Husain's stricken expression. There was rage there, but shock and alarm, too, and his mouth had tightened as if he were defending himself against a terrible grief. Opening her mouth, she tried to speak. She wanted to say that she was sorry, and ask his forgiveness, but no sound would come. Her throat was as stricken as his heart.

'Come on, honey. As soon as we get back to civilisation, we'll get you out of those rags and find you some ladylike clothes, and there'll be more jewels than you know what to do with.'

'Jewels?' she said huskily, finding her voice at last.

'I said jewels, honey. By my reckoning we're near to them now. No, don't try to stop me!' he growled again as Husain stepped closer, the Sword of God in his hand. 'If you touch me, my men will hack you to pieces.'

'If you take the Jewels of Destiny, then you will condemn my land to death and starvation! There will be no food, no water. The women and children will die, and the old men and the camels. Horses will turn into skeletons and bake in the desert heat . . . you will destroy us all!' Husain's voice was the voice of the tempest's surge, threatening, defying.

Drew Huntington threw back his gilded head and laughed harshly. 'You don't believe all that black magic, do you? Legends and curses! That nonsense – crazy! Finders are keepers and I intend to be the finder.' The blue eyes narrowed.

'I shall die before I let you steal the jewels!' Husain advanced upon Drew, the Sword of God glittering in the sunlight.

Again Drew gave that harsh and mirthless laugh. 'How do you intend to stop me? Try to interfere and my men will see that you stay here for eternity.' The blue eyes were hard as gunmetal.

'I shall fight you all . . . I shall not stand by and let my land be laid waste . . .'

Mishaal cried out a warning, but she was too late. The burliest of Drew's companions had been playing with a coil of rope. She had not realised what he was doing until she saw him whirling the rope round and round, so that it formed an airborne hoop that shot through the air and landed around Husain, pinioning his arms to his sides. He struggled fiercely, thrusting out his arms and flexing his muscles but the rope bit deeper with every movement. Grinning, Drew strolled over to him and tried to wrench the Sword of God from his fingers. After a struggle, two of the veiled men approached Husain and kicked him to the sand. As he lay there, the breath knocked from his body, one of the men stamped on his hand, once, twice, until he was forced to free the sword, whereupon it was placed in Drew's grasp. He smiled down at it delightedly, smoothing a finger along the blade.

Mishaal could not believe what had happened. Her first joy at seeing Drew had been serrated by their argument, by the threats and talk of death, and now this cruelty . . . Drew and Husain, the two men whom she loved, had loved . . . She put her hands to her temples, giving a cry of agony. She loved them both. She loved them both! She could not bear to see Husain treated like this, to see the murderous hatred on his face when he looked at Drew.

'Stop! Oh stop, I cannot bear this!' She threw herself between them, arms outstretched to keep them apart. 'This is so futile, so stupid. Please, please let Husain go free . . . He will not hurt you, I am sure of it!'

Drew touched her shoulder lightly, yet there was a cold warning in his eyes.

'Didn't you hear him say he would kill me, honey? I believe

him. Look at his face. He wants me dead. I would be a fool to let him go. He would sneak back in the night and stick a knife in me. Arabs are like that.'

'Yes, I would kill him, Mishaal,' Husain growled. 'Stay out of this. We must settle it between us.'

'It's settled already, Arab. You stay trussed up and I get the jewels.'

'No, you will never have the jewels!'

'They are mine already.' Drew's eyes glittered.

'Please, Drew, please let him go!' Mishaal pleaded, hanging on to his arm, but he behaved as if she had not spoken, patting her hand in an absent fashion and turning his back on Husain.

More ropes were added to the lassoo, and soon Husain's wrists and ankles were rubbed raw as they travelled, their prisoner slung over the back of one of the camels in the most humiliating way.

Mishaal fought back her tears. Her pleas had been ignored and Drew was intent upon Husain staying as he was, a helpless prisoner, until they reached the temple and the jewels. Nothing she said had moved him; once, he had looked at her with pained eyes and said, 'But I thought you loved me, honey? Do you want him to kill me? You were his prisoner, weren't you? Don't you want your revenge on him?' She had hung her head, unsure, stricken at the turn of events that had made ashes out of glory. She could not look in Husain's direction without her eyes welling with tears and so she ceased to look and, as the hours passed, her mind went over and over all the possibilities of the next day or so.

If she behaved as if she still loved and trusted Drew, perhaps she could sneak out in the darkness when everyone slept and cut Husain free? That would surely be the simplest method. If she let Drew suspect, then she would never be allowed the freedom of movement. But why did she speak as if she no longer loved Drew? Seeing him again had revived all her old feelings for him; how she had adored him and yearned to be his wife, and she was shocked to discover that she was torn between the two men, that she appeared to love them equally. She was in turmoil.

The journey was an agony of the heart for her; she could not wait for nightfall. When they made camp, having ensured that the little knife she carried in an inner pocket of her cloak was still safely there, she struggled to behave normally. Food was handed round, and she took hers as if she were ravenous.

Drew sat cross-legged beside her, his knee touching hers, his eyes glinting in the light from the camp fire.

'Isn't this romantic? Just you and me and the stars . . . you always did have a fancy for them, didn't you?'

Flushing, she nodded, lifting one of the shiny brown dates and putting it to her lips. It tasted of dust and decay; she wanted to gag on it and spit it out. A few yards away, Husain was sitting with his ankles tightly bound, his arms freed so that he could eat. The moment that he had eaten and attended to a call of nature, they trussed him up again for the night, the silent, veiled thugs who obeyed Drew's every word.

She managed to swallow a little water, but nothing else. Drew put his arm around her, and she leaned her head on his shoulder.

'When this is over we'll have all the time we need just to ourselves,' he whispered, his hand brushing her breast. To her dismay she felt herself respond. She wanted him to hold her and kiss her, yet how could she feel like that? How *could* she? She was betraying both Husain and herself. Self-loathing rose inside her, acid, scalding.

The night grew blacker and the men settled to sleep. Drew lay down on his sheepskin, Mishaal beside him. She could barely breathe, she was so watchful. The figures of the sleeping men rose like glowing black arches from the sand, weirdly illumined by the force of her tortured imagination; she was sure that their eyes were upon her, that they could see in the darkness, and so she waited longer than she had planned before carefully creeping out from Drew's side, and, with the little knife in her hand, slowly, cautiously approached Husain.

Placing her hand over his mouth, she whispered his name in his ear. She felt his body jolt, felt the hope rise in his breast; in that tense moment, she was feeling his feelings, thinking his thoughts. Swiftly the little knife sliced through the bonds and his arms were free so that he could take the blade for himself and hack at the ropes around his legs.

Tears filled Mishaal's eyes as she saw the ropes falling away. Soon he would be free . . . and she? Until that second, she had planned to free only him, not herself; she had wanted to stay with Drew, hadn't she? Now, she did not know . . . Yes, she did. She could not let Husain vanish into the night without her; what if she never saw him again? Oh God help her, what should she do?'

'Neat, but not quite neat enough.'

The voice came at them like a weapon, and then Drew's hand was taking Mishaal's and dragging her to her feet, and she saw the little blade kicked from Husain's fingers as he struggled to cut away the last few bonds. With a massive effort, he tried to leap to his feet, untangling the ropes as he moved, but the veiled men were upon him, all of them, silent and merciless, and Drew pulled her towards him so that she could not see what they were doing.

'You little idiot! Do you want all his hordes riding down on us? We'd never get the jewels then . . . What's the matter with you? Surely you don't hold some sentimental feelings for him? Christ, but women can be stupid!'

She listened in a growing numbness, feeling so chilled that she could not reply. If Husain were freed, he would bring back his men to deal with Drew: they would kill her first love and take the jewels. Why had she not thought of that? In the blind emotion of the moment, she had forgotten that possibility. She put a hand to her mouth to stifle a groan. Whatever she did, one of them would die.

Drew had her by the arms and was staring into her face.

'You don't think you're in love with him, do you? He's a savage, my love, an out and out savage! Do you think he would show me any mercy if I were his prisoner? Remember how he split us up and how he treated you then . . . Mishaal, see reason!'

'No, I don't think I'm – I'm in love with him,' she whispered hoarsely. 'I – I felt sorry for him, that's all.'

'Christ! Women!' Drew pulled her close and half-shook,

half-hugged her unresisting body. Stars flashed out of the corner of her vision. As if from a thousand miles away, she heard the sound of Husain fighting the veiled men, but in vain, and then there was silence and she knew that he was bound and gagged again, her beautiful barbarian shackled like a felon.

That night she barely slept; her heart was so divided that she felt as if it had been cut into two aching, bleeding halves, and it seemed to her that she could read Husain's thoughts, feel his agony and frustration, and she wanted to die.

Daylight found them trekking over low dunes, and now within sight of their destination. Like a mirage, in the far distance the temple met their eyes and they fell silent in awe. There were ruins dotted here and there throughout the desert, religious edifices, Roman forts and arenas, ancient, long-deserted townships, yet none of them had ever seen anything quite like the temple that had been taboo for so many centuries. There was an impressive majesty about it, a hardy courage that spoke of a determination to survive, whatever the cost, floods or deluge, drought or earthquake. 'Nothing shall reduce me,' it seemed to say as they stood in the drifting dust, parched and aching with the heat, the taste of salt on their lips, a different tale in each one's heart.

'This is not the same as we saw before,' Mishaal said, wonderingly. 'When we thought we were close before, we could not have been, my Drew.'

'Was that the mirage, or is this?' Drew's mouth twisted, yet his hand round hers was tight, comforting.

'That bright, silvery stone . . . I have never seen its like before.'

He looked at her fondly, thinking that her enthusiasm for new things was one of the most delightful qualities she possessed, then his eyes returned to the temple that he had dreamed about and yearned for during the past long, bitter months. After being thwarted by that darned Arab savage, who had paid him off to keep him from the treasure, he had been attacked by desert brigands and left for dead. He had recovered slowly, but was too weak to travel back to his homeland, so he had to send to New York for money. Then, when he was all ready to set out, the fever had come, the result, so the physician had told him, of his privations in the wilderness. For the rest of his life it was likely that he would have recurrences of it.

As a result, he had vowed that if he must take home the physical weakness that had enslaved him in the desert, then he would also take the Jewels of Destiny and spend the rest of his days in luxury. He would take his beautiful Arabian bride, too. Arabian women knew how to make good wives; they had none of the high-handed independence of so many American women. He loathed their steely pioneer spirit, from the poorest to the most aristocratic. His days with Mishaal had spoiled him for other women; he did not wish to tie himself to a complaining, domineering pioneer girl. He wanted honeyed smiles, warm flesh and rosy kisses and the unalloyed adoration that the little dancer had given him from the first hour they had met. She would be some small recompense for his ordeal. As for that vicious savage who had tried to take her from him, well, it was unfortunate, but he could not let the Arab live. If he went free, he would bring his followers after the jewels and that could not be allowed. It would take Drew and his men some days to escape the desert; they must have time to make their way to safety unhindered.

Staring at the shining white stone of the temple, Mishaal became aware of a rushing sound as if a great wind roared past her ears, yet the desert air was desiccated and still. Ahead of her lay the entrance to the temple, dusty and crumbling, yet in her eyes as stately and magnificent as when it was first built. Dashing a hand across her face, she looked again, knowing that she could not be seeing aright. Her legs trembled; she longed to run back. There was too much agony ahead of her; whichever way matters went, she would be heartbroken. This burden was too much for her: why had she been given it, why?

'Can you not let him go free now, Drew?' she heard herself say, astonished at her own temerity. 'This is no place to fight one another. We are near a place of worship . . .'

'A pagan temple, honey, not a church!' Drew grinned lazily. 'The people who worshipped here didn't know a thing about God. They sacrificed children and animals, and let them bleed to death on the altar in honour of their pagan goddess. The so-called priestesses were whores who gave their bodies to any man who wanted them, lord or beggar, then the local peasants created that ludicrous legend out of their own ignorance.'

'No!' she cried, startling him. 'No! They did not! They were holy women and they loved their goddess and she loved them . . . As for the legend, of course it is true! Of course it is!'

'True if you are a superstitious savage maybe,' Drew's lip curled nastily, 'but not if you're intelligent and educated. Life in America will cure you of all this claptrap, at least it better had. Now come on, follow me.' He returned to his mount, and helped Mishaal to climb up in front of him.

The distant ruined temple never left Mishaal's vision throughout the long journey. They had envisaged reaching the ruins by midday but it was decided that they would pause to eat and rest until the scalding heat of noon evaporated. Drew cursed at the delay, but there was nothing he could do about it.

They flung Husain on to the sandy ground, but this time no one cut free his hands. One of the veiled men held a water flask to his lips, and he drank in painful, searing gulps; then fruit was thrust into his mouth and a chunk of unleavened bread, hard and indigestible. Husain forced himself to think of the strength he would need in the coming hours, trying to keep his thoughts from the woman he loved and who was now ignoring him. She had not looked in his direction since she had tried to cut his bonds; he knew that she was ashamed of the way she had deserted him, but deserted him she had. She must love that American with all her heart to have run into his arms so easily. Allah, how he loved her, but she had never truly been his, he knew that now. Not even during the Days of Heaven had she been his; all this time her heart must have been with the American. So much for Mishaal and the legend, and how she would save his land from drought! He had been a romantic fool, a drooling idiot, and now he was paying the price for his witlessness.

This would be the last time they would halt before they reached the temple. He was racking his brain to think of a way to escape; he had done little else since they had first shackled him, but they had coiled so many ropes round him that he felt as if he were paralysed. Gradually he had been wriggling one or two loose, but it was a slow, tortuous business and he had to stop every time one of them looked in his direction. Now the sun was beating down into his eyes and he could not roll himself over, the ropes were so constricting.

Minute after long minute he worked away at his bonds, tensing his muscles to expand the ropes until he felt that they must surely give, yet with each effort he was disappointed. The ropes had been damped before they had bound him; now they were cutting deep in his flesh, biting like acid, bemusing his mind with pain, but he refused to give in. This was *his* land, not any ruthless stranger's, and the Jewels of Destiny belonged to him and his suffering people, not to this avaricious American.

One of the ropes was on the point of giving; now, he could extricate his hand if he was careful, working slowly so that they would not be attracted by any sudden movement. Cautiously, yet determinedly, he freed first one hand and then the other, elation swelling in his veins at his success. Next his feet. He would have to lie on his side and bring his knees up to his chest as if he slept, while his fingers tugged and pulled at the lower thongs and he kept his ears alerted for anyone approaching him. Hours seemed to pass before the first section of rope loosened slightly. Delight coursed through him. Summoning a patience he did not feel, he glanced cautiously at the group who were sitting round in a circle finishing their meal. They were all laughing, no doubt thinking of the treasure they anticipated finding that day and sharing out between them.

Fury seared him at the thought of strangers stealing the jewels, his anger a greater paralyser than his bonds, for he wanted to leap up and charge at them, knowing that if he did, they would kill him instantly. He had no weapons; the American had the Sword of God. He held it up in the air now and again, always when he was confident that Husain was watching, and swished it through space, or polished the blade with a piece of cloth in a covetous, possessive manner, fully aware that he was making Husain seethe with frustrated rage.

When he had cooled enough to move with wisdom and not impetuousity, Husain lay still until they had settled themselves to sleep through the boiling midday heat and then he began to slide along the ground, agonisingly slowly, biting on his lips, praying to Allah that they would not see he was free.

Mishaal half dozed, dazed with the heat, wild dreams swirling in her mind. She saw Husain bearing aloft the Sword of God in his hand, galloping towards her on Prophet like an ancient warrior king, and she was running to him, arms outstretched, calling his name. And then she knew that if she went to him he would have Drew killed with that very same sword . . . Drew's head would be hacked off; he would lie on the sand with the blood jetting from his neck and draining away into the earth. Somehow his blood was splashed on to her face and breast; she was screaming, looking down at it in terror, and Husain was laughing exultantly at her distress.

She woke with a jolt of shock, feeling her body damp with sweat. Everyone was sleeping; even the restless American beside her had his eyes shut, his body relaxed. Instantly she looked across to the spot where Husain was shackled, and she had to bite back the gasp that came to her lips when she saw that it was empty.

A few yards farther away she saw him slithering cautiously out of sight behind the dune which rose like a golden mountain before them. Her heart jumped hard, and she knew what was meant when people said their heart came into their mouth. There was a twisting alarm of pain through her chest and into her belly. She remembered Drew's cold, frightening guns and the feel of death in them; would he use them on Husain, shoot at him as he tried to run?

Allah, what shall I do? she thought in despair. What shall I do?

Indecision turned her legs to putty; she could not move nor could she find her voice to warn Drew. She knew Husain far better than she knew her American, she realised. There was a better chance that Hussain would allow Drew to go free than Drew Husain. It was disturbing to come to this realisation. Her American might kill Husain, but Husain would only wish to kill him in self-defence.

The sun was scalding; she longed to be able to close her eyes and forget, but she could not. She wanted to watch Husain as he made his escape; there he was, the man she had almost learned to love, the one who had begged her to marry him. Within minutes he would be running free, back to his people, and she would never see his handsome, sun-tanned face again; it would all be over. Over.

She felt the tears though she did not shed them; they lay inside her, a flood of misery, and she was as helpless as a kitten to alter what fate had decreed. The decision had been taken out of her hands; it would be Drew whom she would marry, and America would become her home.

Of all the stupid and inane things to do, he thought later. He, veteran of the desert for a lifetime, so knowledgeable about its animals and insects. In his exhilaration at escaping he had forgotten everything except the thrill of being on the move again and his own master.

When the snake lunged at him for disturbing its travels, he tried to clamp his mouth shut on the cry of agony, but not quickly enough. He was lying sweating and ashen-faced when the first veiled man came over the dune-top. He struggled to move on, to crawl away, but his mind was filled with a vortex of clashing zig-zags and colours and his muscles were slowly constricting, furiously, ragingly tightening so that he could not move; he was shackled again.

His master had said that he wanted the prisoner to see the

jewels being taken; wanted to see the agony on his face when he realised that he had lost the treasure. That was the only reason why Drew's man lunged at the raw, scarlet snake bite and cut deep into Husain's flesh, so deep that the noxious poison was sliced out and flung to one side before the man sucked at the wound and then spat out what was left of the bitter venom.

Consciousness returned within the hour and Husain could focus again. He saw Drew Huntington pacing up and down in the heat, swinging his arms up and down while Mishaal ran after him, apparently begging with him. Faintly he heard her voice.

'Please, my Drew, do not leave him here! Please! He will die! We have only a short way to go now . . . Leave him in the shelter of the temple if you must, but not out here in the open, please!'

For answer, Huntington pushed away her pleading hands where they clung to him, and glared down at her, his face a scowl.

'What gave you the idea I'd leave him here? I want him to see me take the jewels . . . It will be a lesson he'll never forget, my love. When I hold them in my hands and he has to watch them being taken away from him for ever, *that* is what will satisfy me immensely. I would not forfeit that opportunity.'

'Allah be praised!' Mishaal whispered, her colour returning.

'Not Allah, my love, never Allah. Thank the good Christian God, not that jumped-up savage's idol.'

Then the sound faded again from Husain's ears; he could see the lips move but hear nothing. He must have blacked out again because, when he came round, they were moving towards the temple.

Chapter Thirty-Three

Mishaal felt uneasy as they approached the temple; there was a strange and unhappy atmosphere; it was as if time had returned to those ancient centuries before when the heart-broken Zenobia had parted with her treasure, giving it into the safe keeping of the goddess who had once reigned supreme.

Drew was elated, his face glowing, his eyes brighter than she had ever seen them. He was soon leaping down from his camel and vanishing inside the building, his men following close behind, swords at the ready. Mishaal's legs seemed to be as frail as tissue, the muscles shrieking with pain, yet she knew what she must do.

In his excitement at being so close to his goal, Drew had forgotten about the Sword of God. He had two pistols tucked into his belt so he would not need the sword, and he had slotted it through one of the leather thongs on the camel saddle. There it lay, like Excalibur, waiting to be claimed by its true master. Hardly daring to look, she turned her head in Husain's direction. He was staring up at the temple, consternation in his face, and she could see him struggling for strength.

She went to the Sword of God, gently pulled it out of its sheath and with halting steps took it to Husain. Placing the sword into his hand was like switching on some extraordinary force of energy for them both; she felt it even as he did. She saw the colour and health come back into his face and before her eyes he changed from being a man near death into one whose stamina and courage were unconquerable.

'Mishaal,' he whispered her name as if it were a prayer. 'I love you; whatever else happens, believe that.'

'I believe it, Husain, I believe it,' she whispered back, tears in her eyes. 'Escape now, while you have the chance . . . They are inside, their minds on the jewels. Please, my love, go now, please!'

He smiled silently, gripping the sword so fiercely that his knuckles glowed white.

'Leave here now? Never! Do you think I would let him take my jewels and my woman? He shall have neither!' And with that, Husain got to his feet, swaying only once as he righted himself.

'He will kill you!' she cried. 'You must escape now, while they're inside, oh please, please, take one of the camels and go, my love!'

He looked down at her, his fathomless dark eyes bright with determination and zeal, but there was tenderness about his mouth.

'Mishaal, this is our destiny, here, now. We cannot run away like frightened children.'

She was the one of the legend, after all; he knew it now. Through her, his land would be resurrected, but how?

For a few moments they stood hand in hand facing the temple with its massive Romanesque columns, tall, slender and stately; its timeless strength that had withstood the centuries. When this was built, civilisation had been in its infancy, and yet what a glorious childhood, now lost and never to be repeated, when man and woman had held all knowledge in their hands, when out of the dankness of the earth and the limpid skies, the world had been sown, nurtured and brought into flower.

There had been riches then, material and spiritual, and people were so close to the earth and nature that there was a blessed symbiosis between them, gratitude for what the land yielded and reverence for the Earth Mother who provided the vital nourishment that supported life.

How distant humankind was now, after 2000 years of male gods, for with the rejection of Mother Earth, there had been the rejection of all that was vital to humankind, a coldness falling that had displayed itself in centuries of war and battles, with woman subjugated and treated with contempt while man was elevated to a mortal godliness.

The priest must be male; the law was penned and upheld by men who were in the Prophet's image; Allah, Jehovah, both were male. The compassion had been wrung out of the words of Mohammed and Jesus and retranslated according to men's desires. And what was the result? Arabia was divided amongst itself, the tribes warring and avenging one another in bloodshed and venom, and only in the Land of Mirages was there a spurious peace.

Why should there not be a woman beside him now, Husain thought, one of equal strength and influence, to help right the imbalances, to speak for the women of the land and ensure that justice was upheld for them?

A tingling sensation was dancing over Mishaal's skin as she considered what Husain wanted her to do. This place was taboo, forbidden and shunned for centuries, repudiated along with all those other edifices of the Mother Goddess, Inanna, who had been worshipped in the East. Muslims would have nothing to do with idols, or images of the gods, male or female, nor would the Christian religion Drew had taught her about. There had been hundreds of false gods when Mohammed came to prominence and he had banished them all save the one true God, Allah, yet there were no carven images of Him, only the black stone at Mecca, the Ka'ba, made by Abraham, for Muslims to worship and revere.

Soon she would see what was utterly forbidden by the religion of her childhood, false images, idols, decadent and corrupt.

'Whomsoever God has cursed, and with whom He is wroth, He has made of them apes and swine, and worshippers of idols – they are worse situated and have gone further astray from the right way.' The words of the *Qu'ran* rang in her ears. 'Serve your God and eschew idols'; 'idolators shall burn in the fires of eternity.'

'Are you afraid, little *fáhd*?' Husain's richly melodious voice brought her back from her thoughts. 'Do you think you will be condemned if you enter the place that is taboo?'

'I – do not care. I am not Muslim now, you know that.' She attempted one last trumpet of brave resistance. 'How could idols harm me?'

He did not pursue the argument. She would need all her courage to enter the taboo place, whatever fanciful ideas she nursed as to her true religion, and so would he. Destiny awaited them, and to hold it in their hands they must face all that was most fearful.

Here, a homeless, conquered Queen had hidden her crown jewels, the fabled Jewels of Destiny amongst them; here, she had forfeited everything most dear to her. She had lost her beloved husband, her country, her crown, her treasure, and it seemed to Mishaal that her heartbreak echoed from every glittering white stone, irradiating the atmosphere for miles around, sinking into Mishaal's soul so that she shrank back. Oh what tragedy there had been in this place, and might be again . . .

Zenobia. Zenobia. She heard that ancient name and it was as if the long-dead desert queen was speaking directly to her. 'I am waiting, I am waiting.' She heard the words as if they were whispered close by and her flesh tingled. 'Come for me now!'

Shivering, she walked on, stepping on to the Sacred Way, where supplicants and pilgrims had once trodden with reverence, and now Husain's hand was tightly clasping hers. How long the Sacred Way seemed, on and on, endlessly, her heart beating wildly. The last few moments had changed everything, yet still she was undecided. She had wanted Husain to escape, hadn't she? That was the only reason why she had given him the sword, she was sure, and yet her instincts were now telling her otherwise.

It was like a dream, a vivid nightmare; her limbs were frozen and yet there was such an urgency to move that she felt as if her heart would burst.

From inside the temple they heard the noise of a thundering crash. They were desecrating the holy place! Drew and his men were destroying it! Husain grasped her hand and together they entered the dark, arched doorway.

Inside the sun sparkled and cavorted on a million dust motes as they twirled and twisted through the air caused by the fall of the statue brought down by the combined efforts of Drew's men. Mishaal stared at it, aghast for long, unsteady moments. It was an idol, steeped in sin and wickedness, anathema to all Muslims.

'The unbelievers and the idolators shall be in the Fire of Gehenna, therein dwelling for ever; those are the worst of creatures.'

The words of the *Qu'ran* floated in her mind. Stepping closer to the fallen idol, she saw no corrupt and hideous evil but a serene and tranquil face, beautiful, reassuring, and she warmed to it as to a mother returned to her after many years of separation. Reaching out, she touched the lovingly sculpted features, the straight, determined nose, the almond-shaped eyes that stared lucidly and affectionately, the slightly tilted mouth that suggested a tolerant humour.

Inanna, Asherah, Astarte, the Evil One, the pagan goddess of all that was vile and debauched, her worship banned and forbidden by Mohammed in the seventh century. False idol, graven image, handmaiden of Shaîtan, the Devil.

There had been some terrible mistake. Mishaal knew that as she gazed into those affectionate, intelligent eyes. This was no handmaiden of Shaîtan but a wise and motherly goddess, close to nature and the earth, benevolent and protective, bestowing sagacity and content on all her followers.

'Daughter, you have returned to me, now rule as I once ruled.'

Mishaal heard the voice inside her head, the sweet-toned woman's voice gently flowing through her thoughts. In that moment she knew that she no longer wanted to leave this beloved land and go to America with Drew. She had work to do here, to bring man's mind back to the vital qualities of life, the closeness to nature, the gratitude for water and the soil, the rain and the harvest, the honouring of woman as the haven of fruitfulness and the giver of life. Tears of understanding filled her eyes.

Drew and his men were overturning everything in their path, smaller statues and offertory bowls, shiny dishes in which gifts had once been placed for Inanna, and all to no avail, for they had found nothing. The dust was thickening in the air, and broken artefacts littered the aisles. Mishaal's eye alighted on a coiled serpent, its dull gleam catching her attention. It had fallen from the goddess's hand when she was pulled down, and now it lay at Mishaal's feet.

She hesitated only briefly before picking it up, feeling it warm and comforting in her hand, a joyous sensation filling her heart, as if she had found some long-lost and beloved possession.

Looking up, the serpent coiling round her hand, she saw Husain watching her. There was a strange light in his eyes as if he were seeing her for the first time. Colour came into her cheeks and she lowered her head. It was as if they stood in another age, centuries away from the heartless marauders who were wrecking the temple in search of the Jewels of Destiny, an age when learning and wisdom were paramount, and the gentle agrarian arts prized above all things, before war and greed took command. Power flowed between them, richly sparkling in the atmosphere, and Mishaal knew that, separated, they were helpless, but together they could achieve miracles. It was up to her whether the Land of Mirages was rescued from its desperate straits and revived and replenished. Husain could not do it alone, and, from the expression on his face, he knew it.

To the rear of the temple, they came across heaped skeletons, pile upon pile of them, with bloodstains freshly preserved scarlet in the dry air. Here, men had fought to the death, each coveting the Jewels of Destiny, but Mishaal knew that they must be retrieved for the good of humankind, not for any single, selfish purpose. Her throat tightened as she saw the skeletons of the greedy dead, reminding her of the Died-out Place, and she saw Husain's hand go to the medallion at his neck. How alike were their thoughts at times, as if spun from the same web. The last two days of alienation sped away as if they had never been.

On the far side of the skeletons stood Drew, watching them, his mouth curling contemptuously.

'So you found strength to see me take the jewels, savage, and from the look on your face you think you will have my woman in exchange. Over my dead body! She is mine; she has always been mine, and you are dross unworthy to kiss the hem of her gown! When I find the jewels it will be the death of *your* people, not mine. The men of the New World are the rightful owners of the treasure, as they are the rightful rulers of the world they've forged with their grit and tenacity! What have you lazy Arabs ever done to deserve such a prize? God is on *my* side!'

'No, Drew Huntington, He is on my side!' Husain retaliated. 'If He is on yours, then find the jewels and try to take them. Try!'

'So you think I'll be struck down by divine retribution, eh? A thunderbolt from heaven, perhaps? How little you superstitious peasants understand about reality. To the just, the spoils, Rashid, that is the law of life.'

'And of my life, but who claims to be just? Do you?'

Drew looked as if he did not know whether to roar with laughter or sneer.

'This inane argument is wasting time, Rashid, but no doubt that's your intention.' Gesturing to his men, he turned on his heel and began to descend the twisting stone steps into the crypt of the temple.

Taking Mishaal's hand, Husain followed him. It seemed that Drew was quite content to let her stay with the Arab he despised. Was it because he thought she would change her mind when she saw the jewels and knew that he owned them? Or in his arrogance did he simply not care?

They passed more skeletons, two locked in battle, the weapons that had killed them still visible, one with a dagger embedded in his bleached ribs, the other with a sword thrust in his side. They must have died within seconds of one another.

In the crypt, that was enormous and at first eerily dark, Mishaal could feel watching eyes upon her, and yet Drew and his men were some yards away intent on finding the treasure. The air itself was alive with thought and feeling, clutching at her, putting ideas into her mind.

'Here is your destiny,' she heard the words whispered into her mind, 'not the hand of an unbeliever, no, but the hand of a woman, only a woman, may free my jewels . . .' Frightened, she clasped her hands to her ears, thinking that she was losing her mind.

This crypt had once housed the treasures of Inanna, brought

to her by the faithful as gifts, and housed in the very same cache where the desert queen's gems had been concealed all those epochs ago. There, as the darkness cleared, stood the great vault waiting to be opened, and, without thinking, Mishaal rushed to stand in front of it, as did Husain. Shoulder to shoulder, they defended the desert queen's treasure, and it was as if an ancient and fearless strength flowed through their bodies.

Drew roared with laughter at the sight of them standing like dolls before the vault.

'Stand aside, enough time's been wasted. Do you think you can scare me off? Mishaal, you belong at my side not with that piece of desert vermin. Come here, girl, and stay out of trouble. Watch that sword of his! If I know Arabs, he'll stick it through your ribs if the fancy takes him. Here, Mishaal, come here, honey.' He spoke to her as if she were an erring child whose mind must be made up for her.

At his words, his men cocked their guns, directing them towards Husain.

'I am not a hound to be ordered to do your bidding!' Mishaal jutted her jaw. 'I stay here with His Highness the Amir.'

'His *Highness*? That hoary old title? It means nothing, my precious, nothing but empty vanity. He hasn't a stone to hang round your neck. You'll wear rags for the rest of your life if you stay with him, but I don't believe you're foolish enough to do that, are you? Playing hard to get, eh? Heard that it inflames a man's passions . . . Well, you could be right, to a point. Now come on, step out of the way, honey, I don't want you hit by a stray bullet. You, Rashid, have as little hope of protecting the jewels as a jerboa on a leash! Unless you want the little woman harmed, it would be wiser for you to stand out of the way.'

Mishaal did not know whether it was a threat or a promise, but she saw Husain's face tighten and his cheeks blanch with anger. There was nothing else he could do but obey, for he was surrounded by guns that were aching to be fired. He and Mishaal exchanged agonised glances but she kept her hand tightly in his, the coiled serpent in her palm giving her an added courage.

Drew stepped triumphantly towards the vault, the second treasure map in his hand, the one that had been concealed for safety in his boot. One of his men had lit a torch and it was flaring above them brightly, causing hideous shadows to cavort on the walls of the crypt like primeval cave paintings of terrifying devils and demons. Consulting the map, Drew began to work the concealed spring that would reveal the jewel hoard. He was grinning widely, excitement searing his veins. This was the moment of triumph, the greatest moment of his life. He had found the treasure hoard and he was going to be a millionaire!

There was a scraping, whirring sound of stone being rubbed against stone, and Drew was grinning even more exuberantly, head thrown back, eyes glittering acquisitively. Any moment now he would see them . . . the fabled Jewels of Destiny.

The scraping sound increased, scratching against their eardrums so that Mishaal flinched, and then suddenly came the sound of rocks slipping, falling, crashing down, and there before their eyes was the treasure hoard, the Jewels of Destiny blazing, gleaming, a miniature mountain of gold and gems beyond price.

The rocks were beginning to fall outside the vault, a deafening, grinding noise filling the crypt, the first rocks crashing from above them, directly over Mishaal. Screaming, she flung up her hands, but Drew did not even glance in her direction for he had seen the stones tumbling down over the treasure and he knew that it was a trap, that the hoard would be covered for ever more by rock and he would lose his fortune for all time.

In that terrible moment, as Drew rushed to the jewels not caring that she could be killed, and Husain rushed to save her, thrusting aside the falling rocks with his bare arms as if they were papier mâché, and sweeping her up into his embrace to carry her to safety, she realised the truth.

Drew Huntington was the savage noble, and the man who had saved her, Husain ibn Rashid, was the noble savage. Tears flooding her eyes, she clung to her Amir, for she had heard the heart-tearing screams as Drew fell beneath the trap that had been set for unbelievers.

Warily she gazed in the direction of the vault, seeing it illuminated by the flaring torch that suddenly seemed to be brighter and more luminous. Huntington lay half in and half out of the entrance to the vault, his arms full of gems, blood oozing from the corner of his mouth, the rocks almost covering him. His men were standing over him in horror, their arms bent up, their fingers splayed. They could see that it was too late to save him. He was dying.

His last words whispered sibilantly round the crypt, a death knell for Mishaal and Husain.

'Kill the Arab and the girl, so they – they – tell no one. Take the – jew-els to-o Lord Tav-Tavenish in Am-er-ica as we plann-ed.'

Then Huntington's head sagged and the breath deserted his body in two loud, gasping exhalations. Slowly, the men turned, guns at the ready. They had been primed beforehand by their hirer and they knew exactly what to do with anyone who tried to interfere.

But the Sword of God was in Husain's hand and the men were unbelievers, the accursed ones who are fated to live for ever in the Fires of Gehenna. Sweeping through the air, the sword flashed a startling candescent silver, the engraven legend gleaming in the shadowy gloom. Seeing it, the man bearing the torch gave a gasp of dismay, the torch slipping from his nerveless fingers.

In the sudden dense and formidable blackness, Mishaal heard the retort of gun fire ricocheting round the crypt so deafeningly loud that she thought her eardrums had been shattered. Clamping her palms to her ears, she moaned, imagining her beloved Husain lying dead on the floor, blood running from his wounds. Then she heard his voice, telling her to lie down and she knew that he was still alive, a groan from the far side of the crypt telling her that one of the villainous Arabs had been wounded.

Obeying her lover, she prayed as she had never prayed before to Allah the one true God, and, although she did not fully understand why, to the gracious and loving goddess whose temple this was, to male and female she prayed, with all her heart and soul and being, for male is not whole without female, nor female without male.

The Sword of God struck steel in the darkness and there were shouts and more gunshots, cracking against her ears like bunched fists and piercing her whole body with pain and sound. She wished that she could find where the torch had fallen, but even if she did, she had no way of lighting it.

At last she found the courage to stare into the ebony pit before her, astonishment rising as she saw the Sword of God, eerily luminous in the dark, swaying and dancing through the air as if propelled by Allah himself. Husain was everywhere at once, leaping, ducking, swirling on his heel, dashing to left and right, avoiding the bullets as if he were invisible, and now there were only two of the villains left to fight him.

Her prayers were being answered.

She was on her knees now, not knowing whether, in the dark, she faced Mecca. She was sure Allah would forgive her if she were wrong this one time. She was a believer, and that was all He cared about.

'Allah the most merciful the most generous, please I beg of you, save the man I love, save him, I beg!' she prayed, willing her words into reality.

There was another cry, and the skittering sound of a cold metal gun skidding across the stone floor, but in the opposite direction from Mishaal. Now her eyes were becoming accustomed to the darkness and she could see the shadowy figures fighting, Husain, and the one brigand who was left alive.

Fists crushed to her lips she dared not breathe. She was willing her beloved to fight on and survive this final fraught battle. She had never seen anyone move with such strength and agility; it was as if Husain were a god possessed of supernormal energy and abilities. How could she ever have existed in the belief that she did not love him? How stupid and idiotic she had been holding him off. She loved him, oh, how she loved him, her handsome, valorous and beloved prince, Husain ibn Rashid, Allah save and protect him unto the end of time! She was meant for him and he for her; she would never leave him now, or the Land of Mirages. She loved it as devotedly as did he; they would rule together, as he had wanted, if only, sweet Allah, he would survive this battle!

Then she heard the sibilant whispering voice again.

'He is yours, daughter, he is yours. Guide him and love him in the ways of righteousness and wisdom, and your land shall flourish in water and verdancy until the end of time and your wells shall never run dry . . .'

Then the brigand made the error of thinking that Husain was exhausted, that he could not possibly continue at that speed, and he grinned, his broken-toothed mouth splitting evilly, the dagger in his grip lunging down towards Husain's chest in one violent, sweeping movement. But Husain's arm swept up at the same second, the Sword of God sinking into flesh and muscle and cutting through bone as if it were paper, and the man groaned, slumped to the ground and lay still.

Racing into Husain's arms, crying out his name and how she loved him, Mishaal clasped him as if he were her child, feeling the burning heat of his body, the sweat that coated him in a fine, limpid veil.

'Beloved one,' she sighed. 'Oh my darling, beloved one, you are alive. How I love you!'

Tears in his eyes, Husain held her tightly, unable to speak for emotion and relief. The men were dead; Mishaal loved him. There lay the Jewels of Destiny, just a few feet away and they were waiting for the believer who would lift them out of the vault. He knew it would not be him; that it must be a woman, and not simply any woman but an extraordinary and exceptional one: the one who was crushed in his arms at this very moment, whispering his name like a benediction.

When they were recovered, he gently released her hands and went in search of the torch which he lit with the tinder box and flint he found in the *djellaba* of one of the dead villains.

Tensing, Mishaal tried not to look in the direction of the vault as the torch illuminated the crypt. There lay the man who had loved jewels and gold more than he could ever love her; while beside her was a man who loved her more than he loved the preservation of his land and his amirate.

Gently, he took her hand and led her to the vault.

'Do not look at him. Pretend that he has been there for years, that he tried and failed centuries ago to find the treasure, my little *fáhd*. Now it is your turn to lift out the jewels. Do it now, my darling, do it now.'

In silence, Mishaal went to the entrance, while Husain held the torch aloft so that she could see the Jewels of Destiny glinting and gleaming in vibrant hues of crimson, emerald, blue, purple and gold, dozen upon dozen of them, ropes of rubies larger than any she could ever have imagined hanging on thick gold chains; black pearls piled one upon the other, each one worth enough to keep a Beduin family for three years; emeralds, pale green and dark green, rich as the colours of nature, filigree chains of purest yellow gold, bracelets and rings, anklets, earrings studded with pearls and amethysts, diamonds and mellow lemon citrines.

One by one she lifted out the gems, her whole body trembling with emotion and disbelief. It was like a dream: how could this be real? Yet as she removed the gems, she felt the atmosphere grow lighter and easier, joy singing through the air, and in her heart. Now the jewels were back with their rightful owners: the desert people of the Land of Mirages, Husain's people, and they would ensure that they were put to wise use.

Last of all was the solid-gold coronal, three-tiered and thickly-studded with huge rubies, the crown that had once graced the beautiful head of Queen Zenobia. Mishaal felt her heart twist as she looked at it, the symbol of a long-forgotten and ancient majesty that she had rediscovered.

Her throat tight, she gently placed the crown in her looped-up skirt, adding more of the gems to it before accompanying Husain out of that wretchedly dark and haunting place, he with his robe and cloak crammed with the remainder of the treasure.

Up the worn stone steps they went and into the blazing, eye-scorching sunlight. They had almost forgotten that it was day, and that there would be such brightness. The sun was painfully sharp, yet it warmed them through and through, and as their eyes adjusted, they saw that the golden rays were directed on to the statue of the goddess, playing around her mouth so that she appeared to be smiling, her eyes alight with pleasure and exultation.

Gesturing to Mishaal to wait, Husain went to the statue and began to set it upright once more, as if it were featherlight, with barely any effort on his part, and then he told Mishaal to kneel before the Mother Goddess.

Not knowing why, she obeyed, her eyes filled with love and trust. This man was beloved above all others; his courage and nobility were the most beautiful and inspiring that she had ever known, or would ever want to know.

Wonderingly, she saw him lift up the ruby-studded crown, Queen Zenobia's crown, and how it glittered in the swirling silver-gilt dust and sunlight of the temple, as if newly polished in readiness.

Gently, adoringly, he placed it on Mishaal's bowed head, her whole body trembling with delight.

'You are now my queen,' he said, his voice thick with emotion, 'and the queen of my people, and we shall never be apart from one another again, ever. I vow before the one true God – and His consort.' A smile curved his lips.

Taking her hand, he raised Mishaal to her feet and kissed her reverently, and then they gathered the jewels together, marvelling at their colour and beauty, and went outside into the desert where they chose the two sturdiest camels left by Drew's men, and packed their saddle bags with gems and gold.

Helping Mishaal on to her camel, Husain grinned at her broadly, she grinning back. Once she had been unsure and nervous in the saddle but now she was secure and graceful, and as they headed back towards Husain's camp and their future, they continued to smile at one another, again and again, still not daring to believe and accept that they had found the legendary Jewels of Destiny.

A few hours' ride away, their people would be searching for them, Mishaal's people now as well as Husain's, and they would have food and water in plenty, for miracuously the dried-out wells were gushing water and the rain was tumbling from the skies to fill the valleys and rivers to flooding point.

And for Mishaal there would also be the heady joy of finding her foster mother waiting for her at the camp, Rhikia not knowing until she saw her face that the Amir's bride was her own darling Mishaal returned to her for the rest of her days.

It was the Prophet Mohammed Himself who, when asked what was the greatest gift that can be bestowed had replied, 'Water', and this Mishaal had now bestowed upon the Land of Mirages for eternity. In return, she would enjoy a lasting love and her rightful heritage as Amira beside the man whom she adored.

Spurring on their mounts, they gazed dotingly at one another. Never had man and woman loved more, or been more willing to die for one another. From this hour forward, they would share everything: their bed, their happiness, their amirate, and their children when they came, born of a love that was alredy legendary and whose fame would travel down the centuries to inflame and inspire as no love had ever done, or ever would do, before or since; Amir and Amira, passionately, indivisibly one.

The wilderness and the solitary place shall be glad for them; and the desert shall rejoice and blossom as the rose.

Isaiah, XXXV, 1.